Pow(

E

Playing With Fire

SF Mazhar

Also in the Power of Four series

Run To Earth

ISBN-10: 1508479658

ISBN-13: 978-1508479659

Dedicated to my family and friends.

Playing With Fire - to act in a way that is very
dangerous and to take foolish risks

- English Cambridge Dictionary

ACKNOWLEDGEMENTS

When I first sat down to write the beginning of Aaron's adventure, I never imagined it would get the kind of response it did. For this reason, I would like to first and foremost thank everyone who read Run To Earth. To all those wonderful people who gave my book a chance, thank you from the bottom of my heart.

Playing With Fire would probably still be in my head and not on paper, if it wasn't for a few very special people in my life. Thank you to my mum and dad for their unconditional love. Thank you to my wonderful husband, Mazhar for encouraging me to keep on writing. A big thank you to my sisters; to Yasmeen for always being there for me, and to Samena for being the one I can always come to. To my M&Ms, mummy couldn't be more proud of how supportive you all are. To my friends, thank you for being the best friends a girl could ask for and for sharing my excitement.

A massive thank you to Gerard Donnelly from Ginger Creative Agency, for designing the gorgeous cover. Thank you to Melissa Hyder for editing Playing With Fire, and for going beyond the call of duty to answer all my questions.

And a big thank you to all the readers that are prepared to go with Aaron on his journey.

1

A Ruined City

The purr of the motorbike cut through the air. Stationed outside the main doors of the impressive manor, the three vamages stilled, superior hearing strained to catch the growing sound. They moved as one, stepping down the stairs and onto the lush garden, to see the single bike coming towards them.

"Get Machado," one of them instructed when he recognised the bike, and the dark-haired boy riding it.

One of three vamages turned and raced inside. The other two tensed as the bike came closer.

"Smell that?" one asked.

The other cursed. "Does he do it on purpose?"

"I wouldn't be surprised," the first replied. "Torturing us is his pastime after all."

The doors behind them opened and Daniel Machado, the right-hand vamage of Hadrian, stepped out. His glittering blue eyes fixed on the biker approaching them. The heir to the Aedus bloodline, the only son of their leader, the boy others referred to as the Scorcher – but to Machado he was, and always would be, the insufferable Kyran Aedus.

Kyran came to a stop and cut off the engine. He lifted himself off his bike and began walking towards them.

Machado heard the starved growl behind him. "Easy," he warned in a low voice. "Control your hunger." He could smell the blood too, but he had learnt long ago to lock his thirst when it came to the Aedus heir.

Seeing the smirk on Kyran's face, Machado knew the boy could see the strain on the vamages as they tried to hold back and not give in to their bloodlust. It was an old game for Kyran, but one he loved playing nonetheless.

Machado turned his head. "Leave," he instructed. The two vamages practically ran indoors with relief.

"What's the matter?" Kyran asked. "They squeamish? Can't stand the sight of a little blood?"

Machado's sharp gaze had already picked out the bloodstain on Kyran's chest, but his enhanced sense of smell told him there were more injuries elsewhere. He grinned. "I see the charade is over," he said. "What happened? How'd they catch you out?"

Anger glinted in Kyran's eyes. "You should ask your *men*," he hissed as he passed by, heading indoors.

Machado turned to follow after him. "My men wouldn't talk," he said. "The ones that know of your identity are trustworthy."

Kyran stopped to glare at him. "Trustworthy? Vamages?"

Machado smiled at the familiar jibe. "We're more loyal than you think, Kyran," he said. He scanned the boy from head to foot. "We just need a *worthy* enough leader. One who would deserve our allegiance."

Kyran took a step towards him, green eyes bright with anger. "You have no idea what I'm capable of, Machado."

Machado chuckled. "You can scare the others, Kyran, but you can't touch me and we both know it." Machado drew himself taller. "It's a shame you're nothing like your father. You carry his legacy, hold his power, but you're not half as talented as him. If you were, we'd obey your every word too."

"Father is welcome to command you lot. I have no interest in it," Kyran said. A slow smile spread across his lips before he reached into his pocket. "And as for how talented I am?" He pulled out a pendant and held it up for the vamage to see. "I guess *this* is enough of an answer."

Machado stared with disbelief at the purple gem dangling from the chain. "You...you got it?" he asked. He stepped forward, his gaze fixed on the gem – the key that would unlock Hadrian's powers. "How did you do it?" he asked, reaching towards it. The key was rumoured to always be around the neck of the fierce and powerful leader of the mages – Neriah Afton.

Kyran pulled his hand back and pocketed the gem. "I told you – you have no idea what I'm capable of." He took a step closer, right up to the vamage's face, holding Machado's gaze. "And if you know what's best for you and your *men*, you won't make the mistake of testing me."

Machado didn't say anything. Kyran gave him a last look full of loathing and walked away, heading straight to his father's room, slamming the door closed behind him.

***

The City of Salvador was in ruins. Buildings lining both sides of the street had been darkened by fire. The residents were left dazed and shaken by the events of the last few hours. The Controller, Scott Patterson, and his Hunters were standing in a huddled group, talking to Neriah.

Watching from a window was Aaron Adams. It had been four months since the fourteen year old had come to the City of Salvador in the mage realm. In that time, Aaron had seen and done things he could've never imagined. He'd fought demons, he'd learnt how to split the ground with his powers, he'd learnt how to use a gun, how to fight and defend himself, and he'd learnt it all from the boy who had turned out to be their greatest enemy – Kyran.

Kyran was the one who'd taken over Aaron's training when Skyler Avira used it as an excuse to beat him bloody on a daily basis. It was Kyran who spent hour after hour teaching Aaron how to aim and fire his weapon, how to send ripples through the ground, how to control the element of Earth.

Before coming to this realm, Aaron had no idea what being a mage meant. He didn't know mages had powers so they could fight against demons. Aaron wasn't even aware that he was in fact an Elemental – one of the four families with complete power over an element.

In a strange world of mages, demons and elemental powers, Kyran was the only one that Aaron felt somewhat comfortable around. Aaron had even dreamt about Kyran before meeting him. It was a strange friendship that Aaron had developed with Kyran, one that he didn't share with anyone else, not even his childhood best friends, Sam and Rose Mason.

Aaron turned to see Rose sitting on her bed, in the room they all shared, head leaning on her brother's shoulder. Her bloodshot eyes made Aaron look away, his heart clenching painfully. Rose had just started a relationship with Kyran, only a day before she found out who he really was.

He's the Scorcher.

Zhi-Jiya's voice rang in Aaron's head. Kyran was the Scorcher, the son of Hadrian, the leader of the vamages – a hybrid species, part mage and part vampire. It was a group of vamages that had killed Sam and Rose's parents, when Aaron had unknowingly brought the vamages to his street on the dawn of his fourteenth birthday. Kyran, it had been revealed, had been there too that night.

Not only was he there when your parents were murdered, he didn't do a thing to stop the vamages – who obey his every command.

Skyler's taunt to Rose echoed in Aaron's head, making his insides go cold again. Kyran had come with the vamages. He could have stopped the attack. He could have saved Mr and Mrs Mason, but he hadn't. He'd let the vamages kill them. Why?

Because he didn't care. There was no other explanation. Kyran didn't help the Masons because he didn't care about them.

The door to their room opened and Aaron looked over to see his mum walk in, several empty duffel bags in her hands.

"Gather your things." Kate addressed all three of them, throwing a bag each their way.

Aaron looked from the bag at his feet to his mum. "What?" he asked.

"Pack your things," his mum said. "We're leaving." She stepped out of the room.

Aaron got up and hurried after her. "Where are we going?" he demanded. "I thought Salvador was the safest place in all the realms."

"Salvador *was* the safest," she said, walking downstairs. "It's been compromised now."

"Compromised?" Aaron followed her into the living room. "How is it compromised?"

Kate turned to look at Aaron with surprise. "The Scorcher can get past the Glyphs on the Gate," she said. "That means he can drop the Gate and let his vamages in. For all we know, he could be leading his army here as we speak."

Aaron had to force himself to stay still and not flinch at the idea of Kyran leading an attack on them. Each and every time Aaron had found himself in trouble in this realm, it had been Kyran who had come to his aid. Despite what had happened a few short hours ago, Aaron still couldn't accept that Kyran was, and always had been, the biggest threat to the mages.

The front door opened and Aaron's dad, Chris, walked into the living room, two packed bags in his hands. "Ready?" he asked.

"Not quite," Kate replied. "Aaron, go upstairs and pack."

Aaron stood where he was. "Where are we going?"

"Where it'll be safe," Kate replied.

"For how long?" Aaron asked. "We're leaving Salvador because it's been compromised, but what are we going to do when the same happens to other cities? Where do we go then? The entire realm is under threat, Mum."

"We don't have time for this," Chris said. "I'll go and pack his things."

"No!" Aaron turned to snap at him. "I'm not leaving!"

"Aaron." Kate stepped forward. "You can't stay here. Neriah has ordered only Hunters to remain in Salvador."

"You're forgetting that I'm a Hunter too," Aaron said.

Kate's eyes narrowed at once. "No you're not!"

"You don't get to decide that," Aaron fought back.

Kate looked like the last strand of her patience was about to snap. She took in a breath, pumping her hands into fists.

"Aaron. Go upstairs. Gather your things, or so help me, I'll–"

"What?" Aaron challenged. "You'll do what? Yell at me? Raise your hand again?" His green eyes slit with rage. "Go ahead. Maybe this time you'll actually hit me."

Kate stilled. Pink spots coloured her cheeks but she didn't say anything.

"Kate?"

Aaron turned to find his dad looking at his mum in shocked disbelief. At this point, Aaron didn't care about his reaction either.

"So this is it?" Aaron asked. "You're planning on running, leaving the rest of the mages to their fate again?"

Chris's eyes moved from Kate to Aaron, with an intensifying expression of anger. "If I have to run to keep my family safe, then that's what I'll do."

"What about everyone else?" Aaron asked. "What about the rest of the mages with families? You don't see them running to hide."

"Aaron." Chris stepped right up to him. "Things have changed in the last few hours. Kyran–" He choked on the name a little, but pushed past it. "He's got the key that will unlock Hadrian's powers. This war just became more dangerous than you can imagine. You may think you're a Hunter but you don't have the training to face Hadrian or his vamages. It's not safe to stay in Salvador. We're leaving in the next half hour–"

"No, Dad." Aaron stepped back. "You might be leaving in the next half hour, but I'm not. I won't abandon the other mages." He held his dad's stare. "I'm not repeating the mistake you made. I'm not running out on them."

Leaving his dad looking hurt and stunned, Aaron headed out of the cottage, slamming the door shut behind him.

***

The street was filled with mages. Aaron saw a few of the younger kitchen and orchard workers carrying their belongings in cloth bags, following Hunters towards the open Gate. But as some mages were leaving through the shimmering cut in the air, more were arriving – long streams of bikers entered Salvador; Hunters arriving in the aftermath chaos of Kyran's escape. The Hunters parked their bikes in the street and hurried towards Neriah, looks of bewilderment on their faces.

Aaron stood in the middle of the street, just watching them as the story of Kyran's betrayal was repeated. He saw the disbelief and horror replace their confusion. After a few minutes, Neriah began to walk away, with Scott by his side. The Hunters followed after them.

"We need to make the arrangements," Aaron heard Drake Logan, his dad's best friend and ex-Hunter, say to 'Mother' Mary, as they passed him, following behind Neriah and Scott. "Neriah shouldn't have to deal with this. We'll sort out Ella's funeral."

Aaron's heart lurched. Just for a brief moment, he had forgotten about Ella's death.

Neriah suddenly stopped in his tracks. He turned to seek out Drake, having overheard him. The look on Neriah's face was frightening. His violet eyes had darkened and his jaw clenched in fury.

"You have enough to worry about." Drake spoke directly to Neriah. "Despite tradition, no one should have to bury their own."

Scott rested a hand on Neriah's shoulder. "He's right," he said. "We'll take care of Ella's funeral."

"Stop it!" Neriah thundered, shoving Scott's hand away. "She's not dead."

A ripple of surprise went through the crowd. Aaron stepped closer, hoping against hope Neriah was right and not just in denial over the death of his niece.

"But," Mary started, confused, "I saw her lying in the middle of the ring. Scott said Kyran had—"

"He broke her neck," Neriah seethed with anger, "but that didn't kill her. I can still feel her. She's not dead, only unconscious."

Tremendous relief swept up in Aaron, making his knees weak. Ella was a part of Neriah's bloodline. If she had died, Neriah would have felt it. Throughout the chaos of Kyran stealing the key and escaping, no one had thought to go to Ella. They all just assumed that she was dead.

"The way you reacted when she fell," Scott said, "I thought...it looked like she had died and that's why you lost it and attacked Kyran."

Neriah's expression was terrifying. His strong form was rigid, hands curled into tight fists. When he spoke, even his voice was tense and strained. "He broke her neck. It may not have killed her, but he still hurt her."

Scott nodded before suddenly going still. His brow furrowed before he looked up at Neriah. "That means," he started, "Kyran's a mage. That's why his attack didn't kill Ella."

Aaron remembered what he had been told by Ella.

...part of our bond as a mage is that we're all linked to each other. That's why we can't kill each other. We can do what we like: stab, cut, shoot, hurt each other all we want, but we can never kill one of our own, except of course by the ritual...

Aaron understood the ritual was to be shot in the spot between the eyes with a personalised bullet. That was the only way for one mage to kill another.

"I don't understand," Scott said. "How did Kyran get out of the inhibitors if he's a mage? And why would Hadrian not turn his own son into a vamage?"

Neriah looked away. "I don't know," he said, "but I'll be damned if I don't find out."

Something must have caught Neriah's violet eyes, for his expression changed, concern replacing his anger. Aaron followed his stare and his heart missed a beat. A group of Hunters were making their way up the pathway. A disgruntled-looking Skyler was leading them, with Zhi-Jiya and Omar behind him. By Skyler's side, as always, was Ella.

Aaron's joy at seeing Ella again, alive and well, was such he almost ran over to her. He restrained himself, just watching as Neriah took long strides to reach his niece. Ella was shaking her head at him, grey eyes stormy and filled with fury.

"I swear I'm gonna track him down and break *his* neck! See how he likes it," she said the moment Neriah reached her.

Neriah didn't say anything. He took Ella in his arms and held her close, leaning down to kiss the top of her head.

Aaron let out a relieved breath. He was thankful he hadn't had the heart to tell Sam about Ella's presumed death. He didn't want to imagine the anguish he would have brought to his friend, only for it to be a misunderstanding.

A warm hand touched his shoulder and Aaron turned, thinking his parents had followed him. But it wasn't his mum or dad. It was Michael.

"Uncle Mike," Aaron breathed, and in an instant he had his arms around him.

Michael hugged him back. "How you doing, kiddo?" he asked.

Aaron didn't answer, choosing instead to tighten his arms around Michael. When Aaron pulled away, he saw the fatigue on his uncle. Michael's vibrant, bright blue eyes were dull, with dark circles under them. His face seemed thinner and his usually neat hair was dishevelled.

Michael looked around the busy street before back at Aaron. "What's going on?"

Aaron didn't know what to tell him.

"Where are your mum and dad?" Michael asked.

"They're inside," Aaron replied, nodding in the direction of the cottage. "Where were you? Why didn't you come back with Mum and Dad?" Aaron hadn't seen his uncle in four months.

Michael had left with Chris and Kate, but he didn't return until now.

Michael closed his eyes, letting out a sigh. "In hell," he muttered. Opening his eyes, he saw Aaron's expression. He smiled, reaching out to ruffle Aaron's hair. "Not literally, Aaron. Don't look so scared." He grinned at Aaron's messy locks. "You need a haircut."

"It's the last thing I need," Aaron said.

"Seriously, what's going on here?" Michael asked, glancing up and down the busy street.

Aaron opened his mouth to try to start explaining.

"Aaron Adams!"

The shout had both Aaron and Michael looking around at the open Gate. Aaron spotted Patrick Sweeney, the Lurker he had met only a few days ago, standing with fellow white-robed men. Patrick broke away from the group of Lurkers to hurry down the street towards Aaron.

"I just heard," Patrick said, coming to Aaron's side, looking rather ashen-faced. "Kyran – he's the Scorcher? I can't believe it."

Aaron couldn't find anything to say.

"Scorcher?" Michael's eyes widened. "As in, the son of Hadrian?"

Aaron looked around at him. "You know about him?" The fact that Hadrian had a son was only discovered two years ago, when Michael was still in the human realm with Aaron and his parents.

"I heard the stories when we were looking for Neriah," Michael explained. "Horror stories," he corrected.

Aaron's heart twisted as a mental picture of Kyran flashed in his mind. A part of him was still in denial, refusing to believe that all the death and destruction accredited to the Scorcher had been carried out by Kyran. Aaron couldn't bring himself to think Kyran could be that cruel.

"Is that why there's so much commotion?" Michael asked. "We found the Scorcher?"

Aaron shook his head. "He escaped." Then taking in a deep breath, he added, "He took the key to unlock Hadrian's power."

Michael's eyes widened, his face rapidly losing colour.

"What?"

"He was living here," Aaron continued. "He stayed in Salvador for a year, waiting for a chance to get to Neriah."

"The Scorcher was here? In Salvador?" Michael asked. "How is that possible? He can't get past the Gate."

"He's not a vamage," Aaron said. "He's a mage."

Michael looked like he was struggling to speak. His mouth opened and closed a few times but no sound came out. He ran both hands through his hair. "I...How? I – I don't understand."

"None of us do," Patrick said. "But we don't have the time to work it out. Hadrian's got the key; he'll have his powers back in no time." He looked to the Gate, through which more Hunters were arriving. "Neriah's gathering all the teams. Hopefully we can get together a decent defence before Hadrian attacks." He turned to face Michael. "I don't think we've met." He held out a hand. "Patrick Sweeney, Head Lurker, rank twelve."

Michael shook his hand. "Michael Williams," he said. "Ex-Hunter."

It took a moment for it to hit Aaron. "Wait." He turned to Patrick with a frown. "You don't know him?" he asked, gesturing to Michael. "You said you knew my uncle, that you worked with him and my dad." It was only a few days ago that Aaron had met Patrick, and he remembered their conversation well.

Patrick looked confused. He glanced to Michael before looking back at Aaron. "I meant your other uncle," he said. Seeing Aaron's confusion, he elaborated. "Your paternal uncle, Alex Adams."

Aaron stood still. Patrick's words echoed in his head, fighting to make sense. Slowly, Aaron looked over to Michael. His uncle was staring at him, his face shadowed with guilt. He couldn't hold Aaron's stare for long. Patrick was looking between them in confusion.

"Did I miss something?" he said. "Aaron, you okay?"

Aaron didn't say anything. He took a step back and turned, walking away.

"Aaron! Aaron, wait!" Michael hurried after him. He grabbed Aaron's arm, and forced him back around. "Listen to me."

"Why?" Aaron snapped, pulling himself out of Michael's hand. "Do I have more family I don't know about?" he seethed. "More uncles? Aunts? Grandparents, even?"

"I know you're mad," Michael said. "You have every right to be."

Aaron shook his head, moving back a few steps. "You know what? I get that mum and dad didn't tell me about being a mage. I get that they kept this world from me, kept the fact that I'm an Elemental hidden, but not to tell me about my own family?" Aaron was so angry his hands were shaking, his fingertips buzzing. "That's it. I'm done with them. I'm done!"

"Don't say that," Michael pleaded. "At the very least, hear them out—"

Aaron let out a bitter bark of a laugh. "Hear them out? Yeah, okay, I'll hear them out. Problem is, they won't tell me anything."

"Yes they will," Michael said. "This time they will. And if they don't, then I will."

Aaron paused, staring at him, unsure if he believed him.

Michael took a step closer. "I've always wanted to tell you, Aaron. I urged Chris and Kate to tell you the truth but they couldn't bring themselves to do it. It's not my place to tell you what happened." He reached out to hold on to Aaron's shoulders. "But if they don't give you answers today, then I will. I'll tell you *everything*, I promise." He held Aaron's gaze. "But give your parents one last chance to do right by you."

Aaron tried his best to push his anger down, to bury it for now so he could face his parents. He stuck his trembling hands into his pockets and hunched his shoulders before nodding.

***

Sam and Rose were still upstairs – whether or not they were packing, Aaron didn't know. He was in the living room, seated on the sofa with Michael. Both his parents were in front of him, apparently too wound up to sit. Aaron didn't say anything. He sat in silence as his mum and dad shared uneasy looks. Neither of them started the conversation. Aaron turned to give Michael a look.

"He's waited long enough," Michael said to both Chris and Kate. "Don't make him wait any longer."

Chris nodded at Michael before looking at Aaron. He shook his head slightly. "I don't know how to start this," he said, betraying his honest hesitation.

"How about you start with family?" Aaron said, trying and failing to hide his anger. "Why don't you start with *Uncle Alex*?"

The colour faded from Chris's face.

"Why didn't you tell me?" Aaron asked. "Why keep family a secret? Why not just tell me I have an uncle–"

Michael reached out and held on to Aaron's arm. He shook his head at him. Aaron looked back at his dad, to see what could only be described as pain flash across his features.

"I'm sorry," Chris said, his voice reduced to nothing more than a whisper. "I should have told you."

Kate came to his side, her hand slid into his and Chris closed his eyes, drawing quiet strength from her.

"Alex," Chris started, "was my brother." He opened his eyes to look at Aaron. "You *had* an uncle, Aaron, but we lost him." Chris struggled to go on. He dipped his head and his grip tightened on Kate's hand. When he looked up, Aaron's breath hitched at the raw pain glistening in his eyes. "I lost my brother," he continued in a strained voice, "the same day you lost yours."

2

THE PAST

It took Aaron a moment to fully understand what his dad had said. Brother? He had a brother? No, he'd *had* a brother.

Aaron looked from his dad to his mum. Both had the same look – pained expressions and shadowed eyes. Chris sat across from Aaron, pulling Kate with him, but she refused to sit. She stood by her husband's side, her hand clasped in his.

"I promised you I would tell you everything," Chris started, fighting to compose himself. "God knows I never wanted to hide any of it. I was only waiting for the right time, for you to be older when I told you." He took in a deep breath. "I lost both my parents when I was ten. The only family I had was my younger brother." Aaron could read the grief on his dad. "Alex was only three when our parents died. I brought him up, looked after him. The other Elementals looked out for us." Chris paused. "Do...do you know about the Elementals?"

Aaron nodded. Rose had shown him the book she found that detailed the four Elemental families that descended from Aric. Each family had complete power over one of the elements.

Chris went quiet, then pushed on. "We lived in the City of Marwa – the city of the Elementals. Both my parents had been Hunters, and when I came of age, I followed in their footsteps. That's how I met your mum."

Aaron's wide-eyed gaze darted to Kate. "You were a Hunter?" he asked.

She shook her head. "Lurker," she said quietly. "I worked with your dad on his hunts."

"We got married and your mum moved to Marwa to live with me," Chris continued. "Then we had Ben." Aaron could see the small smile touch his dad's lips. "Ben." Chris uttered the name again softly. "He was...something." His smile blossomed. "Always jumping around, could never sit still. He was so full of life."

Kate shifted, pulling her hand out of Chris's and turning around, her back to them.

"It was Ben's fourth birthday," Chris said. "He wanted to go to the Halloween fair. We went every year." He fell quiet. His hand came up to rub at his forehead and he took in a deep breath. "Marwa was supposed to be *safe*." His voice was barely above a whisper. "It had every Glyph known to magekind. But somehow they found a way in."

"Who?" Aaron asked, forcing the word out.

Chris's pain-filled eyes locked with Aaron's. "Lycans."

Aaron's heart twisted with fear, his mouth suddenly dry. The image of the terrifying beasts flashed in his mind. With their deadly fangs and sharp claws, Lycans were one of the most dangerous demons the mages hunted. Aaron stared at his dad, not sure he wanted to hear the rest.

"They came out of nowhere," Chris continued. "There were so many kids at the fair, so many mages, but not enough Hunters."

Aaron saw his mum's shoulders tremble a little.

"They went straight for the kids," Chris said. A muscle twitched in his jaw, his hands balled into fists. "We tried to push the Lycans back, away from the mages and the kids but–" He faltered, squeezing his eyes shut. "But we were outnumbered."

Aaron listened with mounting horror, unable to peel his eyes away from his dad's agonised face.

"Your mum," Chris continued in a harrowing voice. "She...she was pregnant with you." His eyes lifted to meet Aaron's. "She tried to run, tried to protect Ben, but...but the Lycans surrounded her."

A stifled sob interrupted him and all eyes turned to Kate. Her shoulders were hunched, head dropped, and the way she was trembling made Aaron's heart twist in his chest. Chris was up on his feet, both hands on his wife's shaking shoulders as she tried to suppress her tears. Without a word, Aaron got up and walked over to his mum, coming around to face her. Her eyes were clenched shut but tears still managed to cut down her cheeks. It was the second time in his whole life that Aaron had seen his mother cry. The first had been a flesh memory, taken from the letter she had left for him. That time Aaron hadn't been able to do anything. This time, she was standing before him.

"Mum?" Aaron called, reaching out to her. His previous anger towards her had been washed away by her tears. "Mum?" He tugged at her arm to make her look up at him.

Kate didn't meet his eyes. "He took him," she sobbed in a near whisper. "Right out of my arms."

Chris wrapped an arm around her, burying his face into her hair, kissing it.

"It's not your fault," he whispered but it only made her cry harder.

"I couldn't stop it," she said. Her wide, pain-filled eyes met Aaron's. "They killed him. They killed my son right before me and I...I couldn't do anything."

Aaron moved in and hugged her. Kate held on to him, tighter than she ever had and cried.

Aaron felt, more than saw, Michael come to their side, to calm his sister down. It took several long minutes before Kate's embrace loosened from around Aaron. Michael and Aaron led her to the sofa to sit down between them. No one spoke. The only sound was that of Kate's hiccupping sobs.

"Mages are all connected," Chris said quietly.

Aaron looked over at him, but his dad was focusing on the ground.

"We have a connection, a bond that ties us all together," he continued. "But when it comes to family, this bond becomes an actual presence. You know your family, you can sense them. You can feel their connection deep inside your core." He faltered, before pushing on. "When someone...dies, their family feels it, feels that connection break."

Aaron wanted to tell him that he already knew this. But remembering *who* had told him made him change his mind. He didn't want to mention, or even think about, Kyran right now.

"The moment Ben took his last breath, I felt it deep in my core." Chris raised his eyes to Aaron. "I felt my son die."

"We all felt it," Michael said quietly.

Aaron could sense his mum's tremors at his side, but he didn't look over at her. He didn't have it in him to see her tears again.

"I was trying to get to Ben," Chris said, his eyes glazed over, no doubt replaying the horrific memory. "The Lycans were throwing him from one to the next like he was nothing more than a chew toy." His fists clenched. "I was trying with all the power I had to get through the Lycans and reach my son. But when I felt him die, I stopped. It was just for a moment, barely longer than a heartbeat, but I came to a stop. The pain, it...it halted me, almost brought me to my knees." He closed his eyes and a tear rolled down his cheek. "All I knew in that moment was that they had taken my son from me and I wanted to kill them, all of them."

Chris sucked in a breath and paused. The pain was evident in every line of his body. He looked up at the ceiling, as if asking an unseen force for help. "A-Alex," he choked on the name. "I don't know how, but he managed to get ahead of me. He raced after the Lycans, blinded by rage." He stopped, unable to say what had happened but Aaron could easily figure it out.

Chris kept his eyes fixed to the table as drops fell from them, trailing down his cheeks. "When I felt Alex die, it almost killed me too. It was like my back had broken. I couldn't stand. I couldn't walk. In a matter of minutes, I had lost my son and my brother." He turned his head and looked at Aaron with bloodshot eyes. "All I had left was your mum and you."

Aaron stared at him, not knowing what to say.

"The Lycans had attacked your mum," Chris continued. "She was seven months pregnant with you. I had lost Alex and Ben. I wasn't going to lose my wife and unborn child too." His eyes steeled. "So I took my wounded, pregnant wife and I ran, leaving behind the fight, the city, this realm."

Aaron couldn't hold his dad's gaze. He looked down, staring at the ground.

"Michael came with me," Chris said, "and the three of us crossed the mage realm through a tear and came to the human realm. We had no other choice. There were no portals open that could take us into another city and I was close to losing the rest of my family. The attack on your mum had put her life and yours at risk."

Aaron snapped his head up, his mouth impossibly dry as the timeline caught up with him. This had happened on Halloween, fourteen years ago...

Chris nodded at his unspoken realisation. "You were born a few hours later."

Aaron couldn't believe it. He came into the world hours after his family had suffered so much loss.

"You were two months premature," Chris continued. "At first I didn't know what was going to happen, if you would make it, if you had suffered because of the attack. But you were perfect – healthy, tiny but breathing, safe and sound." Chris's expression hardened, his eyes darkened as he glanced at Kate and Michael. "And the three of us swore that day, that no matter what, you would always be safe. We would do whatever we had to, pay whatever price for your protection. We made the decision not to go back. We stayed in the human realm. We forgot we had powers and lived as humans, ignoring the world that we had left behind."

Guilt hit Aaron like a slap in the face. His parents had done so much, sacrificed their world and their way of life, all to make sure he was out of danger. And he had gone out with the mages, risking his life, hunting down demons with barely any training.

"I know that everyone blames me for running out on them," Chris said. "I know that I'm labelled a coward and a traitor, but I did what I had to, to keep my family safe. I've already lost half my family to this world." His eyes glistened. "I don't have it in me to lose any more. So if keeping what I have left of my family out of danger makes me a coward, then so be it."

Aaron shook his head weakly in protest. "You're not a coward, Dad."

Chris got up, so he could kneel before Aaron. One hand cupped his cheek. "I don't care what anyone calls me, or even thinks about me. The only thing I care about – what I have *always* cared about – is you," he said. "Staying here in Salvador is no longer safe." His eyes filled with desperation. "Please, Aaron," he urged. "Don't fight us. Don't make leaving this place harder than it already is."

Aaron couldn't find his voice to argue. Truth was, he wasn't sure if he even wanted to. Learning what had happened in the past, to his brother and his uncle, had sapped Aaron's bravado. He was left feeling ill, his insides cold at the thought of the loss his parents had suffered. His mum's grip on his hand tightened.

He looked around to see quiet pleading in her watery eyes. Holding her gaze, he gave a brief nod.

Chris pulled Aaron to his chest, a hand on the back of his neck. "Thank you," he whispered. He let go of him and smiled, but it did nothing to the pain lingering in his eyes. "Go and grab your things. I want to leave before it gets dark."

Aaron got up wordlessly, his legs weak. He walked to the door and pulled it open. He stopped at the sight of his two best friends, standing just beyond the door, looking shocked and saddened at what they had heard.

***

When Aaron stepped out of the cottage, he saw the street was packed with even more mages. Everywhere he looked, all he could see were armed Hunters, and Lurkers in various coloured robes, standing in huddled groups. Some looked furious, others pensive, and some looked downright scared. Aaron scanned the crowds but couldn't spot Neriah, nor Ella.

There was a group of older-looking mages near the table, crowding around Scott. Aaron recognised Mandara in their midst. The chief of the City of Balt was deep in conversation with Scott. Aaron didn't have to think too hard to figure out what everyone's topic of conversation was. The infamous Scorcher – Kyran – was all anyone could discuss.

Aaron walked down the path with his family and friends by his side, horribly aware of the packed bag in his hand. The sun was already setting, but it wasn't dark enough for them to leave unnoticed – which was the point, he guessed. He figured his dad didn't want anyone to think the Adams family waited until dark to sneak away.

Aaron followed after his dad, who was keeping his eyes ahead, not looking at anyone. His mum and uncle were behind him, while Sam and Rose were by his side. As the group headed down the street, mages stopped to turn and stare. Aaron saw the hostile glares of mages he had never met. He heard the murmur of 'Adams' ring in the air. It reminded Aaron of his first time in Salvador. Four months ago, when he had stepped into this city, mages had whispered about him, stared at him, given him unfriendly looks, but at the time Aaron had had no idea why. Now, he understood the reason, and he couldn't blame them for their bitterness.

The Adams were Elementals. They were one quarter of the power that protected this realm and they had run away, hidden in the human realm for fourteen years. It angered the mages, hurt them that while they were left behind to suffer and fight the war against demons and Hadrian, the Elementals of Earth were living a quiet, peaceful life in a world that wasn't theirs. Aaron understood their anger, just as he understood his parents' decision to do what they did.

Aaron caught sight of Alan Kings. The other boy's eyes trailed to the bag in Aaron's hand before lifting to stare at him in shock. Aaron wanted to speak, to tell him he didn't want to leave but that he had to. Before he could open his mouth, Alan's eyes turned cold and he walked away, heading to the Stove with his head dropped and fists clenched.

Slowly, the residents of Salvador – the ones Aaron had spent the last four months with – noticed him heading towards the Gate, packed and ready to leave. No one spoke to him. No one called out. They simply stood and watched.

Near the Gate was a bruised Skyler, seated on one of the bikes, surrounded by his gang of Hunters – all except Ella. Skyler's gaze moved through Aaron's group, starting with Michael and Kate, then moving to Sam and Rose before pausing on Aaron. His stare went to Chris and the air chilled around them. Skyler looked back at Aaron, his jaw clenched, the icy blue of his eyes cutting into Aaron.

"See you in another fourteen years," he growled in a low voice as Aaron passed him.

Aaron stopped to face Skyler. He opened his mouth, but no words left him. Skyler tore his gaze away, looking disgusted. Aaron turned to the Hunters around Skyler, to Zhi-Jiya and Ryan who stared back at him with the same disappointment as the rest. Aaron felt Sam's nudge against his shoulder, to prompt him to start walking again. Aaron followed his dad out of the Gate of Salvador, leaving behind the first city he had seen in this realm – the place that had taught him who he was.

***

The portal that sat in the woodlands outside the Gate of Salvador had been destroyed by Kyran after he raced through it to escape. Scott had set up a new one, allowing those leaving Salvador to do so quickly and safely. Aaron made his way through the dense forest, head lowered as he followed behind his dad.

The glow of a portal made him look up. Aric's mark – a circle with an inverted V inside, holding a spiral between its legs while three wavy lines sat behind it – glittered against the darkness, inviting them in.

Aaron paused when his dad walked past it. "Dad?" he called.

"It's not ours," Chris replied. "This one is for the City of Jharna."

Aaron felt his mum's hand gently push him from behind. He hurried after his dad. "Where are we going?"

He could only see his dad's back, but even so he could sense the tension in him.

"We're going home, Aaron," he replied.

Aaron's gaze shot to his two friends. They couldn't go home. Sam and Rose had the Trace – something that would get them

32

killed if they set foot back in the human realm. Sam frowned in return. Aaron turned his head to look behind at Kate and Michael.

"Not the human realm," Kate said, reading Aaron's expression. "The home we once had in this realm."

Chris came to a stop, halting the rest. Before him sat a smaller portal, but still in the glowing form of Aric's mark. Aaron stared at it, inexplicably nervous.

"You mean," he said, "we're going to...?"

Chris faltered. "Marwa," he said at last. "We're going to the City of Marwa."

He turned to take Aaron's hand, and Aaron quickly hoisted his bag onto his shoulder to take Sam's hand. Kate had Michael's hand in one of hers and came forward to hold on to Rose, who was already clutching her brother's hand. As one, they walked to the portal and passed through it, leaving the woods behind, to arrive at another Gateway.

Aaron took a moment to study his surroundings. The pathway under his feet was made of perfectly smooth concrete, stretching as far as the eye could see, like the one leading to the Gate of Salvador. But this one was different – it was a glittery white-stoned path across a vast lake. Aaron looked at the deep blue water on either sides, with something akin to mesmerised shock, as the calm water licked the edges of the pathway. When Aaron lifted his gaze, he saw rocky mountains in the far distance on one side of him and a magnificent waterfall on the other. He could see the clear stream gush down, raising little clouds of mist as it hit the waterbed.

His dad pulled at his hand, leading Aaron down the path. They walked for a few minutes before a towering Gate appeared out of nowhere, materialising in the blink of an eye. Aaron watched the familiar marks flash on the glistening mass –

symbols depicting demon forms, numbers that represented the four elements and the outlines of various weapons.

Chris stopped at the Gate but never let go of Aaron's hand. He reached out and placed his other hand on the door. Kate did the same, as did Michael.

"Christopher Adams."

"Kate Adams."

"Michael Williams."

The Gate flashed and a light washed over all of them. The numbers and symbols disappeared, until all that was left was Aric's mark, pulsing on the surface of the Gate. A click and the Gate slid open, disappearing into itself.

Aaron couldn't help the sense of déjà vu as it washed over him when he stepped out of the blinding daylight into a darkened, sleeping village oblivious to their presence. Lanterns floated in the air. Rows of houses lined either side of the street. There was even a long table in the middle. Aaron's heart skipped at the sight.

As they made their way down the cobbled path, Aaron realised that the layout might have been the same, but Marwa was not Salvador. Even the darkness of the night couldn't mask the big houses with their perfectly kept gardens. The table that sat proudly in the middle of the street was not a scrubbed wooden one; the lanterns gave enough light for Aaron to notice the rich mahogany. The very air spoke of elegance and wealth.

Chris, Kate and Michael led the younger three along the street, passing one impressive house after another. Aaron noted that Sam was giving his surroundings a curious look but Rose wasn't. Her eyes were on the ground, walking slowly, being led by Sam's grip. For a moment Aaron worried Rose wasn't aware of what was happening. Was she in some kind of shock?

A sudden gasp made Aaron look away from Rose. He came to a stop, because the adults before him had too. They were in front of a house – a big, square, detached villa, one that must have once stood with great pride but now was wrapped in thick vines.

Aaron gaped at the sight. The glow of the lanterns above was enough to see the vines that ran not only up but also vertically around the house, encasing it, like thin branches of a monstrous tree that had grabbed hold of it and refused to let go. The doors, windows, every part of the house from the bottom to the roof was held fast.

Kate was staring at the house with an open mouth, eyes wide and filled with hurt. "Oh my God," she breathed.

Michael stepped forward. "What is this?" he asked.

"I'm guessing it's a reaction to our disappearance from the neighbours," Chris said, his voice forced into an even tone.

Aaron looked over at his dad to see flickers of anger in his eyes as he stared at his home. But Chris only let out a tired sigh and handed his bags to Michael before rolling up his sleeves. He raised both hands, aiming at the house. The vines shuddered and slowly, *very* slowly, they started to unwind and inch backwards. A minute passed and Aaron watched as his dad's eyes narrowed, a faint sheen covering his forehead.

"Damn, they were angry when they did this," he muttered, flexing his fingers.

Without a word, Aaron dropped his bag to the ground and went to stand next to his dad. Chris looked at him in surprise. Aaron didn't meet his gaze but raised both hands and focused on the vines. From the depths of his mind, Aaron heard Kyran's voice echo, no matter how much he tried to block it.

You're an Elemental, Ace. You can use the power of Earth as you see fit...Take control...Free your mind from the constraints of how to do something. Focus instead on what you want.

Aaron pushed his power forward, feeling his fingertips tingle. He glared past the darkness, focusing on the vines, willing them to pull back, to fall away.

…Command, Aaron, don't ask…

A strange pressure built inside him, squeezing his heart. *Fall back!* He called mentally. *This is our house. Leave it alone!*

The vines recoiled. When the last of the vines withered away and freed the house, Aaron lowered his hands. He felt jittery, his fingers still buzzing. He braced himself before glancing at his parents. They had never witnessed him using his powers before. His dad had a strange look on his face, something between pride and regret. Michael was smiling. His mum, on the other hand, didn't look happy at all.

***

The air was musty and stale but Aaron expected that; the house had been sealed for fourteen years. They walked into the silent, dark house, coming to stand in the hallway. Michael raised a hand and small flames suddenly danced in the lamps on the wall. Aaron looked around at the dark wood panels and what once must have been cream walls, but now the paint had changed to a mouldy yellow. There were doors leading to rooms on either side of him. The only piece of furniture was a rectangular sideboard, the top of which held half a dozen framed photos. Everything was caked in a thick sheet of dust. Cobwebs gathered like little clouds in the corners.

Kate and Chris were staring at their home, the place they had once happily lived. Kate's gaze stopped at the far end of the hall, where a small, colourful toy truck lay, tucked in the corner. Aaron saw it too. It suddenly occurred to him that his parents had left during the attack that killed his brother and uncle. They never got a chance to come back here. The house was exactly as it had been, fourteen years ago, with all of Ben's things where he had left them.

Kate didn't move. She stood where she was, her eyes on the toy. Chris came up behind her, wrapping his arms around her. He kissed her hair and Kate swallowed back her emotions. She pulled herself out of his arms and turned around, facing the three teenagers, fighting to remain composed.

"The bedrooms are upstairs," she said. "I'm sorry about the state they're in–"

"It's fine."

It was Sam who had spoken. His voice was rough but his words held a hint of empathy.

Kate nodded. "You should go and rest. It's been a long day."

Michael led the way, lighting the lamps as he went. Sam, Rose and Aaron followed after him. As Aaron passed the sideboard he couldn't help but glance at the framed pictures. Even through the grime and dust, he could make out images of his young, joyful-looking parents.

He stopped at the first photo of a small, dark-haired baby, smiling cheekily up at the camera. That was him. His brother. The one he lost hours before he was born. Aaron picked up the frame and wiped a hand down the glass, clearing away the dust. Ben looked not much older than two in the picture. Thanks to his mum's love for displaying family photos around the house, Aaron had seen plenty of his own baby snaps, so he instantly recognised how much he looked like Ben at that age. The only difference was the eyes. Aaron had green eyes, Ben had had blue. Aaron's heart twisted as he stared at the photo. If his brother had lived, they would have shared a great resemblance, the kind that told complete strangers they were brothers.

Aaron put down the picture, wanting to follow his uncle and friends upstairs. He passed by the rest of the photos, only giving them a quick glance. He stopped abruptly as a familiar face caught his eye. He turned towards the sideboard, leaning in closer to the gold-trimmed photo of a handsome, dark-haired, green-eyed boy sitting with Ben on his lap. Aaron's breath caught in his chest, his heart hammering at his insides. The boy in the picture was Kyran.

3

THE AEDUS HEIR

The room was dark and quiet. So quiet it was impossible to tell someone was there, lying in bed, fast asleep. A knock sounded on the door and the figure shifted, groaning.

"What is it?" came the sleepy question.

The sharp knock rapped the door a second time.

"Go away," the figure said, turning to his side, settling comfortably.

The door clicked open and Kyran strode inside. "Morning," he called.

A wave of his hand had pulled the thick curtains aside, letting bright sunshine spill into the room. The occupant of the bed groaned louder and pulled the covers up over his head. Sunshine danced in every corner of the room, reflecting off the impressive chandelier to throw patterns on the walls. The gold-plated bed frame gleamed in the light.

Kyran grinned, standing cross-armed next to the bed. "Seriously?" he asked.

The covers inched lower, just enough to expose messy black hair and narrowed hazel eyes. "Sunlight," he croaked. "Burns."

"It does not," Kyran dismissed. "You're not a vampire. Sunlight doesn't bother you."

The eyes narrowed further. "That's not what I meant," he said. "I was sleeping. You know what bright light does to sleepy eyes?"

"Yeah." Kyran smirked. "Wakes them up." He gestured for him to rise. "Come on, get up. I want a demonstration."

"I'm tired," came the reply. "Which means I'm not ready yet. Leave me alone to recover."

"Father," Kyran breathed. "How are you going to build your strength if you lie in bed all day?"

The covers came all the way down this time. Hadrian smirked up at his son, the gold specks in his eyes glittering in the light. "That sounds like a plan."

"You're not spending the day in bed," Kyran said. "Get up."

"I sense there's a role reversal going on here," Hadrian said.

"Or maybe this is payback," Kyran replied. "You used to get me up at the crack of dawn. I, at least, let you sleep till nine."

"How kind," Hadrian said dryly. "But as it stands, *I* am still the father and I'm telling you to get out and leave me alone."

Kyran laughed. "Not a chance," he said. "I didn't spend a year stalking Salvador, waiting to get to Neriah to steal the key that hung from his damn *neck* and unlock your powers, just for you to sleep through the transition."

"It's tiring, Kyran," Hadrian said with a sigh, but he pulled himself to sit up in bed. "The core takes its time, not to mention immense energy, to recover from the damage of being locked for so many years."

"Speed it up," Kyran said.

"I would but it's better for it to happen slowly," Hadrian replied. He smirked at the disappointed expression his heir wore. "How did you think this was going to go?" he asked. "You would hand me the key, unlock my core, and I would surge with unspeakable power, rise up ready for the kill and go on a war path in five seconds flat?"

"No," Kyran replied. "Three seconds."

Hadrian chuckled, his eyes bright with amusement. "Patience," he said, throwing aside the covers to get up. "It's not just a virtue. It's the difference between winning and losing." He crossed the room, heading to the en-suite.

Kyran watched him go, his eyes darting to the partly exposed tattoo on his father's right shoulder blade, peeking out from under his vest. The inked mark had fascinated Kyran from a young age. That was until he grew up and understood what the circle holding an inverted V, three wavy lines and a spiral meant.

"Not much point now," Kyran said. "We've already won."

Hadrian paused and turned to look at him.

Kyran sat at the edge of the bed, leaning back to stretch out his legs. "Your powers are back," he said in explanation. "The war is as good as over." At his father's raised eyebrow, Kyran shook his head. "It's not what I think. It's what the mages believe. They're convinced that once you unlock your powers, you'll win the war in a heartbeat and they'll all end up dead."

Light sparkled in Hadrian's eyes and his lips lifted in an amused smile. "They've got the right idea."

Kyran snorted. "You wouldn't believe the crap I had to hear this past year." The smile slipped from his face and his eyes darkened a shade. He looked over at his father. "Did you find out who made those kills?"

"Raoul and his Lycans," Hadrian replied.

"Figures." Kyran glowered with fury. "It looked like Raoul's work but the mages couldn't be bothered to figure that out. They were more than happy to blame me. The Scorcher burns everything he touches, so it must have been him!"

Hadrian chuckled. "I never knew your reputation meant so much to you."

Kyran snapped his head up, intense green eyes narrowed. "It's not like that," he argued.

"What is it like, then?"

Kyran paused for a moment. "They should find the real culprit," he said at last. "Blame me when it's *actually* me. I don't have a problem with that. I'm proud of what I've done."

Hadrian watched him carefully. "Of course you are."

Kyran shifted in his seat. His right hand, with four silver lines across the back of it, curled into a fist.

"I'm surprised you didn't see that coming," Hadrian said. "They've been doing that with me for years."

Kyran nodded slowly, eyes unfocused, mind going over all he had heard in his Hunter meetings at the Hub. Every time they talked about the Scorcher, pinned another crime on him – one that he hadn't committed – it had made his blood boil. Kyran was surprised he'd managed to keep himself from burning the city to the ground. Well, almost, anyway. His escape wouldn't have been possible if he hadn't distracted them with that fire. He knew it wouldn't do any lasting damage, though – he hadn't put much force into it.

"Don't worry, Kyran," Hadrian said, pulling him out of his thoughts. "We'll make them pay for tarnishing our good name."

Kyran could sense the mocking tone. "Not if you stand around talking all day."

Hadrian crossed his arms over his chest, looking down at Kyran with a smirk. "You planning on being cheeky all day?"

"I have a year to make up for."

Hadrian's smile slipped from his face. "I never anticipated it would take that long," he admitted.

"It was okay," Kyran pacified. "It was mostly tolerable. When they weren't spreading lies about you and blaming me for everything under the sun, it wasn't...too bad."

Her image flashed in Kyran's head – dark hair, big brown eyes and that smile that made him stop and stare every damn time.

"You sound almost nostalgic," Hadrian said.

Kyran looked up at his father to see that teasing smile again. Kyran rolled his eyes. "Yeah, you're right. I miss Salvador," he said. "I especially miss the bullets they buried in me."

The humour left Hadrian quickly. Something flickered in his eyes, his body tightened, even his jaw clenched. Kyran saw it and at once shifted, sitting upright.

"Don't start again," he said.

"Then don't bring it up again."

There was an edge to his voice, one that Kyran knew meant Hadrian was struggling to hold back his anger. If there was one thing Hadrian couldn't stand, it was Kyran getting hurt, and last night Kyran had come home with bullets in his chest and back.

A thought crawled into Kyran's mind and he relaxed, smirking a little. He kept his eyes on his father and shrugged. "All things considered, I got away pretty easily."

He was right. It was the wrong thing to say.

Hadrian's body tightened further but he uncurled his arms, clenched his fists and took a step closer to Kyran. "Easily?" he snarled. "They shot you *three* times!"

"I know, I counted them," Kyran replied dryly.

Hadrian's eyes darkened. "Did you count them last night too, when I had to *dig* the bullets out of you?" he asked, his words underlined with a growl. "Their shots may not have killed you, but they still pierced holes in your flesh. You came to me bleeding and injured."

Kyran kept his eyes on him. "What does it matter?" he said carefully. "As long as you got what you wanted."

That did it. Hadrian's face twisted with rage, the gold specks in his eyes brightened, coming alive until his eyes glowed amber. "Kyran!" he yelled.

Behind him, the entire wall lit up in flames. The roar of the fire filled the room, a manifestation of Hadrian's anger. Then just as suddenly as it had come, the fire died, leaving the wall black and charred. Hadrian turned to glance at the damage before looking back at Kyran, only to see him smirking, looking very proud of himself.

"You did that on purpose," Hadrian said in realisation.

"I got impatient," Kyran said. "I've waited my whole life to see you use what's yours."

Hadrian started to smile, but his expression changed, a flash of pain crossed his face. He stumbled, about to fall, but his son was by his side in a heartbeat, holding him steady.

"Father?" Worry laced Kyran's voice.

Hadrian took in a breath and shook his head, as if trying to clear it. "Look what you've done, you brat," he said in a strained voice. "You tired me out with your little trick."

"Admit it, it was worth it," Kyran replied with a grin.

Hadrian let go of Kyran and straightened up. He narrowed his eyes at his son. "No more of your antics," he warned. "I have to wait for my core to fully restore before I start using my powers."

"Fine," Kyran replied. He stepped back. "And for the record, Neriah and his Hunters could've buried every last bullet into me, and I still would've returned to you with the key. I have yet to fail to do as you ask."

"I asked you to get out and leave me alone," Hadrian reminded playfully.

"And when I go to have breakfast, you'll have your wish."

Hadrian shook his head. He held Kyran's easy gaze but his own was changing, darkening once again. He stood tall. "So," he paused. "Are we going to talk about it?"

Kyran frowned, looking lost. But something in his father's expression told him what he was referring to, and Kyran felt his blood run cold. His expression lost all his previous amusement.

"No," he replied.

"Kyran—"

"There's nothing to talk about," Kyran said quickly. He ignored the frantic beating of his heart, but knew his father's vamage abilities would pick up on it. And then he would *make* Kyran talk.

Hadrian took a step towards him, his eyes softer.

"Kyran—"

"Do you know what I was wondering?" Kyran asked quickly. "How are we going to let the world know Hadrian Aedus is back?"

Hadrian let the topic go, for now. He smiled.

"Don't worry," he said. "I've been planning this for sixteen years." His eyes gleamed in vicious glee. "They won't know what hit them."

***

The sound of gunshots was deafening. Grunts and growls of beasts with sharp claws and bloody jowls surrounded him. Aaron watched in mounting horror as he stood in the middle of the chaos. Hunters were everywhere, fighting to the death with hell hounds. The gruesome, ugly dogs, with matted fur and red eyes pounced at the Hunters.

Aaron tried to focus, to recognise the faces of the mages but none of them seemed familiar. He ducked out of the way of a hell hound's vicious swipe, meant for the Hunter behind him. After a minute or two, Aaron began to realise that no one was coming at him. No hell hound and no Hunter. It was like he was invisible, like he wasn't even there.

The ground under his feet rumbled before cracking. Aaron watched it with fascination as he stood perfectly stable. That's when he looked past the growling beasts gnashing their teeth together, past the Hunters shooting and fighting with great flair, to the glittery white walls. Three walls were locked by grey criss-crossing bars. That's when Aaron knew where he was. It was a Q-Zone – a trap devised by the mages to kill demons – only he wasn't really here because he didn't remember coming on a hunt. Which meant he must be dreaming.

"Didn't you hear him?" someone yelled over the noise of the hunt. Aaron looked for the familiar voice, only to gape in surprise. It was his dad, a young Christopher Adams, fighting a hell hound. He kicked the grisly dog back before his power turned it to stone. He looked right at Aaron. "Get out of here!"

Aaron stared back at him. He opened his mouth to speak, to ask what was going on, how his dad could see him, when someone replied from behind.

"No way! I'm not leaving without you."

Aaron turned in the direction of the voice, but he couldn't tell who had spoken from the crowd of fighting mages.

"Go!" Chris called, drawing Aaron's attention again. He watched as his dad fired three bullets into one hell hound, dodging the rabid fangs of another. "The zone is about to collapse!" He shot two more hell hounds before wiping his arm over his sweating forehead. "Get out now!"

"Not without you!" came the reply.

Chris twisted out of the way of another hell hound's attack before shooting it down. He looked straight up at Aaron, furious. "Dammit, Alex, get out!"

Aaron spun around. The crowd behind him had thinned, leaving only three Hunters. Two Aaron didn't recognise. The third had to be his uncle. Aaron stared at his uncle Alex, only to see Kyran stare back at him.

Aaron woke up breathing hard. Golden light from the setting sun was warming his face, coming in from the bare window. Aaron rubbed a hand down his face, trying to wipe the rest of his sleep away. He rose from his bed, fully clothed with his shoes still on. He had been so tired after helping his mum clean that he had crashed on his bed, intending to just rest but ended up falling asleep.

Aaron ran a hand through his hair, pushing it away from his eyes. He really did need a haircut. He sat on the edge of the bed, his heart still racing from that dream – if that's what it was. It seemed like an actual memory, like he had somehow opened a flesh memory and witnessed a moment from his dad's past. He was in a Q-Zone, a collapsing Q-Zone with hell hounds. His heart skipped a beat when he recalled who his dad was calling out to.

Dammit, Alex, get out!

Aaron held on to the memory of his uncle, his dad's younger brother, a spitting image of Kyran Aedus. Two nights ago, when Aaron had seen Alex's photo in the hallway, he had been convinced he was staring at Kyran. His dad had come behind him to put a heavy hand on his shoulder, staring at the photo too. He had only said two words, 'That's Alex,' before pulling Aaron away. Aaron finally understood why his parents had looked so shocked at seeing Kyran in Salvador.

Aaron shook his head, trying to clear it, but Alex's face refused to melt from his mind's eye. It was impossible for two people to be so similar and not share a blood connection. The same face, the same dark hair, the same green eyes – Aaron paused. No, that wasn't entirely true. His uncle Alex had had bright green eyes, the kind that sparkled when he smiled, evident by the numerous photos he'd seen around the house. Kyran – his heart leapt just thinking about him – had intense green eyes, the kind that made you stop breathing when they narrowed at you.

Why Kyran looked like his deceased uncle, Aaron didn't know. He entertained the thought that maybe Kyran was his uncle's son. That would make Kyran his first cousin. The thought was oddly comforting. But when Aaron remembered the memory Zhi-Jiya had shared with him, he felt his throat close up with fear. Kyran, flanked by two vamages, burning a village to the ground. The memory of those mages' dying screams rang in his head and Aaron was quick to push the thought away. Kyran wasn't his cousin. He couldn't be an Adams. He was too cruel to be from Aaron's bloodline.

He had killed mages, wiped out entire cities, zones even.

He had taken the key to unlock his father's powers, giving Hadrian all he needed to destroy the mage realm, and the human one.

He had stood back and let Sam and Rose's parents die.

It was that last crime which made Aaron's insides twist with hatred. Kyran could have stopped the vamages. He could have saved Mr and Mrs Mason, but he didn't.

Aaron let out a long breath. He glanced out of the window. It looked like late afternoon, the blaze of the sun had turned to a comforting glow. How long had his nap taken? Aaron got up and crossed the threshold of his new room.

He opened the door and headed down the dark-panelled corridor to the wide-stepped staircase. The house was big, far too big in Aaron's opinion. There were two floors with six bedrooms and three bathrooms, and there was also a drawing room and separate living room on the ground floor. The kitchen was three times the size of their old kitchen in the human realm. Aaron had lost count of how many utility rooms there were.

Under other circumstances, Aaron may have been excited to live in such a big place, but the house had been abandoned for almost a decade and a half. Not only was it filthy, it had an entire array of creepy-crawlies taking up residence. His mum had started cleaning the first morning they woke up there. Aaron knew it was too much for her and offered to help. Sam and Rose didn't offer, they just quietly started cleaning on their own, following Kate's lead. Chris and Michael spent most of the first few days out of the house, bringing back supplies.

Aaron paused at the stairs, turning to look at the door at his far right. The years of abandonment had taken their toll but three faded colourful letters were still distinguishable on the wooden door.

BEN

Another reason Aaron had offered to help his mum was because of his late brother's things, lying scattered around the house. Toys in random places, tiny boots tucked under the sofa, a small raincoat hanging behind the door – everywhere Aaron looked there was something of Ben's waiting to greet them. It was enough to almost break his mum every time.

Aaron stared at the door, at his brother's room. He hadn't looked inside, didn't really want to. He had heard his uncle Michael whispering to his dad about clearing it out but Aaron didn't think it was going to happen. Not if his dad's heartbroken expression was anything to go by. They didn't really need to. They had more than enough rooms. They could leave Ben's room as it was, preserving his memory.

Aaron made his way downstairs, but paused. Rose did the same, on her way upstairs. For a moment, the two friends just stared at each other, standing so still it looked like they had been frozen. Then Rose blinked and looked away. She cleared her throat.

"Your mum's looking for you. Dinner's almost ready."

Even though there was a communal table outside in the street, Kate prepared all their meals in her own kitchen. None of them had gone outside, save for Chris and Michael.

Rose turned to walk back downstairs without another look at Aaron. Ever since they'd left Salvador, Rose had been distant with him. At first, Aaron thought she was in shock. She had been left heartbroken by Kyran's deceit. She had liked Kyran, even kissed him, before finding out who he really was and his involvement in her parents' murder. Aaron understood her hurt, her pain, but he didn't know why she was taking it out on him.

"Rose?"

She didn't stop.

"Rose?" Aaron hurried down the steps. "Rose? Hey, wait." He grabbed her by the arm at the bottom of the stairs. Rose whirled around and shoved him in the chest, hard.

"Don't touch me!" she snapped.

Aaron stumbled back. He stared at her in stunned shock. He had known Rose all his life. He had seen her being pushy with Sam, playfully hitting him on the arm or sometimes pushing him away when he was annoying her, but she had never lashed out like this. And never at Aaron.

"What's wrong with you?" Aaron asked.

"What's wrong with *you*?" she retorted. "Why are you grabbing me?"

"To stop you from running away," Aaron said.

"Why?" she bit out.

"Why?" Aaron asked, incredulously. He stepped closer. "Because we're friends, *that's* why. But ever since we've come here, you won't even talk to me."

"What's there to talk about?" Rose asked, her tone sharp, guarded.

Aaron stared at her. His ire melted when he saw past his friend's anger and saw the fear – the desperate desire to lock away her pain.

He stepped closer. "Rose–"

"Don't." Rose backed away. "Don't, Aaron. I don't want to hear it. There's nothing to talk about. I'm fine."

"No you're not."

Rose paused, her eyes continued to burn in anger but her lips pressed together before she shook her head. "I don't want to talk about it," she said. "I don't want to even think about it, about...about..."

Kyran.

She couldn't say his name, but Aaron didn't need her to. He took another step, so he was standing close to her, so close he could see the start of dark circles under her eyes.

"You want to be angry, fine, be angry," he said. "You want to hit me, go ahead. Take out your anger any way you want, but please," his hand reached out to take hers, "don't block me out. Don't be mad at me."

Rose's shoulders slumped, the anger left her eyes and remorse replaced it. "I'm not...I'm not mad at you," she said. "I'm just–" She took in a breath. "I'm just mad."

Aaron nodded. "I get it."

Rose looked at him, right in the eyes and Aaron realised that he, in fact, didn't get it. He had developed a friendship with Kyran, a kind of camaraderie he'd never had with anyone else.

Rose had fallen for Kyran.

A knock on the front door distracted both of them. They turned and looked at it with a frown. Kate walked out of the kitchen, her eyes narrowed with cautious suspicion. Chris and Michael hurried out of one of the rooms; Sam came out of another. They gathered in the hallway, just staring at the front door. It had been four days since they arrived. Until now, no one had knocked on their door.

Chris went to answer, as Michael stationed himself behind the door. Kate moved to stand at the foot of the stairs and it took Aaron a moment to realise she was shielding him. Chris opened the door a crack before he paused. A breath caught in Aaron's chest when his dad didn't do anything but stand there. Then Chris swung the door open fully to reveal a woman. She looked to be in her late thirties, maybe early forties. The auburn hair at her temples had turned grey but the rest of her hair shone in the setting sun. She was just standing there, her brown eyes still on Chris, mouth parted slightly. Then her gaze moved to Kate and she choked out a gasp.

"Kate."

"Jane?" Kate's voice carried her surprise.

The woman – Jane – stepped into the house, slowly looking Kate up and down, shaking her head. "I can't believe it," she said. "You're...you're really here."

Kate stepped forward and hugged her. Then they were crying, letting out small sounds of surprise and sorrow.

***

Jane Boyd, Aaron quickly learnt, was his mum's best friend. The two women were in the living room with steaming mugs of tea while Aaron and the others sat at the table in the kitchen, working their way through a mashed potato and chicken dinner. Aaron's eyes kept darting to the open doorway, where he could see the two women sitting and talking quietly in the living room, looking rather forlorn.

Aaron narrowed his eyes at them. Skyler used to be able to hear him talking from halfway across the street, yet he couldn't make out the conversation happening in the next room.

"Mages have good hearing, right?" Aaron asked.

Chris and Michael looked up from their plates. Sam and Rose tensed, but didn't say anything.

"What?" Chris asked.

"Mages," Aaron said. "They're supposed to have good hearing. But I can't pick anything up."

Chris looked conflicted before Michael nudged his hand and tilted his head at Aaron.

Chris sighed. "You're supposed to use the air."

Aaron waited but nothing followed. "How exactly?" he pushed.

Chris's eyes darted to the next room, to his wife and her friend, before resting on Aaron. "Eavesdropping is wrong, Aaron."

"So is keeping secrets."

Chris dropped his fork on his plate and leant across the table to look at Aaron. "Don't do that," he warned. "Don't get cheeky with me. We didn't tell you about our past because we didn't want to upset you."

Aaron held his gaze. "I had a brother and an uncle I never knew about," he said. "No matter how painful it is, I deserve to know about my family."

The pink spots in his dad's cheeks told Aaron he was ashamed. He didn't say anything for long minutes. And when he did, his voice was so quiet, Aaron almost missed it.

"I know."

***

In the living room, Kate and Jane talked while their tea went cold.

"I heard rumours," Jane said. "For months there was talk about the Adams being back. I came by the house but it was still blocked so I figured the rumours were just that. I didn't think much of it. Then I heard that the vines were gone and I...I had to see for myself." She held Kate's gaze. "I never thought I would see you again."

"Do you know who did it?" Kate asked. "The vines?"

Jane shook her head. "No. I found your house like that, when...when I came back."

"Came back?" Kate shifted in her seat, leaning forward. "What do you mean?"

Jane's haunted eyes glistened. "I know what everyone thinks of you," she started. "Everyone has something to say about the Adams. But I know why you did it, why you left. I understand. Truth is, everyone did what you had. Everyone ran after the attack. The difference is, they ran to hide in this realm. You chose the human one."

Kate was quick to sit tall, raising her head. "We did what we had to."

Jane nodded and looked at the dark-haired boy in the kitchen, helping tidy the table after dinner.

"You did the right thing," she said, staring at Aaron. "You had already lost too much."

Kate didn't say anything. She waited until her friend looked back at her. "Where did you go?"

"Everywhere," Jane said. "Lived almost ten years going from city to city before I gathered the nerve to come back here."

Kate's eyes widened. "Ten years?"

"I wasn't the only one," Jane said. "The attack on Marwa left everyone shaken. If the City of the Elementals wasn't safe then what city was?" She shook her head slowly, eyes brimming with tears. "You don't know what it was like after the attack. The entire city emptied. No one wanted to stay in Marwa. This place was like a ghost town. For years, the city lay in ruins, abandoned, not a soul living here. Everyone was terrified the Gate was defective, that it would allow more demons in, so they refused to come back. Even Neriah didn't return until five, maybe six years later."

Kate was surprised but she didn't say anything.

"When Neriah came back, a small community followed him," Jane continued. "I think they felt...secure with Neriah here." She quietened for a moment. "But Neriah didn't stay. He couldn't. He began moving from city to city, always on the move. Some say he did that to avoid being tracked, others just assumed he needed to travel from one place to another to keep on top of things." She paused before swallowing heavily. "But I know why. He left Marwa because he couldn't live here, not with all the memories—" She broke off suddenly, taking in a breath to stop the tears. "He changed, Kate." Her voice quivered. "Neriah changed."

"He had to," Kate said quietly. "He was the only Elemental of his generation left in this realm." She met Jane's eyes. "He had to change, so he could take control."

The guilt was heavy and noticeable but Jane didn't say anything. Instead, she wiped at her cheeks and sniffed, turning to look at Aaron in the kitchen again. She watched him silently for a moment before smiling.

"He seems like a lovely boy," she said. "He looks so much like Chris."

Kate smiled at the sight of Aaron helping Sam with the dishes.

"What did you name him?" Jane asked.

Kate paused before replying quietly, "Aaron." She had to force her voice steady. "I named him Aaron."

Jane didn't say anything but looked at Kate with wide eyes, which were filling fast with tears. Kate didn't blame her. She was finding it difficult to keep them out of her eyes too.

***

Jane left shortly after Aaron had given up on eavesdropping and went upstairs to his new room. It was a big room, with a double bed and a four-door wardrobe against one wall. A small but fancy glass chandelier hung from the ceiling. But the room, much like the rest of the house, was in dire need of a good clean and Aaron had only half-heartedly attempted to clear away the dust and filth. In Salvador, he had shared a tiny room with Sam and Rose. Here there were so many rooms they got one each, but Aaron found himself wishing he was back in that small room with three beds crammed inside. At least he'd got to talk with his best friends there. He could always go to Sam or Rose's room but he was holding back. He wanted to see if they would come to him first. If they wanted to see him too.

Eventually, Aaron gave up. He opened his door and took one step when two doors simultaneously opened, and Sam and Rose walked into the hallway. They stopped to stare at each other. Small, awkward smiles came to all three.

"I was just coming to see you," Sam said to Aaron.

"Same here," Aaron said.

Rose stepped towards Aaron. "I was coming to say sorry," she started. "About before."

Aaron shook his head with a smile. "Already forgotten."

Rose smiled back at him.

Sam looked between the two. "What am I missing?"

"Nothing," Aaron said.

A knock sounded on the front door again. All three glanced to the stairs.

"How many friends does your mum have?" Sam asked.

Aaron frowned. There was something decisively different about this knock. Jane's knock had been hesitant, almost afraid. This one had a sense of power behind it. Before the second knock came, Aaron was halfway down the stairs. He saw his mum hurrying to answer it, no hint of the previous apprehension on her. She obviously thought it was Jane again.

"Mum," Aaron called from the stairs. "Wait—"

The door opened and everyone froze.

Neriah Afton stood at the threshold. His unusual violet eyes moved from Kate's shocked form to Aaron.

"Evening." His deep baritone voice boomed across the house. "May I come in?"

4

LEGACY HOLDERS

For a moment no one spoke. No one moved. All eyes were on Neriah, the leader of the mages. Neriah's gaze moved from Aaron to the shocked Kate.

"If you're going to close the door on me, I suggest you do so, or you invite me in," he said. "It's rude to linger in the doorway."

That seemed to bring Kate around. She moved, opening the door wide. "Come in." Her voice was quiet, guarded – afraid.

Neriah stepped inside. Kate didn't close the door. "Are...are they not coming in?" she asked and Aaron could hear the tremor in her voice.

"No, Skyler and Ella would rather wait outside," Neriah replied.

Aaron came down a few more steps, craning his neck to see, but his mum had closed the door before he got more than a glimpse of Skyler's ivory coat. At the sound of the door, Chris and Michael came out of the living room. They paused mid-step, staring wide-eyed at their unexpected guest.

"Neriah?" Chris said. "What are you doing here?"

Neriah smiled but his eyes remained cold. "Let's not play this game, Chris. You know why I'm here. It's why you gathered your family and left Salvador, is it not?"

Chris didn't reply. He straightened up. "Aaron," he called, but kept his eyes on Neriah. "Go upstairs."

Aaron stood where he was.

"Aaron, *now!*" Chris stressed.

Kate hurried towards Aaron, looking like she was going to drag him by the hand and stand guard in front of his door.

"Stay where you are, Kate," Neriah instructed and to Aaron's surprise, Kate obeyed, halting mid-step.

Neriah walked over to the stairs, all the while staring at Chris, his look clear to read: *stop me if you dare.* But when his violet eyes turned to Aaron, they softened, the anger dissipating a little.

"If you have a few minutes," he said. "I would like to talk to you."

Aaron didn't know what to say. What could Neriah want from him? He opened his mouth but before he could get out a word, his dad had stepped between them, facing Neriah.

"No," Chris said, his voice low and determined.

Neriah only glanced at him before focusing on Aaron again. "It won't take long," he said.

"Go to your room, Aaron," Chris repeated. "Don't come out until I say."

"But–" Aaron started.

"Go!" Chris snapped.

Aaron looked over at his mum and she nodded at him. "Go," she urged quietly.

Aaron turned to climb the stairs, glancing at his uncle, who was staring at Chris and Neriah, looking more than a little worried.

"You'll want to hear what I have to say, Aaron," Neriah called, halting him.

"You won't be saying anything to him!" Chris seethed. "I told you, Aaron's not going to be a part of it."

"He already is," Neriah said.

"Dammit, Neriah, leave him out of this," Chris said. "I don't want him involved."

"That's just the thing." Neriah turned to look at Chris at last. "It's not up to you."

"Neriah." Kate's voice was quieter, softer. "Please. He's only fourteen. Don't drag him into–"

"If I wanted to *drag* him, I would already have done so," Neriah cut her off, but his eyes remained on Chris. "The decision to get involved lies with Aaron, not with you, or with me – only him."

"Neriah–" Chris started.

Neriah raised a hand and Chris quietened. "You've forced your son to be a mute all his life, Chris," he said. "For once, let him speak." He looked past Chris to Aaron. "How about it?" he asked. "Do *you* want to hear me out?"

Aaron looked from his parents to his uncle before meeting Neriah's gaze. He knew what they wanted him to say, but that was the direct opposite of what *he* wanted. He took in a breath and met Neriah's waiting gaze.

"Yeah," he said. "I do."

***

Aaron sat on the sofa in the living room, facing Neriah while his dad hovered in the corner, watching them like a hawk. His mum and Michael hadn't been allowed to come in. It was a strange sight for Aaron to witness, for a guest to tell the owner of the house they weren't allowed in their own room.

Aaron tried his best not to fidget as Neriah's eyes stayed glued on him. It had been almost two minutes but Neriah hadn't spoken a word.

Aaron cleared his throat. "So, what is it you came here to talk to me about?" he asked.

In the hallway, Neriah had looked angry. Now, sitting across from him, he was a lot more relaxed. A small smile even tugged at his lips. "You look very much like your father," he said.

Chris glowered at him from behind but didn't speak.

Neriah turned his head to the side. "Let's hope your heart isn't anything like his."

Chris took a step forward, fists curled, but he stopped, restraining himself.

"You came all the way from Salvador to insult my dad?" Aaron asked. "Wow, that's some dedication."

Neriah was the leader of the mages. He was the oldest Elemental. His very presence demanded respect and Aaron was happy to give it, but not when he was taking digs at his dad.

But Neriah didn't get mad. He didn't even get upset. Instead, he smiled. Then chuckled. "I came to see you, Aaron," he said. "I never got the chance to speak much to you in Salvador."

"With all due respect," Aaron started, "I hardly think now is the time to make social visits."

"I never said the visit was social." Neriah's gaze hardened. The smile fell from his lips. "I spoke with Ella and she told me about your..." he paused, turning his head to the side again, "lack of knowledge about all things mage."

Chris's angry gaze was so sharp, it could have pierced holes into Neriah's back. Aaron shrugged, even though a flash of anger went through him. He knew why his mum and dad kept him away from the mage realm, but that didn't mean he didn't resent them for keeping secrets.

"I got the basics," he said.

"But the basics are not enough." Neriah shifted in his seat, pulling himself to the edge so he could lean towards Aaron. "You understand that you are an Earth Elemental?"

"Yes," Aaron replied.

"Do you understand that's not all you are?"

Aaron frowned. His palms became clammy and he felt his heart rate pick up. "What do you mean?"

Neriah held his gaze, his unusual violet eyes glinted with anger, or was it annoyance?

"I mean, you are the only Earth Elemental of your generation," he said. "And that makes you the legacy holder for Earth."

Aaron was confused. "I'm sorry," he said. "I don't know what that means."

"Of course you don't," Neriah said and his voice steeled. "That's why I came here. I had very little faith that your parents would explain any of this to you."

Chris was now pacing by the door, looking like he would explode if he stayed still.

"You understand where Elementals come from?" Neriah asked.

Aaron nodded. "Aric's bloodline."

Neriah looked momentarily surprised. "There can be many Elementals," he started, "but for each element, there is only one mage who carries its legacy. If there is more than one of each Elemental in a generation, the legacy chooses the one with the stronger core. It's passed from one generation to the next, from parent to child." His head inclined to the fretting Chris behind him. "Your father held the legacy for Earth. Now it's with you."

Aaron looked from his dad back to Neriah. "What does that mean?" he asked. "Holding the legacy? What does it do?"

Neriah smiled, but it held no humour. "It marks you," he said. "For great power – and for death."

Aaron swallowed back the fear that bubbled up. He saw the way his dad was raking his hand through his hair, ready to tear it out. "That sounds like a rough deal," he said. "Power but with a death sentence."

Neriah's eyes glinted, a look that Aaron didn't understand. "Most things that are worth having come at a price," he said. He straightened up, shaking whatever moment had come over him. "Being born an Elemental is a privilege, but being a legacy holder is an honour."

"Why?" Aaron asked.

"Because legacy holders are the only ones who can wield the Blades of Aric." Neriah smiled at Aaron's frown. "I'm not surprised that you're confused. I was certain you wouldn't even know about Aric, never mind his Blades."

Aaron's gaze flickered to his dad, in time to see the pink spots appear in his cheeks.

"Legend has it that after Aric's fourth child was born, Aric melted his mighty sword to create four smaller blades," Neriah explained. "Each one was blessed and carved by Aric's own hands. His eldest four were given a sword each and those became the Blades of Aric. Each Elemental family has its own blade."

Aaron remembered the conversation he'd had with Scott, the day he learnt about the Scorcher. Scott had said something about the Scorcher wielding the *Blade of Aedus* and that only Hadrian's son could do that. He forced back the memory of Kyran, seated right next to him while the discussion was taking place.

"These swords are not like other weapons," Neriah continued. "The Blades of Aric are extremely lethal. There is nothing in this world that could block them, defeat them." He held Aaron's gaze. "Mages were made for the sole purpose of fighting evil. The Blades were created to make sure legacy holders didn't fail that task. When a legacy holder raises their Blade, nothing can stand in their way."

Aaron nodded. So far, he was following. "So how does the death sentence come into it?"

"The legacies are our power, our future – they're passed from one generation to the next," Neriah started. "Legacies give power to the mages who share an affinity for their element. So as long as the legacies exist, every mage and Elemental will stay strong. The legacy holder is the only one able to use the Blades of Aric – the most powerful weapons against demons." He paused for a moment, collecting himself. "Look at it through the eyes of our enemy, and you'll see why legacy holders make such tempting targets."

Aaron stiffened, his eyes growing wide. His dad was still pacing, looking closer and closer to losing his nerve, but Aaron couldn't focus on anything but Neriah.

"But legacies are like anything else – they strive to survive," Neriah continued. "If a legacy holder dies before leaving an heir, the legacy races back up the bloodline, going to the former holder. If that person isn't there it will go further back. If it can't find a previous holder, the legacy will try to attach to another in the same Elemental bloodline. If it can't find anyone, only then will the legacy die."

"What happens then?" Aaron asked.

"Without an active legacy, all those that shared that element's power would grow weak and lose their powers."

"They would become human?" Aaron asked with shock.

"No, Aaron," Neriah said quietly. "They would die. Our powers are our life. Take them away and we have nothing to sustain us." He took in a breath. "Which is what the demons want."

Aaron stilled in horror.

"Three hundred years ago," Neriah continued, "the leader of the Lycans decided the way to cripple mages was to hunt down the legacy holders and kill them. If they got rid of the legacies, the mages would grow weak by themselves and die."

Icy fear crept down Aaron's back, making him shudder.

"But it's impossible for the Lycans to know the identity of the legacy holders," Neriah explained. "So they target all of the Elementals." He took a moment to continue. "Mages, they mostly ignore, but Elementals, they hunt down and kill."

Something clicked in Aaron's mind and his heart dropped like a stone.

"The City of Marwa," he started in a hollow voice. "The City of the *Elementals*." He held Neriah's pained and saddened gaze. "That attack, the one that killed my brother and uncle, that was by the Lycans. That's why they attacked Marwa, because they knew the Elementals lived there."

Neriah didn't say anything but his grief-stricken expression was enough to answer Aaron.

They went straight for the kids.

His dad's words rang in his head.

"That's why they attacked the children," Aaron said. "They were targeting the legacy holders."

"A legacy transfers from the parent to the child once the child's core awakens at the age of thirteen," Neriah said. "Lycans didn't want to wait for that to happen. They killed the Elemental young so the legacies wouldn't have anywhere to go and would die when the parents did."

Aaron closed his eyes and dropped his head, slowly shaking it. Everything was making sense. That's why the Lycans had targeted his brother, because Ben would have been the legacy holder for Earth.

"Isn't there anything we can do?" Aaron asked. "A way to safeguard the legacy holders?" It didn't register with him right away that he was talking about himself.

"Of course there is," Neriah said. "Train them. Make them untouchable."

Kyran forced his way into Aaron's mind at the word *untouchable*. The memory of his easy confidence, his graceful but lethal fighting, the way he taunted the demons but never allowed them to get close – yeah, Kyran was pretty untouchable. Which made sense now, as he happened to be the legacy holder for Fire.

Once Aaron managed to force all thoughts of Kyran away, he realised what it was Neriah had said, and what that meant for him. "That's why you're here," he said. "You want me to train?"

"I want you to learn to defend yourself," Neriah explained. "You're the legacy holder for Earth." His eyes stayed locked on his. "You are the *only* one that can use the Blade of Adams and help us in this war."

Aaron didn't say anything. He honestly didn't know what to say. He found he didn't need to figure out a response, because his dad was suddenly standing in the middle of the room, blocking Aaron.

"No," he growled. "He's not fighting."

"That's not your choice to make," Neriah replied at once.

Chris had both hands clenched. "You're asking a fourteen year old to risk his life–"

"No, I'm asking him to learn how to safeguard it," Neriah corrected, rising to his feet. "I don't want Aaron to fight this war, not until he's ready." His eyes flickered to Aaron before snapping back to Chris. "But there's no time to waste, and you and I both know what he could do with the right Blade in his hand."

Chris bristled, like he had been burnt. "No." He forced the word out from behind clenched teeth.

Aaron thought he could feel the ground tremble under him, or maybe it was just his heart that was beating so hard it was making him shake.

"Chris." Neriah's tone was one of warning.

"You can forget it!" Chris bit out. "I'm not losing any more of my family."

Neriah looked stunned. His eyes widened before narrowing. "Your family?" he asked. "*Your* family, Chris?" He stepped closer, his eyes darkened with anger. "What about the rest of us? Have we not lost family? Have we not suffered?" His expression was fierce, fury filling every inch of his being. "Have I not lost family, Chris? Hasn't Drake? What about Thomas? He was found hanged, drawn and quartered. Did his widow take her son and run?"

Chris stood silently as Neriah's fury escalated. Aaron turned to see the windows had begun to ice over.

"Or how about Joseph's *eight*-year-old son," Neriah continued, "who was forced to watch as his family was butchered? Did Skyler leave this realm?"

Aaron's heart leapt in his chest. He remembered Skyler's bitter words to Rose, only a few months ago.

You think you're the only one to lose your parents? Count yourself lucky you didn't watch them die. You didn't hear their screams.

Skyler was a git, a bully and a general pain, thought Aaron, but no one, *no one*, should go through that. No one should watch their family die.

"You're not the only one to lose someone, Chris," Neriah said. "Every *single* one of us has suffered but no one else got up and left!"

A tremor ran through the ground, rattling the furniture. Aaron quickly stood up.

"What can I say?" Chris's words were strained, coming from his tight jaw. "I'm not as brave as the rest of you. I can't risk my family and I'll do whatever I have to in order to protect them."

"What about the others?" Neriah yelled. "The families in Hadrian's zones? The ones who are tortured *every* day? What about them Chris? Who protects them?"

The ice covering the windows cracked, taking the glass with it. The ground shook violently in response, the chandelier swung dangerously overhead.

"Stop it!" Aaron yelled, somehow managing to come between the two mages without tripping on the shaking ground. "Stop! Just stop!" He grabbed his dad's arm and pulled him back. "Dad, *stop!*"

The shaking ceased. The chandelier swayed overhead, the tinkling of the glass droplets and the quick breaths of the Elementals who continued to glare at each other filled the room.

Aaron turned to Neriah. "I think you should go," he said quietly. "Please, just...just go."

"I'm not going anywhere until I get an answer."

"I already told you—" Chris started.

"From *Aaron*," Neriah snapped. He turned to the fourteen year old. "I want an answer from *you*."

Aaron paused. He could feel his dad's arm tense under his hand. Aaron took in a breath. "I'm sorry," he said to Neriah. "I can't help you."

Neriah kept his eyes on Aaron. "Is this your decision?" he asked. "Or are you only saying what you know your father wants?"

Aaron couldn't help but glance at his dad in guilt, but he didn't say anything.

Neriah straightened up, standing tall. "I'm staying in the city tonight," he said. "I'll leave first thing tomorrow morning. If in one night you can gather the courage to do what *you* want, then come and find me."

***

Morning crept along. Chris hadn't slept. He couldn't, not with Neriah's words spinning in his head. He picked up his mug and took a gulp of coffee. Kate was fixing breakfast. She hadn't slept much either, joining her husband in the kitchen just before daybreak.

Aaron had been very quiet after Neriah left. Chris didn't know what to say to him and so had left him alone. Until the early hours of the morning, he had heard voices coming from Aaron's room – Aaron whispering with his friends about Neriah, no doubt. Chris had wanted to go upstairs and tell them off, scold them to get some sleep, but he didn't have the energy, or the heart. He told himself that at least Aaron was talking to *someone*; he was getting his feelings out, which could only be a good thing.

Kate put a plate of pancakes in front of him but Chris didn't have the stomach to eat.

"Hey." Kate ran a hand through his hair, caressing him gently. "Don't think too much about it," she said. "Neriah's not forcing Aaron to fight. That's all that matters."

Chris nodded. "Yeah," he said. He rubbed at his eyes again. "Yeah, I know."

Kate slid into the chair next to his. "When I saw him at the door with the other two Elementals, I thought he was here to take Aaron away, one way or another."

"He's the oldest Elemental," Chris said. "If he really wanted to, he could have taken Aaron, even against his will." He shook his head. "But Neriah's not like James had been. He doesn't force, he gives a choice."

Kate didn't say anything and picked up her mug of tea.

"He's desperate," Chris said quietly. "It won't be long before Hadrian's core awakens. Neriah needs all the power he can gather before then."

Kate was looking at him with a frown, her eyes narrowed. "You want to go."

It wasn't so much a question as it was a statement.

"Want isn't the right word." Chris pulled in a breath. "I *need* to do this," he said. "I need to fight, to stand with the rest and do what I can to stop Hadrian." He looked at his wife. "The world can think what it wants, Kate, but I'm not a coward. I didn't run from a fight. I ran to protect what I couldn't afford to lose. But now that Aaron's older and he knows the truth about who he is, I can leave him with you and go join the war." He held her blue-eyed gaze. "These last fourteen years haven't erased who I am. I'll always be a Hunter." His hands flexed, itching to close around his familiars. It had been almost a decade and a half since he held his weapons. "Neriah wants the Blade of Adams. I know I can't use it. The legacy is now with Aaron. But that doesn't mean I can't use another sword." He held Kate's stare. "I need to help, Kate. I want to stand against Hadrian. I'm fighting this war."

Kate was silent, watching him. She nodded at last, before breathing out a sigh. "I know." She smiled at him. "And so am I."

"You need to stay with Aaron, Kate," Chris said.

"I have just as much right to protect this realm as you do," Kate said.

"I never said you don't," Chris replied. "But if both of us go away to fight, who will take care of Aaron?"

Kate dropped her gaze. "Family," she said quietly.

"Michael won't stay back," Chris said. "He wants to fight too. He told me just the other day he was thinking of going to Salvador to speak to Neriah."

"I didn't mean Michael," Kate said.

Chris frowned. "What other family do we have?"

Kate looked at him. "Family doesn't always mean blood."

Chris's eyes widened with realisation. He looked away.

"Chris," Kate reached across the table to touch his hand. "We need to go and see her. We should've by now."

Chris shook his head. "I don't think I can face her."

"Alaina has every right to be mad at us," Kate said. "But she won't hold anything against Aaron. She will take care of him, and Samuel and Rosalyn too."

Chris shook his head. "Kate—"

A door closed somewhere above them, then they heard footsteps down the stairs, coming steadily towards them.

"We'll talk later," Kate said, getting up from the table.

She pulled out another few plates and turned, about to lay the table for the three teenagers when the door opened. Kate froze, the plates in her hands. Aaron was standing there, wearing his heavy jacket, with a packed duffel bag in his hand.

5

MAKING CHOICES

Aaron watched as Chris stood up, surprised eyes on him, taking in his attire – heavy boots, jeans, hooded top under his jacket. Aaron could almost see the realisation as it swept over his dad. A Hunter – he was dressed as a Hunter. Chris's stare moved to the bag in Aaron's hand before snapping back to his face. Aaron almost flinched.

"What are you doing?"

It was his mum who asked the question, standing with a stack of plates forgotten in her hands. Aaron walked further inside, and Sam and Rose trailed in after him, clutching their own bags. Aaron put the duffel bag on the table.

"I'm leaving," he said. He looked straight at his dad. "I'm going with Neriah."

The plates hit the worktop with a hard *crack*. The next thing Aaron knew, his mum had grabbed his arm and yanked him around to face her. "Have you lost your mind?" she seethed. Her eyes were wide, mouth twisted in outrage.

"Mum–" Aaron started.

"NO!" Her shout reverberated in the kitchen. Her grip tightened on Aaron's arm. "You're not going *anywhere!*"

"Kate?" Michael appeared at the door, looking surprised. "What's going on?"

Kate didn't answer him. She was too focused on Aaron. "You listen to me." Her voice was beginning to shake, clear blue eyes clouded with fear. "You're not stepping one *foot* out of this house. You hear me?"

Aaron rested his free hand on hers, on top of her tight fingers clenched around his arm. "Mum," he said quietly. "You know hiding like this isn't right."

"*What?*" She was livid. "You think risking your life is the right thing to do?"

Aaron held her gaze. "Mages were brought into existence to fight demons."

Kate's grip loosened. She pulled away, eyes still wide, mouth open in surprise.

Aaron turned to look at his dad. He was standing with his back rigid, jaw clenched, eyes fixed on him.

"If we don't fight, if *I* don't fight, then what does that make me?" Aaron asked.

"Aaron." Chris's voice shook. "We already explained to you. We can't lose–"

"I know," Aaron stepped towards him. "I get it, Dad, I do. You've been through so much, you've lost your brother and your son, you don't want to risk losing me too." He paused to take in a deep breath. "But that doesn't mean we get to sit back while *everyone* else is left fighting."

"Yes, you do," Kate said. "*You* do. Your dad and I will fight. We will do what we can to help defeat Hadrian but *you* will stay out of the way."

Aaron's eyes narrowed. "What?" he asked. "You both are joining the fight?" He looked at his dad. "When were you going to tell me this? Or were you planning on leaving in the middle of the night again without saying a word to me?" He turned to his mum. "Was I going to get another letter? How long would I have to wait this time to see you again?"

"We left you in Salvador the way we did because we had to," Kate said. "There wasn't time to explain everything to you. We needed to find Neriah. If Neriah found out we had returned to the realm but made no contact with him, he would've been within his right to execute us."

Aaron's surprise showed in his expression.

"Neriah wouldn't–"

"He didn't," Kate said. "Doesn't mean he couldn't have." Her voice dipped. "We will fight for Neriah. But you need to stay as far away from this war as possible."

"I can't," Aaron said. "I've spent all night trying to talk myself into doing what you want. I told Neriah I wouldn't help him, but I can't sit back and watch as the world crumbles around me, especially when I know I can bring something to this fight."

"Aaron." Michael came to his side. "I admire your courage, but you're not of age yet. Until your core matures, you won't be much good to anyone in the war."

"What if I have the Blade of Adams?" Aaron asked.

Michael hesitated. He looked to Kate but didn't speak.

"You said you always wanted to tell me the truth," Aaron reminded him. "Now's your chance. I'm asking you, would the Blade still be effective if I use it now?"

Michael dropped his gaze and gave a reluctant nod. "Yes," he whispered unhappily. "It wouldn't be anywhere near as powerful as it could be with a mature core, but – yes, the Blade would still be pretty lethal."

"Then why shouldn't I use it to help?" Aaron asked.

"Aaron," Michael's voice held a pleading note. "You're too young."

"Mages younger than me are out hunting."

"That doesn't make it right!" Chris snapped. "Just because Neriah's lost his mind, sending kids out to face down demons, doesn't mean I'll let you do the same!"

"Those *kids* are the ones who have been protecting not only this realm but the human one too," Aaron said, unable to hold back his growing anger. "And they've been doing it for the last *fourteen* years."

"It's going to be different now," Michael said. "With Hadrian back–" He paused, sucking in a breath. "Aaron, you have no idea what you're getting yourself into."

Aaron held his anxious gaze. "I guess I'll find out."

"You can say what you want," Kate said in her usual end-of-matter tone. "You're not leaving."

Aaron stilled for a moment, before reaching out to pick up his bag. "Yes I am," he said.

Kate stared at him and Aaron could see the realisation hit her then, that she could no longer force him into obedience. Her lips thinned and eyes started to water.

"Aaron, *please*," she begged.

"I know you're scared, Mum," Aaron said. "Truth is, I am too. But we don't get to sit this out. We're not the only ones to have lost family. It's happened to the others too but they're fighting back and that's what we should do." He turned to look at his dad. "We're Elementals. We need to help. We *should* help." Chris didn't say anything. Aaron stepped towards him. "Come with me." This time, it was Aaron that was pleading. "We can all go back, all of us join the fight." He took another step forward, inching closer to Chris. "Please, Dad, don't fight me on this. You can teach me–"

"No," Chris said. "You're not fighting. You're staying here."

Aaron stared at him. His mum had yelled the same words minutes ago, but it was his dad's quietly spoken command that tore his heart open. Aaron swallowed the rest of his words, pushing them deep down. He stepped back, not trusting himself to speak. The hurt was quickly turning to fury and he knew if he didn't leave right now, he would say something all of them

75

would later regret. He shifted the heavy bag in his hands and turned.

"Don't you dare, Aaron!" Kate called after him.

"Sorry, Mum," Aaron said quietly. "Come with me or not, I'm leaving." He walked away.

Sam and Rose followed him.

"Where are you two going?" Michael asked.

Sam paused and looked back at him. "With Aaron."

Aaron and the twins headed to the front door. They stepped out to find Neriah waiting for them.

Aaron was taken aback at the sight of the leader of the mages, standing at his gate, waiting for him with a smile on his lips and a look of triumph in his eyes. It only served to further annoy Aaron.

"What are you doing?" he asked, as he made his way towards Neriah.

"Waiting for you," Neriah replied simply.

"You were that sure I would come?" Aaron asked.

"I was sure that the boy who fought his way into a Q-Zone, a mere few months after coming to this realm, wouldn't give up the chance to fight."

Aaron stopped just before the gate. "Scott told you?"

"He had to tell me."

Aaron shifted under the intense gaze. "You should know I didn't go into that Q-Zone to fight. I went because–"

"Because your friends were there." Neriah glanced at the twins before looking back at Aaron. "Yes, Scott told me that too." He didn't look mad. If anything, he looked rather amused. He didn't say any more on the subject, though. He moved to allow the gate to swing open. "Come, we should leave."

Aaron held on to the metal gate but turned back to look at the house. The door was firmly shut. No one had come out after him. They were actually going to let him walk away like this, angry and hurt.

Aaron caught Sam's eye; his friend simply nodded his encouragement. They had spent the whole night discussing this decision. They had all agreed that no matter what happened, they were taking part in the fight against demons, against vamages – against Hadrian. Sam and Rose were human. They had no elemental powers, nor did they know how to wield a sword or use a gun, but they were willing to do whatever they could to help the mages defeat the vamages – the demons that murdered their parents.

Aaron turned and pushed open the gate. He walked behind Neriah, with Sam and Rose beside him, all heading down the street.

"Where's Ella and Skyler?" Aaron asked, partly just to have something to say.

"They're waiting at the Gate," Neriah said. His gaze went to the long table that sat in the middle of the street. Something flickered in his eyes but he looked away before Aaron could figure it out. "They don't have much tolerance for Marwa."

"Why is that?" Aaron asked.

Before Neriah could answer, the sound of a door slamming shut made them turn around. Aaron gaped at the sight of his mum, dad and uncle Mike, hastily packed bags in hand, coming down the path. They looked beyond livid, lines of anger on their faces, eyes blazing. His mum blasted the gate off its hinges, without even touching it, before heading down the street towards them.

Neriah stepped past Aaron, coming to stand before him. It took Aaron a moment to understand he was standing guard, protecting Aaron from his parents. The absurdity of the situation would have made him laugh if he wasn't so keyed up.

"What's going on?" Neriah asked, directing his question to Chris.

"What's it look like?" Chris snarled. "We're coming too."

Aaron's relief was short-lived, because almost at once, Neriah shook his head.

"I don't want you," he said.

"I don't care," Chris replied.

Neriah stared at Chris, before a half-smile came to his face. "I guess having you in Salvador is better than here." He glanced back at Sam and Rose before meeting Chris's eyes. "You three can take Aaron's friends to Salvador."

"Why?" Kate asked quickly, stepping forward. "Where are you taking Aaron?"

The panic in her voice made guilt surge in Aaron. He pushed it down.

"Aaron will accompany me to retrieve his Blade," Neriah replied.

Aaron tensed, sharing a nervous look with the twins.

"We want to stay with Aaron," Sam said at once.

"We're coming too," Kate added.

But Neriah shook his head. "If too many go to get the Blade it will attract attention."

"Mike," Chris called. "You and Kate take Samuel and Rosalyn. I'm going with Aaron."

Kate let out a noise of protest but Michael had grabbed her hand, already pulling her towards the twins.

Neriah didn't move, his gaze still on Chris.

78

"You can't come with us," he said.

"Yes I can," Chris stubbornly argued. "You may be the oldest and the leader, but I'm an Elemental too. You can't stop me. I have every right to come with you."

Neriah let out a humourless laugh. "You sure you still deserve to be called an Elemental after shirking your responsibilities for fourteen years?"

Chris got impossibly close. His eyes were blazing, jaw clenched so tight Aaron was sure it must be hurting.

"I'm going with my son," Chris said very quietly, taking his time to say each word carefully. "Elemental or not, you can't deny me that much."

When Neriah didn't speak, Chris moved past him. He walked by Aaron without a word. He didn't even look at him. Sharing a last glance with Sam and Rose, Aaron walked away, following his dad and Neriah to Marwa's Gate, where Skyler and Ella stood waiting.

***

Aaron walked in silence, the only sounds came from the crunching and snapping of leaves and twigs under their feet. Skyler and Ella were behind him, climbing up the path. His dad trailed them. Leading the way was Neriah. No one had uttered a word in the last two hours.

Aaron shifted his bag; it was getting uncomfortably heavy at this point. He climbed the steep hill, panting slightly at the exertion. He could feel beads of sweat gathering under his collar. When he had followed the others out of the Gate of Marwa, there had been two portals ready. One led to the City of Salvador, which his mum, uncle and friends took. The other, Aaron had presumed, would take them straight to wherever the Blade of Adams was. Instead, he had passed through the portal only to land in the middle of a dense forest. They had been quietly trekking their way through it ever since.

Aaron came to Neriah's side when he paused, to let the others catch up. Then, when he continued forward without saying a word, Aaron couldn't hold back any longer.

"What's with the nature walk?" he asked. "I thought the portal would take us straight to the Blade."

"You thought wrong," Neriah replied.

"Like always." Skyler's quiet comment came from behind. Aaron turned to glare at him.

They walked for another few minutes in silence.

"Why didn't you set up a portal closer to the Blade?" Aaron asked.

"Portals leave behind trails," Neriah said. "And trails can be followed."

Aaron considered this. "Who would want the Blades of Aric?" he asked. "They're useless to anyone other than legacy holders."

"Our enemies may not be able to use the swords," Neriah said, "but if they found the Blades, they could stop *us* from using them."

Aaron felt like an idiot, so he kept quiet and continued walking. It was another half an hour before they came to a clearing. The group paused, bringing out bottles of water to replenish that which the sun had forced out of them. Aaron didn't have any water; he hadn't packed essentials like that. All he had in his bag were his jeans and tops, and an extra pair of shoes – all useless for quenching his raging thirst.

As if to mock him, Neriah held out his empty bottle for Aaron to take. Aaron grabbed it, with every intention of hurling it into the air. Before he could though, Neriah held his fingers against the bottle and water began filling it.

No matter what Aaron had seen these past few months, water magically pooling out of thin air stole his breath. He brought the full bottle to his mouth, letting the cold, cool water rush down his dry throat. He drank almost the whole thing before remembering his dad was there too, and in his haste to follow Aaron, probably hadn't packed a bottle of water either. Aaron turned around to find his dad next to Ella, taking the bottle she was offering. He brought it to his lips and, like Aaron, he almost emptied the entire thing.

Aaron turned and gave the bottle back to Neriah. "Thanks."

Neriah didn't say anything. They continued walking. Aaron kept up with him, walking in step with the leader.

"How can you do that?" he said. "The water? How can you make it from nothing?"

Neriah smiled. "I'm not making it," he said. "Water is my element. It comes to me when I ask."

"How?" At Neriah's look Aaron quickly added, "I'm sorry, it's just…I don't quite understand how we can do…what we do."

Neriah's eyes had that same glint Aaron had seen the day before when they were talking about legacies – a strange mix of anger and annoyance…and maybe a little pity.

"Mages have what we call *cores* inside us," he started, slowing his pace to allow Aaron to keep up. "Our core is what defines us, what decides which element we will have an affinity with. In a sense, our core is the root. It's what makes us a mage." He looked at Aaron and waited for his nod of comprehension, before continuing. "Our core pulls energy from the elements. The stronger the core, the more energy it pulls, making the mage that much more powerful. You don't know your core is doing it, but it's working all the time."

Aaron looked around him, at the trees surrounding him, the soft ground under his feet. "You mean, I'm drawing the power of Earth right now?"

Neriah smiled. "Just as I am drawing water from the moisture in the air, the clouds overhead, and the lake that's six miles west from here." He chuckled at Aaron's gob-smacked expression. "It's an involuntary action, like breathing. You don't think about it, you just do it. We do it from the moment we're born. We practise while our cores are asleep. When they awake, they already have a store of energy."

Aaron tripped on the overgrown root at his feet, such was his concentration on Neriah.

Neriah steadied him with one hand and continued. "Our core utilises this energy, giving us the ability to manipulate the elements. When I fill a bottle with water, I'm not making it out of thin air. I'm merely directing it from one source to another." He gave a pointed look to the sky, where white fluffy clouds hung overhead.

Aaron grinned. "That's awesome."

"Glad you approve." Neriah smiled.

"So when I want to make the ground split open?" Aaron asked.

"You're not redirecting anything then," Neriah explained. "You're bending the element, making it bow to your will. It's different."

"Not to mention difficult," Aaron muttered.

"It's only difficult because you haven't had much practise," Neriah said. "You are a legacy holder. You are capable of much more than you think."

Aaron fell quiet. After a moment he looked around at him. "Does holding the legacy make your core stronger?" he asked.

"It's the other way around. Legacies choose those with a strong core," Neriah replied. "But having a legacy connected to the core does give the holder an ability to manipulate their element with more ease."

Aaron shifted his bag uncomfortably between his hands. He certainly didn't find using his Elemental power easy, but then again, he hadn't started training until he was fourteen. Most mages started at ten, three years before their cores awoke.

"Yesterday you said something about legacy holders giving power to the mages who share an affinity for their element," Aaron reminded him. "I don't understand that."

"Each legacy keeps the power of their element alive," Neriah said. "Your legacy is for the element Earth, so every mage that uses the power of Earth can do so because of your legacy. The legacies are what connects the mages. You are the legacy holder for Earth, so you share a connection with all those who use Earth as their element. I am the legacy holder for Water, so my legacy calls to all those who use my element." He looked at Aaron. "But you and I also have a connection, through those mages that use both Water and Earth."

Aaron glanced behind him, to his dad, to see him looking rather annoyed that Aaron was talking to Neriah. Aaron turned back. "This connection is even more powerful when we're related, right?"

Neriah took a moment to answer. "Nothing is more powerful than blood," he said quietly. "Our very cores connect to one another in the same bloodline. They act like links in a chain. When one core is lost, the chain breaks. The rest will stay connected but the link that's missing will always leave a gap, one that can never be bridged."

Neriah's voice held such pain, such heartbreak, that Aaron couldn't look at him. He lowered his head, studying the ground as he walked. They headed deeper into the forest. Tall trees with thick branches were blocking out most of the sun, draping everything in shadow. Aaron followed close behind Neriah, but his thoughts went to his dad, thinking about him and about the brother he lost, the four-year-old son he felt die. They were two 'links' that had been severed from his bloodline chain. The only two Aaron knew about. He realised there must be more – many more. His grandparents, for example. Aunts, uncles, cousins, anyone in his dad's family that died left a break in the Adams family chain.

A pressure closed down on Aaron's heart, making him breathless. His dad had been through so much. It was no wonder he was fighting so fiercely to protect him. The feeling of guilt was fast becoming unbearable. Aaron turned to look at his dad again.

Something crossed Aaron's mind.

"Neriah?" he called, looking around at the Elemental by his side.

"Yes."

Aaron faltered, before pushing on. "Do you have family?"

Neriah almost stopped in his tracks. Then he pushed onwards but didn't answer for several long minutes. "Only Ella," he finally replied.

Aaron had guessed as much. He remembered talking with Ella, the day he had found out that the demon Hadrian had actually been a mage once. He recalled Ella telling him the story of The Mage Who Fell – how Hadrian had given up his purity to become a hybrid, a vamage. It was when she spoke about Neriah that Aaron had asked if he was her father.

Uncle...Maternal. The only family I have left.

If Neriah had a wife and kids, Ella would have mentioned them.

"You said you're the legacy holder for Water," Aaron started. "But if you don't have any kids, who will your legacy go to? What if the legacy doesn't choose Ella?"

Neriah turned to look at Aaron and even in the limited light, Aaron could see the glint of amusement in Neriah's eyes. "No one's had the nerve to question me about my legacy," he said.

"Sorry," Aaron said quickly.

Neriah's deep chuckle echoed in the woods. They continued walking in silence for long minutes before Neriah spoke.

"I'd thought about it, once," he confided. "I had the usual plans – marry the girl I love, have kids, set up a home." He fell quiet, the very air around them spoke of Neriah's remorse. "Some things are not meant to be."

Aaron didn't know how to respond.

"Our powers are our own," Neriah said, and his voice was back to its usual strength. "No one can force us to give our powers, our legacies, away. Only through free will can our powers be given to another." He turned his head to look at Aaron. "When the time comes, I will choose to give Ella my legacy."

Aaron frowned. "I thought you said the legacy chooses who to go—"

Neriah held out a hand, halting Aaron. He had come to an abrupt stop. Aaron stood still as a chill washed over him. Behind him, he heard footsteps stop as well. Neriah's face was in shadow, his body perfectly still. Then he cursed.

Before Aaron knew what was happening, a hand grabbed his arm and hauled him back. He stumbled in the darkness and looked up to see his dad's tensed and worried form next to him. Chris's hand was curled around his arm, tight enough to make Aaron's hand tingle in protest.

"Dad?"

"Shhh!" Chris urged.

Aaron could hear Skyler and Ella getting their weapons ready. No one moved. They barely breathed. But Aaron still couldn't pick up on what had caused the reaction.

He stared at his surroundings until he noticed something moving, straight in front of him. Before his eyes, several big shadows stepped past the cluster of trees. Stray rays of sunshine made their way through the leafy canopy so Aaron couldn't mistake what he was seeing.

Lycans.

A whole pack of them, growling low in their throats with fangs bared, blocking their way.

6

When Dogs Come Out To Play

It happened in the blink of an eye. One moment Aaron was standing, staring wide-eyed at the pack of beasts before him; the next a full-on battle had broken out. Neriah, Ella and Skyler unleashed a fury of attack, while Chris pulled Aaron behind him.

The Lycans howled as they were thrown back by the bullets. It took Neriah and Ella mere seconds to encase several Lycans in ice, holding them immobile, before moving in to shoot them in the back of their heads. Skyler sent whirlwinds of pure power at the Lycans, throwing them to the ground. But the Lycans weren't staying down for long. They leapt back up, standing on two legs, not four, with their fangs and claws bared. The fur on their back bristled as they tensed before darting forward to attack. Some Lycans managed to break out of their iced prisons before they could be shot. More and more Lycans darted out of the darkness of the woods. They all slashed and tore their way closer to the Elementals, trying to get near enough to taste blood.

Neriah pulled back his hand and struck out. Spears of ice flew outwards and impaled two Lycans, pinning them to the trees. Ella sent a flurry of snow at the approaching five Lycans, blinding them long enough for Skyler to blast them back and against the trees, knocking them unconscious. But more Lycans kept coming at them, dodging the bullets and jolts of power.

When two Lycans came at Chris, Aaron's training kicked in. Almost on instinct, Aaron pulled his hands together, ready to send out a ripple and throw the beasts back.

He never got the chance.

The ground trembled under him before Chris threw out his arms. The trees on either side of him uprooted, tearing out of the ground with a monstrous *crack*. Trees as tall as houses flew towards the Lycans, slamming into them. Chris moved forward, swinging his arms like he was throwing punches, sending tree after tree at the approaching Lycans. The beasts darted back, leaping aside to avoid being crushed.

Aaron stared at his dad in a mix of awe and fear. He had never seen anyone attack like that before. He realised belatedly the reason – his dad was the only Earth Elemental other than himself. Even Neriah, Skyler and Ella paused in their attacks for a heartbeat, to watch Chris unleash his power.

The ground shook under Chris's feet, trees swayed and bent into arcs before springing back to hit the Lycans, throwing them across the forest with enough force to break bones.

The Lycans hunched down onto all fours. Their eyes were on Chris, a low growl in their throats. Chris held out both hands and the ground around the Lycans began to sink. The Lycans scrambled to get out but the ground gave way before many could manage. They fell into the fast-forming pit, their howls ringing in the air. But not a moment later, more Lycans thundered out of the shadows, coming at the Elementals from all corners. Aaron turned to see two darting towards him. He held up his hands and sent two perfect ripples through the ground, knocking the Lycans into the nearest tree. Two more took their place. No matter how many they took down, more Lycans kept coming at them, fangs and claws bared.

"Chris!"

Aaron turned at Neriah's shout to see him throwing Chris one of his pistols. Chris caught it and ran towards a fast approaching Lycan. All of a sudden, the Lycan came to an abrupt halt. It jerked, trying to move forward but thick roots had grown from the forest ground and held onto his feet. Chris reached the trapped Lycan but went behind him, before shooting a bullet into the back of the Lycan's head. The Lycan fell to its knees before toppling over, its feet finally released from the ground. It lay unmoving, clearly dead.

"Adams!"

Aaron turned at the sound of Skyler's shout. He saw Ella holding two Lycans immobile, wrapping and rewrapping their bodies in ice as they struggled to break out of their prison.

Skyler met Aaron's gaze before raising his guns and aiming at the back of the Lycans' heads. He fired both at the same time. The bullets penetrated the ice to hit the Lycans. Ella let go and the ice disappeared, leaving the dead Lycans to fall to the ground. Skyler turned his head to hold Aaron's gaze, before throwing him one of his pistols, mirroring what Neriah did with Chris.

"One bullet," Skyler instructed. "Straight in the occiput." He tapped the back of his own head, at the small space between his head and neck.

Aaron nodded and turned, but it was impossible to aim so precisely at the back of the Lycans' heads – at their occiput – when they were moving at such an unnatural speed. Now Aaron understood why Scott always set up Q-Zones to trap and kill Lycans. Collapsing the prison with the Lycans inside was easier than trying to shoot them in such a difficult spot.

Something changed in the air. The Lycans came to a stop and fell back, howling unearthly cries. Aaron didn't know what was happening, and then he saw it – the huge demonic beast that made its way through the pack of Lycans. The other Lycans were tall when they stood up on two legs, with greyish black fur sitting like a coat on their backs. This one easily dwarfed the others. The fur on its back was a deep blood red. Its eyes were a cold cobalt blue, and they were fixed on Aaron's dad.

The ground shook so violently, Aaron was sure an earthquake had hit them. He had to hold on to the nearest tree to remain standing. He turned to see his dad's entire being tense, his face distorted with rage, pure and unadulterated. His eyes were on the red-furred Lycan, who was growling back in response. It let out several loud barks before falling to all fours, and racing towards him.

Before Aaron could do more than steady himself on the shaking ground, his dad took off, running directly at the Lycan.

"Dad!"

"CHRIS, NO!"

Aaron's shout was drowned out by Neriah's furious cry. As his voice bellowed out, so did a cascade of water, sweeping through the forest. It pushed back the Lycans but before it could reach Chris and the red Lycan, the two had met. Aaron had to remember to breathe when he saw his dad take on the massive beast with nothing more than his fists. Then both fell back, the gush of water knocking them off their feet, but it didn't take long for them to get back up. The Lycan howled, its crimson fur drenched, blue eyes slitted. Chris swung a fist and nearby trees uprooted to pound the Lycan. But this one took the hits, knocking them back with just as much force.

The rest of the Lycans were still fighting with Neriah, Skyler and Ella but Aaron couldn't look away from his dad. He had to hold on to the nearest tree for support as he watched his dad pull back to strike the massive Lycan again. The ferocious beast lunged forward, twisting out of the way of Chris's attack, swiping its clawed hand at him. Chris's eyes widened, his mouth open in a silent scream as he arched back – as a long red line stretched across his torso.

Aaron's world tilted when his dad hit the ground. The cut on his chest begun seeping blood, staining his front. Then his body started to writhe, convulsing in agony.

Aaron's ears were ringing; a pressure built in his chest, making it hard to breathe. A strange sound had filled the air. It took Aaron a moment to realise it was a scream – and it was coming from him.

It was his cry that was echoing in the forest, his fury that was pounding at his insides, his fear that was twisting at his heart. He also realised his grip had fallen from the tree and he was now racing towards his dad.

Aaron didn't stop to think what he was doing. All he could focus on was his dad, and getting to his side. He saw the red-furred Lycan come to stand over his dad's fallen body and Aaron's whole being pulsed with panic. His fingers felt like they were on fire. With another cry, Aaron threw out his hands and the ground shifted under his command. The whole forest shuddered. With a monstrous roar, the ground split on the far side of them, the chasm spreading to take down whatever was in its way – trees and Lycans alike.

The red-furred Lycan had to scamper back, the crack forcing him away from Chris. Aaron came to fall next to his dad, but his eyes were still on the Lycan, his hand outstretched towards him – ready to attack, to defend. The Lycan dropped to all fours and licked its jowls. It snarled at Aaron before taking a few steps back, crouching low. It was going to try and jump over the gap.

Before it could take off, though, something hit it with enough force to send it toppling to one side. It recovered and turned with a growl. Skyler waited a moment before curling his fist again and sending a jolt as powerful as a tornado. The beast darted out of the way, narrowly avoiding the power that tore across the forest, demolishing everything in its path. Skyler wasn't done. He sent another jolt, then another and another. The look on his face told Aaron the attack wasn't anything but personal. Skyler's usually cold blue eyes were now burning, his jaw clenched, teeth bared as he hit out repeatedly. His tornado finally caught the red-furred Lycan, blasting him out of sight.

The other Lycans retreated, scampering back to the darkness they had come from. Aaron's attention quickly snapped to his dad, who had fallen still, his eyes closed.

"Dad!" Aaron held on to him. The horrendous cut across his torso had stained the whole of his front with blood, but the rise and fall of his chest told Aaron he was still breathing. He was unconscious but alive.

Skyler manipulated the air to help Neriah and Ella jump across the wide crack in the ground before following after them. They gathered around Aaron and Chris, kneeling next to them. Neriah's hand hovered over Chris's torso and Aaron wasn't sure if he was imagining it or not, but the bleeding seemed to slow down.

Ella was already holding on to her pendant, talking quickly to the only one connected to it – the Controller, Scott.

"We need it now," Aaron heard her say. "He's been infected." She nodded at the response, her brow glistening with sweat. "Okay. I will." She turned to her uncle. "Scott's opened a portal, about a mile west."

"What?" Aaron choked. "A mile? Tell him to open one here!"

Ella's fierce gaze locked on him. "He would if he could."

"Skyler," Neriah commanded, his hand still aimed at Chris's torso. "As gently as you can."

Skyler didn't say anything but stood up and held out both hands. Chris was pulled off the ground, his prone form floating mid-air, lifted up by Skyler's power. Aaron wanted to protest but his voice failed him. His chest felt as if it was in a vice-like grip; just breathing was proving to be a feat in itself. He scrambled to his feet as Neriah rose too, his hand still hovering over Chris's levitated body. Hoping that Skyler wouldn't act on his intense hatred of Chris in front of their leader, Aaron held his tongue but stayed next to his dad's side, in case Skyler decided to drop him.

With Skyler, Neriah and Aaron's attention on Chris, Ella was the only one left to guard the group. Clutching her weapons, she guided them quickly through the forest.

The portal was waiting for them, the same glowing mark of Aric, a beacon of hope in the dark forest. Hurrying through the portal, Aaron arrived at a familiar Gateway – a long road with acres of flat land stretching out on either side of it. Rocky mountains in the distance. The sky tinted a warm orange and red from the setting sun.

It wasn't Salvador or Marwa, but it did seem familiar, though right now Aaron didn't have the clarity of mind to figure out why. All he could focus on was his dad. Neriah had managed to stem the bleeding, but Chris was still unconscious, his lips tinged a faint blue, his face far too pale to be healthy. Skyler kept him levitated, but his pace had quickened. They were practically running down the pathway.

When they arrived at the Gate, they stood before the brilliant white door towering over them. Ella strode forward and placed her palm on the door.

"Ella Afton."

The symbols on the door brightened before fading to leave Aric's mark. The Gate slid open and they hurried into the city. A group of mages were standing ready. They ran towards them, their hands raised, sending a stream of power to gently take Chris's weight from Skyler. Ella and Skyler stepped back but Neriah and Aaron stayed with Chris.

They set off down the street, no doubt heading to the Empaths' hut so the blind healers could save Chris before the Lycan venom killed him. Aaron hurried along with them until he was stopped by a middle-aged woman.

"Stay here," she instructed as the group moved ahead with Chris.

"What?" Aaron asked. He pushed past her. "I'm going with him."

"You won't be allowed in with the Empaths," the woman argued, holding him back.

"I'm his son," Aaron snapped, pulling his arm out of her grip. He made to move forward but was blocked by her again. Aaron's hands curled tight. He was close to shoving her aside. "Move!" he spat.

"Aaron," Neriah called, turning to look at him, even as he kept up with the moving crowd, his hands still hovering over Chris. "Stay."

Aaron wasn't going to do anything of the sort. He pushed past the woman and raced down the street. He followed after them and turned the corner to see them approach a square building – nothing more than a wooden hut with a slated roof. There were other identical huts lining along the street. Aaron figured they must all be the Empath huts.

Neriah was left outside, as was most of the group. Only four entered the hut with Chris, disappearing behind the curtained door. Aaron ran to follow them inside.

"Whoa! Whoa!" A girl grabbed him by the arm, halting him. "Where'd you think you're going?"

Aaron recognised her. It was the red-haired Bella, the Hunter from the City of Balt, the first Hunter he had seen challenge Skyler in the ring to get a chance to fight in the Q-Zone.

"You can't go in there," she said.

"The hell I can't!" Aaron shook his arm free and moved forward.

Bella's hand hit his chest and stayed there. "You deaf?" she asked, her sea green eyes narrowed. "You can't go in there. The Empaths need to do their job."

"That's my *dad* in there!" Aaron said.

Bella's expression changed. Her hand came away and she looked genuinely regretful. "I'm sorry," she said. "But you can't go in. Your dad's been infected. He needs treatment and trust me, it's better for you not to see him go through it."

If she thought that would make Aaron feel better, she was horribly wrong. It felt like her words had pierced his heart, bringing about a new bout of pain and panic to flood his senses. Aaron moved back, his hands going to his head as he paced outside the hut. A hundred and one thoughts raced in his mind, but only one was making his heart bleed – *he was mad at you and you never got the chance to make up with him.*

"Aaron."

He turned to see Neriah, his features heavy with concern. He stood before Aaron, and for a moment it was as if he were out of words. He met Aaron's eyes and reached out to clasp his shoulder with a strong hand. "Trust the Empaths to do their work."

Aaron didn't say anything but gave a weak nod. No matter how much Aaron tried, he couldn't stop himself from replaying the last conversation he'd had with his dad and thinking about how he'd argued with him.

He had fought to go with Neriah.

He had asked his dad to come with him.

If he hadn't, none of this would have happened.

***

It was just under half an hour later when Aaron finally got to see his dad. Walking through the curtained door and into the hut, Aaron was led to a small room which held nothing more than a single bed and a chair. His dad was on the bed, still unconscious, still a little pale, but nothing like he'd been when they first arrived. Aaron hurried over to his side.

"He's going to be fine," said the young Empath who had led him in. "The venom in Lycan claws isn't as potent as their fangs. It still has to be drained out, but it won't take as long. He'll recover in a few days."

Aaron turned to him. "Thank you," he said.

The Empath smiled, his unseeing light blue eyes staring past Aaron. "He'll be asleep for quite some time. If you like, you can go and rest, and come back–"

"I'm staying here," Aaron interrupted. "With him."

The Empath nodded. "Very well. A cottage is ready for you, if you change your mind."

"Thank you," Aaron said again and pulled the chair closer to sit by his dad's bedside. The Empath left, closing the door behind him with a soft click.

Aaron sat in silence, just taking in the sight of his dad sleeping peacefully. His bare chest was covered by a thin sheet. Aaron carefully lifted a corner, wary of seeing the wound, but a part of him needed to know how bad it was. The cut had been lightly bandaged with a thin muslin cloth. Aaron could see a yellow paste had been generously applied under the makeshift bandage. The cut ran from his dad's lower left side, up his stomach and across his chest, ending at his right armpit. But it was the inked mark on the left side of his dad's chest that made Aaron move closer to inspect. It was a simple design – a circle with the letter B inside it.

Aaron never knew his dad had a tattoo. It occurred to him that he had never seen his dad topless before. No matter how warm the summer was in the human realm, his dad had never taken off his top. Aaron stared at the tattoo. The circle was part of Aric's mark, representing Earth. Being the Elemental for Earth, it wasn't surprising his dad would get a tattoo with his mark. After all, Skyler had the spiral inked on his shoulder, representing his element. Even Neriah had the mark for the element of Water on his wrist. Aaron studied the letter B sitting inside the circle. B – for Ben. Aaron didn't need confirmation. He knew that was what the tattoo represented. It was his dad's first born, his eldest son, the child he lost.

Gently, Aaron covered his dad with the sheet and settled back in his chair. His head was pounding, his body sore and heavy. His hands ached, fingers still buzzing from using his powers. He rubbed at his eyes, fighting the fatigue that was creeping up his back and spreading across his shoulders. He could have easily fallen asleep sitting there, but Aaron struggled to stay awake. He couldn't rest, not until his dad woke up. He wanted to talk to him, wanted to make sure he was really okay. He couldn't take the Empath's word for it. He needed to see it for himself.

The faint sound of a commotion outside the room reached Aaron, making him turn around in his seat, just in time to see the door fly open. Kate hurried in, followed by Michael. Sam and Rose were behind them, as was Neriah.

Aaron rose to his feet, taken aback by their sudden appearance. Before he could get out a word, Kate ran to him, her expression one of tremendous relief. She hugged Aaron, her embrace tight and strong.

"Thank God," she breathed. "You're okay. Thank God, you're alright."

"I'm fine," Aaron confirmed, hugging her back.

Kate's gaze moved to her wounded husband lying unconscious before her. She pulled away from Aaron and stood still, just staring at Chris.

Michael was quick to follow his sister and hug Aaron too, expressing his relief with a thump on Aaron's back.

"Scott told us what happened," Michael said, pulling away to look at Aaron. "When we heard the Lycans had attacked…" He paused, his eyes shadowed with fear. "He told us about Chris, but we didn't know if you were okay."

Aaron shook his head. "I'm fine," he repeated. He looked past Michael's shoulder, at his best friends. "Not a scratch on me." His words were for their benefit too, so the identical looks of worry could fade from their faces.

Neriah stepped past them. "Chris will recover," he said, speaking to Kate and Michael. "The Empaths have to keep draining out the venom, but in a few days he'll be completely fine."

Kate turned to look at him. "How did this happen?" she asked. "You left to get the Blade of Adams. How did Lycans cross your path?"

"I don't know," Neriah replied. "The zone we were in was safe. It's not possible for the Lycans to pass its Gate."

"Has the Gate fallen?" Michael asked.

Neriah shook his head. "It still stands. Scott confirmed it less than ten minutes ago."

"Then how?" Kate asked in a choked voice. "How did they get in?"

Neriah took a moment to answer. "I don't know for certain, but I have a suspicion." He glanced once to Aaron, before looking back at Kate. "The Lycans came at us in big numbers, and they all emerged from one main spot. No matter how many we fought, they kept coming." He paused for a moment. "I think it was a new tear."

"What?" Michael turned to face him completely.

"It's not impossible," Neriah said. "Demons tore the barrier once, they can do it again. Lycans can't get past our Gates, so our zones are safe unless a Gate falls. But if Lycans are getting into zones while the Gates still stand, then that must mean Lycans have started making their own back doors. I think they are using the human realm, ripping the barrier that separates our worlds and entering our zones that way. Today wasn't the only time Raoul's led his dogs into a safe zone."

Kate stiffened. "Raoul?" she asked.

Neriah met her eyes and slowly nodded.

Kate looked down at Chris and understanding filled her eyes. "Oh God," she whispered. "He was there? He's the one who...Chris...He – he did this to Chris?"

Neriah stepped closer, his violet eyes fixed on Chris. "The moment he saw Raoul, Chris lost it. His anger clouded his judgement and he got too close."

Kate collapsed into the chair, her head bowed, one hand clutched onto Chris's. Aaron rested his hand on her shoulder.

"Mum?"

Kate shook her head but her free hand came to rest on top of Aaron's. She tilted her head up but her bloodshot eyes were on Neriah.

"You didn't believe us," she accused. "We told you Raoul is after us, after our son. The moment you walked away with Aaron, Raoul came for him–"

"He came for all of us," Neriah corrected. "There were five Elementals there for him to finish."

Kate rose to her feet. "This is exactly why we don't want Aaron involved," she said. "Raoul is after our family. He wants Aaron–"

"Then Raoul's in for a surprise," Neriah said. He glanced at Aaron and a small but proud smile lit his face. "Because the legacy holder for Earth sure knows how to use his powers, despite next to no training."

Aaron didn't say anything. He knew Neriah was talking about him tearing open the ground to force the Lycan away from his dad. He saw the look of utter shock and surprise on his mum's face as she turned to him.

Aaron avoided her eyes, knowing deep down that the reason he knew how to split the earth wasn't because he was naturally talented, but because Kyran had worked two weeks endlessly to teach him.

7

THE PRISONER OF BALT

The afternoon crept by, but Chris had yet to awaken. Michael had to drag Aaron away from Chris's bedside and force him back to a cottage to rest. Aaron begrudgingly left. His mum was going to stay with his dad and had promised to come and get him the minute Chris regained consciousness.

As Aaron, Sam and Rose followed behind Michael, they passed Neriah at the table talking with Mandara. After seeing the red-haired Bella and then the chief Mandara, Aaron realised he was in the City of Balt. That's why the Gateway had been so familiar. He had once come here to accompany Salvador's Hunters on an assignment to survey one of the sub-zones. He could never forget that experience – discovering the demonic race of Abarimons, and nearly being killed by them, was as memorable as it got. Kyran had been by his side throughout the encounter. He had protected Aaron, fought the Abarimons almost single-handedly and even saved a bunch of kids from being eaten alive.

Aaron's already pounding head ached when he tried to figure out why Kyran, the Scorcher – their worst enemy – had risked so much to help him and the young mages being held captive there. Were Kyran's actions simply self-defence, because he'd been stuck in the valley of the Abarimons and needed to kill them to get out himself? Or had it been because he wanted to protect the young mages? Protect Aaron?

As long as I'm around, nothing's gonna happen to Rose, or Sam, or you.

Kyran's voice echoed in his mind and Aaron wished he could do something, anything, to erase Kyran and everything he had said from his memory.

Michael left Aaron and the twins at the door of the cottage and headed back, saying he needed to speak with Mandara and Neriah. Aaron, Sam and Rose walked into a small, brightly lit cottage. Lamps hung in all four corners of the hall. They headed to the only room on the ground floor and sat down on the sofa.

"You okay?" Sam asked, at last having the time and privacy to speak to Aaron.

Aaron nodded, reaching up to rub at his eyes. "Just tired."

"The bedrooms will be upstairs," Rose said. "Why don't you sleep for a bit?"

Aaron shook his head. He didn't want to sleep. He had to stay awake, so when his dad regained consciousness, he could go and see him.

Rose and Sam didn't push him. They settled beside him to make idle chat. They told Aaron what it was like going back to Salvador. Rose told him renovations had started to repair buildings after the fire. Sam mentioned something about the Hunters and Lurkers making up most of the population of Salvador now. Apparently Drake was grumpier than usual, having to chase Hunters out of his orchard to stop them using fruit in target shooting.

Aaron was finding it hard to stay focused on them. His eyes were slipping shut, his head felt too heavy to hold up. His shoulders felt entirely too comfortable pressed into the soft sofa. Before Aaron could fight it any more, exhaustion pulled him into a deep slumber.

***

Aaron's body tensed, his heart raced and he could taste fear on his tongue. Steeling himself the best he could, he forced out the words, "So what are you going to do?"

Kyran pulled in a breath, his head lowered. After a moment's contemplation, he looked up at Aaron.

"What I have to," he replied. His eyes were a poison green as he stared at him. "I have to kill you."

Aaron snapped awake, his heart pounding at his insides. His hands were clammy, beads of perspiration clinging to his skin. He looked around the empty room, not recognising his surroundings. Then it all caught up with him and Aaron forced out a breath. He was in the City of Balt, waiting for his dad to wake up after the Lycan attack. Wiping a hand down his face, Aaron pulled himself up to sit on the sofa. Either Sam or Rose had covered him with a blanket and then left the room, letting him sleep.

Aaron took a moment to just sit. His dream had shaken him. More than that, it had downright petrified him. The calmness with which Kyran had told him that he would *kill* him – Aaron shuddered. The straightforwardness of it only made it all the more creepy and horrifying.

This wasn't Aaron's first dream about Kyran. He'd had many in the last six months now. Some of the moments he'd dreamt about had come true. Would this be one of them?

Aaron pushed the blanket off him, practically throwing it aside. He felt sick, suffocated. Fear clawed its way up his throat, threatening to choke him if he didn't find a way out. He stumbled out of the room, pausing in the hallway. He glanced upstairs.

"Sammy? Rose?" he called in a shaky voice.

No answer.

Aaron hurried to the front door and pulled it open. He found his friends sitting on the kerb, just past the small fence that surrounded the cottage. Aaron paused at the door, breathing in the cool night air. The calm breeze ruffled his hair, drying the remaining droplets of fear on his skin. Nevertheless, Aaron wiped at his face with his sleeve, making sure all signs of his nightmare were erased before walking down the path. He could see the lanterns floating over the table where most of the city's residents were gathered, having dinner it seemed. Sam and Rose had evidently chosen not to join them. At the sound of his footsteps, Rose turned.

"Hey," she smiled. "Feel better?"

Aaron didn't answer but came to sit next to her. "Any news about my dad?" he asked instead.

"Yeah, he woke up," Sam said. "I wouldn't get too excited." He held out a hand to stop Aaron from running to the Empath huts. "He wasn't conscious for long. Michael said he opened his eyes, asked for you and then went under as soon as he found out you were okay."

Aaron looked to the table, seeing his uncle talking with Mandara. He couldn't spot Neriah. His mum wasn't anywhere in sight either. He figured she would be by his dad's side.

"I should go check on dad, just in case he's awake." Aaron said, getting up.

He left Sam and Rose sitting where they were and headed up the street. He ignored the quiet stares, passing the table with his eyes fixed firmly on the bend in the road, past which lay the Empath huts.

"It's no use," a voice called from behind him. Aaron turned to see Ella had left the table and followed him. "Your dad's still out for the count."

"How do you know?" Aaron asked.

Ella smiled. "I've had a few run-ins with Lycans myself," she said. "It's pretty usual to be knocked out for the first day or so." Her eyes softened a little and she tilted her head to the side. "He'll be okay. The Empaths are watching over him. You really don't have to worry."

Aaron nodded but his heart continued to sink with dread. Was it really common to be unconscious for this long after being attacked by a Lycan? He looked past Ella and his eyes found Skyler, seated at the table, a drink in his hand. A lantern floated overhead, illuminating his face. Aaron stared at him and a memory resurfaced – Skyler returning from a Q-Zone hunt, one that had Lycans as their prey. Skyler's face had been scratched, Aaron still remembered it – three long cuts down his face. But a few days later, Skyler was back to normal, no sign of any injuries, no scarring – nothing but smooth, flawless skin.

But the detail that was sticking in Aaron's mind was the fact that right after being scratched by a Lycan, Skyler had ridden back to Salvador on his bike. He had looked tired, yes – exhausted, actually – but he hadn't looked to be in any kind of pain. He seemed perfectly able to walk back to his cottage. He wasn't unconscious for an entire day. He wasn't rushed to the Empaths of Salvador.

"Ella," Aaron called, but his eyes were still on Skyler. "If it's common to be knocked out after a Lycan attack, then how come Skyler wasn't affected when he got scratched?"

Ella turned to look at Skyler. "'Cause Skyler is one lucky son of a Hunter," she said, turning to face Aaron with a grin. "He has the love of an Empath."

Aaron was confused. "What does that matter?"

"Oh it matters," Ella said. "It matters *a lot*," she chuckled. "You probably didn't pick up on it, but Skyler and Armana are together."

Aaron hadn't in fact known that Salvador's best, sweetest, kindest Empath was with the arrogant bully of a Hunter until he'd seen the two of them kissing.

"Empaths don't usually sit in on Q-Zone hunts," Ella explained, "but Armana insists on being there when Skyler goes on one. The rest of the Empaths come to support Armana."

Ella turned to look at Skyler. "That day, when Skyler got attacked, he was completely out. I was trying to reach him, to get him to Salvador, but I didn't need to. Armana reached out for him, healed him from a distance. She drained the poison before it got hold of him, so Skyler got back up with a vengeance." She smirked. "Those Lycans didn't know what hit them."

"How can Armana do that?" Aaron asked. "Doesn't she need to physically touch him to heal him?"

Ella smiled. "They're in love, Aaron," she said. "They share a bond with each other, one that's strong enough to let Armana reach Skyler when he's far away from her. When you have that kind of a connection, you don't need to be physically close to be together."

Aaron stared at her before a smile forced its way across his tired face. He shook his head. "God, Ella. That's the corniest thing I've heard."

Ella shoved him playfully. "Only because you're romantically stunted."

"So I take it most Hunters hook up with Empaths?" Aaron asked. "For the added perks of healing from a distance?"

"Not every relationship works the same way," Ella replied. "Skyler and Armana have an incredible bond, which is why Armana can reach him and help him. Not every Hunter and Empath bond would work like that."

Aaron opened his mouth to make a joke about 'true love' when a flash lit up their surroundings. Ella and Aaron turned to see the Gate of Balt open, and a crowd of boys and girls entered the city. Aaron moved a step forward, trying to peer through the darkness to see what was going on. He wasn't the only one.

Dinner was halted at the table. Every eye was on the newcomers. Aaron wasn't sure but it looked like they were carrying something as they hurried past the threshold. When they came under the soft glow of the lanterns, Aaron saw it was a group of Hunters, and they weren't carrying something – they were dragging *someone*.

Aaron couldn't make out much over the distance and with the terrible light, just the long hair of the unconscious body supported by the Hunters. Chairs scraped the ground as the residents of Balt got up from the table, darting to the Hunters. Aaron and Ella were running too. The group must have returned from a hunt, bringing their injured back with them.

But it was as Aaron got closer that he realised two things didn't fit with that analysis. One, the Hunters didn't look worried for their injured comrade – in fact, they looked rather gleeful. Two, the young woman held tight by the Hunters wasn't unconscious.

Aaron noticed the odd angle at which her arms were bent behind her. Her head was dropped, her hair obscuring her face. She was struggling slightly, as if the strength to fight had long left her but the spirit hadn't.

Everyone was crowded around the Hunters, staring at the captured woman. Even Sam and Rose had joined them, but not all of them were stunned speechless.

"What are you *doing?*" Ella demanded angrily.

The Hunters met her eyes with surprise. A tall blond boy at the forefront answered her. "We got lucky." He grinned. "We've caught–"

"I don't care what it is you've caught!" Ella snapped. "Kill the thing! Don't bring it back with you."

The imprisoned woman stilled before raising her head slightly. The lightest blue eyes peeked out from behind her curtain of dark red hair.

"Did you really deactivate the Glyph to get this thing past the Gate?" Skyler asked and Aaron turned to see the fury on him. He looked ready to blast the whole lot of the Hunters out of the

Gate. Knowing Skyler, he would do it too – without opening the Gate first.

The Hunters visibly bristled at Skyler's tone.

"We had to," the same blond boy replied. "You don't understand, she's–"

"A vamage," Ella interrupted, her expression one of disgust.

The young woman struggled, this time with a little more strength. The chain cuffing her hands behind her clinked. A muffled groan, faint and strained, left her. She reared her head up again before shaking it, throwing her hair away from her face. Aaron saw the metal muzzle tightly strapped over her mouth and jaw. Her pale blue eyes were narrowed at Ella, hatefully glaring at her.

"Actually, she's not," the blond Hunter said.

Everyone stared at him with surprise. The Hunter met Skyler's gaze with a little apprehension but his excitement was clear to see in his smile.

"You know of her," he said. "Probably heard many stories about her, like the rest of us. Considered the last of her species, the one who turned on her own kind and helped eradicate them. The one and only..." He trailed off on purpose, grinning and raising his eyebrows.

Skyler's gaze widened. He snapped his head to the side to look at the woman again. "You're kidding me?" he said. "This? She's...Layla?"

Aaron saw the lines on the woman's brow disappear. Her eyes gleamed. Even with the muzzle hiding the lower half of her face, Aaron could tell she was smiling behind it.

"Yep," the blond Hunter laughed. "Layla, the last of the vampires." His smile got wider as he added, "The special lady in Hadrian's life."

***

Balt sprang into action. The captured woman – the vampire Layla – was dragged to one of the cottages. Mandara stepped outside to briefly reactivate the Glyph that had been switched off. Many of the residents still gathered at the table, but dinner was long forgotten.

With the city's Gate secure once again, Mandara's focus shifted to the prisoner. "You shouldn't have brought her here, Stefan," he told the blond Hunter.

"We didn't know what else to do," Stefan replied. "We didn't expect to run into her. None of us had our pendants, so we couldn't speak to Scott–"

"Why are you lot hunting without your pendants?" Skyler shot into the conversation.

"We weren't hunting," Stefan said. "We ran into her by chance."

"Hell of a chance," Skyler said, eyes narrowed under the heavy weight of suspicion.

Aaron could see the irritation on Stefan. "I don't need to answer to you, Skyler," he said, albeit with his voice shaking a little. He might have been annoyed at Skyler, but that apparently didn't make him any less afraid of the Air Elemental.

Skyler folded his arms and stared at him with steely blue eyes. "Is that so?"

Stefan was spared when Mandara raised a hand. "Elemental Avira, please," he said. Turning to Stefan, he continued, "I will contact Scott and arrange to have her removed. Balt is not safe with her here. There are too many residents, as well as a few Shattereds present."

Aaron felt Sam shift next to him. Shattered was a term applied to humans that were exposed to the mage world. But Aaron found it incredibly insensitive, naming those that had lost everything, as *Shattereds*. Sam and Rose didn't like being referred as such and neither did Aaron.

Aaron wondered if Sam and Rose were the only humans in Balt, or if the city had permanent human residents, like Salvador had with its caretaker, Jason Burns.

Mandara continued issuing orders to Stefan. "You will assist Bella in assembling a team to make the transfer."

Stefan nodded and walked away.

"Is that what Neriah wants you to do?" Skyler asked. "'Cause I'm pretty sure he'd want me and Ella to do the transfer."

"I'm not sure what he'd want," Mandara replied with a sigh. "He's gone. He left shortly after seeing that Elemental Adams had regained consciousness."

Skyler looked as surprised as Aaron felt. "That was sneaky, slipping away like that," he said.

"He had pressing matters that needed to be addressed," Mandara said.

"Yeah, well, now so do we," Skyler replied, gesturing to the cottage where the vampire had been taken.

Mandara let out a difficult breath. "Excuse me while I contact Scott."

He was about to take a step when Skyler stopped him.

"Wait a minute." Something in Skyler's expression made unease flutter in Aaron's stomach. He had that cruel smile again, the one that Aaron knew meant nothing but trouble. "Why are we just standing around, worrying about what to do with Layla?" Skyler asked, his eyes gleaming with excitement. "We *know* what we should do."

"No," Mandara was quick to object. "Not here. Not in Balt."

"Mandara—"

"Do what you like in Salvador, Elemental Avira," Mandara cut him off. "You can interrogate her, extract memories, do whatever you like – but do it in Salvador under the Controller's authority. In Balt, you will respect my wishes."

Skyler straightened up, his eyes cold as ever but his smile was still in place. He nodded. "Of course."

Mandara hurried away, going to the other side of the street, presumably to his cottage to retrieve the pendant that would allow him to speak to Scott.

Skyler turned too with a grin on his face and a glint in his eyes, one that made Aaron's skin prickle with dread. Aaron saw him stop next to Bella and a few other Hunters. He said something to them before walking onwards. The Hunters, Bella included, followed after him.

"What's he doing?" Sam said.

"He's up to something." Rose echoed Aaron's thoughts.

"Come on." Aaron hurried after them.

"Aaron?" Michael called as he passed the table.

"Just going back in for a bit," Aaron said.

Michael got up from his seat, but he didn't follow Aaron when he saw him heading towards their temporary cottage. Michael relaxed and sat down, getting pulled back into the conversation he was having with another mage.

Aaron and the twins changed route when Michael wasn't looking and darted after the group following Skyler. They approached the cottage that was holding the vampire prisoner. Aaron saw the mark of Aric had been freshly inked on the door. Was that to keep the vampire from leaving or simply a way to mark that this was the cottage that held the demon?

Aaron, Sam and Rose stepped into the small house, surprisingly to no protest. The Hunters ignored them as they pushed through the crowd in the hallway to the only room at ground level. Aaron halted at the door. The young woman – or more accurately, vampire – had been chained to a chair. Her arms were still shackled behind her but more chains had been wrapped around her torso and legs, holding her to one of the straight-backed table chairs that had been brought indoors.

The Hunters gathered in the room, staring at her with nothing less than hateful contempt.

Skyler stood before her, wearing a smile. "I have to say," he started, lowering himself to be at the same eye level as her. "After all those stories, I thought there'd be more to you."

Layla cocked her head to the side, her eyes narrowed. The lamps gave a soft light to the room, but it was stronger than the lanterns outside, so Aaron could see the vampire properly. Whatever her age was, she looked young, maybe in her early twenties. She was in a dishevelled state – her long, thick red mane was messy and falling about her, framing her face. Her eyes were indeed a pale blue but they were just as cold as Skyler's – colder, if possible. She was bound and gagged, yet she retained an aura of ease – as if she were merely playing the prisoner. There was no fear in her. She wasn't cowering, she wasn't squirming in her chains. Even the brutal-looking muzzle encasing her mouth and jaw looked like it was barely bothering her.

Aaron felt someone come to stand next to him. His peripheral vision picked up the dark hair with electric blue streaks through them. Ella stood by his side, but her eyes too were on the vampire in the room.

Skyler touched the chains that were holding Layla to the chair. "These are good," Skyler said, turning to speak to the Hunters of Balt, "but not quite enough."

In the blink of an eye, Skyler had taken out a dagger from his belt and jammed it into Layla's leg. She screamed, her head thrown back, eyes clenched shut. Her cry was muffled against the gag but her pain was clearly heard by all.

Aaron's gasp was echoed around the room; several Hunters looked shocked at Skyler's attack.

"Skyler!" Ella cried, taking long steps to reach his side. "What're you doing?"

"Keeping her docile," Skyler replied without taking his eyes off the vampire.

He moved closer to Layla, who was breathing heavily now, her nostrils flared. She grunted, glaring at Skyler, warning him to stay away. Skyler smiled in response.

"I'm going to take this off." He gave the muzzle a sharp tap with his finger. "Then we're going to have a nice, long, very informative talk. You say one syllable I don't want to hear," he pulled his coat aside to show his belt with daggers lined neatly in the slots, "you'll get a lot of unwanted piercings."

Skyler straightened up and gestured to one of the Hunters standing behind Layla. The girl strode forward to undo the clasp at the back of the muzzle.

Aaron hurried to Skyler's side. "Skyler." He pulled at his arm, forcing the older boy around to face him. "What are you doing? Mandara told you not to do anything here," he whispered.

Skyler frowned at him. "Eavesdropping on me is a good way to lose your ears, Adams."

Aaron ignored the threat. "Whatever you're planning, stop before things get out of hand."

"Why don't *you* stop wasting my time?" Skyler said, twisting his arm out of Aaron's grip and shoving him back with one hand.

Aaron watched unhappily as Skyler turned back to Layla, just as the muzzle was unclasped. Skyler pulled the thing off in one go, tossing it aside.

Layla's lips were swollen pink, the bottom of her chin looked bruised, making Aaron wonder how long she had been wearing that muzzle. Layla shook her head to throw back her hair and tilted her face up to look at Skyler. She smiled, revealing normal human teeth, no fangs in sight.

Aaron stared at her, at her thick red locks that hung around her in waves. He noticed her creamy complexion, which didn't match the usual vampire lore of being pale and sickly looking. He couldn't help but be mesmerised by her light blue eyes, encased by heavy lashes that were black, not red like her hair. He couldn't tell if her plump pink lips were always like that or if it was because of the swelling left by the muzzle. She might be a vampire, a demon, but she was – well, there was only one word for it – beautiful.

"You must be Skyler," Layla said. Her voice was silky and smooth. It matched her appearance perfectly. "Your reputation precedes you."

Skyler laughed before leaning down to meet her eyes. "I bet it does." He held on to the arms of the chair with both hands. "Now, how about you tell us what you were doing in Zone L-28?"

Layla was tightly chained to her seat, arms pulled behind her. The dagger was still sticking out of her thigh but she managed to relax into her seat and pull off a nonchalant look.

"Can't a girl go out without being attacked?" she asked.

"Who you calling a girl?" Skyler smirked. "Try blood-sucking monster."

Layla let out an exaggerated sigh. "Fine, I'm a blood-sucking monster." She moved forward, to get as close to Skyler as the chains would allow. "But last I checked, some of your kind aren't so different to me."

"Vamages." Skyler spat the word with vicious hatred. "They're not my kind."

"They are partly."

"Is that what your boyfriend tells you?" Skyler asked. "Hate to break it to you darling, but he's a lying, demonic, scumbag."

"Now you're just trying to hurt me," Layla said, dropping back and faking a pout.

"Where's Hadrian?" Skyler asked, coming to the point of his interrogation.

"Resting," Layla replied simply. "You have any idea how exhausting it is having your core unlocked after sixteen long years?" She smiled at the quiet panic that washed through the room. "It's taking time, but the last time I saw him, his core was almost halfway to being fully restored."

Fear surged in the air, breaths were sucked in and gasps choked out. Aaron felt his own heart flutter against his ribcage. He had no idea how bad things could get with Hadrian back in power, but judging from the reaction around him, he could make a guess.

"Where will we find him?" Skyler asked.

"You won't," Layla replied.

"As sweet as this is," Skyler started, "I'm not feeling the bond of 'true love' between a blood-thirsty fiend and her demon-hybrid boyfriend. So, I'm going to ask once more and if you don't tell me where Hadrian is, I'm going to start adding to that collection in your leg."

Layla was unfazed by his threats. "You know, as amusing as it is—"

She screamed when Skyler stayed true to his word and stabbed another dagger into her leg, just beside the first blade.

Aaron had to look away. His unease was echoed across the room.

Layla was breathing hard. She looked down at her leg, at the two silver handles sticking out of her thigh and let out a haggard laugh.

"You'll regret that!" she heaved out with difficulty.

Skyler smirked. "Yeah? What're you gonna do?"

"I didn't say I'd be the one to do anything." Layla glowered.

Skyler leant in. "I'm not afraid of Hadrian. You can go crying to your boyfriend all you want."

Layla looked at Skyler with fierce eyes. "Hadrian?" She shook her head. "Try going down a generation."

Shock resonated throughout the room. Aaron gaped at the vampire. She wasn't Hadrian's girl, she was Kyran's. Even Skyler looked taken aback. He straightened up before sharing a surprised look with Ella. Then his gaze moved towards Aaron, but Aaron knew he wasn't looking at him. He was searching past Aaron, to the girl standing behind him.

Aaron turned to look at Rose too, in time to see the shock and surprise leave her expression, replaced with nothing but heartbreak. Sam reached out and held her hand.

"You're with Kyran?" Ella asked the vampire with disbelief.

Layla grinned, her eyes gleaming with delight. "I love that look," she said. "The complete and utter shock that comes moments before the crippling fear of knowing who you're going to have to deal with now." She looked to the daggers in her leg before meeting Skyler's eyes. "He's going to rip you apart for this."

Skyler leant in with a very ugly smirk. "Yeah? We'll see who does the ripping."

He pushed away from her, making the chair skid back a little. He gestured to the Hunters to follow and strode forward, taking Ella's hand and walking out of the room. Aaron was forced along with the crowd gathering in the narrow hallway around Skyler.

"What do we do now?" Bella asked, looking genuinely afraid. "It was bad enough when we thought she was Hadrian's." She glanced through the open door to the vampire before shaking her head. "If she's really with Kyran, then–"

"Then we've got a more immediate fight on our hands," Skyler cut across her. "But that's not entirely a bad thing. If Kyran finds out she's here, there's a possibility he'll come for her. We can use that to trap him. But first we need to get the Shattereds and the residents out of here. Scott can send back-up." He met Bella's eyes. "We have a chance to catch Kyran, Bella. We can get him. We just need to make sure we have everything in place first–" He stopped when a tinkering laugh sounded from the room.

Everyone turned to see Layla laughing. She flicked her long red hair behind her and fixed her eyes on Skyler.

"Oh, honey," she cooed. "You don't have time to lay traps." Her eyes were a cold blue as a mocking smile lifted her lips. "He's already here."

8

COMING TO THE RESCUE

No sooner were the words out of Layla's mouth than the sound of complete pandemonium broke outside. People were screaming, footsteps pounded in a frantic hurry. They could hear dishes clattering to the ground, wood breaking, and several gunshots fired.

"There was no flash," Bella said, horrified. "There...there was no flash. The Gate's fallen!"

Skyler went from shocked to full-on leader mode in a heartbeat.

"Ray, Emma and Stefan – you three stay here and guard her." He gestured to the smirking vampire in the next room. "Do *not* let her out of your sight!" He turned to Ella but she already had her pendant in hand, talking to Scott, asking for back-up. Skyler faced the rest of the Hunters. "Bella, go upstairs and empty the cabinet. Bring every weapon you can find." Bella and another two Hunters ran up the stairs. Skyler looked at Aaron. "Stay with them," he said, nodding at Sam and Rose, surprising Aaron. "It's not entirely safe to stay here with *that* under the same roof." Skyler nodded towards Layla. "If you can get out of here and into another cottage–"

"I can," Aaron said quickly.

"Good," Skyler said.

He looked behind Aaron to see Bella and the other Hunters hurrying downstairs with armfuls of guns, daggers and a sword.

"Scott's sending back-up," Ella said. "But it's going to take time. The Gate's fallen, and Scott can't risk a portal on the Gateway, in case vamages use it to get to Salvador.

"Then until they come, we've got to be enough," Skyler said resolutely.

The group distributed the stash of weapons between them while Skyler and Ella pulled out their own familiars. Aaron and the twins stood empty-handed amongst them.

"Alright." Skyler cocked his gun. "Follow my lead and spread out," he instructed the group.

"I would wish you luck," Layla called from the room, "but all the luck in the world won't help you now."

Skyler didn't say anything. He strode forward to the door. Ella hesitated before turning to face Aaron. She held out one of her guns. Her grey eyes darted once to Sam before meeting Aaron's again. Aaron took the gun.

Skyler opened the door and the sight that greeted them would never leave Aaron again. What had minutes before been a quiet, peaceful scene was now a ravaged, devastated street. Many of the buildings were on fire – burning bright against the night. Splatters of blood stained the cobbled street, even marking the broken table and chairs. Chaos had befallen the people of Balt, and they ran every which way, trying to dodge the vicious attack of vamages. Cloaked by the night's darkness, the vamages fired their guns, catching mages in the back, leaving them dead on the ground. Others used their powers, hitting mages with their jolts. The mages retaliated with their own jolts of power but the vamages shrugged them off. Being part-mage gave the vamages immunity so the mages couldn't kill them. The mages could only hope to incapacitate the vamages long enough to get away.

Skyler flew into action, leaving the doorstep of the cottage in a fury, to appear in the middle of the battle in moments. The Hunters sprinted after him, firing shots at the vamages.

Aaron took off running. The cottage they had been staying in had caught on fire, but it didn't matter to Aaron which cottage they took refuge in, as long as he got Sam and Rose into one.

He ran up a pathway, ushering Sam and Rose ahead of him. They were almost at the door when something blazing flew overhead. Rose pulled back with a scream when the door was hit with a fireball. Flames spread across the cottage in seconds. Aaron and the twins ran to the next safe cottage.

They reached it, but couldn't open the door. It was bolted shut. Aaron pounded his fists against the wood, screaming over the noise of the battle. Whoever had locked the door wasn't opening it. Aaron slammed himself into the door but it was no use.

"Aaron!" Rose called. "Look!"

Following her trembling finger, Aaron found his uncle Mike next to the ruined table, fighting back a group of vamages. Aaron's gun was aimed but he didn't pull the trigger. He found he didn't need to. Michael fought effortlessly, knocking back vamages with shots from his own gun in one hand and fireballs from his other, all the while dodging the retaliating attack. The grace and elegance of his movements reminded Aaron strongly of Skyler. They both fought with confidence and apparent ease; even if it was just on the surface and panic was overwhelming them inside, they never let it show.

Of course, there was one other person who fought with just as much confidence and grace, and right now he was the only one Aaron found himself searching the wreckage of the street for. But Kyran was nowhere in sight. *Maybe she was lying,* Aaron thought to himself. After all, how could Layla know for sure if Kyran had come?

Just as the thought settled, Aaron heard the familiar roar of Kyran's bike. Aaron turned, his heart hammering at his insides and goosebumps erupting over his flesh. Through the thick, billowing smoke of the fire that was ripping through the city came Lexi – Kyran's red and black bike. It cut through the air, arching over the heads of the battling mages. Sitting on top of the bike, the ends of his red coat flapping behind him like scarlet wings, was Kyran. His arms were extended on either side, no longer controlling Lexi. With twin pistols clutched in both hands, he fired at the crowd of Hunters, forcing them back from the vamages.

Aaron didn't understand it. He knew which side Kyran belonged to now – he saw him firing at the mages instead of the half-demonic hybrid vamages, but still, seeing Kyran suddenly appear in the midst of the battle filled Aaron with nothing but *relief*. It was a force of habit, an instinctual reaction. For the last four months, every time he'd faced danger he'd known he'd be alright because Kyran was there.

Lexi hit the ground and Kyran swerved to face the Hunters with both guns raised and aimed. The battle between this small group of Hunters and vamages came to a standstill, with every eye on Kyran. The vamages dropped back, wearing looks of triumph as their gaze darted from the Hunters to the Scorcher.

All around them, the fight raged on, with the rest of the Hunters and residents of Balt doing their best to fend off the vamages' attack. These Hunters, however, remained still, staring at Kyran. But Kyran wasn't looking at them. His green gaze was locked with only one Hunter – Skyler.

Kyran lifted himself off his bike, guns still in hands, his aim never faltering as he slowly approached the crowd. Skyler stepped forward with his twin guns aimed right back at Kyran. Skyler's ivory coat mirrored Kyran's long red one, both had their elemental marks studded in silver at the back – a spiral for Skyler and an inverted V for Kyran.

"And here I thought I wouldn't get a proper welcome," Kyran said. His sweeping glance caught sight of Ella, her gun raised and locked on him too. Kyran grinned. "Hey, Ella," he called. "How's the neck?"

"Great," Ella replied. "Why don't you come closer so I can reciprocate?"

Kyran chuckled. "No hard feelings. It was never about you."

"No, it was all about my one and only family member," Ella spat. "Isn't that why you stalked around in Salvador? So you could get to Neriah and steal his key?"

"Steal?" Kyran shook his head. "I didn't steal anything. I only recovered what was taken from my family."

"Taken for good reason," Skyler said, fury leaking from his words.

Kyran smirked and came to a standstill. "And what reason was that?" he asked, in a tone that suggested he knew all too well. "Because my father had enough of James Avira's tyranny? Or because my father decided to do what everyone else *wanted* but couldn't muster up the courage to do themselves?"

The guns in Skyler's hands were shaking. "You don't know what you're talking about."

"I know more than you can possibly imagine," Kyran replied. "I've lived with the truth, not Neriah's lies."

His last words sent an uproar through the Hunters. The few mages who weren't already aiming at Kyran turned their guns on him. The vamages reacted at once, lunging forward, but a single command from Kyran kept them back. Kyran stepped closer, apparently not fazed by being the target of so many. His eyes were still on Skyler.

"You know, spending a year of my life with you, I learnt you're a lot of things, Skyler," Kyran said. "Big-headed, talentless, a waste of potential." He smirked. "But you're not stupid." He glanced at the vamages, standing awaiting his orders. "You know you can't win this one."

Ella's recovery after Kyran's attack proved Kyran was in fact a mage, and the only way a mage could kill another mage was with a personalised bullet. So Kyran's bullets wouldn't kill any Hunters, and neither would theirs fatally wound him, but Aaron figured being shot – especially at close range – would still be enough to temporarily incapacitate them. Kyran's very obvious glance to the vamages was clear to read; Kyran couldn't kill the mages, but the vamages could.

"Make it easier for yourself, as well as for them," Kyran said, tilting his head to the side to gesture to the rest of the Hunters and mages of Balt, still battling the other vamages. He stepped closer, all amusement gone from him when he asked, "Where is she?"

Skyler smirked. "Missing your girlfriend already?" he asked. "You're too late. I've already driven a stake through her black heart."

Kyran didn't move, but the air around him sizzled, small sparks flew out to singe the ground at his feet. "I sincerely hope, for your sake, that you're lying," Kyran warned.

Skyler bared his teeth. "What are you waiting for, Scorcher?" he asked. He beckoned Kyran with his guns. "Come on!"

Kyran paused, his gaze flickered through the crowd of Hunters. He looked almost regretful before he fired, and the battle that had been paused started up again. The vamages leapt at the Hunters, but most of the mages were aiming at Kyran and Kyran alone. There was no way Kyran could avoid every bullet and as the thought penetrated Aaron's mind, he felt his grip tighten around his own gun. He lifted it but his aim wasn't on Kyran. Despite everything, Aaron couldn't watch the Hunters bury every bullet they had into Kyran.

But it seemed Kyran had no intention of becoming a human sieve. The minute he fired his first bullet and became the target of the Hunters, he dropped one gun and threw up his hand. The ground split. A huge slab of concrete broke from the road and stood up tall, which Kyran used as shelter from the onslaught of bullets.

Aaron gaped at the sight. He was sure he had never seen Kyran demonstrate this particular trick during their training.

Skyler threw out a hand and air swirled before him, taking the shape of a small tornado that ripped across the street, blasting Kyran's shelter to rubble. Kyran leapt out of the way just in time.

Aaron was quickly brought out of his shock when a stray bullet almost caught him, piercing the door behind him instead. Aaron ducked, as did Sam and Rose. Aaron glanced around him, at the line of cottages that were either on fire or had their doors sealed shut. He couldn't take the chance of checking every one. They had to get out of the line of fire, quite literally. Aaron was terrified a stray bullet or jolt would catch Sam or Rose. They were human; they wouldn't survive either type of attack. But the entire city was under assault, and Aaron didn't know where to go to keep them safe. Then an idea came to him. He pulled Sam's arm to get his attention, which was currently fixed on Ella battling the vamages.

"Come on!" Aaron shouted, over the gunshots.

They got up and bolted down the street. Aaron led them, his gun clutched in hand, but he didn't need it. The vamages didn't notice him or the twins, not yet. They were too busy battling the Hunters. Aaron kept close to Sam and Rose, guiding them past the burning buildings.

"This way," he said, heading towards the gaping rectangular hole that once held the Gate. "We need to get out of the city."

"And go where?" Rose asked.

"Nowhere," Aaron replied. "We'll have to hide once we get onto the Gateway."

"Aaron!" Rose tugged on his arm, halting him. "There's nothing out there."

"We'll find something," Aaron said, grabbing her hand. "It's better than staying here." He turned, resuming the race to get to the fallen Gate.

The sun had set hours ago. The night's darkness was only partially punctured by the few lanterns floating overhead that hadn't been engulfed by the thick smoke of the blaze spreading through the city. Not being able to see too far ahead of him was panicking Aaron. He couldn't protect or defend himself and his friends if he couldn't see what was coming at them. A hand grabbed his shoulder and Aaron's heart almost kicked its way into his mouth. He turned, knocking back the hand, his gun raised and ready. He was met by a livid-looking Michael.

"What are you doing?" Michael cried, seemingly oblivious to the gun pointed at his chest.

Aaron couldn't find his words fast enough.

"Get back inside!" Michael raged.

"Can't," Aaron finally managed. "The cottages are either locked or on fire."

Michael turned suddenly, drawing back his hands to block the fireballs that came at them, pelting them back at the vamages. Michael gripped Aaron's arm, the heat from his palms seeped into Aaron's skin.

"Get behind me and stay close!" he instructed roughly.

Aaron and the twins did just that as Michael made his way back to the line of cottages, desperate to find his only nephew and his friends a sanctuary. Michael kept his eyes on the battle, ready to fend off any more attacks.

In his panic, Aaron didn't see the odd way his uncle was holding himself, not until Michael made his way to the front of the first flame-free door. He banged his bloodstained hands on the wood and called out for someone to open the door. There was no answer.

Michael was curling to one side, a hand gripped under his ribs, while the other continued to smack at the door.

"Uncle Mike?" Aaron called, cautiously. "Are you okay?"

Michael didn't answer. He simply pushed away from the door. He swayed on his feet before managing to stumble down the pathway and to the next cottage.

"Gotta get you inside," he managed, before his breath hitched and he stopped in his tracks. His expression twisted in pain but still he staggered forward, just reaching the door. He thumped his fist against it. "Open up! Please!" he yelled. "I've got...I've got kids here. They need to...to get—" He slumped against the door with a groan.

"Uncle Mike!" Aaron rushed forward and grabbed him as he fell to the ground.

With great effort, and the help of Sam and Rose, Aaron managed to get his uncle leaning against the door. Michael's face was pale, sweat glistening on his forehead. His breathing was fast and shallow. Looking down, Aaron saw the reason. A large cut at his side was leaking blood. One of Michael's hands was clutched around the wound, but that did nothing to stem the flow.

Aaron felt his insides grow cold with horror.

Michael reached out, holding on to Aaron's shoulder to pull him close. "Get...out of here," he panted with difficulty. "Get...indoors." His eyes were losing focus. Aaron could see them glazing over in pain.

"Uncle Mike?" Aaron called.

"You...have to...be...safe." Michael's hand fell from Aaron's shoulder just as his eyes rolled to the back of his head.

"Uncle Mike!" Aaron yelled in panic. "No! No, no, no!"

Sam was by his side, two fingers held against Michael's neck to check for a pulse. "He's alive, Aaron, he's alive," he said in a shaky voice. "He just lost consciousness." He quickly unbuttoned his shirt and pulled it off, leaving himself in his vest top. "Here," he said. "Help me tie it around him, to stop the bleeding.

Aaron, Sam and Rose wrapped Sam's shirt around Michael's middle, trying to stem the blood loss. Aaron's heart was beating so fast he felt sick. He looked behind his shoulder to see the fierce battle still going on. They couldn't just stay there with an unconscious Michael – they would be sitting ducks. But leaving his uncle alone and unprotected wasn't an option either. Aaron turned to look to Sam and Rose before back to his uncle, coming to a difficult decision.

"Help me lay him down," he said.

They pulled Michael to lie flat on the ground, just at the doorstep of the cottage. Aaron put both hands onto the ground next to his uncle.

"Grow," he commanded and before his eyes, the grass grew tall and thick. "Protect him," Aaron instructed with desperation. "Keep him hidden."

The grass did as Aaron asked and grew tall enough to cover Michael's slumped form. The entire front lawn of the cottage grew to match the rest. With a heavy heart, Aaron got up. He had no choice but to leave and hope no stray bullets or jolts from vamages caught his uncle.

"Come on, hurry," Aaron called to Sam and Rose before running back onto the street, going back to his original plan of getting onto the Gateway.

He raced past the battle, using the skill Kyran had taught him to block and throw back the jolts that got too close. He had just deflected three ice spears that would have impaled him when he found a vamage's attention shift to him. Aaron stopped in his tracks, breathing rapidly, eyes fixed on the bloodthirsty demon that was grinning at him. Aaron raised the gun Ella gave him and shot three rounds, all of which the vamage dodged. Aaron threw down the gun and raised his hands. A ripple tore its way across the ground, hitting the vamage and sending him flying backwards.

"Aaron, move!"

Sam's yell was accompanied by a shove in the back and Aaron hit the ground, just missing the fireball that blazed past his cheek and ear. Aaron turned to see Sam and Rose had to jump aside to avoid the jolts three vamages were sending at them. Aaron was up on his feet in seconds. Two ripples blasted the vamages back. But now the attention had shifted to the two defenceless humans amidst the mages. Vamages turned to seek out the twins, grinning with delight, hunger lurking in their cold, cruel eyes. Aaron deflected the jolts that came towards his friends, but there were too many. Sam and Rose were forced to duck and dive to avoid being hit.

The jolts drove Sam and Rose apart, so much so that Aaron realised he could only protect one of them.

"Rose!" Aaron cried, seeing her pushed even further away from him and Sam by a mighty blast of air that threw her to the ground.

His panicked gaze moved from Rose to seek out which vamage was targeting her so he could fight back. His eyes caught Kyran's. For the briefest of moments, Kyran paused. Aaron felt his thudding heart bruise his ribs as he held Kyran's gaze. A flicker of something crossed Kyran's features before he looked away. His vivid green eyes moved to rest on Rose instead, just as she was picking herself up from the ground.

It felt like time had slowed down when Rose looked up and found Kyran. They stared at the other as the battle raged around them. Then Kyran's eyes darkened and his expression turned to fury. He pulled back his hand and threw out a stream of fire, straight at Rose.

9

BROKEN TRUST

Aaron was sure his heart stopped when the flames raced towards Rose. She stood in stunned stupor, too shocked at Kyran's attack to move out of the way. Aaron's scream bubbled in his throat but didn't make it out in time. His hand lifted and aimed a ripple at Rose, to push her out of the way – but he was too late.

Rose ducked but Kyran's flames hit the ground before her feet. They spread out, encircling her, confining her inside a ring of fire. Aaron's ripple died just as it reached the flames. Rose stood in the middle of the circle, staring in terror and confusion at what Kyran had done to her.

Aaron turned, his fury made him lash out and the ground at Kyran's feet cracked. The gap would have swallowed him whole if Kyran hadn't jumped back in time.

Sam belted towards his sister, screaming her name. Aaron was at his heels. Before they could reach the trapped Rose, a jolt of power came at her from a vamage. Trapped by the ring of fire, Rose could do nothing but duck to try to avoid it. The jolt was about to hit her crouched form when the flames surrounding her roared and shot upwards, forming a fiery wall that swallowed the jolt. Aaron came to a standstill, looking on in disbelief. Rose slowly stood up, staring at the flames that dropped back down to encircle her. They leapt up again to block an ice spear that came at her from the other side.

Aaron turned to seek out Kyran, meeting his blazing gaze. Kyran only held Aaron's eyes for a moment, before turning to fight the Hunters that had taken his moment of distraction to get close enough to attack.

"Rose! Rose, oh my God." Sam's hysterical cries pulled Aaron's attention. "I'll get you out! Don't worry, Rose, I'll – I'll get you out." Sam was drowning in panic.

"Sammy," Rose yelled back, separated from her brother by the fire that leapt up the minute Sam got too close.

"Sam! Sam, wait." Aaron grabbed his arm, pulling him back from the flames. "She might be safer in there."

"Are you crazy?" Sam yelled, tears shining in his eyes. "It's fire!"

"It's protecting her," Aaron said.

"It won't protect her from bullets," Sam cried.

Not a second later, a deflected bullet from a Hunter's gun came straight at Rose. It happened so fast, Aaron wasn't even aware of it until the bullet ricocheted off the wall of fire that leapt up to defend Rose. Both Sam and Aaron stared at the tiny hole in the ground where the bullet hit.

"I guess it will," Aaron said.

The sound of numerous motorbikes cut through the night and Aaron turned to see headlights come out of the darkness. The Hunters of Salvador had finally arrived. Evidently, Kyran noticed them too. He threw back the Hunter he was fighting with a vicious blow, knocking the boy clean out.

Kyran turned, his fierce eyes searching down the line of cottages, most of which were now ablaze. He found the one with Aric's mark on the door. His fists clenched and he let out a thunderous cry.

"LAYLA!"

The window to the cottage smashed and Stefan, one of the Hunters left to guard the vampire, landed on the grass in a bloodied mess. Layla stepped out of the window frame with incredible grace. The chains that had bound her were gone, as were the two daggers in her leg. She flicked her hair behind her and smiled, her fangs now glistening, even in the limited light.

"You called?" she smirked.

The Hunters turned their guns on her and fired. Layla dodged the attack, her movements swift and fluid as she ducked and dived from every bullet. Her speed was phenomenal. In the blink of an eye, she was halfway down the street. Vamages distracted the Hunters, giving Layla a moment to come to a standstill. Kyran was already on Lexi, speeding towards her. He stopped only long enough for Layla to climb on behind him. Her long-fingered hands went around his waist before inching back to pull out his twin pistols from their holsters. Kyran didn't seem to care. He turned Lexi around and rode to the fallen Gate.

Layla shot at the Hunters to keep them from following after them. Even still, the Hunters made a great effort to stop Kyran, but the vamages held them back by their onslaught of bullets, blades and jolts of power. Aaron pushed Sam down onto the ground to save him from the attack. Behind him, Rose's ring of fire came alive, leaping high to protect her.

The vamages were backing away, keeping up their attack on the Hunters as they followed Kyran. The Hunters blocked the attack while trying with everything they had to stop Kyran from racing to the exit. It was somewhat of a miracle that Aaron and Sam weren't hit in the crossfire. It was only when Aaron dared to look up from his crouched position that he saw the reason why. Someone had stepped in front of him and Sam, knocking back the torrential rain of bullets and jolts that came towards them. Aaron's mouth went dry.

"Mum?"

Kate didn't turn to acknowledge him. She couldn't. Her attention was focused solely on shielding her son from the attack, deflecting the bullets and jolts by using her power of air. Her concentration and energy were fast depleting, though.

Aaron could feel it deep in his bones – an ache that didn't belong to him.

"Mum!" Aaron was up on his feet, running behind her to catch her, just as she swayed and fell back.

Aaron lowered her to the ground, but the attack was over. Kyran had sped through the fallen Gate, leaving the city after having taken what he came for, once again.

The moment Kyran left and the vamages retreated, stepping out of the city and onto the Gateway, the ring of fire trapping Rose died, freeing her. The Hunters gave chase, darting after the vamages but Aaron stayed where he was, with his mum's pale, shaking, barely conscious form in his arms.

Sam shot to his feet, reaching out to his sister as she shakily stepped over the black-charred ring on the ground.

"I'm okay, I'm okay," Rose said, pushing Sam's concerned hands away and hurrying over to Aaron.

Sam followed after her and both crouched next to their friend, not knowing what to say in the aftermath of an attack that left an entire city devastated.

***

Aaron was more than surprised when he learnt the attack on Balt had lasted only fifteen minutes. It had felt endless. But even in fifteen short minutes, Kyran and his vamages had left plenty of lifeless bodies in their wake. More were injured, so many so that there was hardly any room left in the numerous Empath huts.

The Hunters had survived the attack, except two of the three left to guard the vampire, Layla. Ray and Emma were found in the cottage, their heads almost torn off their bodies. Stefan had been bitten and thrown out of the window, since Layla couldn't use the door that had been marked with Aric's symbol.

Aaron could see Stefan's unconscious form laid out before two Empaths as they worked to heal him. That was until an Empath moved to stand in front of the gap between the curtains. Aaron turned his head, focusing on his mum, who was being checked over by the same Empath that had helped his dad.

At last the Empath pulled away with a tired smile, and let go of Kate's hand. "You'll be fine with some rest," he said. "It was just exhaustion from using your powers for too long."

"I told you I was fine," Kate said, quickly getting off the bed. "Your time and touch is needed elsewhere."

The Empath's smile slid away. His head tilted towards the commotion of various mages coming in or out of the huts – some injured, others moderately healed. "Unfortunately," he said, "that is true." He excused himself politely and left to help the injured Hunters.

Kate turned to Aaron, and for a moment neither spoke. Then Kate walked over to him and wordlessly wrapped her arms around him, holding Aaron close for long, silent minutes. Aaron returned the hug. When Kate pulled away, she cupped his face in her hands.

"Don't you ever scare me like that again, you hear me?" Kate's blue eyes were dark with worry. "If there's any sign of a fight, you find a place to take cover and you *stay* there." She shook her head. "When I saw you standing there, right smack in the middle of the battle–" She paused to hold her breath, as if collecting herself before she could go on. "I tried to get to you but...but there was so much going on. I thought I wasn't going to reach you in time."

Aaron didn't say anything. He had no idea his mum was involved in the battle. He had thought she was still in the Empath's hut, safe from the attack.

"I'm sorry," he said.

"Good," a voice said from behind him. Aaron turned to see a disgruntled, but otherwise perfectly healthy-looking Michael. "You should be sorry."

Relief swept up in Aaron at the sight of his uncle. He hurried over to him and Michael opened his arms to hug his nephew. "You're such an idiot," Michael chastised in a quiet, emotionally exhausted voice. "You know that? You could have really got hurt."

Aaron pulled away, his gaze going straight to the bloodstained side of his uncle. Sam's shirt was gone, but then, so was the wound. "You okay?" Aaron still asked, to make sure.

"I'm fine," Michael said. "I got a little ambushed and stabbed in the process, but I'm not going down that easily." He gave a small, half-hearted smile.

Kate went to her brother's side to embrace him gently, and to reassure him that she was perfectly fine, since he'd come looking for her in the Empath hut.

"I tired myself out," Kate explained as the three of them left the hut. "It's been a while since I've used my powers. It got a little...overwhelming."

Aaron looked at her but didn't say anything. His parents had spent fourteen years living in the human realm, suppressing their powers in a bid to live a human life and protect him from this war. Aaron pushed back the familiar wave of guilt as it threatened to engulf him. But when he looked around, at the devastation and the charred remains of the street, his guilt withered away. Everyone deserved to be protected, not just him.

The mages of Balt were slowly picking up the pieces of their city, fixing what could be salvaged and mournfully letting go of what couldn't. The fires had been put out, though most of the buildings were still left smoking. Broken plates and furniture littered the street. But the sight that took hold of Aaron with a gut-wrenching grip was of the bodies lined to one side of the street, covered from head to foot with sheets. How Aaron kept walking he didn't know, but his eyes stayed on the morbid image of the dead mages. There were twelve of them, lined side by side. Aaron's stomach rolled and had he eaten anything substantial that day, he would've turned and retched in the street.

His gaze moved from the covered bodies to the figure kneeling beside them. He recognised the powerful build of Neriah as he crouched next to his fallen people, his head bowed. Daylight was steadily turning the dark sky to a pale, cloudy blue, so when Neriah lifted his head slightly, Aaron clearly saw the heartbroken expression on his face. Aaron watched as Neriah slowly rose to stand but his violet eyes remained on the bodies. He stood there until Ella came to his side, slipping a hand into his. Gently she pulled her uncle away and they started walking up the street.

Neriah raised his head, and came to a standstill. His expression changed, eyes fixed to something in the distance. Aaron followed his gaze and stopped in his tracks as well.

"Dad?"

Kate and Michael turned at Aaron's voice. They all saw Chris, slowly and very painfully, making his way forward. He had his bloodstained shirt on but left it unbuttoned, so the bandages wrapped around his torso were visible. Chris didn't look concerned for himself, though. He was distracted by the ruined city around him. He stared at the street with wide, rueful eyes until he met Neriah's gaze and Chris too came to a standstill.

For a moment, no one moved. Not a word was said. The essence of sorrow hung like a thick curtain between the Elementals – so much so that Aaron was sure both men were about to step forward and hug like mourning brothers would after a death in the family. But Chris and Neriah didn't hug. They didn't grieve together. They stood and stared at the other.

Chris was the first to look away. He shook his head and held out his hands, gesturing to the charred street on either side of him. "Do you need any more evidence, Neriah?" he asked. "Or will you believe me now?"

"They weren't here for him, Chris," Neriah said tiredly. "They came to take the vampire Balt was holding."

Chris didn't believe him. It was clear to see in his expression. "My son steps out of Marwa and is attacked by Lycans. Then the city he takes refuge in is attacked in a matter of hours—"

"By vamages," Neriah cut across him. "Not Lycans, Chris. Vamages. This was at the hands of vamages and their Scorcher."

Chris looked taken aback. His pale face seemed to lose more colour. "He was here?" he asked, and Aaron knew he meant Kyran.

Neriah didn't answer, but stepped forward, walking over to him. "Open your eyes, Chris," he said. "Look around you. This isn't for Aaron. The vamages didn't come for your son, and neither did Raoul and his Lycans."

Chris's expression hardened, his eyes a cold piercing green. "You still won't believe me."

"Believe *what*?" Neriah snapped and his voice boomed across the street. "Your ludicrous story about Raoul having a personal vendetta against your family? That he was hunting the Adams? Wake up, Chris. Raoul is after *all* of us, all of the Elementals."

"I never said he wasn't," Chris retorted, "but he's actively searching for Aaron, and your stubbornness to have him fighting in this war is going to put my son on the front line."

"We're all on the front line," Neriah said. "We always have been. You think I want to endanger Aaron? He's a legacy holder. I want to keep him safe as much as you." His violet eyes gleamed with anger. "But the way to protect him isn't to hide him. It's to teach him to fight, teach him to defend himself."

"You don't want to *defend* him, Neriah!" Chris yelled. "Admit it. You just want to use him. You want Aaron to pick up the Blade and fight, so you have a chance to fix the mess that *you* made!"

With a snarl, Neriah grabbed Chris by the collar of his shirt. Aaron's breath caught in his chest. He darted forward, but Ella held on to his arm.

"Don't," she whispered. "This is long overdue. Let them fight."

But the two Elementals didn't throw jolts of power at each other. They didn't even exchange punches. They stood where they were, Chris with his arms by his side, angry tears in his eyes, staring at Neriah, who gripped Chris by his shirt but didn't strike him.

"I made a mistake," Neriah said in a voice not much louder than a whisper. "I admit it. I should have *killed* him." He shook Chris. "You think I don't regret it? That I don't know we're in this mess because I hoped to fix him? To make him *Hadrian* again?"

"He could never be *fixed*," Chris said quietly but no less furiously. "Hadrian was gone. All that was left was a monster, one that *you* should have put down the day he turned on James." Chris held Neriah's eyes. "You didn't listen to me. You ignored everyone and did what you deemed right in the hopes of saving someone you loved." He held Neriah's eyes. "So why do you judge me for doing the same?"

Neriah let go of Chris and stepped back, shaking his head. "It's not the same, Chris. It's not the same and you know it," he said. "You don't want to fight? Then go. Leave. No one will stop you." His expression shifted and for a moment, his hurt was visible. "You turned your back on me once, left me alone to fight this war. Go ahead and do it again."

The anger melted from Chris. His shoulders dropped and tired green eyes filled with pain. "Neriah," he breathed, stepping forward. "I'm not saying I don't want to fight. I'm with you, all the way. I'll fight this war. I'll do whatever you ask of me." He paused and Aaron could see the desperate plea in his expression alone. "But let my son go. I can't risk him. He's all the family I have left."

Neriah was silent for a moment before he smiled sadly and shook his head. "Family?" he asked. "We were a family too, Chris. You, me, James and Hadrian. We were a family, or don't you remember?"

Chris didn't speak.

"We lived in the one place," Neriah continued. "We ate from the one table. We fought together, we won together." His eyes searched Chris for a silent moment before quietly adding, "You're not the only one to lose them that day. Alex was just as much my brother as he was yours."

Chris flinched at Alex's name but still remained silent.

"You and Alex were my brothers, not by blood but in spirit." Neriah said. "You lost one brother, but I lost all of them. Some to death, one to banishment," his eyes glinted, "and one to abandonment."

"I didn't abandon you," Chris said. "I left to protect my wife and unborn child–"

"Yes, you did," Neriah cut him off. "You left to save them, to protect them. I understand that. *Everyone* understands that. I would do the same." His eyes darkened. "But I wouldn't have waited fourteen years to come back."

"I had to stay away. Raoul was targeting my family–"

"Raoul's been targeting *every* family!" Neriah spat. "He's the leader of the Lycans. This is all they've known for centuries!"

"This is different," Chris insisted. "It's personal."

"No, Chris, it isn't," Neriah said. "It isn't." The anger was gone, leaving only bitterness. "They mess with one of us, they mess with all of us."

Chris reacted like Neriah had punched him. His breath left in a choked gasp and his eyes widened as he staggered back a step.

"That's what we used to say. That's what we believed." The rest of Neriah's words were left unspoken but they hung in the air just the same.

This is our fight, not just yours.

You should have stayed by my side.

***

Aaron found Rose sitting by herself on the kerb outside the ruined cottages.

"Hey," Aaron said, coming to sit next to her. "Where's Sam?"

Rose nodded towards the broken table in the middle of the street and Aaron turned to see Sam helping the mages clear away the debris.

"He said he was tired of sitting around," Rose explained. "He wanted to help." She looked at Aaron. "Did you get to speak to your dad?"

Aaron shook his head with a sigh. "When I first got there, the Empaths said my dad was having the poison drained out some more, so I couldn't go in to see him. I waited outside for an hour. When I finally got in, Dad had fallen asleep. I waited with him, hoping he would wake up so I could talk to him, but he was pretty out of it."

"He shouldn't have left his bed," Rose said. "He's still recovering. Think it took a lot out of him."

Aaron didn't say anything, but he knew it was the argument with Neriah that had worn out his dad. He turned to look at

Rose. His soft green eyes studied her intently, looking past her exhaustion to see how badly she was hurting, but not in the physical sense.

He gently touched her arm. "You okay?"

Rose avoided meeting his eyes. "Yeah," she said quietly. "I'm fine."

Aaron nodded. "I deserved that," he said. "I asked a stupid question. Of course you're not okay."

Rose shook her head. "Really, Aaron. I'm fine."

"Rose," Aaron breathed. "Don't do that. Please don't tell me you're fine when I can see you're not."

Rose met his eyes then. She gave a small shrug but it did nothing to displace the pain of heartbreak in her eyes. "What do you want me to say?" she asked. "He lied." Her voice broke a little, but she pushed past it. "He lied about everything. About who he was, about his past, about everything. Then why is finding out he's with someone else surprising?" She shook her head, looking away. "He never cared, Aaron. He was only amusing himself. I was nothing more than a joke to him, someone whose feelings he could play with until his time in Salvador came to an end."

Aaron didn't know how to say what he wanted to. He focused on the charred ground at his feet.

"He protected you." He could feel Rose tense next to him. "That ring of fire kept you safe. He didn't have to do that if he didn't care—"

"Aaron," Rose cut him off and her voice shook, as if her emotions were close to breaking the surface of her forced calm. "He stood by and watched as vamages murdered my parents."

Aaron's heart sunk at the reminder. He looked into Rose's hurt brown eyes, filled with tears as well as anger.

"For all I know, he might have been the one to order the attack on my house," she said.

"Rose, no," Aaron said at once, his insides going cold at just the thought.

"You saw how the vamages obeyed him. They didn't move a muscle until Kyran ordered them." Rose was trembling, as if her anger had jostled every cell in her body. "He may have protected me today, but he let my parents die. He could have saved them. He could have told his vamages not to attack. He could've–" She stopped, her breath caught in her chest. She clenched her eyes shut and shook her head. "I don't want to talk about this," she whispered. "I can't. I'll drive myself crazy if I keep on thinking about everything he *could* have done."

Aaron held on to her hand and gave it a little squeeze. "Okay, we'll not talk about it, or talk about him."

Rose gave him a ghost of her usual smile and leant in, resting her head on his shoulder. "You okay?" she asked after a minute.

"Yeah," he said. "I'm fine."

"Stupid question," Rose echoed him. "Of course you're not okay."

Aaron smiled. "No, I think I really am," he said. "After seeing the attack, I'm more determined now than ever."

"About what?"

"About what I have to do," Aaron replied. "I need to go with Neriah and claim the Blade of Adams."

Rose lifted her head to stare at Aaron with surprise. "What?" she asked.

"You saw what the vamages did," Aaron said. "And Kyran didn't even have his Blade with him today." He recalled the memory Zhi-Jiya had shared with him, the one where Kyran had destroyed an entire village with a sword that set the place on fire. He knew that must be Kyran's family blade, one of the Blades of Aric.

Rose touched his arm, bringing him out of his thoughts. "Aaron?"

He met her eyes. "We need the Blades, Rose," he said. "Kyran is too strong. Even without the Blade of Aedus, he managed to burn down half the city. I need to get my Blade and use it to fight this war."

Rose's grip tightened on his hand. "So...so you're still going to fight?" she asked. "Even after hearing what your dad said about the Lycans being after you?"

Aaron had to force out a breath to remain calm. He reminded himself it wasn't just him. All the Elementals were at risk from Lycan attacks. If the rest were fighting, then why shouldn't he? He looked at Rose, holding her terrified gaze.

"Yeah," he said. "I'm still going to fight."

10

LONG WINDED TRIPS

Two days passed and the City of Balt slowly recovered from its devastating attack. Most of the debris had been cleared away, restoration of damaged buildings had started and the dead had been buried. Aaron was glad he didn't see the burial; he didn't have it in him to watch twelve bodies go into the ground.

The end of March was bringing a chill in the air, but Aaron still preferred to sit with Sam and Rose outside, near a small pond in a quiet and secluded part of the city.

"When are you leaving?" Sam asked.

Aaron had to squint against the afternoon sun to look at Sam. "Tomorrow," he replied. "Neriah said he's sending you two back to Salvador with Ella at some point today. We're going to leave early tomorrow morning."

"I don't get why we can't come with you," Sam grouched, playing with the small pebble in his hand. "I know what Neriah was saying, about attracting attention and all that, but you've got a big enough crowd already. How much trouble could two more cause?" He drew back his hand and threw the pebble.

Aaron watched the stone plop into the pond and leave ripples across the surface. He smiled. "When it's you two, a lot."

"The whole point of us leaving Marwa was to go with you," Rose pointed out.

"Exactly," Sam said. "I don't want to sit around doing nothing in Salvador. I'd rather do something, anything, to help."

"I agree." Rose nodded.

"I think we should ask Neriah if we can come too," Sam said.

"He'll never agree," Aaron said at once.

"He might," Rose said. "I mean, he's letting your mum and Michael go with you when he didn't even want your dad going the first time around."

"Dad didn't exactly give him a choice," Aaron said. "And I don't know what Mum said to Neriah to convince him, but it obviously worked."

"Maybe this time Neriah's just going to use a portal that goes straight from here to wherever that sword is," Sam suggested.

"If that were an option I don't see why Neriah wouldn't have done it the last time," Rose said.

"Why isn't it an option?" Sam asked. "Why make a long-winded trip when you can practically flash in and out of the place?"

"I don't think it is a choice," Aaron said. "Scott set up a portal a mile away when my dad was wounded and needed immediate help. If he could've gotten one closer he would have."

"So you reckon there are only certain spots where portals can open?" Rose asked.

"Seems like it," Aaron said. He recalled the very first Q-Zone hunt he had witnessed in the Hub. He remembered Drake telling him about portals and how Scott used them to help the Hunters trick demons into the Q-Zone. Scott was using the round white table – the Hub – to control the portals, opening them in several locations and linking them to the one in the Q-Zone.

"So Scott is going to open the portal closest to wherever that special sword is kept?" Sam asked.

Aaron shook his head. "Neriah said portals leave behind trails. He doesn't want anyone following us. He's planned a different route, since we ran into Lycans on the last one."

"I don't get it," Rose started. "Why haven't they secured the swords before now? If they're so protective of them and don't want anyone else getting to them, why don't they keep the swords in a locked room in the middle of a safe city, like Salvador?"

"'Cause Salvador isn't safe."

Aaron and the twins turned at Skyler's voice to see him standing behind them, smirking in his usual condescending way. "I think your ex proved just how reliable and secure Salvador is," he said to Rose, who glared back at him, but didn't say anything. "And even if we could move the Blades of Aric, putting them in a city would be a pretty dumb thing to do."

"Why?" Aaron asked.

Skyler looked at him but didn't answer. He turned to Sam and Rose. "Ella's waiting for you two. Scott opened the portal to Salvador and the sooner you pass through it, the better."

All three got to their feet.

"Where's Neriah?" Sam asked.

"Why?" Skyler frowned.

"I want to speak with him," Sam replied.

Skyler gave him a long look before replying, "He's waiting with Ella."

Aaron turned to Sam. "You're not really going to ask him if you can come with me, are you?"

"Why not?" Sam shrugged. "Can't hurt to ask."

"I wouldn't be too sure," Aaron said. "I'd imagine a wave of water hits like a hammer."

Skyler gave a sharp whistle to get their attention. "Hey, chatterboxes, get a move on."

Sam and Rose walked away, leaving Aaron behind. For a moment, Skyler didn't move, but just stared at Aaron. He looked like he was contemplating something.

Then he straightened up and said, "I'd gather my things, if I were you. We're leaving at the crack of dawn tomorrow." He turned to go.

"Hey," Aaron called and Skyler looked back at him. "I've been meaning to say something to you."

"Let me guess: *I told you not to interrogate that vampire, you should've listened to me, blah, blah, blah.*" He narrowed his eyes at Aaron. "You can save it, Adams, 'cause Balt would've been attacked regardless of whether I questioned Layla or not. The only thing I regret is not staking that piece of filth when I had the chance. It would have saved two Hunters' lives if I had."

Aaron took a moment to reply. "Actually, all I wanted to say was thanks."

For once, Skyler looked surprised. "What for?"

"For remembering that Sam and Rose were here during the attack," Aaron said. "And caring enough to tell me to protect them."

"They're human," Skyler said. "Protecting them is our priority." He smirked and added, "Doesn't mean I have to like them."

Aaron rolled his eyes. "Of course it doesn't."

Skyler turned to walk away.

"Hey," Aaron called again.

Skyler stopped and faced him, this time looking annoyed. "What?" he bit out.

"I owe you another thanks," Aaron said. "For bringing my dad here."

Skyler's expression was one of agitation. His eyes grew cold, the lines on his brow deepened with resentment. "Don't think too much about it," he said. "I would have left him there to bleed." His eyes locked with Aaron's. "But Neriah asked me to help him, so I did."

A part of Aaron knew this was how Skyler would react. What other response did he expect from a harsh, cold-hearted bully? But a smaller part of Aaron felt rather let down. He had hoped Skyler could be decent, especially when Aaron was trying to be nice.

"Whatever your reason," Aaron said, "you got my dad here in time for the Empaths to heal him. For that, I'll always be thankful."

For a heartbeat Skyler looked lost, like he didn't know what to do with Aaron's gratitude. He fidgeted uncomfortably before shrugging. "Whatever, Adams. Pack up your things."

He walked away, leaving a bemused Aaron smiling after him.

***

The hot water cascaded down his aching muscles, easing the tension out of them. Kyran closed his eyes, feeling the heat sear through his flesh, warming his bones. It was always like this for him. Ever since he was a young boy, he couldn't use the element of Water as well as he could the others.

He could direct water, manipulate it in a basic manner, but when it came to controlling the temperature, he always failed. It was always a notch hotter than he liked. His father teased him by saying it was his element that was getting in the way. His core called to Fire like a person pulled in air to breathe. It was instinctual, an action he wasn't even aware of doing at times. No matter what other element he tried using, fire would always make its presence known. It had taken Kyran years to practise control, but even so, there were some things he couldn't do, like cooling down water in his shower.

Kyran waved a hand and the water stopped at once. With a towel wrapped around his waist, Kyran walked out of the en-suite and into his bedroom, where a visitor was waiting, spread out on his bed.

"I'm not in the mood to play games, Layla," he said, walking over to his wardrobe. "Get out."

Layla purred like a cat and stretched on Kyran's covers. "You're never in the mood," she said. "Come on, Kyran. You saved my life. You must be a little eager to let out some stress."

Kyran slammed the door shut and turned to glare at her. "You think this is funny?"

"No." Layla propped up an arm and rested on it, her light blue eyes fixed on the agitated boy before her. "But I do think it's odd that you came to my rescue and, forty-two hours later, you've still not come looking for my blood." She paused before waving a hand. "Figuratively, of course."

Kyran smirked at her, a cold glint in his eyes. "Maybe that's because I've thought up a better solution."

Layla grinned. "Ah yes, the lock-her-up-and-throw-away-the-key idea you presented to Hadrian?" She sat up on her knees. Waves of red hair framed her as she tilted her head and smiled at Kyran. "He'll never do it. He needs me."

"Unfortunately," Kyran said. "But guess what? He needs me more."

Layla chuckled. "Oh, so did you give him a rendition of your anthem, 'It's either her or me'? 'Cause to be honest, I'd be a little disappointed if I missed it."

Kyran shook his head and walked over to his dresser. "You're such a bitch."

Layla gave a playful shiver. "Oh, I love it when you stick with the classics."

Kyran forced himself to turn his back on her and opened the top drawer. He was too tired for this. He had spent the entire day training. He hadn't slept for two days and the last thing he needed was his father's little demonic pest egging him into a fight. He pulled out dark bottoms, snapped the drawer shut and turned around, only to find Layla right in front of him. Her pale blue eyes gazed at him.

"What's with you, Kyran?" she asked, her voice quiet, undeniably seductive. Her long fingers reached out to ghost over the black circle on his chest. "You've not been the same ever since you came back from Salvador." Her hand trailed down his front to touch the top of the towel wrapped around his waist.

Kyran's hand snapped around her wrist, stopping her. Layla held his furious stare until he shoved her hand away, making her stumble back a step. She grinned.

"There we go," she said. "Think I'm getting somewhere."

Kyran took a step forward to get in her face. "I'm warning you, Layla," he said. "I'm getting closer to the point of not giving a crap and staking you in that place your heart supposedly is."

Layla smiled. "I don't believe you," she said. "I know you won't kill me, and you won't let anyone else try either because Hadrian needs me." She arched up, bringing her face close to Kyran's. "And I need you," she whispered.

Kyran smirked and leant in – and for a moment it seemed like he was about to brush her lips with his own – but he only inched closer to whisper back, "Not in this lifetime."

He walked away, leaving Layla swaying at the sudden loss. She took a moment before turning around to smirk at him. "Is this any way to treat your girlfriend, Scorcher?"

Kyran glared at her. "I wondered what Skyler was going on about."

Layla giggled, looking immensely pleased with herself. "I had to say something to stop them hurting me. Telling a room full of Hunters that I was the sweetheart of the feared Scorcher got them to back off."

Kyran gave her a disgusted look. "You're pathetic," he said and headed back to the en-suite.

"That I am," Layla said with a shrug. "But you know what else I am?" She paused until Kyran came back into the room, wearing the dark bottoms instead of the towel. "Intuitive," she said.

Kyran ignored her and walked to his wardrobe again. Layla smiled and continued. "When I lied that I was your girlfriend, all the Hunters looked shocked, but a few of them immediately turned to seek out this one girl."

Kyran tensed. Layla saw it in the muscles of his bare back. "It was strange – the look on her face," she continued. "I can't quite figure it out. It was a mix of surprise and..." She tilted her head, eyes narrowed as they stayed on Kyran. "...heartbreak."

Kyran turned, his jaw locked. His fists clenched and his fierce green eyes darkened.

"I've been thinking about it," Layla said, stepping closer. "Why did the Hunters turn to her? Why would she care? Why would she get so upset at finding out I was with the Scorcher? Then I came to a conclusion...the only one there can be." She bared her teeth in a dazzling smile. "Really, Kyran? A *human* girl? A mundane, defenceless—"

Kyran was across the room in a heartbeat, a hand around Layla's throat. "Enough," he growled. "I swear it, Layla. You go anywhere *near* Rose and I'll bleed you out, drop by drop!"

Layla held up both hands and Kyran let go, shoving her back. He was breathing hard, his chest heaving, eyes blazing.

"Don't worry, Kyran, I won't go after her," Layla said. She turned to walk to the door, pausing only when her fingers were on the handle. "I won't have to." She looked back at Kyran with serious blue eyes, all amusement gone. "All I have to do is wait until your father finds out his prized prodigy is crushing on a Shattered." She smiled. "Wonder what he'll do?"

She opened the door and left, leaving a seething Kyran alone in his room.

***

Aaron trudged up the hill, feeling a sense of déjà vu in his actions. Just like before, he was following Neriah, who was leading the way through a dense forest. Skyler and Ella were behind him, but this time his mum and uncle Mike were following them. That was the difference. That and the fact he had both his best friends by his side.

Aaron still couldn't figure it out; why had Neriah allowed Sam and Rose to come with them? It made little to no sense. Neriah had been paranoid about his dad coming with them before, for fear of attracting unwanted attention, but now he was indifferent to most of Aaron's family and friends accompanying him.

It was fast approaching dusk. They had spent the entire day trekking through the woods. Before long there would be nothing but the moonlight to guide them.

"Just a minute," Aaron whispered to the twins either side of him, before hurrying over to Neriah.

"How long will it take to get to the Blade?" he asked.

"Not long," Neriah replied.

"We won't get to it before the sun goes down, will we?"

Neriah looked at Aaron with a small smile. "Seeing as the sun is about to dip out of view, I would say no, we won't."

"Are we going to camp out here for the night?" Aaron asked.

This time Neriah laughed. "No, I don't think that would be safe."

"Sooo?" Aaron waited but Neriah didn't volunteer anything. "What are we going to do?"

Neriah sighed. "Trust me, Aaron. I know what I'm doing."

"Then why won't you just share it with me?" Aaron asked.

Neriah's eyes sparkled with amusement when he looked around at Aaron. He pointed ahead. "Another two miles and we'll reach the Gateway to the City of Hunda. We'll rest there for tonight and complete our journey tomorrow."

Aaron nodded, satisfied, and began slowing down his pace so he could join his friends again. Neriah's quiet chuckle halted him.

"You are very much like your father," Neriah said. "He was inherently curious too, always asking questions, getting involved." He went quiet, his mood abruptly shifted. "How a person can change."

Aaron tried to keep silent, but it was a battle he lost within moments. "It's not like that," he said. "Dad was only trying to do what he thought would keep us safe."

"And as commendable as that is, your dad ignored the fact that he had a responsibility to keep the mages of this realm safe too," Neriah said.

Aaron couldn't find anything to say to that. He dropped his head, his steps slowing down, losing their pace with Neriah. In response, the leader of the mages slowed down to match him.

"I don't blame Chris for running," he said, surprising Aaron. "I came to Marwa after the attack had ended that day. I saw what was left of my city. To have endured the attack, watched as mages fell to the Lycans' fangs and claws–" He stopped talking, visibly gathering himself. "I understand why he took his wounded wife and unborn child out of that situation." His jaw clenched and his violet eyes gleamed in the setting sun. "But he didn't come back. He knew what state he left the mage realm in. He knew the implications of the war. He knew about it all, but he still didn't return. That's where my blame lies."

"Because he left you alone to deal with it all," Aaron added.

Neriah looked sharply at Aaron, but it didn't last long. The anger melted from him, replaced with hurt. "It would be impossible for you to understand what life was like before this war," he said. "The Elementals were a family, in every sense of the word. Chris, Alex, James, Joseph and Hadrian…" He paused. "They were my brothers. There was very little we didn't do together." He looked over at Aaron. "Your uncle, Alex was the youngest Elemental. He wasn't just a baby brother to Chris, he was that to all of us. We indulged him, looked out for him." He raised his head to the darkened sky and inhaled deeply. "I had to bury him, as well as what was left of little Ben."

Aaron's heart lurched in his chest. He looked down at the ground. He wanted to ask Neriah about Kyran, to see what theories the oldest and wisest Elemental could give as to why the son of Hadrian shared such an uncanny resemblance with his uncle. But Aaron couldn't find it in him to talk about Kyran, not now, not when Neriah sounded so weighed down with grief.

"Your dad didn't just leave me to deal with Hadrian and this war," Neriah said. "He left me alone to bury the family we'd lost." He met Aaron's eyes. "Above all else, it's this that I can't forgive him for."

Aaron didn't say anything. There was nothing he could say to that.

11

THE TALE OF THE WAITING BLOOM

The City of Hunda was a small but friendly place. The moment Neriah led the group past the Gate, the residents of Hunda welcomed them with great passion, cheering and applauding. Aaron knew the jubilation was for their leader, for Neriah, but it was still nice to experience it, especially after his depressing talk.

They were quickly ushered to the long table in the middle of the street, where platters of fish and rice were served to them. Aaron watched as Skyler, Ella and Neriah spent very little time at the table. They took a few mouthfuls before disappearing into a hut with a short, squat man – who Aaron figured was the chief of this city.

After dinner, the residents of Hunda gathered around a fire while mugs of sweetened tea were passed out. Aaron sat before the crackling flames, his mum and uncle on one side of him, Sam and Rose on the other. The smell of cinnamon lingered in the air, faint wisps of steam escaped from the cups as trays were hovered before them. Aaron declined the offering, feeling too full after his meal.

The City of Hunda shared some similarities with Salvador, like the communal table in the middle of the street, but where Salvador had lines of cottages, Hunda had rows of small huts. Aaron could see many mages retiring for the night, climbing up the few wooden steps to enter their straw-roofed shacks.

His mum's hand touched his arm, getting his attention.

"We should go and rest," she said. "We're leaving early tomorrow."

"You go; I'm not tired," Aaron replied.

Kate's brow furrowed. "I would rather we all go in together."

"Mum, it's cool," Aaron said, a slight bite to his tone. "I'm not going anywhere. I'll be right here." His tone softened at her surprised look. "Go and rest. I'll be sharing a hut with Sam and Rose anyway."

Kate glanced at the twins before looking back at him. "Michael is sharing with you and Sam. I'll share with Rose."

"If Sam and Rose are okay with that, then fine," Aaron said.

Kate's brow knitted, and for a moment Aaron was sure she was going to argue – tell him he wasn't the one making decisions and to just do as he was told. But Kate's annoyance rushed out of her with a resigned sigh. She patted his arm. "Goodnight," she said quietly.

Aaron nodded. "Night."

Kate got up and left, leaving Michael in conversation with the residents of Hunda.

Aaron watched as one of the mages led Kate to the hut that was prepared for their overnight stay. He saw a group of girls around the huts, wide baskets in hand, talking to the few mages there. Gradually, the girls made their way over to the group sitting around the fire. They spread out, going to different people, holding out their baskets. One of them, a girl who didn't look much older than Aaron, came to kneel next to Sam and Rose.

"Would you like one?" she asked.

"What is it?" Rose asked, peering into the wicker basket.

"They're bands of waiting blooms," the girl replied, holding one out.

Rose took it, examining the strip of white silk. In the middle was a small glass dome, filled with water. Floating inside was a tiny ivory bud.

"Strange design for a wristband," Aaron said.

The girl peered up at Aaron. "You don't know what these are?" she asked. "Pardon me, but are you Shattereds?"

"No," Aaron said, and his voice took on a steely edge. "I'm a mage and they are *human*, not Shattereds," he said, gesturing to the twins. "Start using the proper term."

The girl's eyes widened. "A thousand pardons, sir," she said quickly. "It was not my intention to anger you."

"Yeah, well, you just did," Sam said. "You mages always think you can get away with insulting the rest of us."

"Oh, but I'm not a mage," the girl said.

The three of them stared at her with surprise.

"You're not?" Sam frowned.

"What are you, then?" Aaron asked.

"I'm a Peregrin," the girl replied.

"What's a Peregrin?" Sam asked.

"We're travellers," the girl explained. "We go from one city to the next, gathering things from one place and selling them in another."

"Selling them?" Rose looked at the silk strip in her hand. "How much can you make from them?"

"Enough to survive," the girl smiled back. "These are very special, though. These weren't picked up, they were crafted by our hand."

"What do you do with it?" Aaron and Rose asked together and then chuckled at their synchrony.

"You tie it onto the wrist of your beloved, or have them tie it to yours," the girl said. "If it's true love, the flower will bloom."

Rose looked sceptical. "What are the chances of the flower blooming?"

"Why don't you tie it and see?" the girl replied. She gestured to Aaron. "You both make such a lovely couple. I'm certain it's true love."

Rose and Aaron looked at each other with stunned, embarrassed smiles.

"No, no," Rose shook her head. "I'm not with him."

"She's like my sister!" Aaron said. "I've grown up with her."

The girl looked surprised. She turned to Sam.

"She *is* my sister," he said. "So don't even go there."

The girl blushed, dropping her head. "My apologies." She turned to Aaron and Rose. "You asked about the waiting bloom together so I assumed–"

"We were just curious what they were," Aaron said.

"These are replicas of the original waiting bloom," the girl explained, taking the silk strip back from Rose. "It's an exceptional story. Almost every mage knows of it." She caressed the glass dome. "It's one of the greatest love stories of this realm."

That got Sam's attention. He looked to Aaron and Rose before scanning the crowd around the fire. Ella was nowhere in sight. Remembering how much of a fan Ella was of love stories, Sam turned back to the Peregrin girl with a grin. "Alright, then, let's hear this story?"

The girl settled onto her knees, her basket before her.

"The Peregrins heard the tale of the Waiting Bloom from the Pecosas, who swear they heard the story from the mages involved," she started. "It's the story of a girl, rumoured to be the prettiest in all the realm. She had hair as dark as night, skin that glowed like the moon. Her eyes were pools of—"

"Yeah, yeah, we get it. She's really pretty," Sam interrupted. "Get on with the story."

"Sam," Rose chastened with a frown.

"I wanna get to the good stuff," Sam said.

"Please keep going," Aaron said to the girl. "And just ignore him." He waved a hand at Sam.

The Peregrin dipped her head with a smile. "The girl didn't have much of a family. She lived by herself. She was a peaceful creature, for a mage." She gave Aaron and the twins a mischievous smile. "But she was at times deeply troubled; for she had fallen in love with a mage — a daring, brave warrior, who faced all sorts of perils on a daily basis."

"A Hunter," Aaron guessed.

The Peregrin nodded. "The girl used to beg him to give up his role, to settle with her in a peaceful existence."

"If all Hunters did that, there wouldn't be a peaceful existence," Sam joked.

"Funny, that's what the boy would reply," the girl said with a laugh.

Sam looked oddly proud of himself.

"As time passed, the girl began to fret for the safety of her lover," the girl continued. "She would look to the skies, waiting for them to turn dark, for thunder to clap and lightning to cut through the air. Whenever it did, the girl would fall deep into despair, for she knew her lover was fighting demonic forces."

Aaron realised she was referring to the phenomenon that occurred in the mage realm when a Q-Zone opened. He himself had witnessed the weather changing during the first Q-Zone hunt he had followed at the Hub in Salvador.

"She wouldn't sleep, couldn't eat, not until she saw him again," the girl went on. "Sometimes it would take days for him to come and see her, to assure her that he hadn't perished in battle. He couldn't take her despair and worry, so he gifted her with a pendant, one he had created himself, representing both of their elements. He told her to hold on to the pendant and think of him, whenever she fretted for his safety. If the flower bloomed, she was to understand that he was alive and well. Many times she held the glass dome and whispered his name, smiling with relief when the flower blossomed into a full bloom. On one fateful day, when there was a great unrest in the realm, she took the pendant and whispered his name. The flower blossomed, only to wither mere seconds later. The ivory shine turned grey, the petals crushed by an unseen hand. The water in which the flower floated turned crimson and she knew…she knew he was gone, taken by the enemy's sword."

Aaron had guessed the ending the moment the girl mentioned the pendant with the flower that only bloomed if the girl's lover was alive, but it still struck him as tragic. He gave a sideways look to see that even Sam and Rose looked moved.

"So you make the bands in remembrance of their love?" Aaron asked.

The Peregrin smiled sadly and shook her head. "You've not heard the part that makes this the greatest story of the realm," she said. "The girl attended her lover's funeral. She watched as they buried the battered, broken body of the warrior deep into the earth. She knew her lover was dead, but she believed her love wasn't."

Aaron frowned. "I don't understand."

"She believed in her love, in the bond that they shared. He was gone but she believed she could still see him – find his shadow in the house they lived in, hear his voice in the whispers of the wind."

"How?" Sam asked. "That makes no sense–"

"Echoes," Rose said softly, thinking about the ghost-like forms she had desperately wanted to see of her own parents. She looked at the Peregrin. "She was waiting to see his echo?"

The girl nodded. "Legend has it that she sat outside her house and waited to come across his echo for forty days, without sleeping, barely eating. She became ill, so much so that her friends had to bring an Empath to her, as she couldn't move. Everyone told her if she couldn't see his echo in those first forty days, then she never would. That maybe their love wasn't as strong as she believed. But she never gave up. She insisted she would see him again, that her love was strong enough, that their love was true and that one day he would find his way to her. She kept the pendant, with the belief that one day it would bloom again, the moment his echo finally reached her." She looked down at the band. "To this day, she sits and waits for him, and that is why we call it the Tale of the Waiting Bloom."

Aaron waited to hear more, but the girl didn't speak, having finished the story.

"That's it?" Sam asked, looking disappointed. "What happened? Did she see his echo? Did the flower thing bloom?"

The girl looked at Sam. "It would no longer be a *waiting* bloom, then, would it?"

"That sucks!" Sam said. "The poor girl needs some closure." He shook his head, looking unimpressed. "It's a good story but has a crappy ending."

"It's real life, Sammy," another voice said.

Sam turned with Aaron and Rose to see Ella standing with her arms crossed, a small but saddened smile on her face. "And life doesn't always permit happy endings," she continued. "Especially when it comes to matters of the heart."

Sam fell quiet.

Ella looked at Aaron. "It's late. We're leaving early tomorrow morning." She nodded to the huts. "Call it a night."

"Okay," Aaron replied.

Ella gave Sam another look, before her eyes darted to the Peregrin holding the basket. She gave the silk band a long look before turning and walking away.

Sam stared after Ella before taking in a breath. He turned to the girl. "How much for one?" he asked.

The girl offered him the band. "Whatever you can give, sir."

Sam paused, as realisation dawned on him. "I…I don't have anything."

"But you have someone in mind?" the girl asked. "Someone you would like to give this to?"

Sam stared after Ella but didn't speak.

The Peregrin followed his gaze. She smiled and placed the band in Sam's hand. "How about you take one in the name of love?" she said. "Maybe your tale can have a happy ending."

"Here's hoping," Sam said with a grin. "Thank you."

The girl inclined her head. "My pleasure." She stood up and moved away, going throughout the crowd with her basket.

Sam took in a breath, his eyes on the band, and then got to his feet.

"You seriously going to do this?" Aaron asked.

Sam paused, before shrugging. "Yeah," he said. "I'll play it cool. Don't worry." He took off, hurrying after Ella, who had almost reached the huts. "Ella! Hey, wait up!"

Ella turned. "What is it, Sam?"

He came to a stop before her. Steeling himself the best he could, he thrust the band at her. "Here," he said.

Ella looked at the band and then up at him. "What are you doing?"

"I heard the story about the Waiting Bloom and...and I thought of you."

Ella folded her arms and gave Sam a long stare. "Really? Why?"

Sam's comfortable smile began to slip. "Well, I...I mean, you like love stories, right? So I just thought...I figured you'd want this." He held up the band. "It reminded me of you, just 'cause you like sad stories and stuff – not the actual story itself. I'm not trying to call you sad or anything."

Ella was staring at him. Not too far away, Aaron and Rose were unashamedly listening in.

"That's him playing it cool?" Aaron asked.

Rose cringed, shaking her head.

"Anyway, I just thought you'd...like this." Sam said. Ella didn't speak and Sam slowly dropped his hand. "Yeah, stupid idea. It probably doesn't even work." He stuck the band into his pocket. "It's late, so I'll...I'll see you tomorrow, yeah?" He walked away, trying not to run.

"Sammy?" Ella called after him.

Sam stopped and turned around.

Ella paused for a moment, before saying, "You have to put it on me."

Sam stared at her in shocked surprise. Ella walked up to him and held out a wrist, her lips twitching to hold back a smile. "It doesn't work otherwise."

Slowly, Sam took out the band and wrapped it around the offered wrist. The moment the silk straps touched Ella's skin, the bud began to bloom, opening up to a full and beautiful silver rose. The flower shimmered, as if minuscule dewdrops on the petals had turned into diamonds.

Sam gaped at it, his wide brown eyes fixed on the flower.

"I wouldn't get too excited," Ella said. "It's set up to bloom once every day."

Sam couldn't quite mask his look of disappointment. Ella smiled and walked away. But she didn't take the band off. Instead, she carefully held it, softly caressing the glass dome that held the blossomed rose.

***

Aaron couldn't sleep. The hut was oddly warm and stuffy. Aaron turned, trying to get comfortable on the small mattress, but he had his uncle on one side of him and Sam snoring on his other, the latter of which had fallen asleep almost instantly, wearing a smile that stretched from ear to ear. Aaron couldn't wait to tease him into insanity about it tomorrow.

Eventually, Aaron gave up. He couldn't sleep – not in there, in any case. He slipped on his shoes and crept outside.

He sat down on the steps of the hut, letting the cool breeze wash over him. The entire city was asleep. No one, except Aaron, was outside. He savoured the stillness of the night, the quiet of the slumbering city. The longer Aaron sat there, the more he didn't want to go back in and sleep. He knew he should. They'd be leaving early in the morning and God only knew how much more trekking Neriah had planned. If he didn't sleep, he'd be tired to the bone the next day. But the cool air had woken him up and Aaron wasn't one to lie around wide awake. Maybe if he went for a walk, he would tire himself out.

Aaron headed away from the huts, careful not to wake anyone up. His feet led him to a small pathway through a dense forest, almost of their own accord. Aaron went along, trusting his instincts. Maybe his core was calling out to its element.

Aaron walked through the lush, green forest, his footsteps muted on the soft, mossy ground. Aaron stuck both hands into his pockets and walked slowly, thinking about the journey to come, contemplating what would happen once he got the Blade of Adams. Would Neriah train him? Would his dad?

Aaron tried not to think about his dad. He hadn't had the chance to speak to him before he'd left. Ever since the argument with Neriah, Chris hadn't been able to get up from his bed. It was as if that fight had left him drained and unable to stay awake. Aaron shuddered at the thought of his dad waking up to find his wife, son and brother-in-law all missing. He would be beyond furious. Hopefully they would get to the sword soon, maybe even the next day, and they could get back to Balt quickly.

Aaron's foot caught on something and he stumbled. Or rather, he was about to. It was dark, but the bright moon showed Aaron his feet had somehow got caught in twigs and overgrown roots. Worse, he couldn't free them. He felt something scratchy crawl around both his wrists before suddenly they were pulled up. Branches from the tree behind him had encircled his wrists, holding them high above his head.

"What the–?" Aaron was rendered speechless with shock. He pulled, but the branches held tight, stretching his arms. "Let me go!" he instructed, but the forest held fast. Aaron struggled as hard as he could, but he couldn't free himself.

A low chuckle sounded. "You know, it's not everyday you see an Elemental caught up in his own element."

The voice stilled Aaron, his erratically beating heart skipped. He looked up, peering through the darkness.

He saw Kyran, casually leaning against a tree with his arms crossed at his chest.

"Then again, we don't get many Elementals like you, do we, Ace?"

12

SCORCHING CHATS

Aaron's hands curled into fists above his bound wrists.

"Let me go."

Kyran smirked. "Free yourself," he said. "You are the Elemental for Earth after all."

Aaron struggled. Anger was fast replacing his surprise, but that didn't give him any better control of his element. "I said, let me go!"

Kyran straightened up and sauntered closer to Aaron. "When are you going to get it, Ace?" he said. "*Control* your element. Seize it and bend it to your will. Force it to obey."

Aaron's eyes narrowed with fury, blood pounded in his ears. It was one thing to play a Hunter training another to keep his cover in Salvador, but quite another for Kyran to openly mock him like this. To remind Aaron of how he pretended to be his friend, when all along he was the enemy.

Aaron's jaw clenched. The branch of the tree behind Kyran twisted back and sprung forward, aiming for Kyran's head.

Kyran just tilted his head, moving the bare minimum to avoid the collision. He turned back to eye the tree.

"Not bad." He turned around to face Aaron, only to see he had freed one arm.

Aaron swiped his hand and Kyran was forced to duck out of the way this time, as a branch – thick as Kyran's neck – came hurtling at him. Aaron tugged his other hand out of the loosened grip of the vines he had managed to command and turned all his attention to the twigs and roots that were still holding on to his feet. No sooner had he freed himself and stumbled forward than he raised both hands and sent a powerful ripple at Kyran, who jumped out of its way.

Aaron raised his hands again, ready to throw another ripple at him in case Kyran retaliated. But Kyran didn't lift a hand to fight back. He didn't even look bothered by Aaron's attacks. In fact, he was laughing as he turned to face Aaron, green eyes bright with amusement.

"You're starting to pack a real punch now, Ace," he said. "Still not enough, but it's a start."

"Stop it!" Aaron yelled and the trees around them shuddered, groaning against the ground, threatening to uproot themselves.

Aaron wished they would. He wanted to throw them at Kyran, like his dad had done with the Lycans. He wanted the trees to lift into the air and hit Kyran – *hard*. He wanted to hurt him for everything he had done, for every lie he had told, for pretending to be his friend – for everything he had done to Rose.

Before he could think past his rage, Aaron launched himself at Kyran. His first strike was dodged by a chuckling Kyran. His second was caught.

"Easy," Kyran said, holding on to Aaron's clenched fist. "You'll pull something."

Aaron saw red. He kicked Kyran's leg, making him let go. In a flurry of movement, Aaron called for more trees to swing forward and hit Kyran, but they missed each time.

"You need to work harder," Kyran said, dodging the attacks. "I'm barely trying here."

"Shut up!" Aaron's anger got the best of him and he went for Kyran again.

This time, when Kyran caught Aaron's wrist, he twisted it, easily turning Aaron around and pinning him against the nearest tree. Aaron grunted, struggling to free the arm that was held behind his back, but Kyran's grip remained firm.

"I suggest you calm down," Kyran said next to Aaron's ear. "You don't want to wake up the whole city."

"Yeah?" Aaron snarled. "*I* don't want that? Or *you* don't want that?"

"Trust me, Ace, you'll want to hear me out."

"No!" Aaron used his free arm to push against the tree and he threw Kyran back, freeing himself.

He turned around but didn't throw anything at Kyran. He simply stood there, leaning against the tree, breathing hard, angry green eyes fixed on the boy he had once trusted.

"I don't want to hear you out," Aaron said. "I don't want to hear *anything* you have to say."

"Why?" Kyran asked.

Aaron's eyes bulged out and he spluttered. "Why? You're asking me *why*?"

"Yeah," Kyran said calmly. "Why won't you hear me out?"

"'Cause all you'll do is tell more lies!" Aaron spat.

"What lies did I tell you?" Kyran asked.

Aaron snapped his mouth shut before he swore at him. Anger thrummed inside him. His fingertips were buzzing, his core ready to feed him more power. He could almost feel the forest ground sitting tensed, ready and waiting for his command. Yet a small part of him readily and greedily latched on to Kyran's words, wanting nothing more than to believe him. He pushed that part away.

"You kept your identity hidden," Aaron said. "You lied about who you were."

"No," Kyran said. "I didn't lie at all. I was asked my name and I replied with the truth. My name is Kyran. No one asked my father's name."

"Neriah asked," Aaron said. "My dad asked, even *I* asked you."

"And I refused to answer," Kyran said. "I didn't lie."

"Come on, Kyran!" Aaron cried with agitation as he pushed away from the tree that was supporting him. "You're not getting out of this on technicalities! You hid the truth about who you are. You hid the fact that you're the Scorcher – you're the one who tore down the Gates. You're responsible for the disasters that hit the human realm! You're the reason so many people have lost their homes – their lives! You've killed hundreds of mages, not to mention the torment of the mages trapped in their own homes, in their own zones because you've let vamages control them!"

Aaron was breathing hard, his chest heaving and burning with rage. Kyran in comparison stood calm and collected, just staring at Aaron.

"It's funny that, isn't it?" he asked.

Aaron was going to hit him. The trees groaned in response to Aaron's fury.

"Which part?" Aaron spat.

"All of it," Kyran said and started walking toward him. "All that pain, the lives lost, the homes destroyed, the zones taken over; it's funny how it all can be pinned on one person." Kyran stopped before Aaron, holding his furious glare. "You'd think I'd struggle to find enough hours in the day for all that destruction."

"It doesn't take long to start fires," Aaron replied. "Especially for a Fire Elemental."

"True," Kyran mused. He leant forward, close enough to whisper to Aaron. "But even I can't start fires without being there."

Aaron blinked at him. "What?"

Kyran pulled back and smirked but his eyes were furious now, no glint of mischief or amusement. "Think back over the four months you spent in Salvador," he said. "Think about how many crimes were said to be the work of the Scorcher. How many times the Scorcher was out killing mages and burning down Gates, yet all that time, I was in the same house as you."

Aaron stilled. His mind flashed through all the meetings he had attended at the Hub. Most of them had started with a new crime report on something horrendous the Scorcher had just done. And every single time, Kyran had been sitting in the same room.

Aaron remembered something the Hunters had discussed shortly after Kyran had been arrested. "You left Salvador every full moon," he said. "Maybe that's when you set up the attacks."

"Oh come on, Ace!" Kyran pulled back and finally lost his smirk, true annoyance lighting his features. "Think about it. How could I set up multiple attacks in one night? And even if I did, the attacks were said to be done by my hand. It was apparently my Blade that burnt cities to the ground. How can that be true if I was in Salvador?"

Aaron didn't have an answer. His mind was fighting Kyran's questions, screaming at him not to fall for another trick of the Scorcher's. He was the enemy. He couldn't be trusted. But Aaron somehow couldn't bring himself to fully believe that. It was easier to think of Kyran as the enemy when he wasn't standing right in front of him.

"Those attacks, the ones they blamed me for, were committed by Raoul and his Lycans," Kyran said. He shook his head. "It wasn't me, Ace. I've never killed a mage. I've yet to burn any city to the ground."

"You're lying," Aaron said, his voice threatening to break. "I saw you. Zhi-Jiya shared a memory of you burning down an entire village—"

"Of Banshees," Kyran said. "Banshees, Ace, not mages. You would have seen that if the entire memory had been extracted."

Aaron stared at him, desperately wanting to believe him. "Why are you telling me this?" he asked.

Kyran paused and his eyes held a strange emotion, one Aaron couldn't figure out. "Because your mind isn't tainted," Kyran replied. "You weren't brought up with Neriah's lies. You haven't lived your life blaming everything that goes wrong on Hadrian and his Scorcher. You have a chance to see things for what they really are." His eyes held Aaron's. "I'm not who they say I am. I'm not the monster Neriah wants you to believe, and neither is my father."

"Your father is a vamage," Aaron said.

"That doesn't make him a monster."

"But it does make him demonic."

Kyran quietened and straightened up. "You've still got a lot to learn about mages and demons, Ace," he said. "I would advise you to make quick work of it, so you can recognise who's pure and who's demonic."

"Is that what you are? Pure?" Aaron asked.

Kyran shrugged. "Not completely, but I'm not demonic either." He pocketed both hands and tilted his head to stare at Aaron. "You remember the map at the Hub?"

Aaron was thrown at the sudden topic change. "Yeah."

"You remember how many zones Hadrian has?"

"It's hard to forget," Aaron replied. He could still clearly see the map of the mage realm in his mind, with its blue zones outmatched by the red.

Kyran smiled. "Here's a little maths teaser for you," he said. "If there are twenty-six zones in our realm and my father supposedly has control of nineteen of them, how many of those nineteen reflect Neriah's deceit?"

Aaron frowned. "What?"

"Neriah's been lying," Kyran said. "He's been lying for years. We don't have nineteen zones. We have nine. Ten zones belong to demons."

Aaron stared at him with shock. "How?" he asked.

"Demons have found a way past the Gates," Kyran said. "They've been fighting mages for centuries – long enough for them to find ways to outsmart the mages and their defences." He took in a long, somewhat troubled sigh. "Raoul and his Lycans have been sneaking into cities without the Gates falling. How they're doing it, I don't know, but they're getting in and then forcing the chief of the city to bring down the Gate so they can take over."

"Neriah said something about them too," Aaron started. For a fleeting moment, Aaron forgot all about the animosity he had for Kyran. It felt like they were back in Salvador, discussing the threats to their realm like Hunters would. "Neriah seems to think the Lycans are making new tears, creating their own back doors," he said.

Kyran snorted. "I'm surprised Neriah noticed," he said. "He's been so busy blaming my father and accusing me of tearing down Gates. I thought he'd never figure out who the real culprit is." Kyran held a hand to his chest. "I never took any zones from the mages. Raoul took them from Neriah and I took them from him. I've cleared demons out of more sub-zones than all of Neriah's Hunters put together. It was me and my father's vamages that drove Raoul and his Lycans out of six zones and secured them with Gates."

Aaron's eyes widened. "What?" he asked.

"Yeah, that's right," Kyran said, his eyes blazing with anger. "Contrary to popular belief, the nine zones in my father's name are all Gated. I put the Gates up myself."

Aaron's head was swimming. There was too much being thrown at him for it all to make sense but Aaron understood one thing – there wasn't only seven safe zones after all. There were sixteen. Hadrian's zones *and* Neriah's zones were Gated. So it was only the ten zones under the demons' rule that were open zones. They were the ones that allowed the flow of elemental power to seep through and disrupt the human realm.

"I don't get it," Aaron said. He looked up to meet Kyran's eyes. "Why would Neriah lie?"

Kyran let out a harsh laugh. "Can't you see it, Ace? He made Hadrian public enemy number one, so others would do what he couldn't."

"What's that?"

"Destroy him."

Aaron didn't know whether or not to believe him. Everything Kyran had said could very well be true. Then again, it could be nothing but lies.

"You risked getting caught to come and tell me this?" Aaron asked. "Why would you care if I know the truth or not?"

Kyran smiled. "I thought we were friends, Ace."

Aaron felt like he had been stabbed, straight through his chest. "I thought so too," he said. "But we're not friends, not if you're against the mages."

Kyran shrugged. "I'm not against them. As long as they pledge their allegiance and submit to my father's rule."

"Even if I were to believe you only have nine zones, and all nine are Gated, Hadrian is still a vamage," Aaron said. "He killed James Avira – an Elemental that was supposed to be like family to him. How can you think he's fit to rule the mages? How can anyone pledge allegiance to someone like that?"

"There's always two sides to a story," Kyran said.

"For some stories it doesn't matter," Aaron replied. "There's always a right and a wrong. A few days ago, you came with your vamages to the City of Balt and let them kill twelve mages. How are you going to spin that one, Kyran? You going to tell me that was right?" He stared at Kyran with angry eyes. "I was there, I saw what your vamages did. *You* might not have killed anyone, but you didn't stop your vamages, just like you didn't stop them from murdering Sam and Rose's parents."

The air around them chilled, raising goosebumps on Aaron's flesh, but he didn't care. He stood in front of Kyran, whose hands had curled into fists and eyes darkened to a poison green.

"I didn't hurt them," Kyran defended.

"It doesn't matter," Aaron fought back. "You didn't save them either."

"I tried!" Kyran snapped. "If I had got there sooner, I would have saved them, but by the time I reached the house it was too late."

"Too late?" Aaron frowned. "What are you talking about? You were *with* the vamages!"

"No, I wasn't," Kyran argued. "I arrived afterwards."

"So you just happened to be hanging out in the human realm by yourself that night?" Aaron asked. "You really expect me to believe that?"

"Believe what you want," Kyran said. "I didn't come here to convince you of my side of the story."

"Then why did you come?"

Kyran didn't speak right away. The wind blew past them, ruffling their hair and clothes. The cold seeped into Aaron's skin, chilling him.

"I know what you're planning with Neriah," Kyran said quietly. "Don't do it, Ace."

"Do what?" Aaron asked.

Kyran straightened up. "The last thing you want is to get involved in this war." Piercing green eyes held Aaron to the spot. "The minute you touch that sword, your life will never be the same again."

Aaron's heart jolted with surprise. "How did you know that's what I'm here for?"

Kyran smiled. "There isn't a corner of this realm that's hidden from my father," he said. "We know what's going on, what Neriah is up to. But trust me, he can get all of Aric's Blades, he's still not going to win."

"So you've come to threaten me?" Aaron asked.

Kyran chuckled. "No, Ace. I came to warn you."

Silence settled between the two boys. Aaron couldn't figure Kyran out. His words weren't what he expected from him, neither was his behaviour. He had thought if he ever faced the Scorcher again, they would be hurling jolts of power at each other, not standing around talking.

Aaron opened his mouth to speak when he heard a shout muffled by the wind. Faint as it was, Kyran had heard it too. Aaron turned around as his uncle Mike's call echoed in the air. He was looking for him, yelling his name. Aaron turned back to Kyran. If Michael saw him...

"Go," Aaron said. "Before someone finds you."

"You do realise you're giving up the perfect opportunity to turn me in," Kyran smirked.

Aaron glared at him. "You saved my life," he said. "I'm repaying the debt. From now on, we're even. I don't owe you a thing." He could hear Michael's shouts getting louder. "We're done."

Kyran chuckled as he backed away, letting the dark shadows greedily swallow him up. "Not even close, Ace," he said. "Not even close."

He was gone by the time a worried Michael found Aaron, standing alone in the middle of the dark forest.

13

FOILED PLANS

By daybreak, Neriah and his group had awakened, finished breakfast and left to carry on their journey. They trekked through more woods, with Neriah and Ella leading the way, Kate and Michael behind them, and Aaron and the twins following. Skyler was trailing after them, his gun in hand.

Aaron barely noticed. He walked with his head lowered, his mind replaying the conversation he'd had with Kyran the previous night. If he had slept at all, he would have thought he'd dreamt the entire encounter.

When Michael found Aaron standing alone in the forest in the middle of the night, he had demanded to know what was going on. Aaron brushed it off as a simple, couldn't-sleep-so-went-for-a-walk excuse. It was partly true. But he kept the bit about meeting the Scorcher to himself.

Michael had guided Aaron back to the hut and didn't say any more on the subject, but Aaron knew Michael didn't believe him. Aaron could tell by the way his uncle kept looking at him, his blue eyes narrowed and lips pressed into a line. But Michael didn't speak, didn't ask any questions. He only gave Aaron another long look before turning around to carry on walking.

A warm hand slipped into Aaron's, snapping him out of his thoughts.

"You okay?" Rose asked. "You look tired."

Aaron shook his head. "I'm fine."

He wasn't planning on telling anyone about his talk with Kyran last night, not even his best friends. After days, Rose was somewhat normal again. He didn't want to tell her Kyran had tracked them down. He knew it would only upset her. And Sam would just get angry if he found out Aaron had stood around talking instead of throwing the whole forest at him. Aaron was confused enough about what he should have done to Kyran; he didn't need his friends weighing in.

"Aaron?" Rose called, her eyes and voice full of concern.

"I'm fine," Aaron repeated. "Just didn't get much sleep."

"I slept like a baby," Sam said, a bounce in his step and a grin on his face.

"Meaning you were up every other hour, crying and wanting to be fed?" Rose teased.

"Whatever, Rose." Sam's good mood was not to be deterred it seemed.

Rose threw a look at Ella before asking, "Aren't you worried things are going to be awkward with Ella now?"

"Why would things be awkward?" Sam frowned.

"Well, Ella knows you have a thing for her," Rose said.

"What?" Sam came to a stop.

"You gave her a waiting bloom. That's probably the most romantic thing in this realm," Rose pointed out.

Sam was stunned. He looked ahead at Ella, who was walking alongside Neriah, seemingly deep in conversation. "But I played it cool. I told her I gave her the thing 'cause the story reminded me of her, that's all."

"Yeah, because that's totally believable," Rose said. "She's not daft, Sam."

"Aaron?" Kate called.

Aaron turned to see his mum and uncle standing ahead of him, staring. Aaron felt his heart plummet. Had his uncle told his mum about the forest? Is that why she looked annoyed? Did they somehow figure out what had happened? Whom he had talked to? But wait, that was impossible. How could they work that out?

"Hurry up," Kate said. "You don't want to fall behind."

Aaron breathed out a sigh. She had only called to him because he and Rose had stopped to talk with Sam. He nodded at his mum. "Okay."

They started their slow walk behind Kate and Michael again.

"What should I do?" Sam was asking. "Should I say something? To clear the air?"

"I think you've said enough," Rose smirked. "Let her bring it up. Don't you say anything."

"You reckon?" Sam asked, clearly nervous. "What do you think, Aaron?"

Aaron didn't reply.

"Aaron? Hey?" Sam shook his shoulder and Aaron looked up at him.

"What?" Aaron asked.

"What's up with you?" Sam frowned. "You've not woken up this morning."

"You look like something's bothering you," Rose said. "What is it?"

Aaron caught Michael turning to look at him again. Aaron fixed his gaze to the ground to avoid eye contact and hoisted his bag higher on his shoulder. "Nothing. I'm fine, Rose."

They walked in silence until they crested the top of a hill, where Neriah was waiting with Ella.

"We nearly there?" Aaron asked.

"Almost," Neriah replied, searching the area.

They just stood there, with Neriah scanning the grounds.

"What are we waiting for?" Aaron frowned.

Before Neriah could answer, a shimmer ran through the forest and just a few metres in front of them, a portal opened up. Aric's mark glittered in the sunlight, sitting proud and tall.

"I thought you said we weren't going to take any portals?" Aaron said.

"This isn't for us," Neriah replied. He turned to his niece. "Ella, please take Samuel and Rosalyn Mason to Salvador and wait there for us."

Aaron wasn't expecting that.

"What?" Sam stepped forward with a frown. "I thought we were staying with Aaron."

"You said we could go with him," Rose added.

"I'm afraid, this is as far as you can come," Neriah said. "From this point onwards, it will be only myself, Skyler and Aaron's mother and uncle who will accompany him to retrieve the Blade."

"Why?" Aaron asked and all eyes turned to him.

"Because from this point onwards, you no longer need a mask," Neriah replied.

"A what?" Aaron frowned.

Neriah smiled. "You resemble your father, an Elemental who is well known throughout the realm." He glanced at Kate and Michael. "The rest of your family aren't quite as famous. And when you have two Shattereds on either side," he looked to Sam and Rose, "most would be forgiven for assuming you are also a Shattered, simply on your way to be relocated."

Realisation dawned on Aaron. "That's why you let my friends come with me," he said. "For cover."

"I needed to hide you," Neriah said. "And the best way is in plain sight." Neriah nodded to the portal. "Scott is waiting, Ella."

Ella didn't say a word and strode forward. From her tight jaw and stormy grey eyes, it looked like even she wasn't privy to this plan, and she didn't approve of it. Aaron turned to look at Sam and Rose, who looked just as annoyed as Ella.

"I'll see you soon," he said, before his friends started arguing.

The twins weren't happy at being used and discarded, but they didn't put up a fight. They reluctantly followed behind Ella, before stepping into the shimmering portal. In a flash, the glowing symbol vanished, taking them to Salvador.

"Come on," Neriah said. He began walking down the hill, leading the way forward.

Aaron watched him go for a moment as the others followed after him. A flicker of doubt passed through his mind. Was Neriah as righteous as he thought? Or did the leader of the mages have a side that no one was willing to see? The way he had just used Sam and Rose for his purpose and then got rid of them was downright devious, not befitting for a man who claimed to be fighting the good fight.

As much as Aaron didn't want to hear them, Kyran's words from the night before came rushing back to him.

You weren't brought up with Neriah's lies. You haven't lived your life blaming everything that goes wrong on Hadrian and his Scorcher. You have a chance to see things for what they really are.

Skyler nudged his shoulder and jutted his chin forward, cold blue eyes instructing him to follow. Aaron started walking. Kyran was right about one thing – Aaron could see things for what they were. He just wasn't sure he liked what he saw.

***

180

Aaron walked in silence for what felt like hours. His mum and uncle Mike had moved behind him, to protect him should anyone, or anything, creep up on them. Skyler walked alongside Neriah, leading the way. Before Aaron realised it, Neriah had slowed down to fall into step with him.

"I sense you're annoyed with me," Neriah said.

Aaron was surprised. He didn't think Neriah would care either way. "Is that one of your powers?" he asked sarcastically. "You have a someone-is-mad-at-me sensor?"

Neriah chuckled. "That would come in handy," he said.

Aaron looked around at him. "I don't like you using my friends," he said bluntly.

"I don't like it either," Neriah replied. "But I will do whatever is necessary to ensure your safety."

Aaron looked away and shifted his bag higher on his shoulder. "My safety shouldn't be your concern," he said. "I can take care of myself."

"My concern is everyone's safety," Neriah corrected. "I am the oldest Elemental. It's my duty to protect my own."

Aaron didn't say anything. Little by little, his annoyance at Neriah ebbed away.

"I meant to ask you something," Aaron started. "Only the Elementals can be legacy holders, right?"

Neriah nodded. "Right."

"So is that why Elementals rule the realm?" Aaron asked. "Because they have the most powerful weapons?"

"You could see it like that," Neriah said. "I like to think of it as Elementals ruling the realm because they have the means to protect it, by using the most powerful weapons."

"It's a good thing legacy holders are born with the right to wield the Blades of Aric," Aaron said. "I can imagine others wanting to steal the legacies, so they can use the swords."

"Our legacies can't be taken from us by force," Neriah explained. "There is nothing anyone could do to make you give them your legacy. Our legacies sit in our cores and our core is our life. To give someone your legacy is to literally give them your life. It's only by free will that we can give our life to another."

Aaron remembered Neriah saying that when the time came he would give Ella his legacy. That's what he meant, Aaron realised – he was planning to give her the legacy at his deathbed.

"I thought you said it's the legacy that chooses the core?" Aaron said.

Neriah nodded. "It does."

"But you're going to give Ella your legacy."

"I know Ella's core is strong enough," Neriah said. "The legacy will choose her."

"And if it doesn't?" Aaron asked.

Neriah looked at him. "It will."

Aaron held his gaze. "I know Ella's powerful," he said. "I'm only asking what would happen if, theoretically, it doesn't."

"Ella is the last Afton," Neriah replied. "The legacy has nowhere else to go. But I know how strong Ella's core is." He smiled at Aaron. "There is nothing to worry about. My legacy has a great successor."

Aaron fell quiet and turned to look ahead. He watched Skyler move steadily onwards. The rays of sun caught the studded silver spiral on the back of his ivory coat. It made the mark glisten like crystal. Aaron looked back to Neriah, noting his plain clothes.

"Don't you have a coat like that?" he asked, nodding at Skyler.

Neriah smiled. "I do."

"But you don't wear it?"

"I don't need to."

Aaron frowned at him.

"Everyone knows who I am," Neriah explained.

"That's what the coats are for?" he asked. "To show that you are an Elemental?"

Aaron had seen in a flesh memory that his dad used to wear a similar coat, only it was green and had the mark for Earth on the back. He didn't want to think about Kyran's red one with the silver inverted V.

"Actually, it's to show you are the legacy holder," Neriah replied.

Aaron turned to him with shock. "I thought legacy holders were targeted?"

"They are," Neriah said. At Aaron's confused look, he elaborated. "It used to be a custom. Once a legacy holder was fully trained and able to protect themselves, they were presented with their Elemental coat. But after the Lycans started targeting the Elementals, looking for the legacy holders, the coats were deemed too dangerous." He looked ahead, his violet eyes gleaming. "By the time my generation came to be, we were sick of hiding. All of us, myself, your dad, James and Hadrian, we all used to wear our coats, especially in battles. It made the Lycans crazy, to have their targets before their eyes, but not be able to kill them." He went quiet and the small smile that had come to his face slipped away. "After Hadrian killed James and your dad left, I stopped wearing mine. What was the point? Everyone knew who I was – the only Elemental of my generation left." He looked to Skyler ahead of him. "Skyler insisted on his coat. I presented it to him when his core awoke. He lost his entire family at the hands of Lycans. He's anything but afraid of them."

"I gathered," Aaron said. "Seems like Skyler's not afraid of anything."

"Everyone is afraid of something," Neriah replied.

He came to a sudden stop. Ahead of him, Skyler did the same. Neriah held on to the pendant dangling from his neck. His violet eyes widened, darting to all corners of the dense forest.

"Where?" he asked.

Whatever was Scott's reply, Aaron didn't know, but he saw the colour drain from Neriah's face. He spun around and his gun was already clutched in his hand. He made a gesture with his free hand and in a flurry of movement, Aaron found his mum and uncle by his side.

"Go," Neriah commanded, pushing Aaron into Kate and Michael's hands. "Scott's opened the portal again. Get out of here."

Aaron was pulled into a run by his mum and uncle. Aaron twisted around, just in time to see countless dark shapes emerge from the shadows. There were too many to fight, even for Elementals like Neriah and Skyler. Aaron caught a glimpse of the dark-furred beasts, hunched on all fours as they moved forward, their fangs and claws ready.

Lycans.

Skyler, Aaron saw, was aiming his gun at the slowly approaching beasts.

"Skyler!" Neriah warned, as he backed away.

Before Aaron could process the fear completely, his mum and uncle had dragged him around the corner. They raced back the way they had come until they arrived at the spot Rose and Sam had left with Ella. The portal was back again, sitting open and ready for them. Aaron turned to look behind him when he heard heavy footsteps and saw Neriah and Skyler.

Kate and Michael didn't wait for them. With a firm grip on Aaron, they darted to the portal, leaving the demon-infested forest and arriving on the Gateway to the City of Marwa. No more than twenty seconds later, Neriah and Skyler appeared on the Gateway too. They looked unnerved, and furious.

"What just happened?" Michael asked.

"Lycans," Neriah growled. "Sons of demons got in here too."

Skyler, Aaron noted, was so angry that pink spots had appeared in his cheeks. Aaron could sense how badly Skyler had wanted to fight. He was fuming, pacing the Gateway with white-knuckled fists at his sides. But Neriah had done the right thing. There were far too many Lycans. Neriah had forced Skyler back before anyone had got hurt.

"Neriah," Kate stepped forward. "How are they doing it? That's two different zones they've sneaked into and crossed your path. Raoul can't be tearing the barrier in so many places, it's impossible."

"That word has no meaning," Neriah said. "Demons are capable of more than you can imagine."

He let out an angry sigh before stepping past them and touching the Gate they were standing before. He didn't even have to state his name. The Gate slid open and the city of Marwa stood waiting for them.

"Until I can ensure a safe journey to retrieve the Blade, I want you to stay here," he instructed Aaron.

Aaron could practically feel his mum's relief. She took Aaron's hand and quickly pulled him past the threshold. Aaron went with her, having not much of a choice in the matter. Michael followed them but Skyler remained on the Gateway, and Neriah at the threshold.

They were halfway down the street when Aaron saw the front door of their house open. Chris appeared from inside, looking pale and a little thin. A rush of emotion hit Aaron. He hadn't seen his dad for a few days but somehow it felt longer. Chris hurried towards them and embraced Kate first, holding her close, before turning to Aaron. He didn't speak but his joy was clear to see. Aaron felt his eyes prick. A lump grew at the back of his throat and Aaron had to mentally shake himself.

"Thank God, you're okay," Chris said and hugged Aaron. His relieved whisper made Aaron want to hold him tight and never let go.

"I'm glad you're okay too," he said, his words muffled against Chris's chest.

Chris gave a little laugh. He pulled back to give Michael a quick but warm brotherly hug.

"When did you get here?" Michael asked.

"Ten minutes ago," Chris replied. "Mandara said you would be here." His gaze had already picked up Neriah's presence and turned cold. "But I didn't know Mandara was a rotten liar. I contacted Scott when I arrived and found no one here. Scott told me Neriah had taken Aaron to find the Blade." He looked to Kate. "What happened? Why has Neriah brought you back?" He gave Aaron's empty hands a quick glance. "Without the Blade?"

Kate shared a look with her brother before holding on to Chris's arm. "Come on," she said. "Let's go inside."

She and Michael led Chris into the house, to sit him down before telling him they were ambushed by Lycans. Again.

***

Aaron was sure he wouldn't be seeing Neriah again for a few days, so it was with great surprise that he spotted him later that same day. He saw him when he opened the front door to welcome Sam and Rose from Salvador. Neriah had personally accompanied them for the trip.

After exchanging relieved hugs, the twins passed by Aaron to take their things upstairs. Aaron stood where he was, staring at Neriah's still form at the head of the empty table in the street. He couldn't stop himself from walking over to him.

"Neriah?" he called.

Neriah didn't move. His eyes remained on the table for another few seconds before he took in a deep breath and turned to look at Aaron. "Hello, Aaron," he said quietly. "I came to deliver your friends." He smiled tiredly. "I wouldn't want you annoyed at me."

Aaron smiled. "Thank you."

"And I wanted to assure you that I will return soon to accompany you to retrieve your Blade," Neriah added.

Aaron shifted from one foot to the other. Judging by the chaos his dad had caused after hearing how their path had crossed with Lycans again, Aaron was pretty sure he wouldn't be leaving for the Blade of Adams without a major fight.

But he smiled at Neriah and said, "Sounds good. The sooner I get my Blade, the sooner I can train with it, before Hadrian destroys our realm completely."

Neriah shook his head. "Hadrian won't destroy this realm."

"How do you know?" Aaron asked.

Neriah smiled. He turned to give the table a long look. "Come here," he said and gestured for Aaron to stand next to him. Aaron stepped forward. "Here." He took Aaron's hand and gently laid it flat on the surface of the table.

Aaron looked at him. "I don't–"

"Just relax," Neriah instructed. "Follow me."

Aaron's surroundings melted as his mind was propelled forward into a memory lifted from the table by Neriah. The day turned to night and Aaron found himself still standing where he was, at the head of the table, but this time it was groaning under the food piled on top. Every chair around the table was occupied. The air was one of jubilation. The mages were definitely celebrating something. Lanterns hovered overhead, giving enough light for Aaron to recognise some faces.

The first he noticed was actually a young Neriah, seated next to an older, blond-haired man with serious blue eyes. On his other side was a young, handsome, dark-haired man. Across from them was Aaron's dad. Aaron stared in awe at the young Christopher as he sat laughing with the others, a little blue-eyed baby in his lap. Aaron recognised Ben, his brother. Seated at Chris's right was Alex.

Aaron's heart skipped a beat as he stared at the uncle he never got to know. Alex, looking like the spitting image of Kyran, sat feeding Ben small bits of chicken. From their house came Aaron's mum, hovering a large platter of grilled lamb chops in front of her.

"This is the last of it," she said, settling the dish on the table with difficulty.

"You outdid yourself, Kate," said the dark-haired man next to Neriah.

"The occasion called for it," Kate replied and sat down. She took Ben from Chris. "We had to mark your brilliance somehow."

Laughs of agreement echoed around the table.

"Don't encourage him," the blond-haired man on Neriah's other side said and the chatter around the table quietened. "What he did wasn't only dangerous and reckless, but against the rules."

Aaron watched as the dark-haired man twisted in his seat to look past Neriah.

"You know what, James?" he started. "It wouldn't kill you to pay me a compliment every now and again."

James smirked and Aaron was strongly reminded of Skyler. "You would have to do something worth complimenting first."

"Whether or not James approves," Neriah said quickly, seated between both men, "the rest of us agree that you were downright epic today."

"I second that," Chris said.

"Third," Alex raised a hand.

"Fourth it."

"Fifth!"

And so on it went down the table. Aaron watched as the ire melted from the dark-haired man. He grinned. Neriah flashed him a charming smile.

"Raise your glass," Neriah said and held up his own, "to Hadrian – the best damn Controller this realm has ever seen."

Aaron pulled his hand back and the memory snapped and dissolved before the toast ended. Stunned, Aaron turned to face Neriah. Compared to his younger self, this Neriah looked bone-tired and world-weary. He didn't speak, but then Aaron didn't ask him anything.

They simply stood facing each other until Neriah spoke in a quiet voice. "Sometimes it's the things we love and were once so proud of that can cause our downfall." He looked at the table with glistening eyes. "Hadrian knows this realm like no other. He controlled it for most of his life. The last thing he wants is to destroy it."

"Then what does he want?" Aaron asked.

Neriah met his eyes. "He wants to rule it."

14

PAINS OF THE PAST

The tavern was busy, like most nights. Mages, local and not so local, crowded around rickety tables, laughing and sharing stories. The air was heavy with their chatter, but it was easy enough to ignore if a person really wanted to. The place was dimly lit, with tiny flames burning in the lanterns hanging from the ceiling.

Sitting at the bar on his own, Kyran idly played with the fire of the lantern in the corner. With a mere twitch of his finger, he pushed the flame to rise up, licking at the glass walls hungrily. Then he shrank it down, pushing it to the brink of extinguishing. He repeated the process, causing a flicker on the wall.

Getting bored, he stopped and picked up his glass, taking a sip. It had been three weeks since he met Aaron in the City of Hunda, yet his mind still replayed the encounter. He smiled into his glass at the recollection of how Aaron had tried to fight him. If it had been anyone else, Kyran would have knocked them three ways to Sunday for trying to strike him. But when it came to Aaron, Kyran found his antics more amusing than anything else.

Aaron was obviously angry with him, and Kyran hadn't expected anything different, but he was thankful that Aaron still listened to him. According to his sources, Aaron had returned to Marwa the very next day after speaking with him. That was all Kyran wanted; Aaron safe, back in Marwa, away from Neriah and his suicidal plans for him.

His fingers grasped the cool glass, feeling the drops of condensation seep into his skin. The four silver lines across the back of his hand glinted in the dull light. If Aaron remained in Marwa, so would she.

Kyran lifted the glass and downed the remainder of his drink in one go. He stood up and walked out of the tavern. The cold air of a late-April's night, whipped at his face and hair. Kyran buried his hands into the pockets of his coat, hunching his shoulders as he headed down the street. No matter what he did, he couldn't stop the image of her, of her smile, coming into his mind's eye. Kyran pulled in a breath, willing Rose to leave him alone, to not linger in the corners of his head. It was driving him crazy.

His footsteps were the only sound in the otherwise empty street. Kyran headed towards Lexi, parked at the end of the footpath. He liked coming here, to the tavern in the small village of Zone J-11. It was perfect for him: quiet and secluded in location, but with enough of a crowd to get lost in. He had needed the break today. If he had spent another minute under the same roof as Layla, he would have killed her with his bare hands, which, as it stood, wasn't all that difficult for him.

Kyran grimaced at his own thoughts and shook his head. He was about to pull out his key when he noticed something at the corner of his eye. Kyran turned his head and stilled.

It was him.

Standing on the other side of the road, half-hidden in the shadows, was a white-robed Lurker. Kyran narrowed his eyes. Like always, the Lurker had his hood pulled up so his face was hidden. Kyran couldn't have seen who it was, even if the Lurker didn't have the cover of the night.

Kyran's heart kicked up a gear. He stood motionless, eyes on the Lurker – who in turn was just as still, staring back at him. Ever since Kyran went to Salvador under the guise of being a Hunter, he was certain he had seen this same Lurker on several hunts. Kyran knew all Lurkers wore the same uniform, with the colour of the robes signifying different ranks, so it was very possible he had seen different rank twelve Lurkers. But a strange sense told him it was this same Lurker that he had seen watching him all those times.

The day Kyran ran into the Abarimons, he had seen a Lurker moments before he spotted the back-footed demon. The Lurker had pointed at the path, the one that no one had noticed because of the thick vegetation. But when Kyran had looked back, the Lurker was gone.

Sometimes Kyran would catch just a fleeting glimpse of the white-hooded Lurker. But there were moments when the Lurker would stand, like he was now, and just stare at him until Kyran moved. Then he would take off, with Kyran chasing after him.

It was on such an occasion that Kyran had run after the Lurker, only to lose him through a tear and find himself in the human realm. How Kyran ended up there, in that particular location, he'd never understood. The tear he went through should've taken him to different coordinates, but instead he was on a darkened street, standing facing the back of a house, surrounded completely by vamages.

Kyran forced that memory back, focusing on the Lurker across the street. Slowly, Kyran took one step forward. The Lurker took off like a shot.

"Hey," Kyran yelled. "Wait!" Kyran bolted after him.

The Lurker was running fast, dipping in and out of the shadows.

"Wait," Kyran shouted after him.

The Lurker ran down two streets and then turned the corner. Kyran wasn't far behind him, but by the time Kyran reached the corner, the Lurker had disappeared from sight. Kyran stood panting, sharp green eyes scanning the street, but it was empty.

Kyran cursed. What was going on? Why was this Lurker stalking him? More importantly, since the Hunters and Lurkers now knew his true identity, why hadn't he attacked? Kyran searched his desolate surroundings, watching and waiting for an ambush. Nothing happened. Kyran cursed again. Of course nothing was going to happen. He was in one of his father's zones. Neriah's Hunters and Lurkers wouldn't dare cross their Gate. But then, this Lurker had.

Kyran gave up and turned, ready to go back. He'd had enough for the night. He took no more than a few steps when he heard it, the faint, distant sound of someone screaming. Kyran looked around. He couldn't see anything, but he could hear the cries.

Kyran ran across the street, following the petrified and desperate shouts. It didn't take long to discover the problem. Vamages, two of them, had a young girl pressed against the wall of a back alley, trying to hold her still so they could sink their fangs into her. The girl didn't look much older than fifteen, maybe sixteen, but she was putting up a fight. The air swirled around her, kicking up dust and debris, but it wasn't strong enough to push the demons back. She was screaming herself hoarse, kicking and biting the vamages but she couldn't get free.

"We're the ones that are supposed to do the biting, darlin'," one of the vamages said, then grabbed her by her blond hair, to hold her still and expose her neck.

"You know that's really not fair," Kyran said.

The vamages and the girl looked at him, standing at the mouth of the alley.

"Two against one?" Kyran shook his head. "If you're that scared of taking on mages, why do you do it?"

The girl struggled, tears in her eyes. "Please!" she cried. "Help me!"

The vamages chuckled darkly. "No one's going to help you, darlin'," one said. "He's here to die too."

They glowered at Kyran. They were both from a lower rank. They had heard about the Scorcher, but to their misfortune, had never seen him.

"You wanna make this fair?" the other said to Kyran. "No problem. Come here and even out the numbers."

Kyran smirked. "I was hoping you would say that." He stepped forward, flexing his hands.

***

Being back in the city of Marwa was strange for Aaron. He'd got himself ready for the battle, for the fast approaching war. He had been preparing himself mentally for intense training, for combat, for the fight against Hadrian. Instead, he was back home, helping with the housekeeping, waiting for Neriah to come for him. He had tried asking his uncle Mike if he would help train him, so he could utilise the time. His dad put a stop to it before Aaron could even finish the sentence.

A few days after Aaron had returned to Marwa, the full moon rendered him, his parents and uncle Mike unable to get out of their beds, as it did all mages each month. Sam and Rose fulfilled the chores for that day and even prepared simple meals for the sick mages. The very next morning, after recovering from the draining effects of the full moon, Kate, Chris and Michael carried on in their quest to make the house habitable again.

Three weeks had passed like this, but Aaron hadn't heard anything from Neriah. His parents were acting like everything was perfectly normal, focusing all their time and energy on the house. After it was spotlessly clean, the adults decided to paint and redecorate.

Chris had healed completely from the Lycan attack, evident by his ease of lifting heavy furniture from one room to the other as they rearranged the rooms. They all worked on the house during the day and sat around the table in their kitchen for dinner at night, instead of joining the rest of Marwa at the communal table outside. They talked about everything but the war.

It was slowly driving Aaron mad.

But Aaron's resolve to stay quiet snapped, when all of them sat down to have breakfast one morning and Aaron noticed the empty chair.

"Where's Uncle Mike?" he asked.

Chris took a moment to answer. "He's gone."

Aaron frowned. "Gone? Gone where?"

"To meet Neriah," Chris replied.

"What for?" Aaron asked.

"It doesn't matter, Aaron," Kate said. "Have some pancakes."

Aaron ignored the plate she pushed towards him. "Of course it matters," he said. "Why is Uncle Mike talking to Neriah? Is it about the war?"

"Aaron." Chris turned to him with serious eyes. "This doesn't concern you."

"You know it does," Aaron replied.

"No," Chris said. "I don't care what Neriah says. You're not fighting. You're only fourteen, you're a kid."

"Have you had a look around?" Aaron asked. "There are plenty of *kids* fighting this war."

"That doesn't make it right," Chris replied.

"I agree," Aaron said. "But that's all that's left. The adults have either been killed—" He stared at his dad. "Or scared off."

Chris looked stunned and somewhat offended. "Aaron!"

"I'm sorry, but it's true," Aaron said. "You got scared because of what happened to uncle Alex and Ben, but losing family doesn't give us a right to stand back. Others have lost family too, but they're fighting back. That's what we should do."

Chris leant against the table, his eyes bright with anger. "We will fight," he said. "I will fight. Your mum, Mike, all of us will fight this war, but *you* won't."

Aaron's temper slipped from his grip. "You don't get to decide that," he said. "Not any more. You don't get to order me around."

"Excuse me?" Chris asked with narrowed eyes.

"You can't keep me from being a part of this world, Dad. Not like you've been doing all my life!" Aaron said, his voice rising with his anger.

"Aaron," Rose whispered and tugged at his sleeve but Aaron pulled away, ignoring her.

"I know you're scared for me," Aaron continued. "I get that, I really do. But you can't force your fear on me. I want to fight. I want to stand with the rest of the mages, with the Elementals, and I have that much right. Our family's Blade can make a big difference to this war and I'm the only one who can use it, so why are you stopping me? We're Elementals, Dad. We're meant to help, to protect—"

Kate shot out of her seat and ran from the kitchen. Her abrupt departure made Aaron stop and stare. Chris rose from his chair, as if about to chase after her, but he didn't move from the table.

Aaron took in a deep breath. "All I'm asking is for you to let me make my own decisions," he said, a little calmer. "To let me do what I'm *supposed* to do."

"Supposed to do?" Chris asked, his brow furrowed with anger.

"Mages came to this world to fight," Aaron said. "That's our purpose. That's what you're keeping me from doing."

"Your purpose is to live past the age of *fourteen*," Chris seethed. "Alright? Leave the war to us."

"I can't," Aaron said. "I won't sit back when I know I can bring something to this fight. I'm an Elemental, Dad, a legacy holder. Like it or not, the Blade of Adams is meant for me. I can fight. All I need is some help, some training–"

"No!" Chris smacked his hand on the table. The *thwack* rang through the room, making both Sam and Rose jump.

Aaron stared at him, at the fury in his eyes. "Why?" he asked. "Why won't you help me?" He stood up so he could look his dad in the eye. "I'm your *son*. Don't you want to teach me? You were a Hunter, Dad, a fighter. Why don't you want to train me?"

Chris stood with his hands clenched. "No, Aaron," he managed through gritted teeth. "No. I can't."

"Why?" Aaron asked.

"I'll tell you why," Kate said as she came back into the kitchen. She held a small box in her hands, which she slammed down on the table. Aaron looked at the wooden box, then up at his mum. He was surprised to see angry tears in her eyes.

"You think we're forcing our fears on you?" she asked. "You think fighting alongside mages, alongside *Elementals*, will save lives?" She put her hands down on the table and leant in. "There were many Elementals there that day, the day I lost my son, and not *one* of them could protect my baby boy." Her eyes were brimming with tears, but none fell. "You want to fight Aaron? You want to go out and face demons, like Raoul and his Lycans, or Hadrian and his vamages?" She pushed the box towards him. "Then first see what this offers you. Watch this memory, watch it all, and then look your dad in the eye and ask him to teach you how to fight. Ask him to do to you what he did to Alex, to train you so you think you can take on demons. So you go running out there when a demon attacks, with false confidence and skills that fail you when demons surround you." Her breath hitched in her chest, but the tears still didn't fall.

Aaron looked at the box with trepidation. "What is it?" he asked.

Kate's body stiffened. With great difficulty she pulled her hand off the table and rested it on the box. She didn't speak, but just stood for a long moment. Taking in a breath, she clicked the box open. Aaron saw a wad of cloth, ivory white, folded inside. Kate reached in and gently, softly caressed the cloth. The waiting tears finally fell from her eyes. Aaron saw his dad look away.

Kate lifted the cloth out and it fell open to reveal a small hooded cloak, something a child might wear when playing dress up. Aaron's heart sunk. It was Ben's, Aaron knew it.

"Come here," Kate said, and her voice was barely above a whisper.

Slowly, Aaron walked around the table. He eyed the cloak with dark apprehension.

"Mum, I don't want to see—"

"Neither do I," Kate cut him off, "but you *need* to see this, to see what it is you're risking. To understand what it is you're asking of us."

"No." Chris walked around the table to reach his wife. "I'll do it." He made to reach for the cloak.

Kate held fast. "It's fine," she said. She raised her eyes to meet her husband's. "I live it every day, Chris. See it every night in my nightmares. I can watch it happen again."

Chris didn't say anything, but his eyes too filled with tears. He moved away, grabbed his coat from the hook on the wall and opened the back door, disappearing outside. Aaron looked around at his mum.

"Hold it," she instructed.

Aaron licked his lips nervously and looked to Sam and Rose. They were sitting at the table, watching him anxiously. Sam gave a little shrug, showing his uncertainty as to whether Aaron should watch the memory or not. Rose gave a small nod.

Aaron turned back and met his mum's eyes. She offered a hand, which Aaron took. Her fingers curled around his tightly. Breathing out, Aaron reached forward and held on to the small cloak. Just like Neriah had done with the table outside, Kate pulled Aaron into the flesh memory held on the cloak.

Aaron's surroundings melted, replaced instantly by sunshine and a warm summer's breeze. Aaron had to squint against the light to see where he was. He stood in the middle of the street, both sides of which were lined with small stalls, displaying everything from clothes to toys to sweets. There were so many people around him that some walked straight through Aaron's incorporeal form.

It didn't take long for Aaron to find his family amongst the crowd. His mum and dad were walking down the street, looking young and blissfully happy. His mum was laughing, her blond hair pulled up into a ponytail. One hand supported her bulging belly, and Aaron had a strange moment pass over him when he realised that it was him that she was pregnant with.

He turned his head to look at his mum, standing next to him, watching the memory. She didn't meet his eyes. She was engrossed in the sight of the small boy sitting on Chris's shoulders, gripping his hair with both hands. Aaron took a minute to look at his brother, studying the dark hair and dazzling blue eyes. He definitely had his mum's eyes, whereas Aaron had inherited his dad's soft green eyes. Pulled over Ben's blue shirt and dark jeans was the same white cloak Aaron was holding in his hand to watch the memory.

Aaron heard Ben's hearty giggles and found himself smiling. He watched as Ben pointed to a stall that had stuffed toys hovering in the air above it. Chris and Kate made their way towards it, through the busy crowd.

At the other end of the street, the Gate silently fell. Engrossed in their joy, no one stopped or even paused to look over at what was happening. But Aaron remembered the story. He knew what was happening.

Lycans had entered the city.

In a matter of seconds, pandemonium broke throughout the street. People began screaming, running in all directions, knocking stalls over in their haste to get away. Aaron turned to search the crowd, looking for his mum and dad. Chris had taken Ben off his shoulders and was holding him close to his chest. Ben looked confused; only four years old, he couldn't possibly understand the ramifications of what was happening.

The growls of the beasts echoed in the street, louder and fiercer than the cries of the mages. The Hunters in the midst of the crowd pulled out their weapons and ran to protect their city, their people. Aaron watched as Chris passed Ben to Kate and ran with his gun in hand, joining the fight.

Aaron felt his mum's hand grip tight on his in the present, but he didn't turn to her. He couldn't. He was transfixed in horror, unable to look away from the scene unfolding before him. Through the panicked, fleeing crowd, Aaron saw his pregnant mum run with her four-year-old son in her arms. Ben was clutching on to her neck, crying now as he saw the monsters amongst the mages. Aaron followed Ben's line of sight to spot a young girl, not much older than five or six, hanging limply from the jaws of a Lycan. She was clearly dead as the Lycan shook her around like a rag doll, tearing through her small body. Aaron pulled his hand out of his mum's and turned, doubled over, the cloak scrunched in one hand as he leant on his knees and willed himself not to retch.

Kate's hand rested on his shoulder and Aaron took in several deep breaths before straightening up. Feeling shaky all over, Aaron forced himself to find his mum and brother. He spotted her running, carrying Ben, trying to get away when her path was blocked by several Lycans. Aaron fought the urge to race to her side. He watched in mounting terror as his mum backed away, holding her son close. One of the Lycans – a big, dark beast with a line of silver running down the fur of his back – came at her with claws and fangs bared.

Kate swiped with her hand and the Lycan was knocked back a few steps by a jolt of air. Aaron held his breath, watching as his mum kept up the defence, pushing back any Lycan that got too close. But no matter how good her attacks were, they weren't strong enough to scare off the beasts.

Six Lycans surrounded her, getting closer, tightening the circle. A desperate attack of Kate's managed to push them away once more, but not for long. They came at her again, and this time one of them got too close. Kate pulled back, narrowly avoiding the attack, but the poisonous claws of another Lycan slashed at her back. Kate arched, her features twisting in agony.

Aaron only realised he had made to dart forward when his mum held on to his arm. He looked around at her with wide, horrified eyes.

"There's nothing you can do," she said in a broken voice. "It's already happened. You can't change anything."

Aaron looked down at the cloak that was in his tight, white-knuckled fist. He turned back to watch the memory, blinking through his tears. His mum, wounded and in immense pain, still clutched her son to her chest and tried to fight the Lycans.

From the crowd of screaming mages and growling beasts, came another Lycan. Its fur was crimson, eyes a cruel cobalt blue. Aaron recognised it. It was the same Lycan that had attacked his dad. It was Raoul.

It happened so fast, Aaron couldn't prepare for it. Raoul dropped onto all fours and bounded forward. In the blink of an eye, he towered over Kate before grabbing Ben at the waist.

Aaron's cry mixed with the scream of his mother, fourteen years ago. Raoul ripped Ben out of Kate's arms but she managed to grab on to him. Her fingers closed around Ben's arm and cloak. She was pulling him back with both hands, using all her strength, sobbing as she pleaded with Raoul to let go. But it was the sight of his brother that made Aaron's insides twist with both fear and fury. The little boy was screaming. Raoul's claws had dug into his flesh, causing droplets of blood to seep down his legs. Ben was reaching out for Kate, trying to get back to his mother who wasn't letting go of him. That's when Raoul lifted his leg and kicked Kate, right in the stomach.

A numbness of disbelief fell over Aaron as he watched his pregnant mother assaulted, her vulnerability so disgustingly abused. Kate fell, the brutal attack costing her the grip she had on her son. She was still holding on to the cloak and it ripped from Ben's small form when she hit the ground.

Twisting in agony, Kate raised her head, only to see Raoul throw Ben to its Lycans, like someone would throw a slab of meat to dogs. A Lycan reared back and caught the little boy with its mouth.

Aaron fell to his knees and threw up. He couldn't stop, not even when all that was left to bring up was bile. Sobbing, he lifted his head to see the Lycans throw his brother's bleeding, tiny body from one to the other, fangs tearing him apart. Aaron could see chunks of flesh ripped out from his brother's body.

Aaron clenched his eyes shut and tears cut down his cheeks. He was shaking at the sound of Ben's screams and his mum's cries. Her shrieks, laced with agony, made his insides twist. He refused to watch. He couldn't take any more.

"Stop!" he begged. "Stop, please, stop!"

The memory did, but not quickly enough. The fading sound Aaron was left with, as his surroundings melted back to the kitchen, was his mum and dad's anguished cries at feeling the death of their four-year-old son.

15

INHERITANCE

That night, Aaron was sure all he was going to dream about was the attack he had watched in the memory. What he saw would never leave him. The image of a four-year-old child being so brutally killed by Lycans wasn't an easy thing to forget. And Aaron had watched it happen to his brother.

Granted, Aaron had never known he'd had a brother until a few weeks ago, but that didn't make watching him die any easier. As soon as his mum had pulled him out of the memory, Aaron had found himself kneeling on the kitchen floor. Sam and Rose were by his side, pale-faced and wide-eyed. They hadn't seen what Aaron had witnessed, but they had watched him react to the memory. They heard him cry out, they saw him collapse on the floor and retch. They saw him break.

His mum had knelt next to him and embraced him. Aaron didn't remember ever crying in her arms before. He cried while she pleaded with him to give up the fight.

Aaron understood now – understood with horrifying clarity – why his parents wanted him away from the war. It wasn't because they were afraid to lose him to the war. It was because they had already lost one son; they wouldn't survive losing another.

Aaron had decided then and there to never take the risk of putting his parents through that kind of an ordeal. If that meant staying back while the others went to fight, then so be it. He had nodded and managed a hoarse, "I won't fight. I promise." Kate had broken down then and wept, with Aaron in her arms.

Aaron knew what he watched wasn't the full memory. He remembered his dad saying that after Ben died, his uncle Alex was killed. Aaron didn't recall seeing his uncle in the memory, but then again, his eyes were fixed on his mum and four-year-old brother. He was glad, though. He couldn't handle seeing another death. He told himself his unwillingness to witness his uncle's death had nothing to do with seeing someone look so much like Kyran die.

But when Aaron finally managed to drift off to sleep that night, his dreams weren't plagued by the nightmare he had witnessed. He dreamt of being back home in the human realm. He dreamt about Rebecca, the girl next door he was crushing on. He even dreamt about partying in the Blaze club alongside Sam and Rose, with Rebecca – dressed in her skin-tight catsuit – bringing out a cake with fourteen candles. Then the dream changed abruptly, fading to replace the Blaze with open green fields. Under a large apple tree was Kyran, sitting with his knees pulled up, looking forlorn. Standing before him was another man, but Aaron couldn't see his face, only his back and dark hair.

Kyran took in a deep breath before slowly shaking his head. "I've thought about it," he said.

His voice didn't sound like his own. Aaron couldn't figure out what it was but somehow he seemed...not quite...Kyran. He lacked the usual confidence. He even looked younger.

"Think it over again, Alex," the man said. "You're taking quite a risk."

Aaron stared at the green-eyed boy with stunned surprise. It wasn't Kyran, it was his uncle Alex. Once again, his likeness to Kyran was astounding.

Alex sighed before nodding. "I have," he replied.

The man stepped closer. "Why don't you try talking with Chris?" he said. "Reason with him."

Alex let out a laugh, but it lacked humour. He glanced up at the man and Aaron noticed how much warmer his green eyes were compared to Kyran's.

"You don't reason with Chris," Alex said. "You do as he says." He quietened for a moment. "Problem is, I know what he'll say if I tell him." He shook his head. "But I can't do what he's going to demand."

The man walked over and turned to sit down next to Alex.

Aaron's breath hitched in his chest. He knew that man. He recognised him from the memory Neriah had shown him.

"You know that I'll cover for you," the man said to Alex. "For as long as you need, but things like this don't stay secret for long. Chris *will* find out, eventually."

Alex nodded. "I know," he said quietly. "I know. I just – I don't want him finding out about it yet, not until I can prove to him that I can do this."

"Then Chris won't know," the man said. "Not until you're ready. I'll handle it."

Alex let out a breath and turned to him with a small smile. "Thanks, Hadrian."

Hadrian grinned. "Don't worry about it," he said. "Just promise me one thing. When you do tell Chris, I want a front row seat."

Alex rolled his eyes and looked away, fighting a smile. Hadrian chuckled and ruffled Alex's hair.

Aaron's eyes shot open. He lay in bed for long minutes, wondering what the hell he had just seen.

***

Daniel Machado was not a patient being. It was well known to vamages that to test Machado's tolerance was to invite a painful death. For Kyran, though, pushing Machado to the brink was merely a fun pastime, and one he enjoyed on a frequent basis. Machado, on the other hand, didn't enjoy it as much.

Machado stormed into the main dining room to find the bane of his existence sitting at the table. "What the hell, Kyran?" he spat.

Kyran looked up from his plate. He took in the agitated vamage – with his tight-fisted hands and angry glare – and smiled. "What's wrong?" he asked, with far too much innocence for it to be genuine.

Machado growled. "You know what's *wrong*. You took out two of my men."

Kyran looked up at the ceiling, like he was recalling memories. "Which ones?" he asked.

Machado was spitting like a cat. "The ones you bled out *yesterday*."

"You're going to have to be more specific."

Machado's eyes bulged out with horror. Then he saw the smirk on Kyran's face. "I swear, if I find out you've killed any more of my men, I'll–"

"What?" Kyran asked. "You'll do what exactly?"

Machado was fuming. He could feel the familiar burn of rage fraying the last strand of his patience. "I mean it, Kyran," he growled. "Stay away from my men."

"Tell them to behave, then," Kyran said. His eyes flashed with anger. "In addition to attacking a young, defenceless mage, your two idiots challenged me. What was I supposed to do?"

"Lift your anonymity!" Machado spat. "No one would touch you if they knew you were the Scorcher. The mages know who you are. Why can't all of the vamages?"

Kyran picked up his glass and smiled. "'Cause I like it better this way." He took a sip.

"You listen to me." Machado stepped closer, a shaky finger held up. "I have lost enough because of you. I had to sacrifice more than what was needed for your ridiculous Q-Zone hunt! But I did it so your cover could be kept and we could get the key. It's done now. I won't tolerate any more loss."

Kyran chuckled. "You won't?" he asked. He leant back in his seat. "You think you get a choice?" Kyran's smile faded and he fixed Machado with a sharp glare. "You do what I tell you to. Your men do what I say, otherwise they die."

"We follow your father," Machado bit out. "Not you."

"You don't follow anyone," Kyran said. "If you followed my father, you'd adhere to his rules, like not hurting mages in his zones. You stray from his word, I kill you. It's as simple as that."

Machado was trying to keep himself under control. But it was a fight he was losing. His eyes had started to darken from their glittery blue to a dark red.

"We do what Hadrian needs us to do," he managed to utter through gritted teeth, "but we are vamages. We have instincts that can't be helped. Hadrian knows and accepts that. He has them too—"

"Difference is, my father knows how to control his instincts," Kyran argued. "That's what makes him civilised. It makes him far more superior to what you and your men could ever hope to be. Your blood-lust makes you nothing more than rabid animals – ones that need to be put down."

Machado lost it. His claws slid out. His eyes turned red. He darted towards Kyran with a snarl, his fangs glistening, ready to rip Kyran apart. Kyran leapt to his feet but Machado stopped, standing face to face with the Scorcher.

"Go on," Kyran urged in a deadly whisper. "Go for it." He inched closer. "Give me a reason."

Machado was breathing like a wounded animal, his chest heaving. Kyran stared at him, holding his crimson, blood-thirsty gaze. Machado glanced to Kyran's empty hands and then pulled back. The fangs slid up into his gums, disappearing from sight. The red eyes changed back to blue and his claws retracted.

Kyran smirked and leant in towards him. "You only have to bite once for me to put you down. Always remember that."

Machado didn't speak but his entire being trembled with the effort it was taking not to go in for the kill. Kyran turned to pick up his glass, drained it and walked away, leaving a seething Machado alone at the table.

***

Aaron spent the next week convincing himself to speak to his parents about the dream. His mum and dad had been perfectly normal with him, not mentioning anything about the memory of Ben's death. They seemed at peace with Aaron, comforted by his promise of not fighting in the war. His dad hadn't said a word to him about the upcoming battle with Hadrian. Instead, he discussed his landscaping ideas with him for their garden.

It was as Aaron cleared out the back garden with his dad, forcing the overgrown grass back into the ground, that Aaron couldn't take the questions in his mind any more.

"Dad?" he called.

"Yeah?" Chris didn't look at him, too busy bringing the dead flowerbeds back to life.

Aaron licked his lips. "Were you and uncle Alex close?"

Chris stopped and turned around. His eyes were narrowed, but Aaron didn't know if that was because of the sun's glare or his question. "Why are you asking?"

Aaron tensed and the grass at his feet shrunk completely into the ground. "I had this...this dream." Aaron started. "It was of uncle Alex, but it didn't feel like a dream." He paused. "It felt like a flesh memory."

Chris's frown melted, replaced by a look of understanding. He relaxed. "Right, of course." He walked over to Aaron and put both hands on his shoulders. "Don't worry about it. You're at that age. You'll be getting lots of dreams; some of them may well have Alex in them."

"I don't understand," Aaron said.

Chris chuckled. "No, I don't reckon you do." He pulled Aaron to the steps leading up to their back door and sat down. "From the time your core awakens to the point it matures, mages quite often dream about moments from the past and even the future," Chris explained. "It's referred to as your Inheritance. Some don't get more than three or four dreams, others can have them nightly." He dropped his gaze. "I should have told you about them. I can't imagine how unnerving it must be to have such vivid dreams and not understand what they are." He looked up to meet Aaron's eyes. "I'm sorry. Truth is, I had forgotten you'd be coming into your Inheritance."

Aaron was too distracted to take in his apology. "The dreams are real?" he asked. "So what I dreamt will happen?"

"Not necessarily," Chris said. "The dreams of the past have already happened, but the dreams of the future may not play out as you see them." He rested both arms on his knees and clasped his hands. "There are scholars that argue there are too many variables present to put much faith in future Inheritance. What you see might happen, but a simple change to the events that lead up to it – even a minor one – can alter the future. So what you see in a dream is one of many possibilities." He seemed to enjoy sharing this facet of the mage psyche. His eyes were brighter and a small smile graced his face. "Of course, there are those who argue what you see in a dream is what'll happen. It's our Inheritance; we will come into it, no matter what we do."

Aaron's heart was going a thousand miles a minute. His mind was overloaded, flashing him moments of all the dreams he'd had over the last eight months. The dream of him and Kyran running into the cave full of lava, the moment Kyran refused to help him, the time Kyran was convincing him to use the gun. The last two dreams had already come to pass. He had lived those moments. Did that mean the others would come true too? Like the one where Kyran told him calmly that he would kill him?

Aaron felt like he couldn't breathe. The trees swayed in response to his panic. The ground under him trembled. His dad's hand gripped his shoulder.

"Aaron?" His voice was full of concern. "You okay, son?"

Aaron turned his head to look at him. The green of his eyes was dark with worry. With great effort, Aaron nodded. He forced himself to relax and the tremble in the ground ceased.

"Did your dreams come true?" Aaron asked. "The ones you saw when you came into your Inheritance?"

Chris didn't reply straight away, but studied Aaron carefully. "Why?" he asked. "What did you dream about?"

Aaron swallowed. What did he dream about? The short answer was Kyran. He was the one that Aaron saw – Kyran and, of late, Alex. Aaron decided to start with family.

"I saw uncle Alex," he said. "The first dream I had of him, he was in a Q-Zone with you." He shifted and took in a deep breath. "Last week, I saw him again." He paused. "He was...worried about something. He was talking with–" Aaron faltered, not sure how his dad would take the news. He swallowed. "With Hadrian." He watched his dad closely, but Chris didn't look fazed at all. He nodded slowly at him, as if to tell him to go on. "Aren't you surprised?" Aaron asked.

"Why would I be surprised?" Chris said. "You saw a moment from the past. Back then, Hadrian was one of us. He lived here in Marwa. We were like a family. We fought and bickered all the time, but we were there for each other too." He smiled. "And as for Alex? Everyone was fond of him. He was the youngest Elemental of our generation – a fact he used to his benefit, a lot." He chuckled a little, shaking his head. "Hadrian and Alex were very close. Hadrian used to look out for Alex all the time."

Aaron watched his dad, seeing the light of memories sparkle in his eyes. "What about you and uncle Alex?" he asked, repeating the question his dad never answered. "Were you two close?"

"We were each other's only family for a long time," Chris replied. "Alex was three when our parents died. I was all he knew from that age. I brought him up. So yeah, I guess you could say we were close." He grinned.

Aaron didn't know if he should say any more. His dad obviously had good memories of his younger brother. The last thing Aaron wanted was to tarnish them by revealing his brother kept things from him. He held his tongue and looked down at his lap.

Chris leant in towards him. "Have you seen Alex in other dreams?" he asked. A glint of excitement shined in his eyes and Aaron felt his heart ache for his dad.

"No," he said with regret. "Only those two."

Chris nodded, doing his best to hide his disappointment. "I used to dream every week when I came into my Inheritance," he said. "I think you take after your mum." He winked at him.

"I do get other dreams," Aaron said. "Just not of uncle Alex."

"Oh?" Chris looked intrigued. "How many dreams have you had?" he asked.

"I've had plenty," Aaron said. "Other than the two of uncle Alex, the rest were of–" He faltered but pushed past the awkwardness. "Of Kyran." He closed his eyes and shook his head. "I got such a shock when I saw him for the first time, back when I was still in the human realm. I couldn't understand how it was possible for me to dream about a boy I didn't know, only to meet him a few months later. If I–"

"What did you say?"

Aaron stopped at his dad's whispered words. He looked at him to see the shock on his face. The colour had drained from him, his eyes wide and mouth open. Aaron felt a cold chill creep down his back.

"What?" he asked.

"You...you said you dreamt of...Kyran?" Chris asked.

"Yeah."

Chris shook his head. "That's impossible."

Aaron frowned. "Why?"

Chris swallowed hard. "Kyran wouldn't be a part of your Inheritance. He can't be."

"Why not?"

"Aaron," Chris started in a shaky voice. "Your Inheritance is made up of moments that have passed and moments that could come. They are a heritage." He paused, holding Aaron's eyes. "A heritage that only associates with family."

Aaron stared at his dad. "Are you saying the dreams can only be about family members?"

"It's the way the Inheritance works," Chris explained. "You see moments you shared or will share with your family. Moments you witness that don't have *you* in them will be moments about someone you are related to. Those are the only moments that can have others present, like your dream about Alex talking with Hadrian. Alex is your uncle, but you witnessed a moment he shared with Hadrian because it's one *Alex* experienced, not you. Your moments can only be those shared with someone you are related to."

Aaron felt a strange flutter in his stomach.

"So, does this mean that Kyran is...is part of our family?" he asked, finding himself equally excited and terrified at the prospect.

But Chris shook his head, his eyes still wide. "He can't be. He's an Aedus. He is the legacy holder for Fire. He wouldn't be able to wield the Blade of Aedus if he wasn't."

Aaron's heart broke but he didn't understand why. "But then, how could I have dreamt about him?" he asked.

Chris was up on his feet, pacing the garden. "I don't understand," he said. "How is it possible? He's the legacy holder for Fire, he is Hadrian's son. I saw the Blade of Aedus in his hand." He continued to pace in front of Aaron. "But he looks so much like...And he's a part of your Inheritance. It doesn't make sense."

A thought, small but tremendously troublesome, came to Aaron. He stood up and Chris stopped pacing to face him.

"The dream I had last week," Aaron started. "Uncle Alex was talking with Hadrian about something. He seemed worried and upset, and whatever it was, he was keeping it from you. Hadrian told him he would handle it. He said he would cover for uncle Alex, for as long as he needed." Aaron stepped towards him. "Dad, what if the thing uncle Alex was keeping from you, the thing that Hadrian was helping to keep hidden was...Kyran?"

Chris didn't speak. He didn't move. Then his fists clenched and eyes darkened. He stormed over to tower over Aaron. "Tell me about this dream," he gritted out. "Include *every little* detail."

***

Kate sat with her brow furrowed, a hand to her mouth. She slowly shook her head.

"It's not possible," she said. "Kyran can't be a part of your Inheritance."

Aaron sat in silence next to her.

"Are you sure you saw Kyran?" she asked. "It was probably Alex you were dreaming about. It has to be."

"It was definitely Kyran," Aaron said. "Two of the dreams I saw already came true with Kyran."

Kate paled and her mouth dropped open. "I don't understand," she said. "This...this doesn't make sense. If he's a part of your Inheritance, that makes him an Adams."

Aaron felt a shudder go through him at the thought. He remembered asking Kyran what his family name, his surname was, but Kyran had smiled and replied, *'Trust me, Ace. You wouldn't believe me if I told you.'*

He was right. If he had said he was Kyran Adams, Aaron would never have believed him.

"He looks just like Alex, but Alex wouldn't have hidden the fact that he had a son from us," Kate continued. "And if Kyran *is* Alex's son, how can he wield the Blade of Aedus?"

Across the room, standing next to the window, Chris spoke, "He's not Alex's son."

"Then why is he a part of Aaron's Inheritance?" Kate asked. Chris didn't offer an explanation. Kate took in a breath. "I don't want to say it, Chris, but maybe...maybe Alex made a mistake."

Chris turned to her with a frown. "You're suggesting Alex cheated?" he asked. "You know Alex wouldn't do that, not to Alaina."

Aaron looked between his parents. Alaina? He had never heard of her before today.

"These things happen," Kate said. "Maybe he got someone pregnant and he was too scared to tell us. Maybe Hadrian covered for him. That could be the moment Aaron saw. Maybe Hadrian took the boy in as his own–"

"That wouldn't give him the legacy for Fire, Kate, and you know it," Chris said. He turned back to stare out of the window before letting out a long sigh. "He's not an Adams. He's Hadrian's son. He's an Aedus. The Blade of Aedus in his hand proves that." He took in a breath. "If he was my nephew, I'd be able to feel him." He paused for a moment before facing them. "I can't feel him, Kate."

Aaron had gleaned enough facts to understand that if Kyran was family – if he was Aaron's cousin and Chris's nephew – then his dad would have felt that connection with Kyran. He didn't, so Kyran wasn't related to them.

"What was that dream I had then?" Aaron asked. "What was uncle Alex hiding from you that only Hadrian knew about?"

"I don't know," Chris said and Aaron could see the effort it cost his dad to speak past his heartbreak. "But it wouldn't be the first time Alex kept things from me."

Aaron didn't know what to say. A part of him wanted to probe further, to ask what secrets his uncle had, but he could see how much this was hurting his dad. He couldn't find it in himself to ask and cause more pain. Instead, he asked, "Who's Alaina?"

His dad tensed but didn't answer. Aaron turned to his mum, to see her expression filled with sorrow.

"Alaina was Alex's fiancée," she replied. She looked around at her husband. "We need to go and see her, Chris," she said. "We should ask her–"

"Ask her what?" Chris said and there was a bite to his tone. "Ask her if she and Alex had a baby eighteen years ago and just forgot to tell us?"

Kate dropped her head. "Chris," she said quietly. "If you can't feel Kyran, then he's not an Adams, regardless of being a part of Aaron's Inheritance." She held Chris's eyes. "But we need to go see Alaina. We have to ask for her forgiveness." She gave Aaron a sideways look. "And we have something important to discuss with her."

Chris closed his eyes. "I don't think I have it in me to face her."

"Chris—"

"You know what they call her?" Chris asked, turning to look at Kate with fierce eyes. "The name they've given her?"

Kate nodded. "I do." She tilted her head and bit her lip. "All the more reason to go and see her."

Chris stood with his fists clenched.

Kate held his stare, refusing to give in.

Aaron looked between them.

"What would Alex want you to do?" Kate asked in a whisper.

Chris crumbled. He sat down in the nearest chair and ran a hand through his hair. He gave a small nod.

"Tomorrow," Kate said. "We'll leave first thing in the morning."

16

WITHERED FLOWERS

The moment Aaron stepped out of the portal, a cool breeze swept past him, ruffling his hair and clothes. He could taste the salt in the air and smell the ocean before his eyes adjusted to the bright sunlight. He found himself at the edge of a stone path, a light dusting of golden sand on either side of it. The pathway led up to a single wooden house. Behind the house, Aaron could see the ocean, a deep glistening blue with white wisps of froth floating on the surface.

"Whoa," Sam breathed from somewhere behind Aaron.

Aaron turned to see Rose by Sam's side, staring at their beautiful surroundings. His mum was the last to step out of the portal Scott had set up for them. Chris was standing in front of them, staring at the house with trepidation.

"Dad?" Aaron called.

Chris turned to Aaron and smiled, just a small, tight lifting of his lips. "Let's go," he said and began leading the way.

Aaron and the twins followed. Kate hurried to pass them and matched her husband's pace. She walked by Chris's side, slipping her hand into his.

Aaron studied the house they were approaching. It looked like a holiday beach home on an island – a small, double-storey, wooden building with a triangular roof, set against the backdrop of the breathtaking ocean. Big leafy palm trees lined one side of it. It was a sight to behold, quiet and secluded, a world of its own.

They climbed four steps to reach the porch. Chris hesitated at the door. No one made a sound; there was only the windchimes overhead and the gentle waves lapping at the shore behind them. Aaron saw his mum's fingers squeeze around his dad's hand. With a deep breath, Chris reached over and knocked on the door.

Nothing happened for almost two minutes. Chris knocked again.

"Is he sure someone's in?" Sam asked.

Aaron shrugged.

The sound of faint footsteps came from inside the house, shortly before the door opened.

A woman, not much older than early thirties, stood at the door. Her dark hair tumbled over one shoulder, her big brown eyes stared in shock at her visitors. She had a thin face, with prominent cheekbones and sculpted lips. She was beautiful, there was no doubt about that, but there was a darkness in her eyes – a deep well of pain that shadowed her face.

Her gaze flickered from one face to the next, just a brief glance, before settling on Chris. Her lips which had parted with surprise, closed. She stared at Chris, but didn't say a word.

"Alaina," Chris greeted.

She – Alaina – gripped the door tightly, and Aaron was sure she was going to slam it in their faces. Instead, she swung the door open wider, letting her hand fall to her side. She didn't look away from Chris as she spoke.

"Come in." Her voice was soft, but her tone wasn't. "It's about time."

***

They sat in awkward silence around Alaina's small coffee table. The two-seater sofa had Sam and Rose, while the bigger sofa had all three Adams. Alaina sat on the ground next to the table, making tea. She handed each person a cup and saucer. They all took them but no one spoke a word.

Alaina finished making the last cup, pushed it towards Chris and sat back.

"I didn't know you had returned," she said at last.

"We had an incident," Chris said.

"Oh, so you were forced to come back?" Alaina said. "Makes sense."

Aaron glanced at his dad, but Chris didn't look annoyed. If anything, he seemed abashed. Finding something to do, other than stare between Alaina and his dad, Aaron picked up his cup and took a sip. He almost spat it back out. His spluttering caught Alaina's attention.

"It's Horehound tea," she said. "It's bittersweet." She looked back at Chris. "I thought it would be fitting."

"Alaina." Chris's voice was no louder than a whisper. "Please. Don't make this harder than it is."

"*I'm* making this hard?" Alaina asked. "I'm not the one who ran out on everyone, Chris. I'm not the one who abandoned their family."

"Alaina—"

"You left him!" she snapped. Her eyes, which already seemed too big for her thin face, bulged out with anger. "You left both of them. Everyone who died that day were buried by their kin. Everyone except Alex and Ben. Your name was called three times." Tears glistened in her eyes. "*Three* times, Chris. On the fourth call, Neriah stepped forward and buried them. That wasn't his burden to bear."

"Don't you think I know that?" Chris asked and this time, his eyes were just as full of anger and pain as hers. The ground trembled a little, rattling the furniture. Kate put her hand on Chris's knee.

"Chris—"

"You think I don't regret it?" Chris continued, ignoring Kate. "It was my right to bury my own. A right that was taken from me."

"Taken from you?" Alaina asked, either oblivious to the faint earthquake or bravely dismissing it. "You left and didn't come back."

"I came back," Chris said.

Every eye turned to him in shock. Chris let out a strained breath and the shaking ceased.

"I came back," he repeated quietly. "The next night, I returned, but they had already been buried by then."

Alaina stared at him. She shook her head slowly. "Then why didn't you stay?" she asked and for the first time since arriving there, Aaron heard the pain in her voice instead of bitter resentment.

Chris met her eyes. "Raoul was looking for me, for the rest of my family. He had set a bounty on my head, on any Adams his Lycans could find." His fists clenched into balls. "He said he'd enjoyed the taste and wanted more." He dropped his head and took a few moments to gather himself. When he looked up, his eyes had hardened, his jaw set. "I stayed in the human realm to keep my family safe."

Alaina didn't say anything.

"That doesn't mean we don't know what we did was wrong," Kate said.

Aaron turned to look at his mum with surprise. He didn't think either of his parents would ever admit they did wrong by hiding in the human realm.

"We left you by yourself," Kate continued. "After everything that had happened, you needed us just as much as we needed you."

Alaina didn't speak but her eyes brimmed. She looked away, reaching up to brush her eyes dry.

"I'm surprised you still live here, to be honest," Chris said. "I was hoping you'd be married by now, with a kid or two to run after."

Alaina smiled, but there was no joy there. "You only have one heart," she said. "And I already gave mine away. I don't have anything left to give to anyone else."

"Alaina," Chris said softly, "Alex wouldn't have wanted this for you."

"I'm pretty sure he wouldn't have wanted to die when he did, either," Alaina replied.

The room quietened, tension hung in the air, making it difficult to breathe.

Alaina closed her eyes and shook her head. "I'm sorry," she said. "I shouldn't have said that."

Chris waved a hand, but his inability to talk told of how much her comment had hurt. Alaina turned to look at Aaron, before glancing to Sam and Rose. She reached over and waved a hand at Aaron's cup. It began steaming instantly. She did the same to the rest. She smiled and this time, it was genuine.

"I'll just get some honey for the tea."

***

Aaron studied the photos on Alaina's wall. It was apparent by the numerous framed pictures that Alaina had been an unofficial part of the Adams family, and a part of the Elementals group, for some time. The area above her fireplace had many photos, most of the people Aaron didn't know, but there were a few faces he recognised. Alex was in countless pictures. Aaron spotted Ben in a few, along with his mum and dad. His mum's friend Jane was in one or two photos with

Neriah. There was even one of Hadrian, standing with Alex and Chris on one side and Neriah and a woman on his other. The woman seemed very familiar, but Aaron didn't realise why until Sam let out a splutter and pointed at her.

"Bloody hell," he muttered. "How much does she look like Ella?"

As soon as he said it, Aaron saw the resemblance. She had Ella's long dark hair, minus the electric blue streaks, Ella's grey eyes and even her nose.

"Maybe she's her mum," Aaron said.

"Or her twin," Sam offered.

"Her twin?" Rose asked. "Look how young Neriah is in the picture."

"Maybe she's Ella's older twin." Sam grinned, messing with his sister.

"Shut up, Sam," Rose said, annoyed.

Sam chuckled. "Whoever she is, she's damn beautiful."

Aaron glanced behind him to see Alaina in the kitchen with his mum and dad. They seemed a little calmer now, talking in quieter tones as Alaina prepared some snacks for them. The photos proved Aaron had been right. Alaina used to be stunningly beautiful, but the loss she suffered sapped the glow of her beauty, took the light from her eyes and the warmth from her smile.

"Looks like Alaina was with your uncle for a while," Sam said from Aaron's side.

Aaron turned to see the frame Sam was staring at. Alex looked to be not much older than thirteen, maybe fourteen years old. An equally young-looking Alaina was wrapped in his arms.

"They were childhood sweethearts," Aaron said.

"Teenage sweethearts, by the looks of it," Sam corrected.

Rose, Aaron noted, was making an effort not to look at any pictures of Alex. Aaron didn't blame her.

"I can't believe she never went with another bloke," Sam said. "It's been how long?"

"Fourteen years," Aaron murmured, staring at a picture of a laughing Alaina, with Alex at her shoulder, his tongue sticking out at the camera.

Reading the story told by the pictures, it didn't seem very likely that his uncle would cheat on Alaina. They seemed happy. Seeing the devotion between Alex and Alaina made it clear that Kyran, despite the way he looked, could not be Alex's son unless Alaina was his mother.

Aaron turned to study Alaina. She didn't look old enough to be Kyran's mother. Aaron rubbed at his head. He had to stop doing this. Kyran wasn't family; his dad's inability to sense him in the bloodline chain proved that.

"I feel so sorry for her," Rose said, coming to Aaron's side, looking at the collage. "She seemed so happy."

Aaron stared at the main picture, a large framed photo sitting in the middle of the cluster of smaller frames. It was of Alex and Alaina, sitting on the porch of this very house. Alex had his arm around Alaina, holding her close, while Alaina rested a hand on his leg. They looked like a newly married couple on their honeymoon. Alaina even looked like a beaming bride, in a simple white flowing dress. Something caught Aaron's eye and he moved closer, staring at the picture.

"Aaron?" Rose called. "What is it?"

Aaron narrowed his eyes. Around Alaina's neck was a thin silver chain, holding a small pendant. It was difficult to tell in the picture, but Aaron was sure the pendant was a small glass dome with a white rose inside, in full bloom...

Aaron turned around to see Alaina in the kitchen. His eyes sought out the thin chain, still around her neck. He couldn't see the pendant; it was hidden under her dress. The story he heard from the Peregrin girl came back to him.

...it's the story of a girl, rumoured to be the prettiest in all the realm. She had hair as dark as night, skin that glowed like the moon...she lived by herself...she had fallen in love with a mage – a daring, brave warrior...

Aaron turned back to look at the photos of his uncle, a Hunter.

...he couldn't take her despair and worry, so he gifted her with a pendant, one he had created himself, representing both of their elements...

Aaron looked at the picture of the pendant. A rose, to represent his element, floating in a pool of water, to represent hers.

...she knew her lover was dead, but she believed her love wasn't...he was gone but she believed she could still see him – find his shadow in the house they lived in, hear his voice in the whispers of the wind...

His dad said he was surprised she still lived here. There were enough pictures to show she stayed here when she was with Alex. Is that why she was still here? Waiting to see Alex's echo?

...she kept the pendant, with the belief that one day it would bloom again, the moment his echo finally reached her...to this day, she sits and waits for him and that is why we call it the Tale of the Waiting Bloom...

Aaron could hear Sam and Rose calling him, he even felt Rose's hand on his arm, shaking him, but all he could do was stare at Alaina. The intensity of his gaze made Alaina stop and turn around, to meet his eyes with a questioning look.

"It's you," Aaron breathed. "You're the Waiting Bloom."

Alaina didn't say anything. Sam and Rose turned to stare at her in shock. Aaron saw his mum and dad look at him with a mix of anger and surprise, obviously wondering how Aaron knew about the Waiting Bloom.

Alaina reached up and carefully lifted the pendant from under her dress, resting it in her hand. Aaron saw the glass dome with the ivory bud inside. The water around the bud was clear, not crimson like the story had stated, and for that small mercy, Aaron was grateful. He didn't know how he would feel, seeing the blood-stained water that signified the death of his family member.

"It's strange how the world works," Alaina said. "What is a tragedy for one becomes a great story for others."

Aaron could feel heat spread through him, like a fire had started somewhere deep inside. He was suddenly angry, furious at the Peregrins for going around selling copies of the gift his uncle had privately given to his fiancée. He was enraged with the mages for allowing the story to spread, to turn what happened to his uncle and would-be-aunt into a tragic love story. Above all, he was infuriated with himself for enjoying the story when he'd first heard it.

"Why do you stand for it?" Aaron asked her. "Why don't you tell them to stop talking about you, to stop selling those imitations?"

Alaina smiled. "Because it doesn't matter," she said. "They can tell what story they want, sell whatever they like. I don't care."

"How can you not care?" Aaron asked, fury making his hands curl into fists.

"I don't have the heart to care for anything other than who I am waiting for."

Aaron stilled. "Uncle Alex's echo?"

Alaina looked a little thrown before she grinned. A small laugh escaped her. "*Uncle* Alex?" she asked. "I've never heard anyone refer to him as uncle before."

Aaron felt some of his anger abate. She had a lovely laugh, even when it was tinged with sadness. "What did Ben call him?" he asked.

Alaina's smile turned wistful. "Lex," she said quietly. "Ben used to call him Lex."

Kate let out a laugh, choked full of tears. "For some reason, Ben loved dropping the first letter in names," she explained. "She was 'Laina' and he was 'Lex'. Ben could say Alex perfectly, he just preferred Lex."

Chris smiled. "I think Alex preferred Lex too."

Aaron felt himself smile.

Alaina was staring at Aaron before slowly shaking her head. "You're just how I imagined Ben would look, if he..." She faltered and fell silent. She ducked her head and took in a breath before looking up and forcing a smile. "I never thought I would ask Alex's nephew this," she said as she walked over to him, "but what's your name?"

"Aaron," he replied.

Alaina's smile slid from her face. She stared at him with complete shock, before turning to look at Kate and Chris. Aaron frowned at her reaction. When Alaina turned back to face him, tears had slid out of her eyes.

"A-Aaron?" she repeated.

"What's wrong?" Aaron asked.

Alaina reached out with a trembling hand and cupped his cheek. Her hands felt soft and warm.

"Nothing," she whispered. "Nothing's wrong." She turned to look at Kate and Chris again.

"What is it?" Aaron pushed.

Alaina brushed away her tears and sniffed, before turning to give Aaron a watery smile.

"We all had different ideas when it came to choosing a name for you," she said. "Your parents liked Eric. I suggested Xavier. Even Ben had picked a name for you." Her eyes fast filled with tears again. "Alex wanted Aaron."

***

The portal had left Aaron and the others at the Gateway of the City of Marwa. The group made their way across the path, with the water below reflecting the perfect blue of the sky above. But no amount of beauty could distract Aaron today. Thoughts spun in his mind like a whirlpool – meeting Alaina, seeing those pictures of bliss around her home, learning the famous mage love story of the Waiting Bloom was about his uncle and his fiancée, and finally, learning why he was named Aaron.

He cast a small glance at his dad as they walked to the Gate. He wondered what it must have felt like, mere hours after losing your only brother and eldest son to a horrific Lycan attack, to hold your newborn son in your arms and think what to name him. It really was no surprise that his parents chose the name Alex wanted. What better way to always keep Alex in their memories? Aaron knew every time his name came to his mum and dad's lips, they must think of Alex.

Aaron found it strangely endearing, that before he was even born so many of his family members discussed what to name him. They were clearly excited for his birth, yet his uncle and brother never got to see him. Alaina had had to wait fourteen years to meet him.

Aaron had never put much thought into why he was so named. He believed Sam, who said his parents were lazy and named him Aaron because that was the first name in the baby names book. The fact that he was named to honour the memory of his fallen family was both touching and heart-breaking.

Chris and Kate opened the Gate and led the three teenagers into Marwa. Aaron had barely walked ten steps when he spotted the figure waiting in front of their house. He came to a stop, his heart lurching horribly in his chest.

Neriah saw him too and smiled.

Chris and Kate quickened their pace, heading towards their waiting guest. Aaron and the twins followed after them.

"Neriah," Chris called. "What are you doing here?"

"I've come for Aaron," Neriah replied.

Aaron was afraid of exactly this. He had promised his parents he wouldn't fight. But deep inside his longing to save this realm, to protect the human world, was still furiously burning.

If anyone could sniff out that fire, it was Neriah.

17

FIRE IN THE SKY

"What do you mean you've come for Aaron?" Chris asked, taking a step closer to Neriah with curled fists. "I already told you we'd all reached a decision: he's not fighting."

"And if Aaron tells me the same, I'll leave," Neriah replied.

Every eye turned to Aaron, waiting for an answer. Aaron felt Sam and Rose shift behind him, coming to stand by his side. Rose held on to his hand and gave it a tight squeeze. He appreciated the gesture of comfort.

Aaron glanced from his parents to Neriah. He had promised his mum he wouldn't fight, but seeing Neriah again brought it all back – the need to fight despite the risks.

"Aaron?" Kate encouraged. "Tell him you're not fighting."

Aaron met Neriah's eyes and took in a breath. He opened his mouth but the words wouldn't come. Neriah smiled and looked back at Chris, who was staring at Aaron with a furrowed brow.

"Aaron?" he called.

Aaron glanced to his dad but didn't speak.

Kate took a hurried step towards him. "You promised," she reminded him quickly. "You promised you wouldn't fight."

"I know," Aaron said, "and I want to keep my promise, I do. But...it's...I just..." He took in a deep breath. "I don't know if that's the right thing to do when there's a weapon out there that only I can use, and it can make a difference to this fight."

Kate and Chris stood staring at Aaron, their jaws clenched. Neriah stepped forward, addressing Aaron.

"I've mapped the safest route for us to retrieve your Blade," he said. "I've had Lurkers searching the surrounding area for weeks. It's all clear." He was ignoring both Kate and Chris, speaking directly to Aaron. "After we collect the Blade, your training will begin right away. I think it's best if you stay in Salvador. I've arranged a spot for you to store your Blade, so it's more convenient for you to train with it on a daily basis."

"Wait, wait." Aaron was blind-sided by Neriah discussing his plans, even before Aaron had properly agreed to participate in the war. "Why would I travel to the sword every day? Why can't I keep it with me?"

"I'll explain on the way," Neriah said. He held out a hand, gesturing to the Gate.

Aaron's gaze darted back to his mum and dad. Both of them had taken a step forward, ready to stop Aaron if he moved.

"I can't leave like this," Aaron told Neriah quietly. "Not without their agreement."

Neriah let out a tired sigh. "They will never agree, Aaron. You do what *you* want to do, what your heart and soul are telling you to do."

Aaron glanced to his mum. "My heart is telling me not to hurt my parents."

Neriah looked agitated. "Don't fall for their guilt trip," he said. "You are doing the right thing, Aaron. You are the legacy holder. The Blade of Adams is waiting for you. A weapon of such calibre as a Blade of Aric is a tremendous waste if not used in the war."

Aaron's dilemma was worsened when he felt Sam and Rose hold on to his arms and whisper in his ear.

"Think about this before rushing into anything," Sam said.

"This is your life you're talking about risking," Rose added. "Don't let anyone talk you into doing something you're not ready to do."

"I'm not forcing you to do anything," Neriah defended. "But you clearly have the desire to fight this war. That is why I'm here, to help you."

A loud crash shook the earth under them. It sounded like a mighty clap of thunder but when Aaron turned, he saw it was a line of trees behind his dad that had crashed to the ground. Seeing the murderous expression on his dad's face, it made sense.

"That's why you're here?" he repeated. "Why don't you just be honest, Neriah? Tell him you're *using* him. You're risking his life, just to have another Blade of Aric against Hadrian!"

"You can't deny him his destiny, Chris," Neriah said. "He's an Elemental. He's got fight in his blood. He's the last in a long line of Hunters."

"He's *fourteen*!" Chris cried. "What is wrong with you? Why can't you understand that he's just a kid?"

"A kid who is the legacy holder for Earth," Neriah said. "He can level entire cities with one swipe of his Blade and you know that. Why can't you accept the power he holds?"

Chris shook his head with disdain. "That's all this is about, isn't it?" he asked. "Power. It all comes down to power."

"In times of war, power is all that matters," Neriah said.

"No," Chris argued. "All that matters is family, and I'm not prepared to lose mine."

"No one is prepared for loss," Neriah said and his eyes had darkened to a deep purple. "No one wants to lose their family, but to gain victory, lives have to be put at stake."

"Yeah?" Chris seethed. "And just how many lives are you prepared to devastate?"

"As many as it takes," Neriah replied. "I'll do what I must, but I *will* defeat Hadrian."

"You will never defeat him!" Chris was so angry, the ground was trembling under him.

"Chris…" Kate tried to calm him but it seemed his rage had deafened him to her calls.

"You had your chance and you lost it!" Chris continued. "If you couldn't kill him when he was powerless and at your mercy, how are you going to kill him now, when he has his powers back?"

"I'll do whatever it takes!" Neriah spat at him. "And if you're not with me, Chris, then stay out of my way."

"Keep my son out of this first!" Chris said.

"Your son has a mind of his own," Neriah shot back. "And he's choosing to be by my side. He wants Hadrian gone. He wants to fight. He wants to fulfil his destiny. He wants to be a better man than his father!"

Chris bolted for Neriah, lost in his fury.

"Chris, no!" Kate ran to stop him.

She didn't get to him and Chris didn't get to Neriah.

The ground between Neriah and Chris cracked and tilted, throwing Chris bodily backwards.

Everyone stilled before turning to the one who caused the phenomenon.

"Aaron." Sam reached for his arm, but Aaron shrugged him away. He was raging, his hands curled into fists and eyes narrowed.

Aaron could feel the power of the Earth seeping into him, feeding him energy, readying him for a fight. His angry gaze moved from his shell-shocked dad to rest on Neriah.

"You're wrong," he said and the words came from between clenched teeth. "Everything you just said. That's not why I'm willing to fight. I want to fight to save lives. It's got *nothing* to do with fulfilling destiny or any crap like that! I just don't want Hadrian taking over because he's part demon."

Neriah shook his head. "You only say that because you don't know Hadrian—"

"I don't care!" Aaron spat. "I'm fighting so Hadrian – a *vamage* – doesn't take over the realm. So the human realm doesn't fall into chaos because of us! I don't want our elemental powers seeping destructive energy through the tears and destroying the human realm. It's got absolutely nothing to do with having fight in my blood or wanting Hadrian gone." His eyes slitted. "And it sure as hell has nothing to do with my dad. He did what he did to protect the ones he loves – that itself makes him a better man."

Chris was staring at him, but he didn't speak. Kate had reached his side, but her eyes too were on her son.

"I'm not a fighter," Aaron continued. "I may come from a lineage of Hunters, but that doesn't mean I like hunting. I want to fight to protect lives, not because I enjoy ending them."

"You can't deny there is an honour in fighting," Neriah argued.

"What honour?" Aaron asked. "Dying senselessly in war? Is that it?" He stepped closer. "Understand this, Neriah. I'm not fighting for honour, or for any kind of a prize. I'm willing to fight so millions of lives, human and mages alike, aren't lost in Hadrian's battle for power." His angry eyes held on to Neriah. "I don't care what your agenda is and, I'm sorry, but I never will."

He walked away, ignoring Neriah, his parents, even his best friends, until the heat biting at his insides diminished and the burning of his fingertips stopped. He was afraid if he'd stayed a moment longer, he'd have lost control and cracked the ground wide open, letting the gap swallow the whole lot of them.

*****

Aaron was surprised to find the City of Marwa had a lake too. It was smaller than the beautiful lake in Salvador but it was just as serene and peaceful. It invited Aaron to come and sit at its bank. Small fish, silvery white, broke the surface a few times, only to go back down instantly. Aaron watched them, following their path until he accurately guessed where they were going to pop up next. How long he sat there he didn't know, but the tranquillity of the lake helped extinguish the fiery rage inside him.

Aaron let out a breath and leaned back, resting on his elbows as he stretched out his legs. He heard the heavy footsteps approaching but he stayed as he was, unwilling to move. Neriah settled next to him.

"You know, if you wanted to hide from me, at the bank of a lake isn't such a good idea," Neriah said.

Aaron could hear the smile in his voice but it only served to irritate him.

"Why would I hide from you?" he asked, without looking at Neriah. "I'm not afraid of you and I'm not sorry for what I said."

"Oh, Heaven forbid." And this time, there was a small chuckle at the end.

Aaron turned to glare at him, but Neriah only looked amused. "Aren't you angry with me?" Aaron asked. "For disrespecting you."

Neriah turned his head to look at the lake.

"Respect has to be earned. Besides, you spoke your mind. How can I hold that against you?" He smiled. "You know, you reminded me of someone today."

"Let me guess," Aaron started tersely, sitting up. "I reminded you of you when you were my age."

"Not at all." Neriah looked at Aaron for long minutes. "You reminded me of Hadrian."

Aaron bristled and looked at Neriah with indignant surprise.

"He was like you in many regards," Neriah continued. "I'm pretty sure he once said words very similar to what you just said."

Aaron was glaring at him, so angry he struggled to talk at first. "You know what, Neriah? If you want to insult me—"

"I'm not insulting you," Neriah said with a shake of his head. "Hadrian wasn't always corrupt. He was pure once – a mage, an Elemental. He was the Controller, and he was passionate about the mages, about the war with demons. He was a protector, much like you. He fought the war against demons and he did it for no gain other than to save lives."

Aaron stared at Neriah. "How does someone go from being like that to a power-hungry demon?"

Neriah's smile was gone. Pain filled his eyes and he let out a long breath.

"Life is not only cruel but sometimes ironic, not to mention a little twisted." He gave Aaron a sideways glance before dropping his head. "I know that I upset you with what I said," he started quietly, "but I meant every word. You are a fighter, even if you don't know it yet. I see in you what I once saw in your dad. You have that spark that I used to see in Hadrian when he spoke about securing the fate of our realm." His eyes were back to the impossible shade of violet as he held Aaron's gaze. "You are the only Adams of your generation. The legacy resides in you, Aaron. The Blade of Adams is waiting for you and the power you could bring to our fight is phenomenal."

Aaron took in a breath. "I want to help," he said, "but I promised my parents I wouldn't risk my life." He looked down at the ground and steeled himself. "I saw what happened to Ben." He had to clear his throat, pushing back the horrid images that would haunt him forever. "I can't put them through something like that again. They had to watch one son die, that's enough."

"Ben was an infant; he was defenceless," Neriah said in a quiet, hollow voice. "Once you have Aric's Blade, you will have true power at your fingertips. I'm going to train you, teach you how to use the Blade so nothing can stand in your way." He paused. "What happened to your brother happens to children in Hadrian's zones all the time. There are no Gates to protect the mages. Hadrian leaves the zones open and all sorts of demons, including Lycans, find their way inside to torment and kill the mages there."

Aaron remembered what Kyran had claimed, that they only had nine zones and all nine were Gated. He watched Neriah carefully, trying to catch something, anything, that would suggest he was lying. But Neriah's sincerity was shining through his very skin. He believed in what he was saying. So did that mean Kyran was the one lying? Or perhaps that Neriah didn't know about Hadrian's Gates?

"This fight will end the suffering of thousands, hundreds of thousands of innocent mages," Neriah said. "With Hadrian finally defeated, we can protect all the zones of this realm. The human realm will no longer pay the price of our battles. Isn't that what you want?"

"It is," Aaron said. "But I need my parents to agree first. I need their acceptance and help."

"You don't need their help. I'll help you," Neriah promised.

"No offence, Neriah, but I would rather have my parents backing me up than just you."

Neriah paused before smiling. "It wouldn't be just me," he said and his tone was one of playful teasing again. "Ella would back you up too, even Skyler."

Aaron laughed. "Yeah, that'll be the day."

Neriah watched him before letting out a sigh. "I meant what I said. I'm not going to force you. The decision to fight or not is yours to make." He stared at Aaron intently. "But we really could use your help."

Aaron didn't know what to say.

A flash lit up the sky and, for a heartbeat, the entire city glowed red. Aaron whipped around, as did Neriah.

The sky was on fire.

Leaping up to their feet, Aaron and Neriah watched in mounting horror as a wave of fire, brilliant orange and red flames, spread across the sky. The next moment, the flames tightened, coiling themselves to form a symbol. Two adjacent lines, tilting towards one another until they joined at one end: a blazing inverted V burned in the sky.

"What's going on?" Aaron asked, his heart kicking at his insides.

"It's a message," Neriah said, staring at the symbol for Fire in the sky.

"A message?" Aaron asked.

"From Hadrian. He's telling us it's time," Neriah said. He turned to look at Aaron with darkened eyes. "Hadrian's core has fully restored."

18

THE SWORD IN THE STONE

The journey was made in complete silence. The only sound was the crunching of dry leaves and snapping of twigs under their feet. Aaron glanced at Neriah's back as he led the way, once again, through a dense forest. Skyler and Ella were behind Aaron, and on either side of him, were Aaron's parents.

Moments after Hadrian's message had blazed in the sky, Aaron had found both his parents, Sam and Rose rushing to his side. They had all stood and stared at the fiery symbol for long minutes, each contemplating the fate of the realm now that what they had most feared had happened. Hadrian's core was restored, after being locked for sixteen years. Hadrian had his powers again. A full Elemental with demonic powers – what exactly would the mages be up against?

Aaron couldn't stand back, not now, not when the war was afoot. Hadrian had sent his declaration. If the mages were going to survive, they had to gather their forces and ready themselves for the battle.

Aaron had turned to his parents with eyes full of pleading, but before a word passed his lips, his dad had nodded at him and stepped forward, hugging him tightly. Seeing Hadrian's symbol blazing above their supposedly safe city had shaken all of them. There was no time left for reservations. They had to fight. All of them had to fight.

Sam and Rose had been escorted to Salvador that same day, and by nightfall the trip to retrieve Aaron's Blade was arranged. They left at daybreak, with Skyler and Ella joining them. They all took the portal Scott set up to arrive in the middle of a dense forest.

It felt like they had been walking for half a day when Aaron caught sight of something glittering in the distance. He squinted, trying to make out what it was. His eyes widened in complete and utter shock at the sight of a Gate, sitting in all its glory in the middle of the woodland. There was no Gateway for this Gate. It was just a great big towering door amongst all the trees.

Neriah stood before it, waiting for the rest of them to catch up. Once everyone gathered before the Gate, Neriah placed his palm on it and said his name. The Gate slid open and Aaron was disappointed to see what lay ahead was more of what he left behind. The forest looked just the same on the other side of the Gate, which meant they had more trekking to do. Neriah turned to look at Aaron. He didn't say anything but his gaze moved to meet Chris's before he turned and walked over the threshold. Kate and Chris entered with Aaron, leaving Skyler and Ella to follow after them.

Neriah continued to lead the way. It was hot and humid this deep in the forest. Aaron's clothes were beginning to stick to him. Beads of sweat had already gathered on his forehead. He wiped at his brow and trudged along. The further he walked, the more breathless he felt, like the air had suddenly thinned. Thinking he was just getting tired, Aaron ignored it and pushed on. He pulled his backpack higher on his shoulders and walked with his head lowered. His feet felt heavy, every step cost him more effort than it should. A strange weight settled on his shoulders, almost like invisible hands were pushing him to the ground. Aaron came to a stop, breathing heavily. He looked up to see Neriah had come to a rest too, catching his breath.

A hand squeezed his shoulder and Aaron turned to meet his dad's eyes. His face was covered in perspiration. He nodded at him. "It's okay," he said. "It just means we're...we're close."

"The...the Blade is doing this?" Aaron asked, surprised.

"The Blades of Aric are powerful creations," Neriah said, somehow managing to retain his graceful composure, even when his skin glistened with sweat and his voice shook slightly against the strain of breathing in thin air. "When you get close to them, you feel their presence–" He stopped. His body snapped straight with tension. He turned, watching the forest with narrowed eyes.

Not a word was uttered but Skyler stepped forward. His platinum blond hair was plastered to his head. He brushed his hand over his face, wiping at the moisture clinging to his skin. He scanned the grounds with intense blue eyes before turning to the right.

"There," he said. "It's over there."

In the blink of an eye, everyone had their weapons in hand, everyone bar Aaron.

"It's next to the stream," Ella said, and just like that, everyone was moving – heading to the right of the woods. Skyler cocked his gun and pulled out his sword, charging forward on one side of Neriah, while Ella was on the other.

Aaron was taken aback. He had thought they would retreat and ask for Scott to send a team before going off to hunt whatever was out here. But Neriah, Skyler and Ella moved swiftly through the forest without a moment's pause. Kate kept hold of Aaron with one hand, while her other gripped a silver semi-automatic. The sight of the weapon in his mum's nimble hand brought a shudder to Aaron. He met her eyes but quickly looked away.

"Come on." Chris tugged at Aaron's other arm and they hurried after Neriah.

Aaron didn't see much, other than tall trees and lots of vegetation, but he heard the stream before he saw it. The sound of water running over rocks, a soft melody in the quiet woods, led Aaron towards it. Kate and Chris were careful to not let

Aaron get even one step ahead of them. They stayed by his side, guns in hand, alert and ready. Neriah, Ella and Skyler had slowed down and were approaching the edge of a hill with caution. Aaron followed them, struggling to quieten his heavy breathing and slow his racing heart.

Neriah, Skyler and Ella pressed themselves into the soft, mossy ground and peered over the edge of the hill. Aaron, Kate and Chris did the same. The first thing Aaron noticed was the thin, sparkling stream running through the forest. Sunlight bounced off the dazzling water, as if crystal jewels lay under the surface. Staring at the river, Aaron realised just how thirsty he was.

Then he saw what everyone else was looking at.

It was a woman with long white hair, crouching over the edge of the stream. Her pale grey dress hung off her skeletal frame. Aaron saw her thin, wrinkled arm extend to cup water in a trembling hand. Aaron glanced at the area around the old woman, but couldn't see anyone else. Yet, everyone was staring in her direction with unblinking eyes.

Chris was the first to move. He brought up his arm and aimed his gun at the frail old woman.

Aaron couldn't stop himself. "Dad?" he whispered. "What are you doing?"

Chris snapped his head around to look at Aaron with alarm. Everyone stilled. Breaths were pulled in but not let back out. Skyler cursed. Aaron turned to see the woman at the stream freeze, her hand halfway between the stream and her mouth. She whipped around and Aaron almost stopped breathing. Her face was barely more than thin skin stretched over bone. Her eyes glowed an eerie yellow and the moment they landed on him, she opened her mouth and screamed.

Only it wasn't a human scream.

The sound that filled the air was one that made Aaron swear his ears were bleeding. A high-pitched screech, so intense it made Aaron's teeth rattle, rang around them. Such was the volume of her cry that Aaron didn't hear the guns go off next to him. The screaming stopped, and the woman turned and ran. Neriah raced down the hill after her, Skyler and Ella hot at his heels. The old, weak-looking woman bolted through the woods at a speed that left Aaron gaping in shock. There was no doubt as to what she was now. She wasn't human and she wasn't mage. Elementals were hunting her. She must be a demon.

Aaron stood up and spotted her past the trees, a little distance ahead. Aaron raised both hands, aiming a ripple at her, to slow her down.

Nothing happened. The ground stayed as it was. His fingers didn't even tingle like they usually did.

Perplexed, Aaron looked at his hands, turning them over to examine them. He raised them again.

"It's no use," Chris said quietly by his side.

Aaron turned to him.

"Our powers don't work here," Chris explained.

"What?" Aaron asked. "Why not?"

"No power works on the ground that holds the Blades of Aric," Chris explained. "The Blades draw power to themselves from the elements that surround them. If a mage gets too close, the Blades pull power from them too. That's why we can't open portals near them. The Blades would just swallow that energy."

Aaron was stunned. "How am I going to use the sword if it drains my powers?"

Chris shared a look with his wife. "When you hold the Blade it will connect with the legacy inside you. Then the Blade will give you power rather than take it."

A heavy sigh made Aaron turn to look at his mum. She didn't look happy, in fact, she looked downright miserable at the prospect of Aaron wielding the Blade.

"Mum?" Aaron stepped towards her, reaching out to hold on to her arm.

"It's your birthright," she said quietly. "I know that. I just–" She shook her head and closed her eyes. "I wish you were older before you were forced into all of this."

Aaron's hand dropped from her arm. "No one is forcing me, Mum," he said. "I want to be a part of this fight. I *want* to do this."

"We know," Chris said. He gave Aaron a small smile. "You're not going to back down, we've accepted that now. If we can't stop you, then at least we can protect you. You can take the Blade of Adams, but our job–" he gestured to himself and Kate "–is to make sure no one gets near enough for you to use it."

Aaron stared at him. "Dad–"

But Chris looked over Aaron's head and his expression changed. He stepped past him and Aaron turned to see the group of Elementals making their way back, guns clutched in their hands.

"Did you get it?" Chris asked.

Neriah shook his head. "It got away. We injured it, so it won't get too far."

"The Lurkers did a full sweep. They said it was all clear," Skyler said, annoyed.

"It was alone. It must have wandered away from its nest," Neriah replied.

"What was that thing?" Aaron asked.

"A Banshee," Ella replied, scrunching up her nose. "Nasty things."

Banshees. That's what Kyran had claimed had been in that village he burned down.

"I thought Banshees were bad omens," Aaron mumbled, trying to get Kyran and his words out of his mind.

He recalled an assignment he had to complete on folklore last year. His mum had made him focus in particular on Banshees. He remembered reading that their screams were their defence mechanisms, but some folklore suggested it was an offence. When they were attacked or killed, their screams were normal-sounding human cries that caused no damage. But according to different myths, their Banshee scream could do anything from kill, to warn of approaching death.

"They *are* bad omens," Skyler said. "Considering they eat those they meet, I'd say they're the worst type of omens."

Aaron threw him a glare but otherwise ignored him.

"Come," Neriah said. "We don't have time to waste."

He led the way back. Aaron and the others followed after him. Ella jogged forward to fall into step with Aaron.

"Hey," she called. "You doing okay?"

"Yeah," Aaron replied. "I'm good."

"You should know, Banshees have a super sense of hearing," she said. "That one heard you whispering."

"I'm sorry," Aaron said. "I didn't realise–"

"It was already pretty weak, it won't make it too far," Ella said. "At least we know there's a nest somewhere in the vicinity." She smiled. "Maybe later on, you can come with your Blade and hunt it out." She elbowed him in good humour.

"Are Banshees really all that dangerous?" Aaron asked. "That one didn't look like it could do much." He couldn't stop thinking about how thin and frail it was.

"Looks are deceiving," Ella replied. "Banshees are really vile creatures. They feast on mage flesh. They usually prey on babies and infants. Their screams paralyse the young, so Banshees can easily carry them back to their nest to feed on."

Aaron shuddered at the thought. "So, pretty dangerous, then."

"Not as bad as some, but yeah, Banshees are plenty troublesome," Ella said.

Aaron thought for a moment. "Who are the *really* bad ones?"

Ella looked over at him. "I think you already know."

"Vamages," Aaron said, hating how the word now associated with his mental picture of Kyran.

Ella nodded. "And Lycans."

As soon as she said the name, Skyler looked around at both her and Aaron with serious eyes and a furrowed brow. He didn't say anything and turned back, following behind Neriah.

"Skyler's sensitive to that word," Aaron commented.

"Why wouldn't he be?" Ella said quietly. "He lost everything to Lycans."

Aaron remembered what Neriah had yelled at his dad – how Skyler was forced to watch as Lycans murdered his whole family. He felt pity well up inside him.

"He's not the only one," Ella continued, her voice barely above a whisper.

Aaron looked at her. He knew Neriah was her only family.

"What age were you when...?" Aaron faltered, wondering how best to ask such a personal question.

"My father died before I was born, in one of the worst attacks by Lycans," Ella said. "My mother..." She closed her eyes and took in a breath. "She was killed by Lycans a year later."

Aaron felt a sharp pain sear his chest. "I'm so sorry, Ella."

Ella didn't say anything but gave a small nod.

Neriah and Skyler came to a stop in front of a cave nestled at the base of a large hill. The mouth of the cave was almost closed by thick vegetation.

Neriah and Skyler cut away at it with their swords until there was enough room to squeeze into the cave. It was dark inside, even with the sunlight trying to flood in through the entrance. Neriah ran his hand over the walls until he found a small torch. He dug out a lighter from his bag and lit it.

Now that they had some light, Neriah made his way deeper into the cave. Aaron and the rest of them followed. The further they went, the more Aaron's heart dropped. His mouth was incredibly dry and he was feeling light-headed. He wasn't sure if that was the effect of the Blade or his nerves getting the best of him.

Their steps landed on stone, echoing in the small cave. Aaron tasted the stale, damp air when he took in a deep breath. Neriah stopped them suddenly.

"Wait here," he commanded.

Aaron watched as Neriah walked over to the wall and held the torch up high, looking for something. He found it quickly – another torch. Neriah lit it, bringing a little more light into the cave. Aaron watched as Neriah made his way around the cave, lighting several torches. A warm glow filled the chamber. Only when Neriah stepped away from lighting the last torch did Aaron notice what lay before them.

Wedged in the stone ground, in the middle of a tremendous crack, stood a sword. Aaron had seen plenty of swords during his time in Salvador. The artillery hut had an entire wall dedicated to them. Even Kyran had a narrow, white-hilted sword in the weapons cabinet in his old cottage. But this sword wasn't like anything Aaron had seen. Even with a part of it buried, what he could see was almost as long as Aaron's arm. Symbols were engraved across the entire length of the gleaming silver. The light was too dim in the cave to make out exactly what they were. On the black hilt, set in tiny white stones, was Aric's mark. It shone in the limited light, like the moon on dark nights. The Blade radiated power, an unseen force pulsating from the ground. Aaron could feel it, the pull of energy the Blade was demanding from the Earth. It made him dizzy to feel so much power around him.

Neriah came to rest next to Aaron. "Just walk over and pull the Blade out," he instructed quietly.

Aaron's gaze dropped to the end of the sword that was buried in the ground.

"Pull the sword out from the stone?" he asked.

"Yes," Neriah replied.

Aaron smiled. "Like King Arthur?"

Neriah turned to give him a long look. "Who's King Arthur?"

"Never mind." Aaron shook his head. "But if Sam and Rose were here, they'd appreciate the humour."

He stepped towards the Blade but paused to turn to his mum and dad. His dad looked worn thin with worry, but he managed a small nod and a shadow of a smile. His mum had pressed her lips into a line, her eyes gleaming in the limited light as she stared back at him. The orange flicker from the torches threw half of her face into shadow, but Aaron still saw the fear in her expression. He didn't know what to do to dispel that fear. They knew, as did he, that from this day onwards, Aaron was going to be a major player in this war. Their plan to stay by his side, acting like shields, was their way of dealing with it, but that didn't make watching him claim the Blade of Adams any easier. Aaron gave his mum a smile, trying to assure her that everything would be okay. He turned and began walking towards the sword.

The closer he came to the Blade of Adams, the more he felt his power seep out of him. By the time he reached the Blade, a fine sheen of sweat had covered him, leaving him feeling shaky and ill. But even so, when he stood before the sword, he found himself examining it closely. It was magnificent in every sense of the word. Despite being centuries old and left in this cave for what Aaron assumed was at least fourteen years, if not more, the sword looked like it had just been carved out of liquid silver. The engravings were symbols that didn't make much sense to Aaron but they were mesmerising to look at.

His vision blurred suddenly and his knees threatened to buckle under him. Aaron had to fight to keep himself upright. He blinked to clear his eyes. His heart was beating against his ribcage with force, his breathing felt tighter. Aaron looked up to see Neriah standing with his mum and dad, waiting. Skyler and Ella stood to the side, watching him.

Neriah nodded at Aaron. "Push past it," he instructed. "You're standing close to the Blade, that's why it's affecting you. The moment you touch the sword, all the power of the Blade will connect with your legacy."

Aaron swallowed and nodded. He extended his hand, trying to keep it steady. He almost touched the hilt before he stopped. He looked to his dad.

"Will it hurt?" he asked and he hated the way his voice shook at the question.

Chris smiled, his eyes gleaming. "No," he replied with a shake of his head. "It will feel like a part of you that's always been missing has finally clicked into place."

The tight coil in Aaron's chest loosened a little and Aaron nodded. He pushed out a breath and fixed his eyes on the Blade. He reached for it again and out of nowhere, Kyran's voice boomed in his head.

The minute you touch that sword, your life will never be the same again.

Aaron paused. His life had already changed irreversibly. What else was there left to fear? The Blade of Adams was his by birthright. At some point in his life, he was meant to stand here and pull out this sword. He was destined to wield one of the four most powerful weapons in this realm.

Aaron pushed away Kyran's warning, locked away the bubbling fear, and took a hold of the hilt.

The second Aaron's hand closed around the grip of the sword, a tremendous wave of agony tore through him. It felt like fire had entered his veins and was spreading throughout his body, intent on burning him from within. With a cry, Aaron let go of the sword and stumbled back, gripping his hand.

"AARON!"

He could hear his mum and dad's yells, and the sound of pounding feet told him they were running towards him, but Aaron couldn't call back. Screams were ripping out of him. Something was tearing his insides apart. White-hot agony swept through him, clouding his vision. The pain brought Aaron to his knees before he fell, face forward onto the stone ground, sending him reeling into unconsciousness before his parents or Neriah could reach him.

19

BEING READY

The rays of daylight peeked in through the net curtains, warming Aaron's face, urging him to wake up. Aaron wanted to roll over and hide his face under the pillow and go on sleeping. He was so tired, his bones were aching. Did he have the flu? Why was he so sore? Was it the day of the full moon already? Or did Skyler give him a good thrashing again, under the pretence of training? Wait, Kyran was his teacher now. He had been training with him for months. No. Kyran wasn't his teacher. Kyran was the Scorcher. He was the enemy. He came to Salvador to steal Neriah's key so he could unlock Hadrian's power and destroy this realm and take the human one down with it. But Kyran had also come to warn Aaron, to tell him not to fight the war. He told him not to touch the sword.

The sword.

One of Aric's Blades.

The Blade of Adams.

The memory of the agonising pain that flooded him the moment he touched the Blade came back to Aaron and he snapped awake. He was breathing fast, his heart racing. His vision was still cloudy with stubborn sleep, but when he blinked a few times he made out the strangely familiar ceiling.

He was lying in a comfortable bed, in a quiet, peaceful room but Aaron's heart was pounding like he had woken up in a dank dungeon. Every part of Aaron's body hurt. A dull ache pounded in his head, in time with his heartbeat. He felt jittery and ill, weakened and sore.

Slowly, Aaron lifted his right arm, blinking at his hand. It looked perfectly fine – no burn, not even the faintest mark – yet Aaron could swear he'd felt his skin sear with heat when he held on to the sword. Had he been burned? Or was it just his imagination? Or had he been hurt and now healed?

"What happened?" Aaron asked himself out loud, his voice sounding scratchy to his own ears.

"Aaron?" a soft voice called, and Aaron turned his head to see a beautiful, fair-haired Empath at the door. "You're awake already? I thought you would sleep well into the night."

"Armana?" Aaron croaked in surprise. He looked around the room, finally figuring out where he was and why it looked so familiar. "How did I get to Salvador?"

Armana smiled and made her way over to him. "You were brought here a few hours ago," she said. She felt the chair with her hands before sitting at his bedside. "Sensing how drained you were, I was certain you would be asleep for at least half the day."

"The Blade," Aaron breathed. "That's what drained me?" He looked at Armana to see her gentle smile fade a little. "What happened?" he asked. "Why did the sword drain me?"

Armana shook her head. "Don't you worry about that," she said. She held out her hands. "Here, let me check–"

"Armana," Aaron called. "Tell me what happened." He swallowed past his dry throat. "Please."

Armana pulled back her hands, letting them drop in her lap. Her unseeing gaze went past Aaron.

"Don't get upset," she said quietly. "This happens sometimes. It doesn't mean anything's wrong."

"What?" Aaron asked. He pulled himself to sit up and the room spun. He closed his eyes and forced out a breath.

"What...what do you mean?" he asked in a shaky voice. "What happens? What's wrong?"

"You need to rest," Armana said, her voice laced with concern. "Are you sitting up? You need to lie back down."

"No." Aaron pushed the covers back and tried to get out of bed, but he couldn't manage it. "Not until you tell me what's happening?" His body protested to the minimal movement and Aaron had to fight not to collapse onto his back.

"Aaron," Armana started, leaning forward, her hands outstretched for him. "You're in pain. I can feel it in your voice." Her pale blue eyes were glistening. "Lie back, please."

"I will," Aaron said. "But first, tell me the truth. What happened? Why did the Blade drain me?"

"Because you're not ready."

The voice came from the other side of the room. Aaron turned to see Neriah, looking weary and tired. He walked into the room and Armana quickly got to her feet.

"I'll come and check on you later," she said to Aaron. "Please, lie down and let your body heal."

She left, passing Neriah, who came to stand at the foot of Aaron's bed. Aaron didn't do as Armana asked. He stubbornly stayed sitting, fighting with the last morsel of strength he had to stay upright.

"What do you mean, I'm not ready?" he asked.

Neriah walked to the seat Armana had vacated and sat down. He rubbed a hand over his face before letting out a sigh. "It's not very common," he started, "but it's also not unheard of for the Blade to reject its holder."

Aaron locked his arms at his sides to keep himself sitting. "That's what that was? Rejection?" he asked. He closed his eyes and sighed. "No wonder it was so painful."

Neriah didn't smile.

"So what now?" Aaron asked, looking at Neriah. "How do I get the sword to accept me? What do I have to do to be deemed *ready*?"

Neriah didn't speak right away. "Aaron," he said in a quiet voice. "If a legacy holder isn't ready, it's because their legacy isn't awake yet. That's why the Blade rejects them, because it can't connect to the legacy, so it drains them like it would any other mage who tries to wield it. Legacies are supposed to awaken with the core, but sometimes they don't until the core matures." He held Aaron's eyes. "Your core matures when you come of age."

The impact of his words hit Aaron like a physical kick to the gut. "When I'm of age?" he asked. "You mean, I can't use the Blade until I'm eighteen?"

"Nineteen," Neriah corrected quietly.

Aaron stared at him. "Will there be a war left to fight in five years?"

Neriah smiled, but it was a sad, heartbroken one. "God, I hope not," he breathed. He sat back in the chair with his shoulders dropped. "I've been fighting this war for far too long. But now that Hadrian's powers are unlocked, the battle will truly start." He held Aaron's eyes. "And I don't expect it to last very long."

Aaron swung his legs over the side of the bed, but his body refused to be pushed to the point of standing.

"You're giving up?" he asked, fear and anger pumping inside him.

Neriah laughed, a deep rumbling sound that filled the room. He tilted his head to the side and gave Aaron a long look. "I'd sooner face death than give up, Aaron."

"So why are you saying we're gonna lose?" Aaron asked.

"I didn't say that," Neriah objected.

"It's what you're implying," Aaron said. His body ached but Aaron shoved that pain aside. He was too angry to care about it. "There must be a way to awaken my legacy now so I can use the Blade," he said.

"There may be," Neriah replied. "But now isn't the time to discuss that. For now, I think it's best for you to return to Marwa with your parents."

Aaron couldn't believe what he was hearing. "Wait a minute," he said, his chest heaving with the effort it took to breathe. "You're the one who came to my house," he said. "*You* came to get *me*. I fought with my parents, finally got them to agree to let me take part, and now you're telling me to go back home?"

"Without the Blade of Aric, there isn't much you can bring to the fight," Neriah said. "I can't send you into the battlefield with a few months of Hunter training. You won't last an hour."

"I'm still an Elemental," Aaron argued. "You can train me to fight."

"There's no time," Neriah said with a heavy heart. "Without the Blade—"

"To hell with the Blade!" Aaron snapped and his whole body shook with pain and anger. "I'm not going anywhere. I'm not a toy, Neriah! You can't just use me when you see fit and then throw me in a corner when—"

A spasm of pain seized him, cutting him off. Aaron's hand shot to his chest and he doubled over, gasping for breath. It felt like a hand had closed around his heart and twisted it.

Neriah was at his side, strong and firm hands gently guided him to lie back. "You should rest," Neriah said. "It's the only way you'll heal."

Aaron grabbed hold of his hand before he could pull away. "Blade or not," Aaron panted. "I'm still fighting."

Neriah smiled and gently pulled his hand out of Aaron's. "Sleep," he said. "Your family and friends are waiting to see you, but the Empaths won't let them in until you're better."

"You came in," Aaron wheezed.

Neriah smiled. "Not many can refuse me." He patted Aaron on the head and walked away.

Before Neriah could even step outside, exhaustion pulled Aaron into a peaceful slumber.

***

"Please, Armana."

"No, Aaron, absolutely not."

"I'll go mad if I have to stay here any longer."

"You've been here a day."

"I'm fine now," Aaron insisted. "I'm sitting up in bed and everything."

Armana's pale blue eyes widened. "You're doing what? Lie back down, right now!"

Aaron sighed. "Honestly, I feel much better. My headache is almost all gone and I don't feel as drained."

"I can tell from your voice that you're still fatigued," Armana said.

"I need to get out of here," Aaron argued. "You won't even let my friends in to sit with me."

Armana perched on the edge of the bed, staring past Aaron's head. "I let Sam and Rose sit with you for half an hour yesterday. That's more than what the other Empaths would allow." She smiled kindly. "Besides, tomorrow is the day of the full moon. I want you to stay here until it passes."

Aaron let out a frustrated sigh. "I don't want to stay here, Armana," he said honestly. "I need a distraction, something – anything – that will take my mind off the Blade."

Armana reached out, searching for Aaron's hand. She held it tightly. "I know you're upset about the rejection, but you just have to be patient."

"You sound like my dad," Aaron said. "He keeps telling me the same thing."

"You should listen to us, then," Armana said with a smile.

"There's no time to be patient," he said. "I have the legacy but if it doesn't awaken until I'm nineteen, then there's nothing I can do to help in this war. It's just down to Neriah and Skyler."

Armana's expression changed at the mention of the Air Elemental but she didn't say anything. She took a moment before tightening her grip on Aaron's hand, squeezing it gently. "I know you want to help, Aaron, but you're just learning how to control your powers. It's not safe for you to fight in this war."

"I know," Aaron said. "Which is why having a Blade of Aric in my hand would have greatly tilted the odds in my favour." He let out a pent up breath. "There must be something I can do. There has to be some way, someone that can help me awaken my legacy. Neriah said now wasn't the time to discuss it, but that means he knows something that can help me."

Armana pulled back her hand.

"You shouldn't force these matters," she said in a quiet voice. "Sometimes it's best to let things happen by themselves. Your legacy will awaken when it's ready."

"Yeah, when I'm nineteen," Aaron grouched. "Not much point then."

"Looking for shortcuts sometimes leads to more trouble," Armana said.

Aaron frowned. "What do you mean?"

Armana took a moment to answer. "Decades ago, the Elementals of that time discovered a presence. It wasn't demonic, but it didn't come from the mages either. They called it the Influence."

Aaron frowned. "The Influence?"

"It was a different force, very powerful," Armana said. "The Elementals thought they could work with it, use the Influence to their benefit." She closed her eyes and breathed out a sigh. "From the very beginning, mages were able to heal themselves from most injuries. It took time and a lot of *rest*..." She stressed the word, but Aaron stubbornly remained sitting. "...but generally we recovered on our own. As the demonic forces we fought got stronger, the mages often found themselves needing days to recover from injuries. When we came across Lycans and vampires, mages couldn't fight the poison from their bites, and would die. The Elementals used the Influence to help, to give them the ability to heal faster, to heal better." Armana paused for a moment, gathering herself. "The Influence gave them what they asked for: Empaths – mages born with the ability to heal others with a simple touch." She held up a hand. "But what the mages didn't know was that the Influence gave the gift of healing in return for something equally precious." Her hand moved to her eyes.

Aaron's breath caught in his chest. The Influence was the reason Empaths were born blind.

"They took our sight," Armana continued. "They didn't say that was the price. They simply gave one ability, and took away another." She dropped her hands into her lap. "After that, the Elementals prohibited the use of the Influence. No matter what the reason, how desperate the need, no one is allowed to use the Influence."

"Has anyone tried since?" Aaron asked.

Armana shook her head. "There's no doubt in anyone's mind that the Influence will give you what you desire, but it will cost you more than you are willing to give." She stood up. "Take my advice, Aaron, let things be with your legacy. When it's ready, it will awaken itself."

***

It was the day after the draining full moon, that Armana gave in to Aaron's pleading. She let him out with strict instructions to sleep and rest. Aaron couldn't do either.

Jason Burns had arranged their stay in a cleaner, warmer and more inviting sanctuary cottage. Ever since Rose's outburst months before, Jason and a team of mages had worked tirelessly to renovate the green-doored cottages so they were more comfortable to the refugees who came seeking shelter.

Aaron, Sam and Rose took one room, Kate and Chris took another. Aaron waited until all of them fell asleep before slipping outside. He walked along the row of cottages, pausing briefly before the blue-doored cottage that had been his home for the four months he had spent in Salvador. It had been renovated, along with the rest of the buildings, after Kyran had set fire to them in a bid to escape.

Aaron walked down to his favourite spot in Salvador – the bank of the lake. The air was cool and refreshing. It whipped through his hair and ruffled his clothes. Aaron closed his eyes and relished the feeling of being out in the open. He remained like that until the sound of footsteps disturbed him.

For a fleeting, heart-jerking moment, Aaron thought it was Kyran. He had always found him sitting at this very spot. But even before Aaron opened his eyes and turned, he could tell it wasn't Kyran. The steps were distinctly different. The glow of the floating lanterns revealed the smirking form of Skyler, making his way over to Aaron, beer bottles in hand. Aaron swore under his breath and looked away, feeling all the tension that had seeped out return to hit him like a tidal wave. He clenched both hands into fists.

"I'm not in the mood to hear any of your crap, Skyler," he said. "Just go away."

The footsteps stopped next to him. Skyler sat down, settling the bottles before him.

"Seriously." Aaron turned to glare at him. "Why can't you leave me alone?"

Skyler grinned and uncapped one bottle. He turned to Aaron and held it out.

Aaron blinked at the offer.

"You look like you need it," Skyler said by way of an explanation.

Aaron didn't take it. He didn't put it past Skyler to spike his drink with something awful, even though he saw him open the bottle in front of him.

"Don't worry, it's the tame stuff," Skyler said.

Aaron still didn't move to take it.

Skyler placed the bottle next to Aaron and uncapped his own, bringing it to his mouth to take a large gulp.

They sat in silence. The only sound was the wind whistling through the trees. After a few minutes, Aaron couldn't take it.

"What are you doing here?" he asked. "What do you want?"

Skyler took a long drag from his bottle, blue eyes staring ahead. "I really thought you would do it," he said quietly. "When you reached out to take hold of the Blade, I thought you were going to rip that beauty right out of the ground." He shook his head. "But no. You got rejected."

Aaron's jaw clenched. "You know what, Skyler—"

"Hurts like hell, doesn't it?" Skyler interrupted. He turned his head to meet Aaron's furious eyes. "Feels like your insides are being torn out, like life itself is being sucked right out from your body and you can't do a thing to stop it."

Aaron's eyes widened. He gaped at Skyler, who seemed younger without his cold, cruel smirk present. The usual ice blue eyes were warmer, staring at Aaron with a quiet intensity. Then Skyler took another mouthful of his beer and looked away.

"I was about your age when I tried my family's Blade for the first time," Skyler said. His gaze was on the calm, dark water of the lake. "I was so sure I was ready. Neriah tried stopping me, told me I should wait, but I knew the legacy usually awakened the same time as the core. My core had been awake for a year, that was long enough." He shook his head, smiling sardonically. "I was knocked out for an entire day." He gestured with his bottle at Aaron. "Be thankful you woke up after a few hours."

Aaron was choked with surprise. He didn't know what to say. Skyler. Skyler Avira. The boy that walked around with so much pride it was a miracle his feet touched the ground. *That* Skyler Avira was rejected by his family's Blade.

Aaron opened his mouth to speak, but couldn't find the right words. He shook his head. "Why?" he asked at last. "Why are you telling me this?"

Skyler looked at him and smiled before shrugging. "Misery loves company, right?" He looked down at the ground. "I've never told anyone about the rejection, except Armana. Neriah knows, and Ella, of course. If it wasn't common for the Blades of Aric to only be used in extreme battles, everyone by now would be suspicious as to why I use a normal sword and not my family's Blade." He rubbed the bottle between his fingers. "Every year, on the day I get a step closer to coming of age, I go to the Blade of Avira and try to claim it." He dropped his head. "I wake up the next day, feeling hollowed out." He gave

Aaron a sideways glance. "You're the only one I know who's been through the same thing."

"You've done this five times?" Aaron asked. He could barely stomach being rejected once. He didn't think he had it in him to keep trying.

"I would do it a hundred times," Skyler replied, "if it meant that eventually, I get to wield one of Aric's Blades." His eyes remained fixed on something in the distance, the half empty bottle in his slack grip. "I'm the only Avira," he said quietly. "The mighty Blade of Avira is destined for me." He took in a deep breath and crossed his arms over his knees. "In four months my core will mature and with it, my legacy will finally awaken." He turned his head to look at Aaron. "Problem is, I don't know if we have four months. Hadrian's powers are unlocked; his core has fully recovered." He paused and Aaron saw the way his fingers curled tightly around the bottle. "When he comes, there's very little that will stand in his way."

"Sounds like you're giving up before the fight's even started," Aaron said.

Skyler snapped his head around to glare at him. "I'm not one to give up," he said quickly. "I'm not an *Adams*. I'll be standing at the front line."

"You won't be the only one," Aaron said. "I'm fighting too, with or without the Blade."

Skyler's eyes lit up and Aaron could almost swear there was pride radiating from him. "That's good to hear," he said before putting the bottle to his mouth and draining it.

"We can't use our family Blades, but Neriah has his, yeah?" Aaron asked.

Skyler nodded.

"So there's one Blade on either side," Aaron said. "Neriah and...and Kyran, both have their Blades of Aric."

Skyler shifted, his jaw tensed at the mention of Kyran. "The Blades won't fight each other," he said. "Aric created the four Blades to work together, not against one another." He let out a breath. "But the damage they can do is phenomenal. I think that's why Neriah was desperate for you to get your Blade. He knows I can't wield mine. He thought if you had yours, we would have two against Kyran's one."

"That's not fair," Aaron said.

Skyler raised an eyebrow. "No? You don't think that's fair?" He leant in towards Aaron. "Hadrian's a Fire Elemental. There's not much that can survive fire."

"Yeah, I know, but—"

"You think Hadrian's going to play it fair?" Skyler cut across him. "Mages can't kill vamages because they are part-mage, but vamages can kill us because they are part-demon. You think Hadrian won't use that to his advantage?"

"I just meant—"

"What?" Skyler snapped. "What did you mean, Adams?"

Aaron stared at him. The moment of vulnerability had passed. The Skyler sitting next to him had gone back to being the same short-tempered bully Aaron knew and despised.

"Let Hadrian fight the way he wants," Aaron said. "We should fight with integrity. Two swords against one isn't fair. If we play dirty too then what's the difference between vamages and mages?"

Skyler let out a harsh laugh. "I honestly don't know whether to get angry at your idiotic ideals or feel sorry for your naivety." He held Aaron's gaze. "This is war, Adams. You fight to win, no matter how you do it. Because what we're fighting for, we can't afford to lose."

20

PLANES OF EXISTENCE

The next morning, when Aaron, his parents and friends stepped out of the cottage, breakfast was already being served at the table in the middle of the street. Aaron looked around at the mages – ones he had befriended, ones he had hunted with. They were all sitting at the table amongst many new faces. It was easy to tell who the Hunters were. They were all kitted out in the usual attire of hooded tops, long coats and jeans. Tattoos were visible on the sides of their necks or wrists. Further down the table there was a large gathering of men and women in various coloured robes – Lurkers, Aaron realised.

Aaron felt strangely comforted by the familiar walk down the cobbled street to go and sit at the wooden table. He was surprised at how much he'd missed being in Salvador.

Jason Burns gave him his yellow-toothed smile as Aaron passed him. "Good tae see yeh, lil Adams," he greeted him.

"Good to see you too," Aaron smiled back.

Zhi-Jiya and Ryan looked up at him as Aaron approached. They went quiet, looking to Skyler for his reaction. Skyler kept his head down and worked through his plate of eggs and toast, ignoring Aaron. Ella kicked out a chair across from her, for Aaron to sit. Sam and Rose sat next to him. Kate and Chris found seats a little further down the table. Ryan waited another minute before giving in. He leant across the table.

"Good to see you're back," he said to Aaron with a grin.

Aaron wished he had come with the Blade of Adams in hand, instead of being rushed to the city while unconscious. He smiled at Ryan anyway and nodded his thanks. He caught sight of the blond-haired Mary, carrying platters of food from the Stove. Behind her were Alan and Ava, her kitchen helpers. Mary beamed at Aaron.

"How you feeling?" she asked as soon as she reached the table.

"Fine, thanks," Aaron replied.

Alan didn't say anything but he did give him a tight nod as he passed. Ava stopped beside him and reached over to put down the platter of toast and eggs on the table. "I'm glad you're okay," she whispered in his ear.

Aaron smiled and ducked his head. "Thanks."

After breakfast, the table was cleared. Alan was taking his time, gathering the dishes, giving Aaron an opportunity to come up to him.

"Hey," Aaron called.

"Hey," Alan replied quietly. He had always been friendly to Aaron, but when Aaron left Salvador, Alan hadn't been able to watch. He had walked away angrily. Now, he was struggling to meet Aaron's eyes. "I heard you got badly hurt," he said, talking to the edge of the table.

"I'm okay," Aaron said. "How are you?"

Alan shrugged. "Same old," he replied.

"You still mad at me?" Aaron asked.

Alan paused and turned to look at Aaron. "No," he said. "And I'm sorry, I didn't have any right to get angry. You can do what you like. Fight or not, it's your decision."

Aaron smiled. "That's not what you really believe, is it?"

Alan hesitated before replying, "It's what Ava's been telling me."

Aaron chuckled. "Well, if it's all the same to you, I'm going to fight."

Aaron had decided he wasn't leaving Salvador until he found a way to awaken his legacy. Even if that meant he had to use the forbidden Influence, then that's what he was prepared to do. Aaron would pay whatever penalty the Influence decided. It was worth it to have his legacy awake and active. Aaron had next to no idea how to actually go about contacting the Influence but he figured if it came down to it, he would find a way.

Alan looked surprised before smiling his usual wide grin. "Good to hear it," he said. He reached behind him and pulled out a small silver pistol. He showed it to Aaron. "So am I."

Aaron was stunned. "I thought you said you couldn't handle guns?"

"I'm learning," Alan replied. "But this isn't for hunting." His eyes were grim and determined. "The battle is about to start, Aaron. Every mage, Hunter or not, is needed if we're going to put up a decent defence against Hadrian."

Aaron didn't say anything. He looked back at the gun. "Have you been training with it?"

"Ryan's been teaching me," Alan replied.

"Whoa!"

Aaron turned to see Sam with Rose. Sam's eyes were on the gun. He looked up at Alan. "Is that in case someone burns the bread?"

Alan chuckled. "It does have to be baked to perfection."

"I thought you didn't want to be a Hunter?" Rose asked as she walked closer.

"He's not a Hunter," Aaron replied. He took the gun from Alan, feeling its slight weight in his hand. "He's training so he can fight against Hadrian."

Sam moved closer, staring at the pistol with curiosity. "What's that?" he asked, pointing to the intricate silver *TK* engraved in the side of the grip.

"It stands for Thomas Kings," Alan said. "This was my dad's gun."

"I thought you said your dad was a Lurker?" Rose asked.

"He was," Alan replied. "But Lurkers carry weapons too." He stared at the gun in Aaron's hand. "My mum kept this, after my dad...After he passed." He shifted uncomfortably. "I never thought I would use it, but after what happened, after finding out that Kyran–" He stopped abruptly. "I figured, now's the time."

Sam smiled. "Couldn't agree more," he said. He turned to Aaron. "Let me have a look."

Sam took the gun from Aaron and every mage in the vicinity stopped what they were doing.

"Sam, no," Alan said quickly. He had paled horribly, his eyes wide and fearful. He held out his hand. "Give it to me. Sam, give it to me!"

"What?" Sam asked, stunned. "What is it?"

"Put the gun down!" Alan cried.

"What is it?" Aaron asked. "What's wrong? He's only having a look."

"What are you doing?" Zhi-Jiya yelled from behind them. "Sam, put the gun down, now!"

"Easy, Sam," Ryan said, holding out both hands, as if Sam was about to shoot him. "Aim at the ground."

Sam stood as he was – stunned, staring from Zhi-Jiya to Alan.

From the crowd, Ella stormed forward, looking beyond furious. She strode up to Sam and swiped the gun from his weak grip. She held up a finger. "*Never* touch another gun, you understand me?"

"I wasn't going to fire it," Sam protested. "I was only having a look."

"Yeah?" Ella stepped forward so she was in his face. "A slip of yours would have killed one of us."

Sam blinked at her. "What?"

"You're human. We're mages," Ella said.

Understanding filled Aaron. Mages could be killed by any non-mage, humans included. Aaron looked to the gun gripped in Ella's hand. If Sam had accidentally set it off, he could have killed whoever he hit, providing it was a solid shot.

"If I see a gun anywhere near you again, Sam Mason, I swear on Aric's honour, I'll break both your hands." Ella glowered. "You hear me?"

Sam nodded. "Loud and clear."

Ella turned and flung the gun at Alan. "Keep your familiars on you, got it?" she snapped.

"Yes," Alan answered quickly.

Ella looked to Aaron. "Neriah wants to see you," she said, her voice still rough. She gave Sam another harsh look before turning to walk away.

Sam slowly turned to face Aaron before his face broke out in a smile.

"Did you see it?" he asked.

"Ella tearing you a new one?" Rose said. "Yeah, Sammy. We all saw it."

Sam shook his head, still grinning. "Her wrist. Did you see her wrist when she had her finger in my face?"

Aaron and Rose shared a look before shaking their heads.

Sam beamed. "She's still wearing the Waiting Bloom."

***

Aaron held up the small vial filled with a clear liquid. He studied it closely before looking over at Neriah. "What is it?"

"A helping hand," Neriah replied, setting a small clock onto the table by Aaron's bed. "It's nothing to worry about," he assured him. "This just helps you get to where you're going."

"And that's a higher plane of existence, right?" Aaron asked. "The thing is, I still don't understand what that means."

"You don't have to understand it," Neriah replied. "You just have to trust me."

Aaron didn't say anything. He glanced to Armana, who was already seated by the chair next to his bed.

"My mum and dad still out there?" Aaron asked, gesturing to the door.

"They never left," Armana replied. "They're insisting on coming inside to stay with you."

"Let them," Aaron said, "but only once I'm on my way. If they see me now they'll try to talk me out of doing this."

"If you want to awaken your legacy, then this is the only way," Neriah said, coming to stand at the foot of the bed. "Naina is the only one that can help you. She will tell you what you need to do."

"And just to confirm, this *Naina* isn't part of the Influence, right?" Aaron asked.

Neriah looked like he had been hit by lightning. "What?" he growled. "No! Why would you...? How do you even know what the Influence is?"

"I'm picking up on all things mage," Aaron replied coolly, hoping Armana would stay quiet and didn't look too guilty. "And I'm sorry if I insulted you, but I just wanted to see how desperate you are for me to use my Blade."

"I'll never be that desperate," Neriah said quietly, his eyes dark and furious. "Nothing good comes from the Influence, Aaron. Remember that."

Aaron nodded. After a moment or two he asked, "So, Naina? Who is she? Or should I be asking, *what* is she?"

"A different being," Neriah replied. "That's all you need to know." He held Aaron's eyes. "Are you ready?"

Aaron played with the vial in his hand. "Go through it once more."

Neriah let out a sigh and reached forward to hold on to the footrest of the bed. "You're getting nervous over nothing," he said. "You're going to drink what's in that vial and go to sleep. Armana is going to guide your spirit to another plane of existence, and no–" he held up a hand as Aaron opened his mouth– "that doesn't mean that you're – how did you put it? – oh yes, *technically* dead." He gave Aaron an annoyed look. "Really, Aaron, how could you think I was suggesting to kill you?"

Aaron shrugged. "You said *spirit*."

Neriah scowled at him and shook his head, before straightening up. "Once you get there, you have to look for Naina. She can help you with a way to awaken your legacy before your core matures. Hopefully she can tell you all you need to know before your time with her runs out and you wake up back here."

"How long did you say I had?" Aaron asked.

"Exactly one hour."

"That's not too bad," Aaron said.

"Time moves differently where you're going," Neriah explained. "It's going to feel mere minutes to you, so act fast."

Aaron nodded. He looked down at the vial in his hand. "Did you send Skyler to see Naina too?"

Neriah looked surprised. He stared at Aaron for a full minute before asking, "You know about his rejection?"

"He told me," Aaron said.

Neriah took a moment to reply. "No. Skyler didn't go to Naina."

"Why not?" Aaron asked.

"Naina chooses who to meet," Neriah said. He nodded to the vial. "So don't keep her waiting."

Aaron's palms felt sweaty as he uncapped the small bottle and lifted it up. He sniffed it first but it was odourless.

"What is this?" he asked.

"It's dewdrops taken from the petals of a special flower," Neriah said. "It'll help you fall asleep."

Aaron looked around at Armana who stood up and came to his side. She sat beside him on the bed, her soft fingertips brushed his arm as she searched for his hand. Aaron reached for her and held tight. He gave Neriah a last look before taking in a breath and bringing the vial to his lips. He downed the liquid. It tasted bitter and burned his throat. Grimacing, Aaron put the empty bottle onto the table next to his bed.

"Lie down," Armana instructed.

Aaron slid to lie flat on the soft mattress. His head felt fuzzy. His eyelids were already heavy. A tingle ran through his body, calming him. His hand was still in Armana's gentle grip.

"A word of warning," Neriah said quietly.

Aaron turned his head to look at him. "Now?" he asked incredulously. "You're warning me now?"

Neriah smiled. "Naina can be a little difficult," he said. "Be patient with her and no matter what, don't—"

Whatever it was Neriah didn't want Aaron to do or say, Aaron never got to find out, as his eyes slid shut and his mind went blank.

***

Aaron stood staring at the house at the end of the path. It looked exactly like he had last left it. His house. His home. The place he'd lived for fourteen years. Aaron reached out and pushed the small gate open and walked up the pathway. He looked over the fence to see Rebecca's garden, perfectly kept as always. Rebecca wasn't there, though. He turned to glance up and down the street. It was empty, not a soul in sight. That was odd, for the middle of the day.

Aaron reached the back door and turned the handle. It clicked open. He stepped into the empty kitchen. Everything was in its place, the worktops spotless, appliances gleaming. His mum kept a tidy house, but it had never been this pristine. Aaron closed the door behind him and walked across the kitchen and into the hallway.

He looked into the living room to see the frames on the mantelpiece, but they were empty. Not one of the photos his mum loved displaying were inside them. Aaron looked around the house. It was his home, yet it wasn't at the same time.

The sound of someone humming reached Aaron's ears. Aaron turned, feeling a flutter of nerves in his stomach. The sound was coming from upstairs. Letting out a slow breath, Aaron climbed the stairs. His bedroom door was partly open, the light on. Steeling himself, Aaron pushed the door wide.

A small girl, no older than five or six, sat in the middle of his room, playing with her doll's house, singing to herself. Aaron blinked at her, not expecting this. He glanced around the room – it was definitely his. There was his bed in the corner, his books stacked neatly on the bookcase, his collection of cars that he'd started from the age of four displayed proudly on his study desk. Yet amongst all his things sat this little girl in a pink frilly dress, complete with matching ribbons in her blond pigtails, playing with her dolls and doll's house.

She stopped her humming and looked up at Aaron with big blue eyes. She smiled sweetly.

"Hello," she greeted him.

"Hi," Aaron replied. "Um...I think...there's been a mistake."

"No mistake," the girl said as she went back to playing with her toys. "You've come to the right place."

Aaron walked into the room, looking at it with wide eyes. "What is this place?" he asked. Like the rest of the house, the room mimicked his bedroom, yet it clearly wasn't. His room had never been this tidy.

The little girl shrugged. "It's your doing," she said. "You wanted to come home."

Aaron knew this wasn't his home. Not really. His house was in the human realm. This place was on another plane of existence. He told himself to snap out of it. Neriah had warned him to act fast.

"I'm looking for Naina," Aaron said. "I was told to ask for her."

"By Neriah," the girl said. She turned to look at Aaron. "You've come to see what you can do to awaken your legacy."

Aaron stared at her with disbelief. "How did you...?" He narrowed his eyes. "You're...Naina?"

The girl smiled. "I am," she said. "And you're Aaron Adams." She gave Aaron a slow head-to-toe look before meeting his eyes. "But you're not who everyone thinks you are."

That snapped Aaron out of his shock. "What do you mean?"

The girl – Naina – went back to playing. "What do you think I mean?"

"I don't know, that's why I'm asking," he said, irritated.

Naina sighed and put down her dolls. "You are a web," she said.

"A what?" Aaron asked.

"A web," Naina repeated, as if that was a perfectly normal thing to say and Aaron was playing dumb.

Aaron stared at her. The miracle that could help him awaken his legacy, the being that lived on a higher plane of existence, the one Neriah was going on about, that Naina – was a little girl? Not only that, she was an annoying little girl who talked complete nonsense.

"Okay, look, I don't know what's going on," Aaron said, taking a step closer, "but I was sent here to find out how to awaken my legacy, so I can use my family's Blade to fight the war—"

"Do you want to fight the war?"

Aaron paused at the question. No one had asked him that. No one had asked if he *wanted* to fight. They were too busy arguing if he should or shouldn't.

Naina waited patiently for his answer, looking up at him with big, innocent blue eyes.

Aaron let out a breath and shook his head. "Honestly...I don't know," he said. "I don't particularly *want* to fight, but I can't sit back and not do anything either."

"Like your parents want you to," Naina said.

Aaron stilled. "How did you know that?"

The little girl giggled. "I know everything, Aaron. Your parents want you to stay away from the war, so you don't get hurt, like your brother did."

Aaron felt a shiver run through him.

"You want to fight," she continued. "You want to feel like a part of something, but you don't want to kill." She tilted her head, looking intently at him. "You want to help secure the realms, both the one you belong to and the one that was your home all your life."

Aaron nodded. "I do."

Naina stared at him before slowly shaking her head. "You shouldn't do it."

Aaron frowned. "What?"

"Listen to your parents," she said. "This war, it isn't for you." Her clear blue eyes fixed him to the spot. "You have another battle to fight, one that's much harder than this war. Focus on that, or you'll lose more than you can bear."

Aaron's heart was racing, his skin prickled with fear at the little girl's words.

"What do you mean?" he asked. "What other battle is there for me to fight?"

"You'll see," Naina said with a small smile. "Soon enough."

She picked up her dolls and started playing again. Aaron waited, but it seemed like she was ignoring him now. Aaron cleared his throat and stepped closer.

"Naina?"

The girl continued playing.

"I came to see if you could help me," Aaron said. "Whether it's the war or this...other battle you mentioned, the only way I stand a chance of winning is if I can use my family's Blade."

"So you want to awaken your legacy now?" Naina asked.

"Yes," Aaron said, with a relieved smile.

Naina stopped playing and took in a deep breath. "No," she said and started playing again.

Aaron's smile fell. "What? Why?"

"Because," she replied.

"Because what?" Aaron asked.

"Just because." Naina shrugged.

"That's not an answer!" Aaron snapped. "I thought you were supposed to help me."

"How can I help you?" Naina asked, pausing in her game to look at Aaron again. "You want what you can't have."

"What does that mean?" Aaron asked.

"You want to awaken your legacy," Naina said. "But to do that, you need to *have* the legacy in the first place."

Aaron stilled. Her words crashed inside his head.

"What?" he asked. "I don't...I don't have the legacy?" He stared at her with wide eyes. "How is that possible? I'm the only Earth Elemental of my generation. The legacy can't go to anyone else."

"The legacy is with its rightful holder," Naina replied. "Legacies choose the Elemental with the strongest core." She looked at Aaron. "Is your core strong, Aaron?"

Aaron faltered in his reply. He didn't consider himself a powerful mage. It had taken him countless tries before he could handle his powers. He still couldn't shoot straight, he couldn't move as fast as the other Hunters, and he had no clue how to work the air to eavesdrop the way other mages did.

"I'm working on it," Aaron said at last. "I'll train harder—"

"A strong core isn't achieved by training," Naina corrected. "A core becomes strong with confidence. Power comes with dedication, with passion, with a belief in what you're fighting for." She looked at Aaron with amusement. "Your core is weak because you lack that dedication. You're so confused, you don't even know which side to fight for."

Aaron was taken aback, his expression morphed to disgust. "I know what side I'm fighting for," he defended.

"Do you?" Naina asked.

"Yes!" Aaron snapped. "I'm fighting for what's right. I'm fighting for the mages, against Hadrian."

Naina stared at him in silence for a moment. Then she turned her doll's house around, so Aaron could see the inside the pink and white three-storey toy. What he saw wasn't the usual house layout with plastic staircases and miniature furniture in tiny rooms. There was just a hollow space, in which sat an image, like a hologram. Aaron felt his breath seize in his chest when he saw what the image was playing, again and again, on a loop.

It was the attack on the City of Balt, when Kyran had come with the vamages to rescue the vampire Layla. But the image was of him – Aaron – standing with Sam and Rose, lifting his gun and aiming at the mages instead of Kyran.

Aaron stared at it, watching himself repeatedly raise his gun and aim at the mages who were about to shoot Kyran.

"Who were you fighting for that day?" Naina asked, with such childish innocence it seemed she genuinely wanted a reply.

Aaron looked at her, but didn't have an answer.

"He–" Naina pointed at Kyran's image– "is not with the mages, despite being one himself. So if you are fighting for him, you're not fighting for the mages, you're fighting against them."

Aaron swallowed heavily. "I'm not – I'm not fighting for him," he said. "I just... He was outnumbered. I didn't want him getting hurt."

"Ask yourself why," Naina said.

"He's my friend," Aaron said, without thinking.

Naina smiled and shook her head. "He's not your friend, Aaron."

Her words hit Aaron hard, like a physical kick to the gut, leaving him pained and breathless.

Naina turned the house around, facing it towards herself again. "Figure out where your loyalty lies," she said. "The day you do, your core will find its strength and the legacy will come to you."

Aaron shook his head, stepping forward. "I know where my loyalty lies," he said. "I want to help Neriah fight against Hadrian, but to do that, we need the Blades of Aric."

Naina was ignoring him and playing with her dolls again.

Aaron took in a breath to keep calm and not lose his temper. "*Please*," he stressed. "Help us. Help me get my legacy so I can use my Blade. We need the power of Aric's Blades to defeat Hadrian."

Naina stopped and stared at Aaron with serious eyes. "Nothing is more powerful than blood," she said. "You mages never seem to understand that."

Aaron opened his mouth to reply when the lights in the room flickered all of a sudden. Aaron looked up, as did Naina.

"That's strange," she said. "It's not time yet."

"Time for what?" Aaron asked.

Naina looked at him with a confused frown. "For you to leave."

Aaron didn't get any other warning. In a heartbeat, the ground was snatched from under his feet and Aaron was pulled back, yanked harshly out of the room. He sat up with a start, gasping for breath, back in the Empath hut in Salvador. Armana's hand slipped out of his. Aaron tried looking around the room, but his eyes felt heavy with sleep, his vision blurred. He made out his mum, standing by his side, holding on to his shoulder and arm. His dad was helping Armana off the bed and into a chair.

"Aaron?" his dad called. "You okay?"

"Aaron?" It was Ella, standing at the foot of his bed. "Hurry up, we need to go."

"What–?" Aaron asked, feeling groggy and disorientated.

"We don't have a lot of time," Ella said. "We need to leave."

There was an urgency in her voice. Aaron forced himself to snap out of his confusion. He blinked and looked around the room, at his anxious and petrified parents and a pale-faced Ella. "What's going on?" he asked.

"The Gates are being attacked," Ella said. "It's begun."

21

THE BLADE OF AVIRA

"Where's Neriah?" Aaron asked, as he hurried out of the Empath hut after Ella. His parents rushed out behind him.

"He's assembling the Hunters," Ella replied. "Lurkers have sent word. The Gates that protect the Blades have been targeted. The one that protects the Blade of Avira has just fallen. We need to get there and protect the Blade before Hadrian's vamages get to it."

Aaron didn't need to look to his parents. He already knew they were terrified at the prospect of him going to a vulnerable spot. If the Gate protecting the Blade of Avira had fallen, then it stood to reason that vamages could be in that vicinity. Maybe they had already got to the Blade.

"I don't understand," Aaron said, jogging to catch up with Ella. "Even if the vamages get to the Blade, they can't take it. Only legacy holders can touch their Blades."

"They can't touch it," Ella agreed, "but they can make sure that we don't either. We need to get to the Gate and secure it, before the vamages set up their defence."

Aaron spotted the swarm of Hunters gathered at the Gate of Salvador. Old, young, male, female, some with swords, others with guns – they all marched to line up in front of the Gate.

Skyler appeared at Ella's shoulder, wearing his ivory coat with his elemental mark studded in silver on the back. "Scott's set the portal," he said. "We're ready to go." He looked at Aaron with narrowed blue eyes. "You know what you're doing, Adams?"

Under normal circumstances, Aaron would have taken his words as nothing more than a jibe. But right now, Aaron knew his words weren't said to be demeaning – right now, he was being genuine.

"Yeah," Aaron replied, speaking past the tension coiled in his throat. "I've to help set up the fallen Gate."

Ella had rushed through an explanation while Aaron gathered his bearings after being abruptly pulled out of his meeting with Naina. The Gates had initially been set up by Neriah and Skyler, two legacy holders, but Hadrian was now targeting them. Being the third legacy holder, Aaron's input into rebuilding the Gate would make it more resilient to any future attacks.

The only problem was that Aaron wasn't the legacy holder. He was an Elemental and while having Elementals set up the Gate still made it powerful, it was nothing compared to one set up by legacy holders.

The worry clouding Skyler's eyes lifted and amusement replaced it. He elbowed Ella and pointed at Aaron. "The kid is finally picking up on how to play the game." He winked at Aaron before hurrying through the crowd to get to the front. Ella followed after him.

Aaron chased after them, but not so that he could be at the front when the Gate opened. His desire to reach the front line was for something else entirely. He needed to get to Neriah and tell him that he wasn't the legacy holder. The legacy was still with his dad. The leader of the mages had to know what Aaron had learnt from Naina.

Aaron still didn't want to believe it. He was the only Earth Elemental of his generation. He was supposed to get the legacy when he turned thirteen and his core awoke. But he had lived a life oblivious to his powers and to who he really was – *what* he really was. Perhaps that was partly the reason why his legacy remained with his dad and had not passed to him. He lacked the passion to hunt. He didn't have confidence in himself, in his powers. How could he, when he'd only learnt a few months before that he was an Elemental mage? But what Aaron didn't want to admit was what Naina had said to him about Kyran. He shook his head, even as he pushed his way through the crowd. He wasn't on Kyran's side. He wasn't fighting for him. He was on the good side, on the side of the mages. But no matter how many times he repeated it, a small part of him failed to fully believe it.

Aaron spotted Neriah, standing in front of the Gate. He looked tense, his violet eyes scanned the crowd with quiet intensity. To his right was Scott, watching his Hunters gather with worried eyes. Aaron could only imagine what Scott was feeling right now. He was the Controller, the Hunters were his responsibility. Aaron could tell from Scott's drawn and pinched face how terrified he was to send his Hunters out into a fight he'd not had the time to prepare for.

Aaron stepped past the line of Hunters to go to Neriah's side. A hand grabbed his arm, stopping him.

"Where are you going?" Skyler asked.

"I have to talk to Neriah," Aaron replied.

"Not now you don't," Skyler said.

Aaron turned just as Neriah raised his hands and commanded a hush across the gathered Hunters.

"We are going today to secure the Blade of Avira," he said. "The portal is ready and waiting for us past this Gate." His eyes swept the crowd. "The Lurkers have not reported it, but Hadrian might be waiting for us."

The name cast a strange effect through the crowd of Hunters. Some tensed, their grips tightening on their familiars, others squared their shoulders, ready for the fight.

"If you cross his path," Neriah continued, "do not attack him."

Aaron looked at him with surprise.

"Leave Hadrian to me," Neriah said and his voice alone told how severe this command was. "Same if you see the Scorcher."

Now Aaron felt unease wash through him. Would Kyran be there? Was he the one who destroyed the Gate? Could he have taken down what Neriah and Skyler had set up? Aaron figured the answer could very well be yes.

"Let's go out there and show Hadrian how strong we really are," Neriah said. "Let's show him that in unity lies true power!"

The Hunters and surrounding mages cheered and gave loud hoots of approval. Aaron felt two people come to stand on either side of him. He looked to see his mum and dad, standing shoulder to shoulder with him.

Scott stepped forward as Neriah turned to face the Gate, ready to lead them out. The Gate slid open at Scott's command and the Hunters rushed forward, ready to fight, ready to protect.

Aaron felt his dad hold on to his hand, stopping him from moving with the crowd. Aaron turned to face him. Chris didn't say anything, but stared at Aaron with a grim expression, before holding out Aaron's set of familiars and holsters.

***

Aaron stepped out of the portal onto dry, cracked land. He surveyed his surroundings, but it was little more than a landscape of barren ground. Dust kicked up in swirls as he and the Hunters followed after Neriah. This was the closest portal Scott could have opened; any closer and the Blade would have swallowed the energy.

They hurried across the empty ground. Aaron had to shield his eyes from the sun's fierce glare, but he couldn't see anyone around them, vamage or otherwise. Looking around again, Aaron couldn't even spot the Blade they had come to protect.

Neriah came to a sudden standstill, staring at something on the ground. Craning his head to look past the crowd of Hunters, Aaron caught a glimpse of what it was. A rectangular stump, protruding from the ground. That was all that was left of the Gate that once protected the Blade of Avira.

Neriah raised his head and marched forward with a purpose. Skyler raced to the front, matching Neriah's pace. They walked on for several tense minutes. Guns and swords were held in tight grips, but there was no one to fight. Aaron looked to his dad but he was busy searching the area with narrowed green eyes. His mum was holding his hand, seemingly not ready to let go.

They continued walking in a tight crowd across the barren ground. The heat was fast becoming unbearable as the sun beat down on them. Hot air blew across their faces and through their hair. Aaron could feel sweat gather under his collar. He wanted to stop and take off his coat, and maybe his top too, but he couldn't bring himself to pause. The crowd of Hunters was following after Neriah with quick, hurried steps.

Aaron's breath very soon became laboured. His chest felt tight, and more than once he felt the need to slow down to a stop. He pushed on. The wind bellowed in Aaron's ears, yet he couldn't feel much air on his sweat-soaked skin. His shoulders felt heavy and sore, his feet struggling to lift and fall.

It took Aaron a moment to recognise the sensation and understand what it meant. They were getting close to the Blade.

The fierce wind whipped through their hair and long coats. A constant roar was in the air, deafening them to all other sounds. It was only when they got to the edge that Aaron realised they were on a cliff. They formed a line, staring at what lay below.

A whirlwind. A spectacular, vertical rotating column of air stemmed from the ground. It was a magnificent phenomenon, glittery white and grey, spinning around and around. Never in his life, did Aaron think it was possible to see something so beautiful and yet equally terrifying.

From their viewpoint, Aaron and the others could see into the eye of the spinning vortex and what lay there was just as breathtaking.

The Blade of Avira hovered in mid-air, nestled in the womb of the whirlwind. Even from a distance, Aaron could see the Blade had markings carved into the silver of the sword, just like the Blade of Adams.

It took Aaron a few tries before he managed to pull his gaze away. As he turned his head, he caught sight of Skyler. Aaron could read the longing on Skyler's face, as he stood staring at his family's Blade. If there was anyone Aaron knew that was strong-willed, confident and dedicated to fighting demons, it was Skyler. So why wasn't his legacy awake yet? What more did Skyler have to do to claim his birthright?

Ella was saying something to her uncle, but it was impossible to hear past the tremendous noise the whirlwind was making. Neriah lifted his hand and gestured to the Hunters to move back. They all gathered in a tight circle, a short distance away from the edge.

"There's no one here!" Ella had to yell at Neriah. "Should we just set up the Gate and leave?"

Neriah shook his head. "This isn't right!" he said. "The Gate was destroyed. There must be something here!"

Aaron gave the surroundings another sweeping glance. He couldn't see anyone.

"Neriah!" Skyler called. "The Blade is safe! We should set up the Gate and leave, before something *does* get in!"

"Too late," Ryan said, before raising his gun.

Aaron turned with the rest of them to see what Ryan was aiming at. Climbing over the edge of the cliff were things Aaron struggled to make sense of right away. They looked like neither man nor beast, but something in-between.

Whatever they were, they were an ugly creation. They were short and squat, their skin thick and a sickly yellow. They had broad, flat noses and wide mouths. Their pointy ears stuck outwards. They were dressed in only trousers, made from animal hide. Thick leather bands of their sword holsters crossed their chests. The stench coming from them was enough to make Aaron gag.

"Dammit!" Aaron heard Zhi-Jiya say next to him. "Orcs."

A moment passed in which no one moved. The mages stared at the army of Orcs that had crawled over the edge of the cliff, just as they stared back with cold black eyes. One of the Orcs, a nasty-looking one with teeth that stuck out from his lower jaw, reached behind for his curved sword. That's when Neriah raised his gun and shot a bullet straight into the beast's chest. The Orc staggered back before reaching with thick fingers to touch its chest, where the bullet had struck the surface. Its leathery skin was like armour, which blocked Neriah's bullet.

A moment of complete silence passed before the army of Orcs swung their swords high above their heads and came at them with a loud battle wail.

The Hunters spread out, guns locked and aimed. Aaron's hand found his pistol, tucked safely in the holster at his side, when his mum and dad stepped in front of him, shielding him. As one, the Hunters fired at the approaching Orcs, but it only seemed to slow them down, not kill them. The Hunters darted in different directions, forcing the Orcs to segregate into smaller groups to fight them. The few Hunters that carried swords pulled them out. The clang of metal hitting metal rang in the air as the Hunters deflected the attacks of the Orcs.

Aaron had his gun in hand, but his parents gave him no opportunity to fight. Both Chris and Kate stood before him, firing at the Orcs that got too close. It took more than a few bullets to get through the Orcs' tough, armoured skin, but when they did, the Orcs fell to the ground dead.

When Chris ran out of bullets, the Orcs took their chance to attack. They swung their swords and all three Adams had to duck to avoid them. Kate continued shooting but Chris pulled out his sword. With a well-aimed swipe, Chris made one Orc fall back, a thin red line across its torso.

It didn't stay back for long. Joined by another six, the group of Orcs charged forward. Three Orcs went for Chris, easily drawing him away from Kate and Aaron. Another three Orcs leapt at Kate with their curved swords, even as she continued to fire at them. They swung their blades and Kate was forced to move out of the way. That left one Orc with a direct path to Aaron.

The Orc let out a gruff grunt before darting towards him. Aaron moved back, his gun in hand. He fired and the bullet just missed the Orc's ear. The beast let out a disgruntled roar and charged at him.

Aaron dived under its arm and turned around before shooting three more bullets. All were easily dodged by the Orc, who moved faster than Aaron thought possible. Aaron shot again and again, all the while moving back. The Orc got closer and closer. Usually, at this point, Aaron would discard the gun and use his powers. He would have thrown a ripple at the enemy, blasting them metres away, but the presence of the Blade had already sapped his power from him, leaving him vulnerable and defenceless without his weapons.

Aaron pulled the trigger and his gun clicked. Horror filled him as he realised he had run out of bullets. Aaron didn't have the time to waste on it. He tossed the gun away and pulled out a throwing knife from his belt. He saw the glint in the Orc's eyes as it surveyed Aaron's choice of weaponry and dismissed it. It slashed its sword through the air and Aaron had to jump back to avoid being sliced in half.

Flicking his wrist just like he had been taught, Aaron threw the knife. It spun in the air before hitting the Orc in the chest. The beast paused for a moment before wrenching the knife out and dropping it to the ground. But in that time, Aaron had another three blades in hand. He threw each one at the approaching Orc until the beast swayed on its thick, clumsy feet. Aaron pulled out another two blades but just as he raised his arm to throw them, a flash of silver – quick as lightning – grazed his arm.

Aaron dropped the knives and staggered back with a hiss, clutching his bleeding arm. He turned to look to the side where the attack came from, and saw another Orc grunting at him, sword in hand. Aaron threw himself to the ground to avoid the swing of its blade. By the time Aaron clambered to his feet, a third Orc had joined the first two. Aaron's hand groped his belt for another blade but he couldn't find one. The Orcs were moving towards him, forcing Aaron to step back.

The continuous rumble, that reminded Aaron of a freight train, got louder as he neared the edge of the cliff. Tremendous wind whipped at his back, ruffling his hair and clothes. Aaron knew he was cornered. He had nowhere to go. Another step back and he would fall off the cliff. The three Orcs knew it too, as they paused briefly to grin at Aaron with mouthfuls of sharp, pointy teeth.

Aaron didn't have any more weapons and his powers wouldn't work being so close to one of Aric's Blades. Aaron's panic made it impossible to think, to figure out what he should do. He didn't dare look away from the Orcs to search for his parents, for Neriah. The Orcs came at Aaron as one, swinging their swords high above their heads. Instinct made Aaron raise his hands to shield himself.

A loud clang resonated in the air as the swords hit a pair of crossed ones. Aaron lowered his hands, staring at the boy that had stepped in front of him to protect him from the Orcs. Aaron didn't need to see his face to know who it was. Even the long red coat with an inverted V studded in silver on the back wasn't needed. Aaron knew with one glance – it was Kyran.

Aaron stood rooted to the spot in sheer disbelief, as Kyran held back the Orcs with his twin swords. Kyran's shoulders lifted and he threw the Orcs back with a mighty push. With a sword in each hand, Kyran battled the demons, easily disarming them. He stabbed one and kicked the other before slashing his sword across the Orc's torso. He swung both swords up and back to impale the third Orc behind him. With all three Orcs dead and on the ground, Kyran turned to meet Aaron's surprised eyes.

Being this close to the whirlwind, Aaron wouldn't have heard anything Kyran said, but Kyran's lips didn't move other than to curl upwards into a smile. He winked at Aaron and turned, twisting both bloodstained swords in his hands before heading to the heart of the battle.

That's when Aaron noticed that Kyran wasn't the only newcomer – vamages were also there. Everywhere Aaron looked, all he saw were dark-clothed vamages, attacking the Orcs with their swords and guns. The mages looked thrown – Aaron saw Ryan and Omar pause to stare, their eyes as wide as their open mouths, before recommencing their battle against the Orcs.

Amongst the Hunters, Aaron saw his mum. She met his eyes with horror and he saw her scream his name, although he couldn't hear it. Her terror snapped Aaron out of his stunned daze and he realised he was just standing there, at the edge of the cliff, defenceless. He swooped down and picked up one of the fallen Orcs' curved blades. It was so heavy, Aaron had to use both hands to lift it up.

He hadn't acted a moment too soon. An Orc came charging at him, forcing Aaron to raise the sword and block the attack. The force of the hit almost made Aaron's knees buckle. He felt the clang run down his arms, spiking pain in his shoulders. The Orc pulled back and swung again. Aaron dodged this time and ducked to the side. The missed strike made the Orc tumble forward and fall clean off the edge of the cliff.

Aaron stood up to find his mum at his side and quickly grabbing hold of his arm. She pulled him away from the edge, her gun in hand, but the Orcs were busy fighting the vamages. Aaron couldn't help but stare at the strange sight of mages and vamages working together to fight another demonic army. The vamages and mages put together easily outnumbered the hideous Orcs. Aaron spotted the blue-eyed vamage – Machado – slicing his way through a crowd of Orcs. A short distance away, Neriah was doing the same.

Kate guided Aaron back to Chris and his parents stood on either side of him, protecting him. But Aaron's gaze was on Kyran, watching him battle the Orcs in quick, smooth moves. He ducked the retaliating attacks with practised ease, swinging both swords, catching any and all Orcs that got too close. Across from him, Skyler was dealing out similar damage, firing his gun with one hand and swinging his sword in the other.

Both boys met the other's eye and their fighting increased with vigour. Kyran was slowly making his way through the crowd, dropping the growling beasts to the ground. Skyler was doing the same, until one Orc caught him, knocking the sword out of his hand. Skyler ducked before pulling out his second gun and firing a stream of bullets into the Orc.

Kyran fought the onslaught of Orcs, stabbing one of his blades into an Orc and leaving it there, pulling out his pistol instead. He fired shot after shot, halting the approaching Orcs before swinging his other sword to cut through them.

Both Kyran and Skyler got closer and closer, until they were but a metre apart. Kyran plunged his sword into the last Orc before twisting around and pulling out his second pistol. Skyler shot down his last Orc and raised both guns to aim at Kyran, just as he swerved around to face Skyler with his twin pistols locked and aimed right back at him.

Watching them, Aaron wasn't sure which one would pull the trigger first. But before either boy acted, a large crowd of Orcs came charging at them, from both sides. Kyran and Skyler shared a look before both turned around simultaneously and began firing at the Orcs. Standing back to back, Kyran and Skyler sent bullet after bullet into the Orcs, dropping them to the ground.

Aaron watched as the two Elementals easily fought the crowd of Orcs, not allowing even one to get close enough to attack. They slipped empty magazines out and replaced them with fully loaded ones in the blink of an eye. The popping sound of gunshots filled the air against the background rumble of the whirlwind. Aaron was vaguely aware of his parents joining the fight, firing shots at the Orcs, but his eyes stayed on Kyran and Skyler.

The crowd of Orcs had thinned, leaving bloodied bodies on the ground. Kyran and Skyler floored the last of the Orcs attacking them and immediately turned around, their guns once again aimed at each other.

For the longest time, neither boy did or said anything.

Then Skyler started in his usual drawl. "You know, I would have thought you'd have used better demon scum as a diversion than Orcs," he said to Kyran. "I'm disappointed with your creativity, Scorcher."

Kyran smirked. "You think I let them in?"

"You dropped the Gate," Skyler accused. "You knew we would come, so you let this filth in to distract us."

Kyran laughed. "Is that so?" he asked. "So tell me, Skyler, if I'm the one who let the Orcs in, why am I here fighting them?"

"You double-crossed them," Skyler replied. "It's in your blood, after all."

Kyran's eyes darkened but his smirk was firmly in place. "You don't know anything about my blood," he said. Then, with a shake of his head, he added, "I didn't drop the Gate."

"Then what are you doing here?" Skyler asked.

"The same thing you are," Kyran said. "I'm here to protect Aric's Blade."

Skyler bristled at the mention of the sword. "Protect it? You want to protect the Blade from its rightful holder?"

Kyran smiled and his eyes seemed to brighten. "Alright then, legacy holder. Why don't you go down there and take the mighty Blade in hand? What are you still doing up here?"

Skyler smirked. "I don't need the Blade of Avira to deal with the likes of you."

Kyran chuckled. "What you need is to wake up and see the lies you've been fed."

Skyler let out a scathing laugh. "So says the master of lies."

Kyran smirked. "I never lied. I just made sure you lot asked all the wrong questions." He tilted his head and surveyed Skyler with great amusement. "I'll admit, though, I enjoyed making an idiot out of you. Not that it took that much effort."

"What about Zulf?" Skyler asked.

Kyran's smile fell.

"Did you enjoy making an idiot out of him too?" Skyler asked. "He was supposed to be your friend. I actually believed you gave a crap about him." He shook his head slowly. "You sabotaged that Q-Zone. You're the reason it wouldn't lock." His gaze was an icy blue. "You got Zulf killed."

"I had *nothing* to do with that," Kyran spat and the guns in his hands shook with his anger.

"What would Zulf have thought if he were alive to see who you really are?" Skyler asked. "I guess you did care about Zulf in your own twisted way. You killed him before he could see your truth and be disappointed in—"

Skyler was cut off when Kyran pulled back and swung his pistol at Skyler, knocking him bodily aside. Skyler staggered but regained his balance almost immediately. He turned and fired, aiming at Kyran's head. Kyran dived out of the way and the battle that had come to a standstill started back with vigour.

Aaron realised then, that all the while Skyler and Kyran were talking, the fight between the mages, vamages and remaining Orcs was still going on. His mum and dad were still by his side, but their guns were lowered, their eyes on Kyran too, watching his fight with Skyler.

Kyran twisted out of the way of Skyler's bullets, retaliating with his own shots, which Skyler dodged.

"You made a mistake coming here!" Skyler called to Kyran. "You're not leaving today."

"Why?" Kyran asked. "You want me to stay for a sleepover?"

Skyler shot three times, all of which Kyran dodged with a smile.

"You're dead, Scorcher," Skyler threatened. "I'm going to kill you myself."

"Then I hope you brought a bullet with my name on it," Kyran replied. "That's the only way *you* can kill *me*."

It was Skyler's turn to smirk. "Believe me. I'll be the one to shoot you between the eyes with a personalised bullet!"

Kyran chuckled. "Big aspirations for an Avira."

Skyler lost it and shot with both guns. His anger cost him his aim and Kyran easily avoided the attack.

Their duelling had led them to the other side of the cliff. As Aaron watched, Skyler got closer and closer, driving Kyran nearer to the edge. Aaron found himself reaching to his empty holster, looking for his gun. Naina's words, spoken not more than an hour or two before, came back to him.

He is not with the mages, despite being one himself. So if you are fighting for him, you're not fighting for the mages, you're fighting against them.

Right now, Aaron found he didn't care about sides. He just didn't want Kyran getting hurt.

But before he could do anything, it looked like Skyler had run out of bullets, because he threw down one of his guns. The next moment, he tackled Kyran, throwing himself at the other boy. Aaron could only watch in horrified disbelief as Skyler knocked into Kyran – and both boys fell over the edge of the cliff, disappearing from sight.

22

Secrets

Aaron found himself running, bolting towards the edge of the cliff where Kyran and Skyler had gone over.

He heard his mum and dad calling his name, hot at his heels, but he didn't stop. A few others had left the dwindling battle with the Orcs and were also racing to the edge to see what happened to the two duelling Elementals.

The sound of the whirlwind holding the Blade of Avira deafened Aaron as he got closer to the edge. Adrenaline pumped inside him, his heart hammered against his ribcage and his mouth went dry at the thought of Kyran dead.

The moment Aaron got close enough to the spot from which Kyran and Skyler fell, he saw, with tremendous relief, a steep hill leading all the way down. There was even a dusty pathway, allowing a person to climb down from the cliff to the ground below. Aaron caught sight of Kyran and Skyler at the bottom, picking themselves up after their tumbling fall.

Aaron's parents, Ella, Ryan and a few other Hunters gathered around Aaron, breathing sighs of relief at the sight of Skyler on his feet. The moment the two boys had straightened up, they had their guns aimed at each other again, though apparently Kyran had lost one in the fall.

Aaron saw Ella take Ryan by the arm to get his attention. She pointed to the hill before moving towards it. Ryan followed after her, climbing down the steep incline with the rest of the mages surging after him, all going to Skyler's aid. Aaron moved too but was quickly grabbed by his mum. Aaron pulled his arm free, turning to stare at her with fierce eyes. He shook his head, signalling he wasn't going to stop, before climbing down the hill, pursued by his dad and mum.

They were almost at the bottom when Aaron looked across to see Kyran and Skyler, standing impossibly close to the ferocious whirlwind. The wind was so strong, it bellowed through their hair and made the ends of their coats flap like frantic wings.

Both Kyran and Skyler stood facing each other's gun, but neither fired a shot. Then, to everyone's surprise, Kyran dropped his pistol. Aaron could see Skyler's frown. Even he was thrown by the strange action. For a heartbeat, Aaron thought Kyran was surrendering, seeing as he was about to be surrounded by Hunters.

Then Kyran smirked and his eyes darkened. His hand shot outward, towards the spiralling vortex of air. From the depth of the whirlwind, the Blade of Avira flew out and landed in Kyran's hand.

The whirlwind died instantly, leaving a deafening silence in its wake.

Aaron's breath choked in his chest. He stared at Kyran, waiting for him to drop the sword and clutch his hand, screaming in pain. But it never happened. Kyran stood with the Blade of Avira in his grip. The magnificent sword gleamed in the light, the engraved symbols shone brightly, as if lit by the glow of the moon itself.

Every eye was on Kyran, staring in utter disbelief. The Hunters climbing down the hill had come to a standstill. Kyran was wielding the Blade of Avira, despite not being an Avira himself. How was that possible? Why hadn't the Blade rejected him?

Everyone's surprise was evident in their open mouths and wide eyes, but the one whose shock was palpable was Skyler. He staggered forward a step, his eyes filled with indignant rage, his gun lowered in his stupor.

"How?" he roared. "How are you holding *my* Blade?"

Kyran smirked and gave the sword a playful twist in his hand.

"This?" he asked with exaggerated innocence. "Is this yours?" His smile was vicious and cruel. "Then come and get her, Avira, if you can *handle* her."

Skyler lost it. He dived for Kyran, his pistol aimed once again.

"Sky, NO!" Ella screamed but it was too late.

Kyran pulled back his arm and swung the Blade. A burst of energy, that held the power of a mighty hurricane, exploded around Kyran, knocking everyone back. Aaron was actually propelled into the air before he came tumbling down to land at the foot of the hill. The fall knocked the breath out of him. The rest of the Hunters landed in a heap around him, along with Aaron's parents.

Aaron turned his head to see Skyler had been thrown halfway across the clearing. Aaron looked back at Kyran, who stood there with the Blade in hand. His green eyes were on something on top of the cliff. Craning his neck, Aaron followed his line of sight to see Neriah and the rest of the Hunters, standing at the edge, gaping at Kyran.

Kyran held out the sword for all to see and recognise.

"Your lies are starting to unravel, Neriah!" he called. "It's time you told everyone the truth!"

The Hunters around Neriah aimed their guns at Kyran. A swipe of the mighty Blade and the crowd were thrown back by the force of a tornado. Many scrambled forward on their hands and knees, guns in shaky hands, and tried to take aim again. But it was no use. Kyran was gone. A moment later, so were the vamages.

***

"What the hell is going on?"

Skyler was beside himself. He had a nasty-looking cut on his temple, which leaked a thin trail of blood down the side of his face, but he didn't even seem to realise it. He was lost in his anger, demanding answers from the oldest Elemental, as they all were once again gathered at the clifftop.

"How can he wield *my* Blade?" Skyler thundered.

"Sky, calm down," Ella said, reaching out for him.

Skyler pushed her away, his fury-filled eyes on Neriah. "He *took* my *Blade*! That sword is mine by birthright. How the hell can he touch it and not have the power drained out of him?"

Neriah stood in silence, head dropped and eyes narrowed. He was working things out in his mind, completely ignoring Skyler and the shell-shocked crowd that had gathered around him.

"Neriah!" Skyler cried. "Answer me! What's going on?"

Neriah raised his head at last and looked over at Skyler. He took in a deep breath.

"We have to set up the Gate," he said. "We'll talk once we get back—"

"NO!" Skyler raged. "We'll talk here! Right now!"

"Sky." Ella grabbed his arm in a tight grip. "Get a hold of yourself."

Skyler didn't fight to get free. His eyes didn't waver from Neriah. The usually cold, arrogant and proud Skyler Avira was close to breaking point, and as much as Aaron had once wanted to see Skyler knocked down a peg or two, he found he couldn't stand the sight of him like this.

Neriah glanced to the crowd of Hunters around them. "We need to set up the Gate," he repeated. "The rest of you keep watch, in case we get any more unwanted guests."

The crowd obediently moved away. Kate shared a look with her husband but followed the rest of the Hunters, leaving only Chris, Aaron, Skyler and Ella with Neriah.

Skyler pulled his arm out of Ella's grip. "How did he do it?" he asked.

"Why are you demanding answers from him?" Ella asked angrily. "What makes you think Neriah knows what's going on?"

"He knows," Skyler said, talking to Ella but his bloodshot eyes stayed on Neriah. "He knows what's going on. I can see it." He stepped forward, even when Ella tried to pull him back. "Tell me," he said to Neriah. "Just tell me what's going on. How can he take my Blade without the legacy?"

"He can't," Neriah replied.

Skyler fell silent, blue eyes wide.

"Then how did he do it?" Ella asked, looking as lost as Aaron felt.

Neriah kept his gaze on Skyler and with every passing second, the violet eyes grew more solemn. "Kyran can't have wielded the Blade of Avira without the legacy for Air," he said quietly.

Aaron watched as understanding fell over Skyler, making him choke and stagger back a step.

"He...He has my legacy?" Skyler asked.

Neriah didn't answer, but there was no need. The sheer grief and guilt on his face gave the answer for him.

"How?" Skyler asked and it looked like the shock was either going to kill him or make him go mad. "How can...What the *hell* is going on?"

"This doesn't make any sense," Ella said.

"Why does that son of a demon have my legacy?" Skyler cried.

Neriah shook his head. "Skyler, I don't–"

"Tell him, Neriah," Chris interrupted.

Everyone stopped and turned to look at him, but Chris was staring at Neriah, his expression sombre and pained. "He has a right to know," he said quietly.

Skyler looked between Chris and Neriah, clearly shocked that Chris – the Elemental missing from their world for nearly the last decade and a half – knew what was going on when he didn't.

"Tell me what?" Skyler asked, and now Aaron could see the fear on him.

Neriah was staring past Skyler, holding Chris's eyes. For a heartbeat, no one spoke. They just stood in tense silence. Then Neriah closed his eyes with a defeated sigh.

"He's right," he breathed. "You have the right to know what's going on, Skyler." He looked at Skyler, Ella and then Aaron. "But what I'm about to tell you stays within the Elemental circle."

Aaron and Ella nodded, but Skyler stood rigid with tight fists at his side.

Neriah took a moment before turning to look at Skyler. "Kyran has your legacy," he said, "because Hadrian took it from James before he killed him."

Skyler reacted like someone had hit him. He flinched back, eyes wide and filled with disbelief.

"That's impossible!" Ella fought back. "You can't force anyone to give up their legacy. And Hadrian already had his own legacy. An Elemental can only have power over *one* of the elements."

Neriah smiled but it was filled with bitter pain.

"Yes," he said quietly. "An Elemental can have full power over only one element. Mages can use all four elements but there is only one they have a strong affinity for. We can't have full control over all four elements. It's not possible, since Aric the Great, married a human, and rendered his offspring with this disadvantage. Our humanity is our weakness. And so on and so on." He looked from Ella to Skyler. "That's what we all believe. These are the facts that we are taught, the rules we are brought up with." He closed his eyes and slowly shook his head. "It's not true." His words were whispered but they rang in everyone's ears. "None of it is true."

Ella stepped forward, looking confused and scared. "Neriah, what are you saying?"

"What you're hearing," Neriah replied. "Our foremother was a human. We have always thought that was the reason mages can't have full control of all four elements." He shook his head. "But it's not true. Our humanity doesn't make us weak. It doesn't stop us from having all four powers."

"So what does?" Ella asked.

Neriah held her eyes. "Aric," he said. "He's the one who split the powers. He *chose* to give one element to each of his eldest four. Afton, Avira, Adams…" He hesitated for a moment before concluding the list. "Aedus. He gave them full power of only one element in the hopes of keeping them together. He thought that by giving his children only one power each, he would keep them forever united in the fight against demons. The Elementals would need one another to stay strong." He quietened for a moment. "It worked. For centuries, we believed that alone we were but one power, but together, we had the power of four. There was nothing that could stand in the way of the Elementals. We ruled the realm, protected the humans, fought the demons. We won because all four Elementals knew they needed each other to remain strong." His violet eyes darkened with pain. "Until Hadrian found out what Aric did, and decided our forefather had wronged us, so he set out to correct that mistake."

"How did Hadrian find out what Aric had done?" Ella asked.

Neriah closed his eyes tightly and brought up a hand to rub at his face. "Because of me," he said heavily.

Ella gaped at him, in too much shock to say anything.

"It's a long story," Neriah said. "One I don't have the heart to tell." He looked at his niece. "It was my fault. Hadrian and I were searching for something else when we stumbled across Aric's secret. We didn't tell anyone what we had found out," Neriah said, looking over at Chris. "Not even the other Elementals. We were young at the time and foolish enough to believe that we held some sort of power over the rest by knowing something no one else did." He closed his eyes and let out a sigh. "If there is anything, *anything*, I regret more than all the other mistakes I've made, it's this. I would give everything I have to go back in time and stop myself and Hadrian from learning what Aric had done." He dropped his head and, for a moment, he simply stood there, weighed down by guilt and remorse. He straightened up but looked like he was fighting to remain composed.

"Hadrian was adamant that if Aric had split the powers himself, that meant mages were capable of holding all four powers. He was desperate to test his theory, to find a way to return mages to what they were *supposed* to be – beings with the power of all four elements." He shook his head. "He became obsessed with it. It was all he would talk about, think about. After a few years of struggling to find a way, he gave up. I thought that was the end of it." His eyes went to Chris and both men shared a look. "But then Hadrian found a reason to go back to his research. He believed that Aric left clues in his sermons, to allow mages to find a way to have all four powers if they were willing to do what was necessary."

Aaron could see the tension in Neriah's strong, broad shoulders. He could read the heartbreak in his eyes, the anger in the tight line of his jaw.

"The one thing that was repeated in almost every sermon of Aric was his most famous saying: nothing is more powerful than blood." Then, quietly, Neriah added, "And everyone knows our powers are our life-source. Power flows in our veins; it's in our very blood."

It all fell together with a click, like the missing piece of a puzzle that Aaron didn't even realise he was putting together in his mind.

"That's it," Aaron breathed. "*That's* why Hadrian turned into a vamage." He looked up to find confirmation in Neriah's pained eyes. *Nothing is more powerful than blood.* That's what Naina had said too, and that mages never understood that. Aaron stepped closer. "Hadrian became a vamage so he could drink blood – blood that holds the power of a mage."

Neriah nodded. "He took Aric's words and twisted them, believing that Aric was hinting at a way to gain all four powers, rather than preaching about the importance of family, of brotherhood. He became a vamage, gave up his purity – put that down as the 'price' he had to pay to become, what he believed, was a mage in its truest form. A mage with all four powers, all four legacies." He turned back to Skyler. "When he attacked James, he didn't just take James's life, he took his power, his legacy from him too."

Skyler stared at Neriah with a broken expression. "You knew?" he asked. "All this time, you knew I didn't have the legacy?" His eyes, which had filled with tears, blazed with anger. "The legacy never passed to my father after Uncle James died. It never came to me because *Hadrian* had taken it. You knew that and you still let me believe I was the legacy holder?"

"You're the rightful owner of that legacy," Neriah said. "I've been trying to get you back your birthright."

"Why didn't you tell me?" Skyler asked. "Why?" he screamed and his rage kicked dust swirls up into the air.

But Neriah didn't use his element in retaliation. He just stared at Skyler with guilt-ridden eyes.

"I hoped I would never have to," he replied. "I wanted to get to Hadrian and take back your birthright before you came of age and realised your legacy was missing."

Skyler shook his head, fury emanating from him in waves. The air around them heated up, making prickling sweat gather on their skin.

"I trusted you." Skyler hissed the words. "I believed you. I believed that my core wasn't strong enough, that my legacy was lying dormant inside me. I worked day and night to get better! I trained, I fought. I went out on *every* damn hunt, all of it to make my core stronger, to get my legacy to awaken." His eyes blazed with anger. "And all that time, you knew I didn't have the legacy. You lied to me!"

"Skyler–" Neriah reached for him but Skyler shoved his hand away, stepping back.

"Why?" he bellowed. "Why did you lie to me? Why didn't you tell me?"

Neriah faltered and Skyler's slitted eyes widened.

"You thought I would leave," he said in realisation. Neriah didn't say anything, but again, his silence confirmed Skyler's accusation. "You thought I would go to Hadrian?" Skyler asked. "Are you out of your mind?"

"Many before you have left to go to Hadrian," Neriah said. "How could I be sure that you wouldn't too?"

Skyler was staring at him with disgust. "I wouldn't align myself with a *demon!*" he spat.

"How do you think Hadrian got so many mages to turn?" Neriah asked. "How do you think his army of vamages came about?" Now anger was replacing the guilt and Neriah once again looked like the fearless leader of the mages. "I kept the truth I learnt about Aric and his purposeful splitting of the powers to myself, but Hadrian didn't. He tells mages they can have all four powers. He turns them using greed, promising them what they can't have as mages. That's why we've lost so many. Who do you know Skyler, that wouldn't give everything they've got to have full power over *all* four elements?"

Skyler didn't say anything, but his fists were clenched tightly at his sides.

"After Hadrian killed James, I told Chris and your father about what Aric had done," Neriah said to Skyler. "All the Elementals knew the truth and all of us decided to keep it a secret, so no mage would turn, like Hadrian did. So no other mage would be tempted to forsake their purity in their greed for power."

"I would never give up my purity," Skyler said. "If you knew me at all, you would know I would rather die than turn into a vamage." He started walking away.

"Skyler–" Neriah called to him.

"I don't know what's more insulting," Skyler said, turning to look at him. "To know that the mage I followed like a father lied to me all my life, or to know he thought so little of me that he believed I would choose to become a *demon* if he told me the truth."

Neriah didn't say anything. Skyler walked away. He pulled off the ivory coat, the thing that marked him as the legacy holder for the element of Air, and dropped it to the ground. He didn't look back even once.

"Sky," Ella yelled. She ran after him and picked up his coat. "Sky? Sky, wait! Please."

Neriah remained where he was, staring at Skyler's retreating form, watching Ella chase after him. He took in a deep breath and turned to face the only two Elementals left. He tried to smile at Aaron, but it came across as little more than a grimace.

"We should set up the Gate," he said. "This one should be a lot more stronger, with two legacy holders setting it up."

Aaron realised that all the times Skyler had set up Gates, they hadn't been as strong as everyone thought. Skyler was an Elemental, the last Avira, but he wasn't the legacy holder.

Chris made to follow after Neriah but stopped when Aaron didn't move.

"Aaron?" he called. "Come on."

Aaron shook his head. After everything that had happened, this was the last thing anyone wanted to hear, but Aaron didn't have a choice. "You don't need me to set up the Gate," he said to Neriah. "Not if you want it set up by two legacy holders."

Neriah frowned, his eyes narrowed in confusion.

"What do you mean?" Chris asked.

Aaron took in a steadying breath. "I mean," he started in a quiet voice. "I'm not the legacy holder, Dad. You are."

23

DANGEROUS PLANS

"Are you certain about this?"

"Yes, sir, completely certain."

Hadrian sat back in his seat, brow furrowed in thought. "Then we can't waste another moment."

Sitting at his left, Machado inclined his head. "What would you like us to do?"

Hadrian didn't speak right away. He tapped his fingers on the rich mahogany table at which he was sitting. "Get together a team," he said. "I want his every move watched. Where he goes, who he meets. I want every minute of his existence under surveillance."

"Yes, sir," Machado replied.

"Don't underestimate him," Hadrian warned. "Raoul may be a Lycan, but he's no fool. And if what you've said is true, and Raoul wants to find the Blades of Aric, then he'll put his full force into tracking them down. If he gets to them, he'll block access to them."

"We have the location of the Blade of Adams narrowed down to one of four possible places," Machado reported. "Both the Blades of Aedus and Afton are with their legacy holders and so are safe from Raoul." His eyes darted to the boy sitting at Hadrian's right hand. "But it would help if *all* of us knew where the Blade of Avira was being kept."

Up until now, Kyran was putting on a good show of acting oblivious to the meeting, but he couldn't quite hold back his smirk at Machado's last remark.

Hadrian turned his head to look at his son and smiled. "Kyran?"

Kyran lifted his head and met Machado's eyes. "It's safe," he said. "When it's time to use the Blade, I can easily get to it. That's all you need to know."

Machado's carefully arranged expression slipped and his annoyance surfaced. "If you can't trust your own, Kyran–"

"You lot aren't *my own*," Kyran interrupted. "And the only one who is, already knows the location."

Machado looked to Hadrian, to see the leader of the vamages give a small shrug. "He wants to keep it a secret," he said.

Under the table, Machado's hands curled into fists. "With all due respect, sir," he started, "this isn't a matter of child's play, where you indulge your son by keeping his *secret*." His glittery blue eyes flashed with anger. "This is a matter of security. The Blades of Aric are a very real, very *dangerous*, threat and treating them as anything less is–"

"I know what the Blades of Aric are and what they are capable of," Hadrian cut in. "The one who holds the legacies knows the location of the Blades. That's all that matters. You don't have to fret over it."

Machado lowered his head but not before giving Kyran another hateful glower. Kyran only smirked back.

"What is the situation with the mages?" Hadrian asked.

Machado dutifully proceeded to give him the update. Kyran went back to ignoring the meeting. He already knew what Machado was going to report – Neriah was on the move, Salvador was gathering Hunters, Lurkers had been dispatched all over the realm and Kyran was pretty certain Neriah was still dragging Aaron around in the hopes that he would claim the Blade of Adams and join the war.

Kyran forced out a breath. He had thought Aaron would be safe after he returned to Marwa. He had hoped Aaron had pulled out of the fight for good; that he wasn't going to take part in the war. But seeing him with the rest of the Hunters the day before killed that hope. Aaron had come to protect the Blade of Avira. He was still involved and Kyran wasn't sure what he could do to prevent that.

"...attack on Salvador."

Kyran jerked his head up, catching the last of Machado's words. "What?" he asked.

Machado and Hadrian turned to look at Kyran. Machado tiredly repeated, "We are ready for the attack on Salvador."

"Wait." Kyran sat up in his chair. "You want to lead an attack on Salvador?" he asked.

Machado looked to Hadrian before turning back. "Am I not saying it clearly enough?"

Kyran's jaw tightened. "Forget it," he stated. "There will be no attack."

Machado frowned. "What?" he asked.

"We're not taking Salvador," Kyran said.

Hadrian turned in his chair, his narrowed hazel eyes on his son.

"And if I ask why not?" Machado enquired.

"I'll tell you it's because I'm saying so," Kyran replied. "For you that should be enough."

"What about me?" Hadrian asked. "Do I get more of an explanation?"

Kyran looked at Hadrian, but dropped his gaze quickly. "There's no need to attack Salvador, not yet," he said.

"Not yet?" Hadrian asked. "So, when do you suggest?"

"When the entire city isn't filled with *Hunters*," Kyran replied tersely.

"We have the advantage of numbers," Hadrian said.

"Not necessarily – you have no idea how many Neriah has," Kyran argued. "I spent a year with them and I don't have a clue how many Hunters there are in total. We'd be going in blind."

"I have ways to find out that information," Hadrian said.

Kyran paused. "I know you do," he said. "But Salvador's not worth the risk."

"Salvador is the city that holds what I want," Hadrian said. "And on top of that, it's Neriah's city. It's the sanctuary he built in response to me." His eyes darkened but the gold in his eyes shimmered. "Naturally, I want it in ruins."

Kyran's expression gave away his unease.

"I think your son may have to sit this one out, sir," Machado said with a sly grin. "It seems attacking the place he called home for almost a year is going to be difficult for him."

Kyran glowered at Machado. "If it's my father's wish to have Salvador destroyed then I will tear the city to pieces myself." He turned to meet Hadrian's pleased eyes. "But if you want to hurt Neriah, then Salvador has to remain untouched, at least for now. Let Neriah have his little sanctuary. Once all the other cities are ours, we'll take Salvador from him." He smiled. "Keep the best for last, father."

Hadrian took a moment to study his son. "We'll leave Salvador for the time being," he said. "But I like the idea of keeping the best for last. The City of Salvador, however, isn't close to being the best in the realm."

He turned to Machado to discuss the remaining points of their meeting, but Kyran couldn't focus on anything that was being said. He had bought Salvador a little time, but he had to act fast, before his loyalty to his father made him do what he didn't dare even imagine.

***

Sitting at their favourite spot in the City of Salvador – at the bank of the lake – Aaron and the twins got the chance to do what they hadn't been able to do for a while: catch up.

"She said what?" Sam asked with a frown. "How many battles are the mages planning to fight?"

"Naina didn't say anything about the rest of the mages," Aaron explained. "She only said that I have another battle to fight."

"Why is that?" Rose asked. "Why is it just you? I thought this war affects all of the mages?"

"It does," Aaron replied. "But I got the impression from Naina that this fight was more...personal. She said I had to focus on fighting this other battle or I would lose more than I can bear."

Rose looked worried.

"She sounds like a regular ray of sunshine," Sam said.

"She wasn't exactly helpful," Aaron said. "In fact, she was a little annoying."

Sam snorted. "I'll say. What did she call you again?"

"A web," Aaron replied. "Whatever that means."

"I'd have said you were more of a thorn in the backside." Sam shrugged. "But whatever."

Aaron punched him on the shoulder and Sam chuckled.

Rose shook her head, deep in thought. "I don't get why Neriah would send you to get advice from a little girl," she said to Aaron.

"She was young but she knew what she was talking about," Aaron admitted. "She knew I didn't have the legacy. She knew that my parents didn't want me involved in the war." He shifted uncomfortably, thinking about what Naina had said about Kyran.

He's not your friend, Aaron.

His heart clenched tightly. She was warning him. By her own admission, she knew everything, so she would know if Kyran was a friend or if he was the enemy. Aaron tried. He tried with every fibre of his being to believe Naina, to take her words as nothing but the honest truth, but he couldn't. Every time Aaron had found himself in trouble, Kyran had come and helped him. He had always been a friend, even when he was supposed to be an enemy.

"Hello?"

Aaron snapped out of his daze to find Sam waving a hand in front of his face.

"That was some heavy thinking," Sam said with a half-smile. "What else did the little girl say?"

Aaron shook his head. "Nothing," he said. "That was about it."

Aaron had told Sam and Rose everything about his meeting with Naina, from where it took place to every word she said, except for the bit about Kyran. Aaron didn't want to share that with anyone, not even his best friends. So he told his friends the same thing he had said to his dad and Neriah: he didn't have the legacy. It was still with Chris.

Keeping his word to Neriah, Aaron also didn't repeat what Neriah had revealed about Aric splitting the powers on purpose.

"So your legacy is still with your dad, right?" Sam asked, after a few silent moments.

"Yeah," Aaron said.

"Does that mean you will get it when you turn nineteen?" Sam asked.

Aaron shifted again. According to Naina, he would get the legacy when he showed where his loyalty lied. He felt a stab of anger at the thought. He was with the mages, he wanted to fight against Hadrian. Why was his loyalty called into question? Just because he'd instinctively tried to help an outnumbered Kyran?

"I don't know," Aaron said, "I don't think so. I think Dad's still got the legacy 'cause he's got a stronger core than me. If I can get my core stronger, then maybe the legacy will pass on to me. If not then I'll only get it if..." He trailed off, not able to say the words.

Sam didn't need him to. He understood Aaron would get the legacy if his dad died. Legacies strived to survive, so no matter how weak Aaron's core was, if he was the only surviving Adams, he would get the legacy after Chris died.

"I hope you never get it, mate," Sam said.

Aaron looked up at him and smiled. "Thanks, Sammy."

"Your mum and dad seem happier," Rose said. "Now that your dad is the legacy holder, does that mean he's going to use the Blade of Adams?"

Aaron nodded. "I heard Dad and Neriah making plans. I think Dad's leaving in a few hours."

"So you're not going to be fighting?" Sam asked.

Aaron let out a sigh and leant back. The air was getting cooler now. The beginning of May had brought colder days. The sun still warmed Aaron's face, though. He closed his eyes and took a moment to gather his thoughts.

"After I explained to Neriah and Dad that I wasn't the legacy holder, I told them I was still going to fight, Blade or no Blade." He paused. "But Neriah said if I can't use the Blade of Adams, then he won't let me join the fight. He said I didn't have the necessary training to take part in the war, and it seems no one has the time to teach me."

Rose watched Aaron for a moment before saying, "Maybe it's for the best."

Aaron looked at her. "I thought we'd all agreed that we were fighting against Hadrian, against the vamages?"

"Not all fights have to be on the battlefield," Rose said.

The sound of soft footsteps made all three turn around. They saw Armana making her way over towards them, both hands held out before her as she judged her steps. All three quickly stood up and hurried over to the Empath.

"Armana?" Aaron called, getting close enough to hold on to her hand. "Are you okay?" he asked, seeing her usually pleasant expression was replaced with anxious concern.

"Does anyone know where Skyler is?" she asked.

Aaron felt sorry for her. The worry looked too heavy on Armana's delicate features.

"I'm sorry, Armana," he said.

Armana looked crestfallen. "He's hurting, I can feel it," she said. "I just wish he would come back. I'm scared he'll do something stupid."

Aaron could easily see it too. Skyler needed very little provocation on most days to pick a fight, but when he was already raging he would need almost next to no excuse to get into it with anyone. If he went looking for something to vent his fury on, he could very easily get hurt. But Aaron wasn't going to tell Armana that. She looked worried enough.

"I'm sure he's just sitting in a pub somewhere, getting as much alcohol into him as possible," he said.

Armana paled. "That's just going to make him even more ready for a fight," she said and her eyes brimmed with frightened tears.

Aaron shared a panicked look with Sam.

"Here." Sam wrapped an arm around Armana. "Why don't we go and see Mother Mary? I'm sure she'll know what to do." He looked at Aaron and whispered under his breath, "And say."

Aaron kept hold of Armana's hand, and both he and Sam led her towards the Stove. Sam turned to see his sister standing where he left her.

"You coming Rose?" he asked.

Rose shook her head. "You go, take care of Armana," she said. "I'm going to stay here for a bit."

Sam gave her a look but then nodded. Rose watched as Sam and Aaron guided Armana down the street. She turned to the calm water of the lake. She stood staring at it for a few minutes before walking in the opposite direction to where the boys had gone. She wasn't going anywhere in particular. She just wanted a walk to clear her head.

Her feet seemed to have a mind of their own because before she knew it, Rose was walking into the orchard, past the trees full with ready-to-eat fruit. She saw very few workers picking fruit and filling baskets. It was that time of the day when most of the work was done and the mages had retired to their cottages for a little rest before dinner.

The telltale sound of a gun going off broke the tranquillity. Rose panicked and turned, but she couldn't see anyone. The mages continued working, ignoring the shots that were being fired at regular intervals. Giving in to her curiosity, Rose hesitantly walked forward, trying to see what was going on. She had to walk deeper into the orchard before she spotted Alan and a few other young mages, hurling fruit into the air and then shooting it. Target practice. Rose let out a breath and smiled.

Standing next to them, encouraging them, was Ryan. He held up a hand and Alan lowered his gun. The rest did the same. Ryan said something, grinning the whole time. The Hunters-in-training shared proud looks. Ryan turned and led the team away. They all went, dropping their guns into one of the baskets on their way out.

Rose waited until they were almost out of sight, before making her way over and peering into the basket. The assortment of black and silver guns made her feel queasy. She stepped back. She turned to look in the direction Ryan had led the young mages, but they had already disappeared out of sight.

Something caught her eye and Rose paused. She stared at the tree, the very same one she had once sat under and talked so casually to Kyran. She walked towards it, breathing in the scent of fresh mangos. She looked up at the dangling fruit – beautiful sun-kissed mangos hanging ready for the picking. She smiled sadly, remembering the time Kyran had fast-tracked their growth and lowered the branches, before picking one out for her. She lifted a hand, trying to get to them but they were out of her reach. She dropped her hand and just stood there, staring at the fruit.

Slowly, very gently, the branch began to dip. Rose felt like her blood had turned to ice. She couldn't move. She stared in shock as the branch lowered, bit by bit, until it was almost touching the top of her head. The mangos swung before her, now at eye level. She could easily take one, but Rose kept her hands firmly by her side. Gathering every nerve she had, Rose turned around, her heart beating erratically in her chest.

She knew he was there, even before she saw him. The branch coming down like that, just like it had once before at his command, was enough to warn her. But more than that, Rose could actually feel his presence. It prickled her senses, making her breath catch in her throat.

She found his vivid green eyes waiting to meet hers the moment she turned. Rose forced in a breath. Standing across from her was Kyran Aedus.

24

DESPERATE PLEADS

Rose didn't move. She stared at Kyran. He looked surreal standing under a tree, dressed in a plain white shirt and dark jeans. His expression was unreadable. Rose would have convinced herself she was imagining him if moments before the branches of the tree hadn't bowed down to her, offering her its fruit.

Kyran lifted his head and it was just that smallest of movements that cemented his presence for Rose. She stepped back, her heart pounding. Kyran's gaze moved to the dangling fruit behind her. He looked back at her and smiled. Rose felt her heart leap and break at the same time.

"Aren't you going to take one?" he asked, gesturing to the mangos.

Rose took in a slow breath, and then darted to the basket Alan and his friends had dumped their firearms in. She pulled out the first pistol she touched and turned to aim at Kyran with shaky hands.

"I'd rather take one of these," she said, her voice trembling as much as her hands.

Kyran didn't move. He gave the black pistol in her hands a small glance before looking at her.

"Rose—"

"How did you get in here?" she asked.

Kyran didn't say anything but gave a pointed look to the ground. Rose saw the white robe, crumpled in a heap at the foot of the tree Kyran was standing under.

"Lurkers have a design flaw," Kyran said quietly. "It's hard to make out who is under the hood."

"Why are you here?" Rose asked, fearing an entire army of vamages had come with him.

"I came for you," Kyran replied.

Rose had to force herself to keep the gun steady.

Kyran took a step towards her. "Rose–"

"Stop," she instructed. "Stop right there."

Kyran paused. "Just hear me out."

Rose shook her head. "I don't want to hear any more of your lies."

"I never lied to you."

A choked breath left Rose, full of hurt and disbelief. "You never lied?" she asked. "I lost my parents when I was very young. I miss everything about them – my dad's strong arms, my mum's laugh–" She stopped, fighting back the sob that was clawing up inside her, desperate to get out. "You didn't *lie*?" she asked again, with tears stinging her eyes.

Kyran didn't say anything.

"You lied to my face about losing your family," Rose said. "How could you, Kyran? How could you sit there and listen to me talk about my parents?" Anger had replaced the shock and fear, giving Rose the strength to say everything that had been eating away at her ever since she learnt Kyran's truth. "How could you face me, talk to me about my parents, when you're the one who...? You..." She had to stop; she couldn't go on.

"Rose." Kyran stepped towards her.

"You took me to their *graves*," Rose cried, angry tears glistened in her eyes. "How sick are you? You took me to my parents' graves when you're the reason they're in there!"

"I didn't do anything to your parents," Kyran said.

"That's the problem," Rose said, and her voice broke. "You didn't do anything, Kyran. You could have saved them but you didn't. You could have stopped the vamages attacking my house." Tears streaked down her cheeks and the pistol was shaking in her hands, but it was still aimed at Kyran. "You were there and you didn't do anything. You stood back and let the vamages murder my parents!"

Kyran's expression hardened. He strode towards her. Rose gripped the gun tighter in her hands, trying to hold the thing steady, but Kyran was already right in front of her. His hand came up and Rose knew he was going to knock the gun clean out of her grip. But instead, his fingers rested on top of the pistol and he guided the gun forward, resting the barrel against his chest.

"If you really believe that," he said in a quiet voice, "then go ahead. Pull the trigger."

Rose stared at him, too shocked to react. His eyes were on her too, waiting, holding the weapon against his heart.

"Go on, Rose," he prompted. "Kill me, if you really believe I would stand back and let your parents die."

Rose's finger was on the trigger. All it would take was one small pull. A shot fired by her would kill him. She could do it. He was surely lying about this, like he lied about everything else. But when Rose looked at him, she saw nothing but sincerity. His eyes were clear, no shadow of guilt lurking there. His grip was on the gun; he could push it away from himself, yet he held it steadily to his chest.

Rose's grip slackened from around the gun, and the sob she had been fighting so hard to keep back broke out of her. She dropped her head, her shoulders shaking as her hand fell away from the pistol, leaving it in Kyran's grip.

Kyran threw the gun aside and then his hands were on Rose's shoulders. He tried to pull her into his arms, but Rose stood rigid, refusing to succumb into his warm embrace.

"Rose..." He whispered her name and Rose cried harder, her heart aching.

"Don't," she pleaded, not sure herself what she was asking him not to do.

Kyran's hand cupped her cheek and he gently lifted her tear-stained face, so she had no choice but to look at him. Vivid green eyes met hers.

"I never lied to you," he repeated. "Everything I told you was the truth. I've always been honest with you." He held her tear-filled gaze. "By the time I got to your house, there was nothing I could do to help your parents."

Rose squeezed her eyes shut, and another wrangled sob came from her. Kyran wrapped an arm around her, leaning in so their foreheads touched.

"I tried, Rose," he whispered. "I tried to help, but it was too late."

He pulled away and Rose looked up at him, wanting nothing more than to believe him.

Kyran's hands touched her shoulders again, before trailing down both her arms, making Rose tremble. He held her hands. "I'm not what everyone says I am, Rose," he told her. "I've not done the things they blame me for. I am the Scorcher, and I am Hadrian's son, but I'm not the monster they all make me out to be."

"What are you, then?" Rose asked.

"My father's son," Kyran replied. "I do what my father asks of me. He wanted the key that unlocked his powers. That's why I came here, to get what was rightfully his."

"His powers were locked for a reason," Rose said.

"Yes, and the reason is more complicated than Neriah would ever admit." He let go of her hands and pulled away a few steps, closing his eyes and shaking his head. "I'm not...This isn't why I came here."

"Then why did you?" Rose asked.

Kyran looked at her for a long minute. "I came to warn you," he said. "You need to leave, Rose. You need to take Aaron, take your brother and get out of Salvador. It's not safe here. You need to go to the City of Marwa. That's the only safe city. *Stay* there," he instructed. "Don't let Aaron leave, no matter what. Stay in Marwa and you'll be safe."

"Why is Salvador not safe?" Rose asked. "What are you—?"

She paused, her eyes widening as she picked up the faint sound of laughter coming from past the trees. Kyran turned his head, intense green eyes searching the orchard. He spotted the crowd of boys coming in their direction, led by a chuckling Ryan.

Kyran turned back to look at Rose. "Please, get to Marwa," he said. "Stay there and you'll be safe."

"Why should I believe you?" Rose asked. "How do I know you're not laying a trap? Maybe Marwa is the city that's not safe."

Kyran looked at her for a moment before stepping closer and resting his hands on her arms. "You don't have to believe anything I say," he said, "but if you can, believe this and this alone." He cupped her cheek gently and whispered, "Believe that I can't stand the thought of anything happening to you."

Rose was sure he was going to lean in and kiss her, but Kyran pulled back. In a matter of seconds, he had picked up the Lurker's robe and put it on, the hood lowered over his face. He was gone before Rose could completely process what he had just said to her.

***

"Go over that again," Ella said. "*Kyran* was here?"

Rose nodded wearily. "He said he had come to warn me. He told me Salvador wasn't safe."

Ella turned to look at her uncle, but Neriah was silent, looking deep in thought. Ella's eyes moved to the only other Elementals in the room, Christopher and Aaron Adams. Both looked shocked. The other person with them in Neriah's cottage was Sam, and he wasn't shocked – he was livid.

"I can't believe this," Sam fumed, pacing the floor, hands balled into fists. "How could he just walk in here?" He paused to look at Ella with angry eyes. "You lot should do something about the security of this place," he said. "It's *severely* lacking!"

"What can we do?" Ella asked. "Kyran's a mage. We can't ward the Gate against mages now, can we?"

Sam didn't say anything and returned to pacing.

Ella turned back to her uncle. "What should we do?" she asked. "There's nothing we can add to the Gate that's not already there. Plus whatever Glyphs we put on, Kyran can easily remove." She paused, biting her lip. "Should...should we start an evacuation?"

Neriah turned to meet her eyes. "Salvador is our sanctuary," he said. "If the place we seek shelter is not safe, then where is?"

"Marwa," Rose said quietly. "He said Marwa was the only safe city."

Ella let out a derisive snort. "Yeah, right. As if Marwa's never been attacked before." She shook her head, her eyes closing tight.

Aaron's heart skipped a beat. It seemed the attack that cost Aaron two members of his family had taken someone from Ella too.

"We have to do something," Chris said, speaking to Neriah. "We can't just ignore his warning."

"Question is," Neriah started, "why is he warning us at all?" He looked to Rose, studying her with sharp eyes. "Why did he come to you?"

Rose gave a small shrug. "I–I don't know."

Ella looked at her but didn't say anything. She dropped her gaze to the floor.

"He's toying with her," Sam said furiously. "He did it before and he's doing it again."

"Sam," Rose started.

"Oh come on, Rose!" Sam stopped to face her. "Tell me you don't see through this. Tell me you don't know this is an obvious trap."

"What kind of a trap?" Ella asked.

Sam turned to look at her. "He told Rose to get Aaron and me, and go to Marwa. It's obvious that Salvador isn't the city they are planning to attack – Marwa is."

Ella shifted, looking unsure of Sam's theory. "Okay, lets just say that's true. Why would Kyran want you three in the target zone?"

"Why the hell not?" Sam asked. "He's twisted. He's been playing with my sister's feelings, all the while knowing what he did to our parents. He probably thinks Aaron's got that...that legacy thingie, so he's trying to get rid of him."

Aaron's protest was halfway out of his mouth, before he realised that what Sam was saying could, in fact, be true.

"I don't know, Sam," Rose said quietly. "It didn't look like he was lying."

Sam stared at her with wide eyes. "What's wrong with you?" he asked. "All he's done is *lie* to you."

"I know," Rose said. "But I'm just...I don't know...I felt–"

"That's the problem," Sam cut her off. "Don't feel, use your head!"

"Alright." Aaron stepped in front of Rose. "That's enough, Sammy,"

"No!" Sam snapped. "It's not enough. After everything – *everything* – that's happened, she still wonders if he's lying or not?" He looked at his sister before taking a few steps towards her. "Rose, he stood back and let vamages kill our parents. How can you possibly think about trusting him?"

Rose opened her mouth to speak but words failed her. She closed her eyes and shook her head. "I...I don't know...I just...He said that he tried to help and I...I don't know...I want to believe him."

"He's messing with you," Sam said. "He's trying to get into your head. You heard what Skyler said. They saw him in that memory they got from that vamage. Kyran was in our house that night. That piece of crap stood there while vamages killed our mum and dad!"

Rose turned to look at Ella.

"I'm sorry, Rose," Ella said quietly. "It was a partial memory. We didn't see more than a few seconds, but Kyran was there."

Rose had tears in her eyes. "He admitted that he was there but...but he said he tried to help–"

"He's lying!" Sam snapped.

"You don't know that, Sam," Aaron said.

"It's obvious," Sam replied. "He's not going to admit he stood back and let his vamages murder our parents! He's lying to cover it up."

"No, I don't think he is," Aaron argued. "He told me the same thing. He said by the time he got to your house, it was too late."

Ella turned to him with a frown. "When did he tell you that?"

Aaron stilled. A sense of cold dread filled him. He hadn't told anyone that Kyran had come to see him in the City of Hunda. He looked around the room to find all eyes were on him, narrowed in confusion.

"Aaron?" his dad called.

Aaron closed his eyes. There was no way out of it. He had messed up. He had to come clean.

"What's going on?" Chris asked.

Aaron turned to him. "I didn't tell anyone, but Kyran came to see me."

His dad was staring at him in stunned surprise. "When?" he asked.

"When I stayed the night in Hunda," Aaron replied. "I couldn't sleep so I went for a walk. I met Kyran there."

At once, the room tensed. Everyone was staring at Aaron in shock. Neriah moved towards him.

"You met the Scorcher?" he asked.

Aaron nodded. "Yeah, but–"

"You met the Scorcher when we were on our way to get your Blade?" Neriah asked, cutting him off. "And you didn't think to mention this to anyone?"

Aaron could see the anger in the oldest Elemental and it was an unnerving sight. He dropped his gaze to the floor.

"What did he say?" Neriah demanded. "Why had he come to see you?"

"He came to warn me," Aaron replied.

"Warn you?" Neriah repeated with a knitted brow and blazing eyes.

"He seems to be doing a lot of that," Ella murmured.

"Warn you about what?" Neriah demanded.

Aaron swallowed, knowing how this was going to go down, but he didn't have a choice. He had to tell them.

"Warn me not to wield the Blade of Adams."

Neriah stared at him, completely still for a moment. Then his jaw clenched and those violet eyes began to darken. He stepped closer, his strong hands curled into fists.

"He knew that's where you were going?" he asked. "And you didn't think this was something important? That it was something I ought to know? That the *Scorcher* knew what we're up to? He could have followed us straight to the Blade!"

"We didn't get to it," Aaron reminded. "We had to return to Marwa because of those Lycans–"

"Which was *just* as well," Neriah yelled. "Otherwise we would have led Hadrian's heir straight to Aric's Blade!"

"Hey." Chris was in front of Aaron in a heartbeat, a hand held out towards Neriah. "That's enough."

Neriah's furious stare stayed on Aaron, but he stepped back. "Ella," he said, and his voice shook with the strain of keeping his anger in check. "Confirm with Scott if he's gathered a team yet. They're accompanying Chris tonight to get the Blade of Adams."

Ella nodded, "Okay."

Neriah's gaze hadn't moved from Aaron. "And Ella, ask Scott to get a portal ready in the next hour." His eyes filled with fury and disappointment. "Aaron's returning to Marwa."

Aaron opened his mouth to speak, to protest, but Neriah had had enough. He turned to the door. "Chris," he called and walked out.

Chris met Aaron's eyes. "We'll talk once I get home," he said and followed after Neriah, presumably to get ready to claim his sword.

The door closed and Aaron was left with his best friends and Ella.

"You didn't tell anyone?" Ella asked, staring at Aaron. "You met Kyran and you didn't tell anyone? What's *wrong* with you?"

With a groan, Aaron sunk into the seat next to Rose.

"That's a good question," he said, rubbing a hand across his face. He shook his head slowly. "I just...I didn't want to say anything. Mum and Uncle Mike were already jittery about me going to get the Blade and I knew if I told them they would freak out and force me to go back." He closed his eyes with a sigh. "And I honestly never thought about Kyran following us, like Neriah suggested. I just...I don't know. I didn't know what Neriah would do and...Kyran sort of...confused me and..." He let out a sigh. "I don't know."

Ella narrowed her eyes. "This was the night Michael found you in the woods, right?"

Aaron nodded.

"And you told him you went out for a walk because you couldn't sleep?" Her eyes grew sharp at the guilt on Aaron's face. "You lied to protect him – to protect Kyran."

Aaron didn't say anything.

"Why?" Ella asked. "Kyran is our enemy. Why would you protect him?"

"He jumped into a collapsing Q-Zone to save my *life*," Aaron said angrily. "He saved my best friend." He gestured to Rose. "I felt I owed him."

"You owe him *nothing*," Ella spat. "Get that through your head before you lose it for showing loyalty to the Scorcher!"

"I'm not–" Aaron forced out a breath to calm down. "I'm not loyal to Kyran, okay? I'm...I just...I didn't want him getting caught, not when he came to warn me."

Ella stared at him. She shook her head. "You're playing with fire, Aaron," she warned. "You can't be on our side and still look out for the enemy. Choose a side and *stick* to it!" She turned and walked out, slamming the door behind her.

The room fell into silence. Aaron rubbed at his head, willing the headache blooming behind his eyes to go away. He let out a deep breath.

Sam turned to him. "I can see why you didn't tell any of them," he said.

Aaron let out a snort.

Sam stepped closer. "But why didn't you tell us?"

Aaron looked up at him, thrown by the question. Sam was staring back, hurt and anger shining in his eyes. Aaron opened his mouth but found he didn't have an answer.

***

The portal for the City of Marwa was set up within the hour. As far as Aaron knew, his dad was due to leave with a team of Hunters in the next few hours. He had heard Ella say the Lurkers had confirmed the Blade of Adams was safe. The Gate was still in operation and no vamages or Lycans had been seen around the area. Hopefully, his dad would be able to get in, grab the Blade and get out.

Aaron, however, was to go back to Marwa with his mum and best friends. He headed down the street, following his mum to the Gate, beyond which stood the portal taking them to Marwa.

A subdued and silent Sam and Rose walked on either side of Aaron.

It was as Aaron passed the Stove that he spotted Armana, wrapped in the arms of the platinum-blond-haired, Skyler. It surprised Aaron how relieved he was at the sight of the Air Elemental. He would never admit it, even to himself, but he had been worried about Skyler. He had stormed off after learning a life-altering truth about how his birthright had been taken away from him. Aaron felt sorry for Skyler, seeing how broken he was at the knowledge that he never was the legacy holder – and worse, that Kyran had his legacy.

Skyler pulled away from Armana before cupping her cheeks with both hands. He was saying something to her, making her smile. She rested her hands on his chest. Aaron found himself smiling too. Armana had been so worried; it was good to see her smile again.

Skyler turned his head and caught Aaron's eye. The sharp blue eyes narrowed and he frowned. Aaron cursed under his breath when he saw Skyler move away from Armana and head over towards them.

Sam looked over to see Skyler and groaned. "I can't be bothered with his crap," he said and hurried to catch up to Kate. Rose stayed by Aaron's side, but she seemed too caught up in her own thoughts to pay much attention to Skyler.

"Where are you going?" Skyler asked Aaron.

Aaron stopped and turned to face him. "Neriah's sending me back to Marwa."

Skyler's eyes lit with fury at the mention of Neriah. "Oh? Why's that?"

Aaron shifted his backpack on his shoulder. "He has his reasons."

"Let me guess, it's because you're not the legacy holder," Skyler said.

Aaron gaped at him. "How did you know that?"

"Ella filled me in."

Aaron should have guessed. "No, it's not that," he said.

Skyler scoffed. "Trust me, it probably is." He turned his head to look at Neriah's cottage. "The leader of the mages does what he thinks is right, to hell with everyone else." He turned back to look at Aaron and the fury in his eyes seemed to lessen. "How long is he sending you away for?"

Aaron shrugged. "Dunno. It seems permanent."

Skyler smirked. "You'll be back," he said. "I give it a few days."

Aaron stared at him, completely thrown by his less antagonistic than usual behaviour. "Why would you say that?"

"Because you're not like them," Skyler said, tilting his head towards Kate. "You're one of us." Pride, clear as daylight, shone through his eyes. "You keep on fighting, no matter what."

"Are *you* still fighting?" Aaron asked.

Skyler frowned. "Of course. Why wouldn't I be?"

"I thought you were angry at Neriah?" Aaron said.

"I am," Skyler replied. "What does that have to do with fighting?"

Aaron shrugged. "I figured you wouldn't want to fight for Neriah any more."

Something shifted in Skyler's eyes. "I was never fighting *for* Neriah," he said. "My fight has always been my own." He gave Aaron a long look. "But you went out to defend my Blade, to set up a Gate, when you knew you weren't the legacy holder. You didn't have to do that. You took a risk to protect one of Aric's Blades." He stared at Aaron. "That right there is the mark of a good Hunter, a great Elemental. We fight to protect; we don't run and hide. And for that, you have my respect." He smiled and clapped a hand on Aaron's shoulder. "They can say what they want, take you wherever they like – I know you'll be back. You're not giving up this fight."

Aaron honestly didn't know what to say.

Skyler pulled Aaron close and whispered in his ear. "And if you're up for it, I'll teach you all you need to know about kicking demon ass when you come back."

Aaron pulled back to stare at him. "Will you still knock me around for no reason?"

Skyler grinned. "Of course," he replied, but the small wink told Aaron he was only messing. "I'll see you soon," Skyler said and turned to walk away.

Aaron was left dumbfounded. He stared after Skyler until he walked over to wrap Armana in his arms again. Aaron found himself remembering what the Empath had said about Skyler, that everyone eventually warmed up to him. Aaron smiled. He would never have imagined it was actually true.

25

FAMILIAR MARKS

Aaron couldn't sleep. Being back in Marwa, back in their house, felt strange without his dad. He lay in bed wondering how far his dad had got in his journey. Had he reached the Blade yet? Was he still travelling to retrieve it? How many Hunters had gone with him? What if he was attacked by Lycans again? Aaron let out a breath, fighting back the fear that was bubbling inside him. Another few minutes of worrying thoughts and Aaron gave up on sleep. He got out of bed and, as quietly as he could, he opened his door and crept downstairs.

The house was dark and still. Aaron crossed the landing, heading to the front door. He figured sitting at the front steps in the open air might help calm his frantic mind. He was about to reach out and open the door when he heard his name whispered in the dark.

"Aaron?"

He turned to find Rose sitting at the window, her silhouette visible in the limited light coming through from the lanterns outside.

"Rose?" Aaron frowned. "What are you doing?"

"Couldn't sleep," Rose replied. "What are *you* doing?"

Aaron stepped away from the door. "Couldn't sleep either." He walked over and sat down on the wide window ledge beside her.

"Must be one of those nights," Rose said.

Aaron took a moment to look at his friend. "I don't think blaming the night is fair."

Rose had her knees drawn up, her arms wrapped around them. She let out a sigh and leant her head against the glass. "You're right," she said quietly. "I can't blame the night." She paused. "I should blame myself."

"Why are you saying that?" Aaron asked. "You didn't do anything wrong."

"Then why does it feel like I did?"

Aaron knew exactly what she meant. He had felt like that too, when he met Kyran in the City of Hunda. Talking to Kyran instead of attacking him or raising the alarm felt like a condemnable act, but only afterwards. At the time, it felt somehow right.

"Ever since I found out who he really was, all I wanted was to look him in the eye and ask him why," she said. "Why didn't he help my parents? Why didn't he stop the attack?" She closed her eyes. "I never thought he'd give me the answer he did."

Aaron felt guilt stab at him. "I'm sorry, Rose," he said. "I should have told you about meeting Kyran in Hunda, about him claiming that he was too late to help your mum and dad."

"What did he say to you?" Rose asked, leaning in towards him.

"Pretty much what he told you," Aaron replied. "He said that he didn't arrive with the vamages, and by the time he got to your house, there was nothing he could do to help."

Rose looked at him with big eyes. "Do you believe him?" she asked.

Aaron paused. He swallowed heavily and shrugged. "I honestly don't know."

Rose pulled back, looking disappointed with his answer before turning away and staring out of the window again.

"Do you?" Aaron asked.

Rose didn't speak for long minutes. When she finally did, her voice was little more than a whisper. "Yes." She bit her lip and even the shadows couldn't hide her pain. "I did, when I met him. I believed him. I *want* to believe him, more than anything." She shook her head, her brow furrowed. "But there's this voice in my head telling me what he said makes no sense." She looked over at Aaron. "He said he couldn't help my parents, but the vamages follow his every command. Why couldn't he stop them? He said by the time he got to my house there was nothing he could do to help, but if he didn't arrive with the vamages, then how did he know they were attacking us?"

Aaron had asked Kyran the same thing, and Kyran hadn't given him an answer. "I know," he said. "It doesn't add up."

Rose looked out of the window, curling tighter against it. "He was lying," she said quietly. "He didn't get there too late. He was there the whole time but he just didn't help." She let out a deep breath and closed her eyes. "God, I'm so stupid."

"You're not stupid," Aaron said at once. "You're the furthest thing from stupid, Rose."

But Rose was shaking her head. "I am. I'm stupid for listening to him, stupid for falling for his lies again. I'm stupid for not shooting him when I had the chance!" She lifted both hands, pressing the heels against her eyes. "And I'm stupid because, despite everything, I can't stop thinking about him," she said in a broken voice. She dropped her hands into her lap, blinking tears out of her eyes. "I can't forget him, Aaron. No matter how hard I try, no matter what I do, I can't get him out of my head. I sleep with him on my mind and I wake up thinking about him. I find myself looking at Gates, waiting for him to walk in." Her tears spilled slowly, drop by drop, down her cheeks.

Aaron's heart broke for her. He reached out and touched her leg. "Rose, don't–"

"I know Kyran's just as responsible for my mum and dad's murder as the vamages that killed them," she said. "I know I should hate him. I should hate him with everything I have but...but I don't." She looked at Aaron with wide eyes. "Why can't I hate him?" she asked. "I want to. God, I want to hate him so badly. I want him to pay for standing back and letting his vamages kill two innocent people. I want justice for my parents' murder, but...but when I imagine Kyran facing execution, I feel like I can't breathe." She shook her head. "What kind of a daughter am I? I can't stand the thought of him getting hurt when he let my parents die. What's *wrong* with me?"

"There's nothing wrong with you," Aaron said. "You're confused, that's all. Kyran saved your life. He looked out for you. That's why you can't hate him. And you're not a vengeful person, Rose. I don't think you could stand the thought of anyone getting hurt."

Rose sniffed, drying her tears with the ends of her sleeves before leaning her head back on the wall. She stared at the dark ceiling. "I wish someone could take away all the complications," she said. "And I could just feel nothing for him."

Aaron nodded. "Yeah," he agreed. "Me too."

***

Using the light of the lanterns that moved along with them overhead, Chris led his team of eight Hunters through the dark woods. Neriah had wanted more Hunters to accompany him, but Chris had outright refused. He still didn't like the fact Neriah had underage mages trained as Hunters, so he had picked a handful of Hunters who were of age and asked Neriah to hold back the rest. Scott had assured him he would have back-up ready, should he need it.

Chris trekked through the forest until he saw the gleaming white Gate that guarded the Blade of Adams. The Hunters around him gave appreciative hoots. Chris shook his head but he was smiling, knowing full well he had once been just as immature.

"Come on," he instructed. "We've not got the Blade yet. The celebration can wait." They continued forward.

It happened in a heartbeat.

With a mighty roar, flames leapt up from the ground and spread out in a brilliant circle around the Hunters. Guns clicked behind Chris, as the Hunters searched the darkness to see who had trapped them.

Two of the Hunters tackled the flames, extinguishing them. For the next few moments, they stood on the smoking ground, looking around the dark woods. They noticed the figure approaching them, walking calmly, ignoring the guns that had turned to him.

When the stranger got close, the light of the lanterns washed over him, revealing his identity. Chris felt his chest seize with pain. The Hunters behind him shifted, drawing closer, guns aimed.

Kyran smiled and came to stop in front of the Hunters, his eyes on Chris. "Christopher Adams," he said quietly. "Out for an evening walk? You might want to go in the other direction."

Chris didn't say anything. His gun was in its holster, his sword in its sheath. His belt was lined with daggers. They were still on this side of the Gate, so they could use their powers – and Chris had all the strength of the mighty earth at his beck and call. And yet Chris felt defenceless, because the one he had to fight looked so much like the younger brother he had loved and lost.

"You shouldn't have come here," Chris said.

"I could say the same to you," Kyran returned.

"It's my Blade," Chris said. "Why shouldn't I come to claim it?"

Kyran smiled. "Why?" he asked. "Let's see. How about because you didn't give a damn and ran out on this realm fourteen years ago?" The green of his eyes darkened. "Is that reason enough?"

"No," Chris said. "It isn't." He stepped forward and lifted a hand, gesturing for Kyran to move. "Step aside."

Kyran smiled. "I was here first."

"I think you're missing something," Chris said. "There's nine of us and only one of you. If you don't back down, you're going to have a problem."

Kyran raised an eyebrow. "Is that right?" he asked.

White clouds hit the ground on either side of Kyran. Out from the swirling mist stepped a whole crowd of vamages. Chris swore under his breath. Their numbers easily outmatched the Hunters three to one. Chris looked back at Kyran, who met his eyes and smirked.

"Looks like you're the one with the problem now."

***

Aaron was still sitting with Rose, comforting her, when he heard someone coming down the stairs. The lamps flickered to life and Aaron saw his mum standing mid-staircase, staring at them. She looked from Aaron to Rose, before her expression softened.

"Can't sleep, either?" she asked.

"Yeah," Aaron replied.

He should've expected his mum to be awake. With her husband away to collect one of the most powerful weapons of the realm, she was bound to be a little nervous and anxious for his safe return. Aaron could see his mum had no intention of sleeping until his dad came home. It was the middle of the night and she was still in her day clothes.

Kate came down the stairs, wearing a smile. "Come on, then," she said. "I'll make us a hot drink."

She headed into the kitchen and started bustling around, putting the kettle on and setting out three mugs. Aaron and Rose followed her in and sat down at the table. Aaron noticed a box on the floor, near the front legs of the table.

"How about some camomile tea?" Kate asked. "It's very calming and can help you fall asleep."

Rose nodded. "Thank you, Mrs Adams."

"Mum?" Aaron called. "What's in that box?"

Kate paused. She turned and glanced at the square box before meeting Aaron's eyes. She smiled but Aaron could see the pain behind it.

"I was trying to be brave," she said. "I've been meaning to clear out some of...of Ben's things." She walked over. "I started this evening, after all of you went to bed." She sat down at the table. "Suffice to say I didn't get very far." She attempted a smile but it fooled neither Aaron nor Rose. "I managed to pack one box, and then spent the next few hours looking through his things."

Aaron's heart ached. He wasn't used to seeing his mum like this. She was the strong, strict one. Until now, Aaron had never understood that behind her strength was her greatest weakness, that her smile was to hide her tears and that her discipline was her way of keeping him safe.

He reached out and held her hand. She looked grateful for the gesture, and gave his hand a little squeeze. Aaron looked at the box.

"Can I?" he asked.

Kate looked surprised and then smiled, a glint of excitement in her eyes. She quickly let go of his hand and lifted the box, setting it on the table. She opened the flaps and looked inside, as if deciding what to take out first. She reached in and pulled out a few framed photos.

Aaron laughed. "You had them in his room too?"

Kate looked almost offended. "What's wrong with that?" she asked. "He liked having pictures in his room."

"How do you know, Mum?" Aaron smiled.

"Trust me," Kate said, "if Ben didn't like something, he would let you know."

Aaron chuckled, shaking his head. He reached out and picked up the first framed picture. He stared at the image of Ben – the cute baby with dark hair and perfect blue eyes – sitting on Chris's lap. Kate was by their side. They looked like the happiest family in the world. Aaron gazed at it for long minutes, seeing the joy on his mum's young face and the bliss on his equally youthful-looking dad.

Rose leant in to have a look and Aaron handed her the frame. She took it and smiled at the picture.

Aaron lifted the next frame. It was a photo taken outside, at the table of Marwa. Seated on top of the table were two little boys. One was Ben, the other was a blond-haired boy. Both looked no more than two years old. Sitting at the table, next to Ben, was Chris with his arms around his son. A young man, with hair so blond it looked white, was doing the same to the other boy, across the table.

"Can you guess who this is?" Kate asked with a smile, pointing at the blond-haired baby.

Aaron stared at the smiling face and clear blue eyes.

"Oh my God." Rose stared at the photo. "Is that Skyler?"

"Yep," Kate laughed. "It's Skyler Avira."

Aaron held the photo closer, even as Rose tried tugging it towards herself.

"Let me see it."

"Hold on," Aaron grinned. "Let me have a proper look."

There was no denying it. Skyler was a darn cute baby. Both Skyler and Ben looked adorable in their small shorts and sandals. Their bare chests and rosy cheeks told how hot the day must have been.

Aaron's gaze moved from Skyler to the man behind him. He had his hands around Skyler's waist, supporting him in case he fell. There was a wide smile on his face as he looked at Skyler with warm blue eyes. There was no question about who he was but Aaron still asked, to be sure.

"That's Joseph, right? Skyler's dad?"

Kate nodded, her smile small and sad. "Yeah," she said quietly. "That was Joseph." She took in a big breath. "A world apart from his son."

Aaron looked at the picture of baby Skyler and smiled. "He's not all that bad, once you get to know him."

"Here, let me show you something else." Kate took the frame from Aaron, putting it flat on the table. "Look." She pointed at someone in the background of the photo. Just to the left of the picture, behind Skyler's dad, was a woman. A very familiar woman. Aaron was certain he had seen her before, but he couldn't figure out where.

"Any guesses as to who she is?" Kate asked. Both Aaron and Rose stared at the woman with a little girl in her arms. "That," Kate tapped the photo, "was Lily Afton, Ella's mother."

Aaron realised he had seen her photo on Alaina's wall. She had been standing next to Neriah, next to her brother.

"Ella looks so much like her mum," Rose said, staring at the picture. "Wow, she's beautiful."

"Yeah," Kate said. "Lily really was beautiful, inside and out."

"Is that Ella?" Rose asked, pointing at the little girl in Lily's arms.

"It is," Kate confirmed.

"Oh man." Rose smiled and picked up the frame, holding it close to examine it carefully. "I can't wait to show Sam."

Aaron looked at the photo: at Ella with her mother, Skyler with his father and his dad with Ben. He didn't want to think about how each pair was left broken. Instead, he focused on the smiles and the joy the picture had captured, at a time when all the Elementals were together, living in the City of Marwa.

**

The fight wasn't a fair one. There were too many vamages and not enough Hunters. The darkness of the forest was lit up with gunshots and fireballs. Kyran hadn't stayed for the fight. He had instructed his vamages to 'deal' with the Hunters but not to kill them, before moving towards the Gate.

Chris fought valiantly, taking on two, three, even four vamages at a time. He knocked them out, using the darkness to his advantage by throwing trees at them that they couldn't see coming. The Hunters with him were holding their ground, using their powers and familiars to fight the vamages.

Chris got a moment's pause in fighting and turned to the glowing Gate. His heart leapt in his chest when he saw Kyran about to reach it. Chris grabbed the pendant dangling from the chain around his neck.

"Scott! Where's your back-up?"

"*They've passed through the portal*," came Scott's reply. "*They'll be there any second.*"

"Kyran's about to drop the Gate," Chris said. "I can't wait for the Hunters. I need to stop him."

Chris ignored Scott's warning for him to hold on and wait for the new team of Hunters to reach them, and ran towards Kyran. He saw Kyran lift his hand, about to touch the Gate. He frowned with surprise. He'd been sure the Scorcher would drop the Gate, not simply try to open it. Chris raced forward and raised a hand, taking aim.

The ground at Kyran's feet sunk into itself, taking Kyran with it. How he did it Chris didn't know, but in the blink of an eye, he found Kyran rising upwards. The ground he was standing on elevated back up, the sinkhole gone.

But it was all the distraction Chris needed to get close enough. He came to a standstill, his chest heaving and brow sweaty, and his gun gripped tightly in hand.

"Kyran, stop!" he called, taking aim as Kyran once again reached out to the Gate.

To his surprise, Kyran did.

"I don't want to hurt you," Chris said. "So please don't give me a reason."

Kyran turned to look at him. "You don't want to hurt me?" he asked. "Why is that?"

Chris faltered. He didn't want to mention Alex.

Kyran looked down at the ground and shook his head. "It's funny," he said. "I don't want to hurt you either." He met his eyes. "Doesn't mean I won't."

Chris moved, dodging the jolt of fire Kyran threw at him. It hit the tree behind Chris and the entire thing went up in flames. Chris took refuge behind another tree. He gathered his nerves and told himself he had no choice. He had to stop Kyran. Any second now, the back-up Scott had promised would arrive and the numbers would tilt in their favour. Until then, he had to keep Kyran away from the Gate, away from the Blade. If the Scorcher got to the Blade, no one would be able to get past his defence. Chris took in a breath and leapt from behind the tree.

***

Kate brought out more things from the box. She showed Aaron a toy train that had the letters *B-E-N* on it, a small blanket that used to be Ben's favourite, and a handkerchief that had the words *Benjamin Adams* embroidered in gold thread.

"This was a gift from James when Ben was born," Kate laughed, holding out the handkerchief. "He wasn't very good with kids and what to get them. We used to joke that's why he didn't get married and have any of his own." Her fingers trailed the letters of her son's name and she shook her head. "God, we were so mean."

Aaron looked at her but didn't say anything. He dropped his gaze back to the last framed photo in his hands. He couldn't bring himself to let go. It was a beautiful shot of Ben with Alex and Alaina, on the beach that was outside Alaina's house. They were standing in the water, and behind them was an incredible curved tower of water, a perfect wave surfers would give their arms and legs for. It was caught by the camera at that precise moment, or maybe Alaina had frozen it like that for the background of their picture.

Ben had one arm around Alaina's neck and the other around Alex's. He was sitting on Alex and Alaina's joined hands, held up between them. He was laughing. The jubilation on Ben's face was as stunning a sight as the rest of the picture. Dressed in swimming trunks and a hat, Ben looked close to the age he was in the memory Aaron had watched. Aaron wondered how long it was after this picture was taken that Ben and Alex died. Was it months? Weeks? Days?

He glanced at his mum, but she was busy going through the box, pulling out more of Ben's things. Aaron looked back at the picture. Something caught his eye. He brought the frame closer, eyes narrowed to try to make sense of what he was seeing.

"Rose?" he called. "Where's the photo of Skyler and Ben?"

Rose handed him the frame and Aaron quickly took it, studying his brother. It was there too. The same thing, exactly in the same place.

"Something wrong?" Rose asked, seeing Aaron's expression.

Aaron took a moment to reply. "I'm...I'm not sure." He raised his head and called to Kate, "Mum? What is this?" He held up the photo and pointed to a tiny black mark on Ben's chest.

Kate looked up, her eyes already tearing up as she looked through her deceased son's things.

"That's nothing," she dismissed. "It was a birthmark."

"What kind of a birthmark?" Aaron pressed.

"It was nothing, Aaron," she said. "Just a small spot, though it looked more like a blemish. I swear, the first time I noticed it, I thought something had irritated his skin. There was a strange red outline to the dark spot." She shook her head. "But it was just a birthmark."

Aaron was staring at her, his heart thumping in his chest. He remembered seeing Kyran after he saved Rose's life from the hell hound attack. Aaron had walked in on him before Kyran got a chance to button up his shirt. He had seen what he thought was a tattoo, a simple black circle on the left side of Kyran's chest, with a slight red tinge around it.

'Nice tat,' he had remarked and Kyran had only smiled in return.

Aaron dropped his gaze to the two photos before him, both of them with Ben's exposed torso, both of them showing a small black circle on the left side of his chest.

The sound of his mum's choked sob made Aaron look up. He saw what his mum had pulled out from the box: a plush toy of a monkey, wearing a sleeveless red and gold jacket with matching shorts. A small plaster was on its forehead and a bandage on the very tip of its long curved tail.

"This was his favourite," Kate said quietly, holding the stuffed toy. "He used to love the puppet shows." Kate held the toy in her hands. She smiled even as tears welled in her eyes. "When I was expecting you, we would openly discuss what to name you," she said. "Ben would insist we involve him too. We would ask him, 'What are you going to call your baby brother, Ben?' and he would hug this toy tight to his chest, laugh and say…" She paused. "'Ace,'" she whispered as a tear rolled down her cheek. "'I'm going to call my brother, Ace.'"

Aaron turned to look at Rose who stared back at him with wide eyes. Her hand came up to cover her mouth as realisation filtered through the shock.

But for Aaron, shock didn't even begin to cover it.

***

Chris's attack had knocked both him and Kyran to the ground. Chris managed to get the upper hand and held Kyran down, instructing the roots and vines to grab hold of him. They latched on to Kyran, doing what Chris commanded. Not even a heartbeat later, though, the roots and vines slid away from Kyran, recoiling fast.

Chris's moment of confusion got him a solid hit right across the face, whipping his head to the side. Before he knew what was happening, he was on the ground and Kyran was on top of him, holding him there.

The sound of numerous motorbikes cut through the air and Kyran stilled. Headlights appeared in the woods, cutting through the darkness. The Hunters had arrived.

Taking advantage of Kyran's distraction, Chris swung his fist, catching him across the cheek and throwing him to the ground. Chris took Kyran by his collars, trying to keep him pinned. His rough grab pulled Kyran's shirt, popping several of the buttons. The glow of the Gate they were fighting in front of gave enough light for Chris to see the dark circle on Kyran's chest.

Chris stilled, his eyes widened at the unique mark, at the mark he couldn't possibly mistake. His stare moved to rest on Kyran's face and his fingers slackened their grip.

"Ben?"

Kyran stopped struggling. He met Chris's shocked eyes and, for a moment, he just stared at him. Then the green of Kyran's eyes darkened and he shoved Chris back. Kyran got to his feet, but his attention had shifted to the Hunters that had come roaring to join the fight.

"Fall back!" Kyran commanded the vamages. "Fall back, now!" He turned from the Gate and ran, without giving Chris so much as another glance.

The vamages disappeared into clouds of mist and soared into the sky.

Chris watched Kyran, unable to move, unable to speak. It was as if someone had pulled the earth out from under him and Chris was falling, powerless to stop, unable to find solid ground.

A few of the Hunters ran to him and dropped to his side.

"Chris, are you okay? Are you hurt?" one of them asked.

Chris didn't say anything. Guns clicked next to him and he turned his head to see Ryan and Omar take aim at Kyran's retreating form.

"No!" Chris cried and jumped up, pushing Ryan and Omar back. "Don't shoot!" he said, standing in front of the Hunters. "No one shoot!"

He turned around just in time to see Kyran swallowed up by the darkness. "That's my son," Chris said, his voice breaking. "That's...that's my Ben."

26

The Ones Left Behind

The Elementals gathered in the Hub, along with a very confused Scott, trying to make sense of what Chris had told them.

"It's a trick," Scott said, standing next to the round table, looking at Chris in disbelief. "It must be."

"It's not a trick," Chris said, pacing the floor and running his trembling hands through his hair. "It's him. He's Ben. Kyran is Ben."

"Do you hear yourself?" Ella asked. "Are you aware of what you're actually saying?"

Chris didn't answer and continued to pace up and down the Hub.

"This is perfect," Skyler drawled, the only one seated in the room. He leaned back on his elbows to the bench behind him. "I couldn't ask for better entertainment."

"Shut up, Sky!" Ella snapped.

Neriah looked at Skyler but didn't say anything.

The sound of rushing footsteps echoed from beyond the door before it slammed open. Chris stopped and turned, seeing Kate, Aaron and the twins burst into the room. Kate's face was flushed, her eyes wide and her breath laboured. She ran to him, leaving Aaron, Sam and Rose at the door.

"Chris!" She stopped before him. "Chris, he – Aaron – he, he said..." She couldn't speak. "Kyran...He has – he –" Her hand lifted to touch the left side of her chest. "Aaron said he saw...Kyran has the...the..."

Chris held Kate's hand, his eyes welling with tears. He nodded. "It's him," he said. "It's our Ben."

Kate stared at him. She shook her head a bare fraction. "Chris," she breathed. "I felt him die. *We* felt him die. How...how can he be alive? How could he have survived that attack?"

"I don't know," Chris said, shaking his head. "But I saw the mark on his chest. It's him, Kate. He's alive." He cupped her face in his hands. "Kyran is Ben."

Droplets fell down Kate's cheeks, but her eyes were still on her husband. She trembled and her breath rushed out of her, turning into a sob. Chris pulled her into his arms, holding her close. Kate cried. Muffled words of gratitude left her as she clutched at her husband.

Aaron wanted to go over to them but he couldn't move. The sight of his parents, broken by sheer relief that their son was still alive, was as painful a sight as it was joyful.

"I hate to do this," Ella said, stepping towards Chris and Kate, "but you both need to stop and think about this, okay? Kyran is *not* your son."

Kate pulled out of Chris's arms and turned to look at Ella, her face tear-stained. Chris kept his arms around her.

"I saw his birthmark," he said.

"It was dark," Ella argued. "How can you say for certain what you saw?"

"I saw it!" Chris said angrily. "I wouldn't mistake that mark. It was him. Kyran is Ben. He's my son."

Ella turned to look at Neriah with exasperation. "Neriah, please," she said. "A little help here?"

Neriah took in a deep breath and turned, his hands still clasped behind him. Quietly, he asked, "Can you feel him?"

Chris faltered. Kate stiffened next to him.

"Neriah, I know what I saw—" Chris started.

"What about you, Kate?" Neriah cut him off and looked at her.

Kate swallowed hard and gave a small shake of her head.

Neriah turned back to Chris. "I think that settles it, then."

"He's my son," Chris insisted.

"Then why can't you feel him?" Neriah asked.

"I don't know!" Chris snapped. "I don't understand how...I can't..." He stopped and took in a long breath. "I can't feel him but he has the same birthmark, and his resemblance to Alex, and he's a part of Aaron's Inheritance and...and the way he looks at me..." He held Neriah's gaze. "He's my son, Neriah. I can't feel it but I *know* it."

"Your son was attacked by Lycans," Neriah said. "There is no way he survived. The poison would have killed him, if his injuries didn't."

"He must have been healed in time," Chris said.

Neriah didn't say anything. Ella looked pained, glancing from Neriah to Chris. She pulled in a breath and stepped towards Chris and Kate.

"I get it," she said softly. "I know what it's like. I've dreamt of moments like this; moments when those I've lost have come back to me and it was all a great big misunderstanding, but..." She paused. "But things don't work like that, not in real life. Those who die, don't come back." She held Chris's eyes. "You're desperate to believe your son is still alive, so much so that you're ignoring everything that proves that he is in fact dead. Lycans killed your son. You felt him die. Neriah *buried* him."

"There were many children massacred that day," Chris said. "Maybe Neriah buried another child, thinking he was Ben."

"Chris, come on," Ella said. "Don't you think Neriah would be able to tell if it was Ben or not?"

"To be fair," Neriah said. "What I buried that day was little more than mangled flesh. There was no way to identify him." He looked at Chris, holding his hopeful gaze. "But he was found next to Alex, dressed as Ben had been."

"It could have been anyone," Chris insisted. "Ben's clothes weren't that distinct." His face paled and it looked like he had to force himself to speak, but he pushed on, "When I found Alex, there were a lot of bodies around him. I thought I saw Ben next to him too, but...but it can't have been him, because my Ben is still alive."

Neriah didn't argue, but he looked away from Chris.

Kate suddenly paled, her eyes widened. She grabbed hold of her husband's shirt. "Oh God, Chris!" she cried. "We left him." Her red-rimmed eyes were wide and full of fear. "We...we *left* him. We felt Ben die and we left the realm. Ben was here, all this time. He's been here for *fourteen* years!" She shook her head in abject horror. "Oh God, what did we do? What did we do?"

Chris looked just as broken by guilt. He hugged Kate, unable to say anything as regret consumed him whole. "We'll make this right," he managed to whisper. "We'll do whatever it takes but we will do right by Ben, I swear."

"Alright." Skyler sat up. "I'm just going to go ahead and ask." He pointed a finger at Chris. "If Kyran is *your* son..." He glanced to Kate before looking back at Chris with a smirk. "...why does he look so much like your brother?"

Kate turned to Skyler with wide eyes, first surprised at the question, then outraged at the insinuation.

Chris glared at him. "That's enough from you," he warned.

Skyler held up both hands, grinning. "Hey, look, I'm just asking what everyone else here is thinking."

"Plenty of children are born with a resemblance to their aunts and uncles," Chris said.

"A resemblance, yes," Skyler said. "But from what I hear, Kyran is a spitting image of your deceased little bro." He smirked widely, his eyes moved to Kate. "I can sense there's a story here."

The ground shook and then cracked. It went from the door to Skyler. The bench behind Skyler snapped in two. Seeing red with fury, Aaron shot across the Hub. He would have launched himself at Skyler with everything he had, if Chris hadn't grabbed hold of him.

"No!" he told Aaron. "Don't."

But Aaron was lost in his rage. His slitted eyes were locked on Skyler, who had been forced to his feet, the smirk wiped off his face.

"*Watch* your tongue," Aaron warned. "Or I'll rip it right out!"

Skyler's surprise turned to amusement. "Come on, Aaron," he chuckled. "You can't tell me it's not weird that your so-called brother looks exactly like your uncle and not your dad?"

"That's my mother you're insulting!" Aaron spat, struggling against his dad's hold.

"Well, maybe your mother should do some explaining," Skyler said.

Aaron lost it. "Son of a—!"

"Enough!" Neriah's voice boomed across the Hub, drawing everyone's attention. Neriah turned to Skyler, his expression one of fury. "The next time you open your mouth, it better not be to spew more vile rubbish!"

Skyler held back his smirk and dropped his head. Chris let go of Aaron but stayed by his side, in case Aaron went for Skyler again.

Neriah looked to Chris and Aaron before his gaze moved to Kate. He nodded at her. "My apologies to you, Kate," he said. "I know you cared for Alex like a sister would. Skyler had no right to disrespect you."

Kate shot an angry look at Skyler before turning to Neriah and nodding. "Thank you," she said. "It doesn't make sense, though." She shook her head, reaching up to rub at her forehead, as if warding off a headache. "I always imagined Ben to grow up to look very much like Chris, like Aaron. I don't know why he looks like Alex. He *shouldn't* look like Alex." She held Neriah's gaze. "Ben had my eyes. How can his eyes have changed from blue to green? It doesn't make any sense."

"None of this makes sense," Ella said. "Think about it. If Kyran really is Ben Adams, then how did he get the legacies from Hadrian?"

No one had an answer. They looked to each other, confused.

"There must be an explanation," Aaron said. Like his parents, Aaron too had no doubt that Kyran was Ben, despite Ella and Neriah's argument.

"There is," Ella said. "But it's not the one you want to hear." She turned to Kate and Chris. "Did Hadrian know about Ben's birthmark?"

Chris frowned. "Why are you asking?"

"Maybe the mark you saw wasn't real."

"What do you mean?" Kate asked.

"Did Hadrian ever see Ben's birthmark?" Ella repeated.

Kate shared a look with Chris. "Yes. On warm days, Ben used to run around without his top on. All the kids did. Hadrian lived in Marwa, so he probably did see it at some point."

Ella bit her lip. "Then, don't you think that the mark that Kyran has could be a tattoo?" She looked at Chris. "Maybe Hadrian noticed as Kyran grew up that he shared a resemblance with Alex Adams. Why Kyran looks like Alex I have no idea, but maybe Hadrian convinced Kyran to get a tattoo just like the birthmark Ben had?"

"Why would he do that?" Aaron asked.

"For this exact reason," she said. "Look at us. We're standing around, discussing the possibility of Kyran Aedus, the Scorcher, being Benjamin Adams." She shook her head and turned to look at Chris. "You felt your son die. That right there is all the proof you need to know Ben is dead." She shook her head. "Kyran is not your son, Chris. Being the legacy holder for Fire and for Air, which Hadrian stole, proves he's an Aedus by blood."

Chris held her eyes. "Legacies or not, I know Kyran is my son," he said.

Something clicked in Aaron's mind.

"The legacy," he said, drawing everyone's attention. "Of course, that's why I don't have it."

"Aaron?" Kate held on to his arm. "What are you talking about?"

"I'm not the legacy holder," Aaron said. "It was never supposed to be me. Naina said, *'The legacy is with its rightful holder.'* But she never said Dad was the legacy holder. I assumed it was him, but the legacy has always been with Kyran because he's the rightful holder." He smiled as it all finally made sense to him. "The legacy was Ben's but everyone thought he died and so figured the legacy went back to Dad and then transferred to me when my core awoke. But Ben didn't die. So *Kyran* is the legacy holder for Earth. That's why I couldn't wield the Blade."

Chris turned to Neriah, who looked rather thrown.

"Wait, just hold on a minute," Skyler started, his earlier mirth and amusement gone. "So you're saying that Kyran has the legacy for Earth, Fire *and* Air. He has *three* legacies?"

Ella had her hands in her hair. "This can't be happening," she said. "There's no way Kyran has all three legacies. Please, God, that can't be true."

"It very well might be," Scott said. "I was going crazy trying to figure out how Kyran could've possibly got out of those cuffs. Ella surviving his attack proved that Kyran is in fact a mage, but no mage can break out of the inhibitors." He held up a finger. "But, if Kyran does hold more than one legacy, then he can overpower pretty much any restraining device we have." He looked to Neriah. "A mage, an Elemental, the legacy holder – whoever it is – can only hold *one* legacy, *one* power, an affinity to *one* element. That is the belief we have been working with since the very beginning. And the cuffs are only capable of blocking one power. But Kyran, by wielding both the Blades of Aedus and Avira, proves a mage can hold more than one legacy. That is how he broke out of those cuffs. We were inhibiting one of his powers, but he still had another one – maybe two." He shook his head. "It's no wonder I couldn't lift the rocks he put down when he trapped you in a fight," he said to Neriah. "Being the Controller, I can cancel out the ring when an Elemental sets it up, but I can't cancel out what a multi-legacy holder sets up."

"One of those legacies is *mine*," Skyler said. "And I don't care what I have to do, I'm getting it back from him."

"You're not going to hurt him," Kate said at once.

"I'm telling you, Kyran's not your son," Ella said. "He can't be."

"And I'm telling you he is," Chris argued.

"There's one way to find out," Neriah said. Everyone stopped to look at him. "Chris," Neriah started, "if you can wield the

Blade of Adams, then you are the legacy holder and Kyran isn't your son."

"And if I can't?" Chris asked.

Neriah took a moment to answer. "Then Kyran is the legacy holder for Earth, as well as Fire and Air." He met Chris's eyes. "And that means our problems just got three times bigger."

***

Kyran stormed his way into the bedroom, slamming the door shut behind him. He ran a hand through his hair and cursed, closing his eyes tightly. He pulled off his coat, yanking it away with aggression.

"Whoa, easy there," came a silky voice. "You don't want to rip your iconic Elemental coat of honour now, do you?"

Kyran didn't turn to see who was in his room. "Get out, Layla," he glowered.

Layla smiled and leant against the door frame. "But I just got here."

Kyran turned to her. "I said, *get out*," he growled.

"Or what?" Layla asked. She sauntered over to him. "What're you going to do, Scorcher?" She stopped before him, tilting her head up to gaze into his furious eyes. "Burn me?" She inched closer. "Go ahead," she whispered. "Let those sparks fly."

Kyran grabbed her by the arm and hauled her towards the door.

Layla giggled. "Okay, okay, I was just playing," she said quickly. "I only came to tell you that Hadrian wants to see you."

"I don't care why you came," Kyran said, "but if I find you in my room again, I'll make you pay."

"Don't make promises you can't keep," Layla smirked.

With a snarl, Kyran pulled the door open and threw Layla out. She knocked into a strong chest, and a pair of arms closed around her, steadying her. Surprised, Layla looked up to see who had caught her. Hadrian stood holding her, but his gaze was on his son. Kyran stared back with darkened eyes, his jaw clenched. He turned without a word, but left his door open.

Layla stepped out of Hadrian's embrace but the vamage kept a hand around her arm.

"How many times do I have to tell you?" Hadrian said to her. "Don't aggravate him. Stay on this side of the door."

Layla smiled. "Really, Hadrian?" she asked. "You're going to put restrictions on me when I'm indoors now?"

Hadrian's hand came up to brush her cheek. "I'm only trying to keep you safe."

Layla held Hadrian's gaze. "He won't kill me," she said. "You've instructed him not to, and he would rather die than go against your word. I have nothing to fear."

Hadrian looked at Kyran's room and smiled. "Layla," he whispered. "When it comes to Kyran, you have plenty to fear. Just like the rest of this realm."

He gently pushed her towards the corridor. Layla left quietly, not looking back.

Hadrian stepped forward and knocked on Kyran's open door. Kyran didn't look around at him; he was busy unbuckling the holsters and belts from around his torso and arms, dumping his array of weapons on his bed.

"Let me put these away," he called. "Then I'll give you the debrief."

"There's no need," Hadrian said, walking inside. "Machado already did."

Kyran didn't say anything, but the way he roughly threw his dagger belt onto the bed told of his anger.

"Kyran?" Hadrian started.

"I'll get it," Kyran said, without facing him. "The Blade of Adams will be ours, okay? You don't need to worry."

"I'm not worried," Hadrian said. "But maybe I should be, since my son won't look me in the eye when he makes promises any more."

Kyran turned around with an agitated sigh. "I'll get it," he repeated, holding Hadrian's gaze. "Alright? I'll get the third Blade, so the only one left will be Neriah's. There, you happy?"

Hadrian didn't say anything. He walked over to Kyran. He reached out and lifted Kyran's chin, tilting his face to the side a little, to study the bruise on his cheek. The bruise that Machado reported was the result of the blow Christopher Adams delivered. Kyran pulled away, turning his back to Hadrian. He picked up a handful of weapons and headed to his cabinet to store them.

Hadrian watched him quietly. "Are you going to say anything?"

"What do you want me to say?" Kyran asked, stacking his blades and pistol magazines into the wall-mounted cabinet.

"It's been six months," Hadrian said. "Six months since they've returned and you've yet to say a single word on the subject."

Kyran continued to put away his things. "Because I have nothing to say."

Hadrian stepped closer. "I would rather you say something," he started. "Get it out of your system." Kyran remained silent. "I can't imagine how it must feel," Hadrian said. "After fourteen years, your parents have come back to this realm." He saw the way Kyran tensed. Hadrian watched him closely. "Seeing them again, it must be confusing. I can understand if you want to go to them, talk to them–"

Kyran slammed the cabinet shut with such force the door was left dangling from its hinges. He turned to face Hadrian with clenched fists. "What is *wrong* with you?" he asked.

"You can't fool me, Kyran," Hadrian said calmly. "I brought you up. I can tell you're struggling—"

"Yeah, struggling to figure out what's going on in your head!" Kyran cut across him.

"They came back," Hadrian said. "After fourteen years, Chris and Kate are back. Are you telling me you don't want to go to them?"

Kyran looked like his patience was fraying, thread by thread. "You need to stop this," he said, taking a step towards him. "Alright? Just stop. I'm not going anywhere. I'm always going to be here, by your side."

"Kyran—"

"I'm not their son," Kyran said, his voice fierce, his eyes fiercer. "I'm *your* son and your son alone."

Hadrian smiled. Something shifted in his hazel eyes, brightening them. "You have no idea how good it is to hear you say that," he said. "I was afraid, in the surprise of seeing your birth-parents again, you may have forgotten what it was I asked of you when I took you in."

"I remember," Kyran replied. "I haven't forgotten anything." He held Hadrian's gaze. "There's no struggle on my part, Father. No desire to return to anyone. I'm staying with you."

Hadrian straightened up to stand tall, as if a weight had been lifted from his shoulders. "Good," he said. He turned to go downstairs. "There are a few hours until sunrise. Rest, and I will see you at the table for breakfast."

"I'm not hungry," Kyran replied.

"And I don't care. You *will* eat," Hadrian replied. He stopped at the door to turn and look at him. "And, Kyran?" His eyes darkened and the gold specks glinted. "Heal that bruise before you come downstairs."

Kyran nodded.

"And the next time any being strikes you," Hadrian said, "I expect you to bleed them out, no matter who they are."

Kyran didn't say anything but gave a slow, very reluctant nod.

Hadrian smiled and walked out.

27

TESTING BONDS

The large arch windows facing the back of the mansion were Hadrian's favourite. If he stood close enough to the glass, it seemed as though he was outside. Hadrian was silent, his hands tucked behind his back. He watched as the rising sun streaked the sky red. It was going to be a beautiful day. His eyes scanned the thick, lush greenery. He had chosen to live at this particular location for Kyran, to keep him close to his true element, so he could draw comfort from it. But Kyran very rarely did.

From the day Kyran decided to bury his past and take on a new identity, he had made an effort to distance himself from anything that reminded him he was, in fact, an Adams. At the beginning of his training, Kyran had refused to learn anything that involved the element of Earth. But Hadrian had chipped away at his resolve, urging him to use what strengths he had. Eventually, Kyran gave in.

Under his careful training, Kyran had become a force to be reckoned with. Hadrian couldn't help but beam with pride at how versatile and powerful Kyran had become under his guidance. Three out of the four elements were under Kyran's complete control. He could play with fire, move the earth and bend the air.

But that didn't mean Kyran had made peace with his past. It hadn't escaped Hadrian's notice how Kyran refused to go anywhere near the City of Marwa – the place that had once been his home, where memories of his family remained. Hadrian never pushed him. He was perhaps the only one in the entire realm who understood Kyran's pain. After all, the City of

Marwa had once been his home too. The difference was that Kyran chose to leave; Hadrian had been thrown out.

A knock sounded on his door. Hadrian didn't turn, but called for Machado to enter. He always knew when it was Machado; his knock was always so hurried and urgent.

The door opened and loud steps clicked on the marble floor, but Hadrian still didn't face him.

"Sir," Machado started. "We've received confirmation. Preparations are almost complete. We are set to execute the plan."

Hadrian smiled. "Good," he said. "Ensure everyone understands what it is they have to do. Mistakes won't be tolerated."

"Yes, sir," Machado replied.

Hadrian waited, but Machado didn't take his leave. Hadrian finally turned to see the vamage standing there, looking uneasy.

"Is there something you wish to ask?" Hadrian said.

"Sir, I was just wondering…" Machado swallowed hard. "The Scorcher – it was clear that he's against this. He won't be happy when he finds out." The glittery blue eyes held fast to Hadrian's. "What will you tell him?"

Hadrian took a step towards him. "Are you afraid of Kyran, Machado?" he asked.

Machado dropped his gaze to the floor. "I'm afraid of his capabilities, sir."

Hadrian stared at him. Then the corners of his lips turned upwards. "Good," he said. "You should be afraid of Kyran, and especially of his capabilities." He shook his head. "Go. Do what I've asked of you. Kyran won't touch you – you have my word."

"With all due respect, sir," Machado said, "the Scorcher may not wait to consult with you before taking out his anger."

"Kyran won't do anything to you, not before talking to me," Hadrian said. "And when he does, he'll find what happened was nothing more than a profitable coincidence." His eyes hardened. "I never gave you these orders. You never left with a team. It was an opportunistic attack, one that gave us what we needed the most. Kyran will be pleased with the result, even if he doesn't agree with the way it was achieved." He tilted his head to the doors. "Now go and arrange the happy accident."

Machado nodded. "Yes, sir." He was about to leave when he paused. "Sir, the Hunters we will take care of, but you never stated what you would like us to do with the others."

Hadrian paused for a moment, then said, "Kill them."

Machado nodded. "How many, sir?"

Hadrian's eyes darkened. "All of them."

A smile finally came to Machado's face. He nodded and quickly left the room.

Hadrian turned back to the window, to admire the beauty of the dawn once more, before making his way to the dining room, to have breakfast with his son.

***

The hours passed in a blur for Aaron. He found he didn't do anything the whole day but just sit and think, trying to work his mind through everything he had learnt the previous night.

Absent-mindedly, he watched Ella lead a group of Hunters past the Gate, armed with their weapons, riding their motorbikes. He had seen Skyler do the same not an hour before. He found himself wondering what had happened – what would warrant two sets of Hunters leaving within an hour of each other. On any other day, Aaron would have asked around until he got an answer. Today, Aaron couldn't convince himself to get up. He knew the likely answer, anyway. Hadrian had

363

declared war on them. His vamages were probably wreaking havoc somewhere. It would explain why the Hunters were leaving with haste. Aaron closed his eyes and ran a hand through his hair.

His dad had left earlier that day with Neriah and a whole army of mages, travelling to the Blade of Adams. This was the acid test — to see if Kyran was, in fact, the legacy holder for Earth. If he was, then Chris wouldn't be able to wield the Blade, rendering him drained and out of commission for a few days. If not, then Chris would be returning to Salvador with one of the four mightiest weapons of this realm.

They could do as many tests as they wanted but Aaron knew the truth. Kyran was the legacy holder for Earth, because Kyran was Ben. He was Benjamin Adams, Aaron's older brother.

Aaron couldn't explain how it was that Ben survived the brutal Lycan attack, or how it's even possible for Ben's blue eyes to change to vivid green, and why his parents felt Ben die when he didn't. But somehow, Aaron just *knew* Kyran was Ben. He could feel it, deep inside him, a certainty that no amount of conflicting evidence could shake.

Aaron felt the bite of the wind at his cheeks, but he stubbornly stayed where he was, sitting at the doorstep of their cottage.

The door opened behind him.

"Hey," Kate called. "What are you doing sitting here alone? Where's Samuel and Rosalyn?"

"They're at the Stove," Aaron said. "They wanted to help clear up after dinner."

Aaron knew it was an excuse. Sam and Rose just wanted some space, so they could discuss the possibility of Kyran being Aaron's brother in privacy. Aaron didn't really mind. He needed the solitude to figure things out himself.

Kate rubbed her arms against the chill. "You want to come inside?" she asked.

"In a minute," Aaron replied.

His mum sat down next to him and wrapped an arm around his shoulder, pulling him in for a hug. "I know this is a lot to take in," she started quietly. "It's a lot for us, too. I never thought..." She paused and took in a breath. "Finding out that Ben is alive... It's a miracle that I never imagined."

Aaron wasn't surprised. He could never forget the memory he had watched. He saw for himself how brutally Ben had been attacked. The Lycans had torn chunks out of his body. They had thrown him from one to the other, catching him with their sharp teeth. If not the injuries and blood loss, then surely the poison from the Lycans' fangs would have killed him. How could anyone, let alone a child of four years old, survive something like that?

Kate rubbed his arm, mistaking his trembling for being cold. "You sure you don't want to come inside?" she asked. "It starts to get quite cold in May."

"Weird that," Aaron mumbled. "Supposed to be summer in May."

"In some parts of the human realm," Kate corrected. "But in this realm, it's the end of autumn."

Aaron sat with his mum for long, silent minutes, before clearing his throat.

"I wanted to ask you something," he said. "Dad kept saying he couldn't feel Kyran. How does that work?" He shifted out of her embrace so he could face her. "I mean, how do you know if someone is a part of your family? What is it that you feel?"

Kate took in a deep breath, hugging her arms to her chest. "It's a feeling deep in your bones," she said. "When you're physically close to someone from your bloodline, you have a familiarity that you can't ignore. You're comfortable around them, you feel at ease. But this bond should still be felt when physically away from each other." She closed her eyes. "Right this moment, I should be able to feel both my sons. I should be able to sense Ben's presence, no matter how far away he is." She sighed. "But I can't. The only one I can sense is you." She looked at Aaron. "I feel a void, a deep empty space where Ben's supposed to be." She shook her head, reaching up with one hand to caress her forehead. "I've felt it for fourteen years. I've walked around with a hole in my soul, just like your dad has, but all this time, Ben was right here."

Aaron looked down at the ground, not able to watch the pain on his mum's face. "Tell me more," he said quietly. "About this bond."

Kate took in a breath and dropped her hand into her lap. "Simply put, Aaron, the bond is what tells you who your family is. You can sense when they're around. It's like you can recognise them by their footsteps alone. If they're in trouble, you can feel it."

"And if you call for them…" Aaron started quietly. "If you ask for their help, even if they're in another city, in another zone, they can hear you?"

Kate smiled. "They can't actually *hear* you, in the proper sense of the word," she said. "But that's what it's named, 'hearing calls'. But it's more like they can feel it. If you call out to someone in your family, they know you need them. You don't even need to raise your voice. You call for them in your mind and they will hear you."

Aaron didn't say anything.

"We should go inside," she said. "It's getting chilly."

Aaron nodded but he didn't move.

Kate paused for a moment before leaning over and kissing his head. "Don't stay out here for too long," she said softly, getting up and going into the cottage.

Aaron sat for a few minutes, trying to take it all in. That's why Kyran had come the day Rose got attacked by a hell hound. Aaron, in panicked desperation, had called out for Kyran and he had come running, even though he hadn't been in the same zone. When Aaron asked how he knew they needed help, Kyran had replied it was because Aaron was wearing his pendant – a necklace Hunters wore to keep in contact with Scott and each other during a hunt. But Aaron knew he had lost his pendant before Rose had got attacked. It had been nagging Aaron ever since, how Kyran heard his calls for help. Now he knew. Kyran hadn't heard him; he had felt him. Kyran felt the pull when Aaron, his younger brother, called to him. And just like so many times before, Kyran had come to his aid.

Aaron got up. The wind ruffled his hair. The sun was getting ready to set. For a moment, Aaron just stood there, motionless, eyes staring at the empty street. Then he stepped forward, instead of turning to go indoors, and headed towards the Gate.

Aaron walked through the forest until he was sure he had left the Gateway leading to the Gate of Salvador far behind. He couldn't risk anyone coming to, or going from, Salvador seeing him.

Aaron stopped at a small clearing. The air felt warmer here. Aaron had no idea if it was because he was this deep in the woods or because he had been walking for so long that he had built up a sweat. He went to a short tree stump and sat down. For almost ten minutes, Aaron did nothing but sit there.

The last six months he had been in this realm, he had spent four of them with his brother without knowing it. All his conversations, his time training, every moment he'd spent with Kyran flashed through his mind. The morning after they met, Kyran had interrupted Aaron when he was introducing himself. Aaron had been so surprised that Kyran knew who he was. When he'd asked how, Kyran had smirked and replied, '*You look like your father.*'

Aaron tried to imagine what it must've been like for Kyran, to see his brother and recognise him because he resembled their father – the father that had left him and disappeared from the realm.

Aaron had been forced to wait for four months in Salvador, not knowing where his parents were, when they were going to come back. Kyran had waited fourteen years.

Aaron remembered Kyran trying to convince him to give up on his parents, that they weren't coming back.

'Ace, they've done this before. Your parents ran out on this realm and didn't look back for fourteen years.'

'Yes, but at that time they didn't leave behind their son!' Aaron had replied.

Aaron cringed. He closed his eyes, shaking his head at what he had unknowingly said. He thought about the way Kyran had changed the subject then, taking him away to train. At the time, Aaron thought Kyran had done that for him, to distract him. Now, he wondered whether that distraction was for him, or for Kyran himself.

Aaron let out a heavy breath. Kyran had looked out for him, risked his own life to save him from a collapsing Q-Zone, taken him away from Skyler's beatings, protected him on hunts, stood before him, shielded him – Kyran had done it all, not because Aaron was an inexperienced Hunter, but because Aaron was his younger brother.

'You think that's why I call you Ace?' Kyran had asked. *'To make fun of you?'*

Aaron buried his face in his hands. No, Kyran had never called him Ace to make fun of him, but because that was the name he'd wanted to give his baby brother. Aaron dropped his hands and let out a shaky breath. He closed his eyes and, for a moment, just sat like that.

"Kyran?" he called in a quiet voice. "I don't know if this is just...me being crazy or...or if you can actually hear me," he started. "But I – I really need to see you." He looked ahead, fixing his stare on the darkened trees. "There's so much that I need to ask, so much that I need to know."

He looked around the forest, but there was no one there except for him. He took in a breath. "Ben?" He squeezed his eyes shut and shook his head. That didn't feel right. "Kyran, please," Aaron breathed. "I really need to see you. We need to talk. We need to...I don't know, figure this out."

The minutes ticked by, but no one came. Aaron looked up at the sky, barely visible through the thick tops of the trees. "Kyran, please, I just want to talk," he repeated. "Please, Kyran. I just want to talk."

He fell quiet and the silence of the forest surrounded him.

"Talk, then."

Aaron whirled around. He found Kyran standing a few steps away, his arms crossed at his chest, intense green eyes fixed on him.

"I'm listening."

28

BLOOD BROTHERS

Aaron rose to his feet, staring at Kyran. He had come. Aaron had called for him and Kyran had come. Although this was what Aaron had been hoping for, it still came as a bit of a shock.

Aaron gazed at Kyran, at the brother he never knew he had. But for Kyran, Aaron understood it wasn't the same story.

"You knew," Aaron stated. "From the very beginning. You knew that we were brothers."

Kyran smiled and leant against the tree beside him. "I only have the one brother," he said. "It's kinda hard to mistake him."

Aaron's heart leapt in his chest when Kyran referred to him as his brother. He didn't know why, but he was bracing himself for Kyran to deny it. He stepped forward, his eyes prickling. "Why didn't you say anything?" he asked.

Kyran looked surprised, and then started laughing. "Bloody hell, Ace," he chuckled. "What did you expect me to say? 'Hi, Aaron. You may or may not know that you have an older brother and, surprise, surprise, that's me'?"

"You should have told me," Aaron argued. "I asked why I was seeing you in my dreams. You could have told me then. You could have explained that the dreams were my Inheritance and I was dreaming of you because you're my brother."

Kyran looked closely at Aaron. "Tell me something," he said quietly. "Before you came to this realm, did you even know you had a brother?"

370

Aaron felt like someone had doused him with ice-cold water. He froze on the spot, staring at Kyran. He willed himself to speak, to lie, to tell him that their parents had told him all about their family from the very beginning. But Kyran had already picked up the truth from his silence.

He nodded and looked away. "I thought so," he said.

"Kyran–" Aaron started.

"It makes sense," Kyran said. "They didn't tell you anything about who you are, where you're from, what you can do…" He held Aaron's gaze. "So why would they tell you about the one they had left behind?"

Aaron stared at him. *Left behind?* Wait, so Kyran thought…

"No." Aaron stepped forward. "No, Kyran. Mum and Dad didn't know they'd left you behind. They thought you were…That you had…died."

Kyran's eyes widened, and for a moment he looked truly and completely shocked. Then those vivid green eyes darkened. "Died?" he asked. "Wow, that's…Okay, I admit I wasn't expecting that excuse."

"It's not an excuse," Aaron said. "They said they felt you die."

"Well, then they should get their feelings retuned, 'cause I'm right here," Kyran said.

Aaron held his eyes. "I saw the memory," he said. "I saw the attack, Kyran. I saw what happened, how those…those Lycans…What they did–" He broke off as the image of the four-year-old child being ripped out of his mother's arms and thrown to the beasts to devour flashed before his eyes. Aaron shook his head, struggling with the stinging in his eyes. "How did you survive?" he asked, his voice reduced to a whisper.

Kyran's eyes were a poison green. "By sheer luck," he said. "No thanks to my parents."

"No, they thought you were dead," Aaron said again.

"Oh come on, Aaron!" Kyran snapped. "Wake up already. Stop taking whatever crap they throw your way. They knew I wasn't dead. They knew, but they got so damn scared, they *left* me and ran. They left me to die."

"No." Aaron was shaking his head, hurrying closer to Kyran. "No, Kyran, no. They wouldn't do that. They told me they felt you die. Uncle Mike said he felt it too. That's why Uncle Alex went after the Lycans, because he felt you die as well."

Kyran's expression softened at the mention of Alex. "Alex died fighting the Lycans," he said. "He died the death of a Hunter, of an Elemental." He paused and his eyes glinted with nothing but fury. "Christopher Adams, on the other hand, is a coward who left his dying four-year-old son to save his own skin."

"You can't believe that," Aaron said. "You must know Dad would never do that."

"Wouldn't he?" Kyran asked.

"Dad would never leave someone in need to save himself," Aaron said. "Let alone his *son*."

"Look at me, Ace," Kyran said, holding out his arms. "I'm right here. I'm not dead; I never was." He held Aaron's eyes. "So if they're telling you they felt me die, then they're lying."

"No they're not," Aaron said. "You didn't see them when they talked about how you were attacked. Their grief, their tears, they were all real. They thought you had died, Kyran. They're wouldn't lie."

"Really?" Kyran asked. "They've always been truthful with you, have they? Always told you how it is?" He stepped closer. "Ace, they didn't even tell you that you were a mage. Had you not come to this realm, you wouldn't even know that you have a brother, that I exist."

His words pierced Aaron's heart. He didn't want to admit Kyran was right. "I know now," he tried.

Kyran pulled back, his expression hardening. "It's too late."

"Don't say that," Aaron pleaded. "It's not too late."

"It is," Kyran said. "Ben is gone. There's nothing of him left. He withered away, waiting for his parents to return, being foolish enough to believe they would come back for him." Kyran's eyes were dark, full of pain and anger. "Four years," he said in a voice that almost broke. "He sat and waited for four years, watching the Gateway to his home, calling out to his parents. He spent day after day, just waiting – waiting for the family who ignored his calls and never came for him." The sorrow in Kyran's voice, in his eyes, was killing Aaron. "Eventually, he gave up. From that day onwards, Ben ceased to exist. For the last ten years, there's only been Kyran Aedus – the son of Hadrian."

Aaron shook his head. "That's not true," he said. "Kyran Aedus wouldn't care what happened to Aaron Adams," he said. "Kyran Aedus wouldn't take me away from Skyler's beatings. He wouldn't have risked his life to save me from a collapsing Q-Zone. He wouldn't have taken on the responsibility of training me. Kyran Aedus wouldn't feel the pull every time I call out to him." Aaron paused to steady his voice. "Kyran Aedus wouldn't use the name Ben thought up for his little brother." His eyes stung like crazy, but Aaron didn't care any more. "Somewhere, deep down, Ben is still there," he said. "You're my brother and it means something to you, otherwise you would have just ignored me."

Kyran smiled bitterly. "Your parents may be able to ignore me," he said quietly. "But I can't ignore you."

Aaron's heart broke. "Kyran, please," he begged. "Think about it. Why would they ignore your calls? Why wouldn't they come back for you if they knew you were still alive?"

Kyran held his eyes. "Fear makes you capable of almost anything," he said. "They got scared and left me to die. They heard me screaming their names, every day, for *four* years. They heard but they ignored it, too afraid to come back in case they were attacked."

Aaron shook his head. "They must've not been able to hear you, to feel your calls—"

"It doesn't work that way," Kyran said. "They could hear me, they just didn't care."

"How can you believe that?" Aaron asked. "Why would they not care? Kyran, something must have happened when you got attacked. Some sort of...of misunderstanding. That's why they thought you died. That's why they can't feel you."

"Then why can I feel them?" Kyran asked. "Why can I feel both of them? Feel you?" His gaze searched Aaron's. "Bonds aren't one-sided, Ace. If I can sense all of you, you lot can sense me too."

Aaron didn't know what to say. He pulled in a breath. "Kyran—"

"Can you feel me?" Kyran asked.

Aaron stilled. "I...I don't know what it is I'm supposed to be looking for," he answered honestly.

"When I'm with you, do you feel comfortable?" Kyran said. "When you look at me, is there a familiarity you don't really understand? Can you tell it's me by just the sound of my footsteps? When I'm with you, do you feel safe? Like anything can happen, but you know you'll be okay, because I'm here?"

Aaron didn't say anything, but he gave a small nod.

Kyran looked both relieved and heartbroken. "Don't believe their lies, Ace," he said. "If you can feel me, then they can too. They've known I'm alive all these years."

"No," Aaron breathed. "That's...It...They're not like that. I don't believe they're capable of being so cruel."

"You want to talk about being cruel?" Kyran asked. "They know who I am, Aaron. They knew the moment they saw me, but they pretended not to notice. Your dad stood there, and asked me what my *father's* name was." His eyes were glinting in the limited light, making Aaron's heart clench with pain. "He wasn't asking because he was unsure. He was asking to see if *I* remembered. To see if the four year old he had left behind still recognised him."

"He asked you because you look just like Uncle Alex," Aaron said.

"It shouldn't matter who I look like," Kyran argued. "I'm their *son* – their blood. How can they look at me and not know who I am?"

Aaron didn't have an answer.

Kyran took in a heavy breath and closed his eyes, forcing back his pain. "It doesn't matter," he said quietly. "It's better this way. They ignore me, so I can ignore them."

"Is that really how you want it?" Aaron asked.

A bitter smile came to Kyran. "None of this is how I want it, Ace." He stepped closer and rested his hands on Aaron's shoulders. "I need you to understand something. You may be my brother, but Hadrian is my father." His eyes hardened. "He took care of me, brought me up. Everything I am today, it's due to him. I'm fighting this war for him, and I need you to keep out of it." His grip tightened. "Leave Salvador and go back to Marwa. It's the only safe city. It was Hadrian's home once; he doesn't want to see it in ruins. Take Rose and Sam with you and *stay* there, until the worst is over."

"Until the worst is over?" Aaron repeated. "You mean until Hadrian destroys the realm and kills everyone?"

"That's not his plan," Kyran said. "He wants to fix this realm, not destroy it."

"Come on, Kyran," Aaron said. "We both know he wants to burn it to the ground."

"Sometimes, that's the only way," Kyran said. "To start again and rebuild, so it's stronger."

Aaron pushed Kyran's hands away and stepped back. "You're willing to do that?" he asked with disgust.

Kyran paused for a moment, then straightened up to stand tall. "I'm willing to do whatever my father asks of me," he said. "I owe him more than you can imagine, Aaron. I have never disobeyed him."

"Really?" Aaron asked. "So if I stand in the way and he tells you to kill me?"

A flicker of unease washed over Kyran. "Then I will."

Aaron shook his head. "I don't believe you."

"You should," Kyran said. He stepped back. "Get to Marwa, the sooner the better." He walked away, and it was only then that Aaron noticed the red coat Kyran was wearing, the one that marked him as the legacy holder for Fire.

"Kyran?" Aaron called.

Kyran stopped and turned around.

"How is it that you have the legacy for Fire and Air when you're not an Aedus by blood?" Aaron asked.

Kyran expression darkened. He shook his head. "Trust me, Ace. You don't want to know." He turned to leave.

"Kyran?"

Kyran looked around at him.

Aaron paused. "Will you come if I call for you again?" he asked.

Kyran held his eyes before his usual playful smirk came to his lips. "I guess you'll have to wait and see."

He left, disappearing into the shadows. Aaron stood where he was for long minutes afterwards, waiting until he felt Kyran's presence completely fade away.

***

Aaron made his way back through the dense forest. It had been a mistake going there at sunset. The sky had turned dark and there was hardly any light from the moon. Aaron lost his way twice, coming around in a circle to the same dirt pathway, but he clambered on.

His talk with Kyran had exhausted him, leaving him feeling hollowed out. He wanted to get back to the cottage and speak with his mum. He needed to work out why both his parents couldn't feel the bond with Kyran when he could. What had happened that day, when the Lycans attacked? How could his family feel Kyran die when he was still alive? None of it made any sense.

Aaron let out a deep sigh as he trekked through the darkness, relying on his powers to sense where the trees were so he didn't walk into them. The strange thing was that Aaron wasn't even aware of what he was doing. He was too absorbed in his thoughts.

Kyran believed his parents had abandoned him. He believed his parents had got scared and left, all the while knowing he was still alive. But Aaron knew that couldn't be true. He may not know all the secrets his parents kept from him, but he knew that his mum and dad would never leave their wounded child behind. They would rather die first. The world could think what they wanted about the Adams, but Aaron knew they weren't cowards.

But then a small niggle of doubt wormed its way in. His mum had been pregnant. She'd been attacked. Maybe, just maybe, they ran to get her help. Aaron had watched the memory; he'd seen how brutally the Lycans had attacked Ben. What if his mum and dad had thought Ben was *likely* to die? It certainly had looked that way, with the Lycans throwing Ben from one to another, tearing chunks out of his body. What if his parents had given up on Ben and focused on saving their unborn child?

Aaron pushed the thought out with a firm shove. His parents weren't capable of that. They would've done everything, absolutely everything, to get to Ben and save him. They wouldn't have given up. Aaron had seen how his mum and dad had reacted to finding out that Kyran was Ben. That relief, those tears, that couldn't have been an act. And even if his parents had run to save Aaron's life, knowing that Ben was still alive, they would have come back for him. They wouldn't have lived fourteen years in the human realm, aware of Ben's existence, but not go back for him. They wouldn't have ignored Ben's calls.

His senses told him the trees ahead were thinning out, so that meant he was almost at the Gateway. Aaron let out a little sigh of relief. He peered through the darkness, but he couldn't see anything. It wasn't until a few seconds later that it hit Aaron. He stopped dead in his tracks, staring ahead at the pitch black.

He should be able to see the Gateway. In fact, he should be able to see all around him. It was after sunset in Salvador, but the Gateway was stuck in eternal daylight. The sun was always beaming overhead, the sky a perfect blue with the trees standing proud, shimmering with vibrant colours. The Gate was a towering, glowing beacon of light, brightening the entire area. So why was there no light?

Aaron set off running, darting through the forest, his feet slipping once or twice on the soft ground. Aaron made it past the edge of the forest and stopped on the stone pathway. His heaving breath caught in his chest. At the end of the path, where the Gate should be, was only a gaping rectangular hole.

Aaron's lungs ached for air, but he couldn't breathe. He stared in abject horror, fighting his disbelief to understand what had happened.

The Gate had fallen.

The City of Salvador was under attack.

29

A Lost Sanctuary

Aaron took off, bolting down the darkened pathway, straight for the gap left by the destroyed Gate. He could see through the rectangular cut in the air that Salvador was in chaos. He ran into the city and stopped, horror transfixing him to the spot.

Everywhere he looked, there was fire. The buildings on both sides of the street were set alight. The cottages, the Stove, the bakery – every building was burning. Thick, dark smoke spiralled up into the sky. The acrid smell choked Aaron, and he could taste bitter ash on his tongue when he breathed. The table that used to sit so proudly in the middle of the street was now upturned, broken into pieces.

The floating lanterns in the sky were engulfed by smoke, but Aaron could still see the street was full of dark shadows engaged in battle. Glints of silver flashed in many hands. Gunshots punctured the constant roar of the fire.

It was too dark to see who the mages were fighting, but Aaron didn't care. He staggered forward before breaking into a run. He got close enough to see Gerard, one of the kitchen helpers, trying to fight a tall, beefy man. Gerard was hit, a physical punch had him thrown to the ground. Gerard pushed himself to sit up and used his powers, trying to send out a ripple, but his efforts resulted in small cracks and nothing else. The beefy man went for him, his clawed hands ready to rip the boy apart.

Aaron was too far away, but he held out his hands. His panic and desperation fed into the earth and a ripple tore across the ground. The man was caught and thrown bodily aside. Gerard

380

turned his head to find Aaron. He stared at him with wide eyes, before quickly scrambling to his feet.

Aaron came to a stop but his eyes were on the man who had now sat up on all fours, snarling like a wounded animal. Pale amber eyes met Aaron's and the man smiled, revealing fangs.

Vamages, Aaron realised. They were being attacked by vamages.

The vamage grinned and slowly got to his feet. Aaron stood his ground, meeting the hybrid demon's gaze. In the blink of an eye, the vamage came at him. Aaron was ready. He ducked out of the way and turned, his hands aimed at the ground. Aaron clenched both hands into fists and pushed his power into the ground. A tremendous ripple caught the vamage with force, knocking him back. The vamage hit the ground hard. Before he could get back up, two Hunters took care of him, firing bullet after bullet into him. Aaron was breathing hard. He turned around and found Gerard by his side.

"We need to get to the Hub," Gerard said, grabbing Aaron's arm. "Hurry!"

"Wait." Aaron pulled back, his eyes darting to the duelling mages and vamages around him. "I need to find my mum—"

"You need to go to the Hub," Gerard said, refusing to let go of him. "That's the protocol."

"I'm not going anywhere until I find my mum and friends," Aaron said and pulled out of Gerard's grip.

Ignoring Gerard's calls, Aaron ran across the street. He spotted many mages in the battle, holding their ground against the vamages, but there weren't many Hunters. Aaron felt his already pounding heart speed up in horror when he remembered seeing Ella and Skyler both leave with large groups of Hunters. They had gone to deal with whatever chaos was going on in other cities of the realm. His dad and Neriah had taken a group with them, too. That meant there were only a handful of Hunters, and the mages who had refused to leave Salvador, left to fight the army of vamages.

In the midst of the pandemonium, Aaron spotted the blond-haired Mary, fighting with not one, but two vamages. Aaron was caught off guard at the sight. The woman who mages referred to as Mother Mary had a blade in each hand, which she swung with precision, catching the vamages in the chest, stomach and arms. She ducked and dived from their retaliating attacks, her hair falling out of her bun. In a double strike, she stabbed both vamages and pulled back. The pair of demons fell to the ground, not dead, but dazed enough to no longer pose a threat for the time being.

Mary looked up and met Aaron's eyes. She hurried towards him. "Aaron, you need to go to the Hub!" she said. "Hurry!"

"Mary, where's Sam and Rose?" Aaron asked. The twins had been helping her when Aaron left.

"I don't know," Mary said quickly, "but you need to leave. Go!" She pushed him back.

The sound of several gunshots nearby distracted both Aaron and Mary. They turned to see Alan, pistol in hand, trying to hold back a group of vamages. But no matter how many bullets Alan shot, the vamages continued forward, forcing Alan to back away. They threw fireballs at him, which Alan ducked to avoid. His gun gave its last shot, then clicked. Alan had to drop the gun and use his power to deflect the fireballs the vamages were hurling his way.

Both Mary and Aaron darted forward to Alan's aid. Aaron's hands were already tingling, preparing another powerful ripple to tear through the ground. His ripple hit the crowd of vamages, throwing them back. By the time the vamages recovered, Alan had Aaron on one side of him and Mary on the other.

The vamages stood up and tightened their group, getting ready to attack again. Their eyes glittered with hunger, and sharp fangs peeked from the corners of their vicious grins. Aaron's gaze flitted through the crowd. There were seven of them.

Aaron looked to the ground. For an instant, no longer than a heartbeat, Aaron ignored everything and everyone around him. From the depth of his mind, his brother's voice came to him.

One of the neatest tricks to fight demons is to turn the ground itself into a trap.

Aaron's eyes snapped up and he looked at the vamages. His hand lifted but his aim wasn't the vamages, but the ground on which they stood.

Sink, he commanded.

Nothing happened.

Aaron's entire body tensed. His fingertips were buzzing. His chest felt tight, his breathing strained. He pushed again.

Sink!

The ground shuddered in response. The vamages dropped their shoulders, their clawed hands flexed as they watched Aaron.

"Aaron," Alan whispered with alarm.

Aaron ignored him. The vamages growled in warning, and then darted forward.

SINK! Aaron screamed in his mind.

The ground lurched and then gave in, taking the seven vamages with it. Their cries echoed in the air as they disappeared into the ground. Aaron stared at the dark sinkhole he had created, plunging the vamages deep into the earth. The next moment, he was doubled over, his hands on his shaky knees. He was trembling, feeling like something had sapped all the energy out of him.

"Aaron? Aaron, you okay?" Alan asked, pulling Aaron back up.

"He's fine," Mary said. She stuck her two blades into the belt of her jeans and cupped Aaron's fevered face with her cool hands. "It's just a reaction to using his powers on a large scale. His core isn't used to it." She looked into Aaron's eyes. "Just breathe, Aaron," she instructed. "It'll pass. Just breathe."

Aaron did, sucking in deep breaths, shaking as his body struggled to remain upright. Within a minute or two, his strength returned, ending the quivering of his muscles. Aaron pulled back.

"I'm okay," he insisted. "I need to find my mum," he said. "And Sam and Rose."

"You need to get to the Hub," Mary said. "Now!"

She took out her twin blades and hurried forward to fight. Aaron made to follow her when Alan grabbed him by the elbow.

"We need to go," he said and started pulling Aaron in the other direction. "We don't have a lot of time. We need to get to the Hub."

Aaron dug his feet into the ground and refused to move. "Why?" he asked. "Why the Hub?"

Alan's eyes bulged. "Why do you think they're here?" he asked. "They've come for the Hub itself, the table that controls the realm. If Hadrian gets his hands on it..." His wide eyes shone with fear. "It'll all be over." He stared at Aaron. "You're the only Elemental here. It's your job to protect the Hub."

Aaron's heart kicked at his insides. He pushed back the nauseating fear that came at those words. It was all on him. He had to keep the vamages from taking the Hub. He took off, running through the street, Alan hot at his heels. They raced past the burning cottages and turned, skidding a little on the loose rocks as they headed down the path that led to the Hub.

Aaron could feel a strange pull, deep in his navel, like his stomach was twisting. Something was telling him that his mum was calling out to him, looking for him. Aaron mentally returned her call, having no clue if she would hear him, if it actually worked like this. He told her he wanted to find her too, but he had to help protect the Hub first. Panic, fear and sheer terror coursed through him. He pushed himself to go faster, to get to the Hub. Something hit his legs and Aaron tripped. His head smacked off the ground when he fell. The air was knocked clean out of him, so his pained cry came out as nothing more than a rushed breath.

A dull glow fell over him, lifting the darkness. Aaron realised Alan must have lowered one of the lanterns overhead, so they could see better.

"Good call," Aaron groaned. "Couldn't you have done that sooner?"

"Aaron?" Alan called behind him, sounding afraid.

"I'm okay," Aaron said, sitting up. "I'm okay." He turned to see what he had fallen over and froze.

On the ground was a body. The flickering light coming from the dying lantern Alan had pulled down was enough for Aaron to recognise the lifeless man. Aaron felt as if his heart had come into his mouth.

"Jason?" he called.

Alan was standing still, staring in disbelief at the crumpled body of Jason Burns lying in the middle of the path.

"Jason!" Aaron cried and scrambled forward, sitting on his knees, next to the unmoving body. "No," he gasped. "No, no, no!"

Jason's eyes were still open, his mouth slightly parted. His grey hair was stained crimson, as was his beard. Blood covered his front, stemming from the two puncture wounds at the side of his neck. Aaron's stomach turned, but he couldn't look away.

Alan carefully stepped past the body. "Aaron, come on," he said in a voice that shook. "We have to go." He grabbed hold of Aaron's arm. "Aaron? Come *on*. We can't do anything for him now. We have to go, before it's too late."

Aaron let himself be dragged back to his feet, but his gaze wouldn't move from Jason. Alan pulled Aaron further down the path, until Aaron could no longer see Jason Burns – the human who had lived in the realm of the mages, and served those who came seeking refuge in the City of Salvador.

***

Aaron and Alan reached the clearing. They came to a stop by the artillery and workshops, breathing heavily, staring at the horrifying sight. Vamages were everywhere, battling a handful of mages. The workshops had been ransacked, all kinds of weapons lay scattered across the ground. The mages were fighting valiantly, but Aaron could see they wouldn't be able to hold the vamages back for much longer. The vamages were already pushing their way forward, trying to get to the end of the dusty path, beyond which lay the way to the Hub.

Aaron bolted forward, Alan by his side. Aaron lifted a hand, directing his power towards the trees at the far end of the ground, just at the top of the hill. With a thunder-like clap, several trees fell to the ground, piling on top of one another. Thick vines grew from the ground at Aaron's command, twisting around the fallen trees on either side, and reaching out to the nearest still-standing trees, effectively barricading the way forward. The vamages attempting to slip past the mages' defence came to a stop, unable to go on until they'd cut through the vines and cleared the trees.

Aaron spotted Ava, fighting a female vamage – the first Aaron had seen. The vamage knocked Ava off her feet. Aaron sent a ripple tearing through the ground, but the vamage moved before it could catch her. She turned and flicked her wrist. A blast of air hit Aaron like a punch straight to his chest.

Aaron fell back with a dull thump. His head swam at the impact, having been knocked twice in the space of a few minutes. His moment of disorientation was all it took for the female vamage to sit on top of him, pinning him to the ground. A clawed hand wrapped around Aaron's neck, holding him still. The vamage bared her fangs in a grin.

"Hey!" a voice shouted.

The vamage turned and met a metal rod, right in her face. She was thrown off Aaron, toppling to the side. Aaron turned his head, and to his utter shock found Sam with a rod in his hand, held up like a baseball bat. He extended a hand to pull Aaron up.

"You okay?" he asked.

"Yeah," Aaron gasped. "What are you *doing?*"

Sam looked at the rod and then shrugged. "Fighting," he replied simply. "Now, come on."

Aaron went with Sam, darting through the crowd of mages and vamages locked in battle. Aaron saw Drake sending out ripples with one hand and swinging a sword with the other. He was flooring the vamages. Aaron knew Drake used to be a Hunter, but until today, he never knew how lethal a fighter he was. He was leaving the vamages dazed and bleeding on the ground.

Aaron looked over to see vamages burning through the vines and levitating the trees he had used to block the way forward. Aaron hurried in their direction with Sam, Alan and other mages behind him. Aaron swung his arm and the trees closest to the vamages rumbled and shook before their branches swept forward to knock the vamages clean off their feet. But not even a heartbeat later, more vamages had replaced them.

The mages around Aaron were all throwing out jolts of their power – fireballs, shards of ice that cut like glass, blasts of air – but the vamages stood strong and fought back, while a few continued to push the trees back, trying to clear the way. Aaron's body was aching, but he took aim again, ready to send more power into the ground to stop the vamages. The forest floor shook, but it wasn't Aaron's doing.

Bright headlights appeared from the darkness, accompanied by the roar of several motorbikes rumbling against the earth as they raced closer. Aaron turned and caught the glint of silver on an ivory coat as a bike passed under a lantern, and Aaron's breath rushed out of him with relief. Skyler was here, and so were the rest of the Hunters.

With a thunderous cry, the Hunters fell head first into the battle. Many jumped off their bikes, others chose to use them to run over vamages. Aaron found Ella by his and Sam's side in an instant, a sword in one hand and a gun in the other.

Aaron turned his attention to the vamages at the edge of the path. Most were standing ready to fight the Hunters. One vamage, Aaron spotted, was climbing over the last remaining tree to get to the other side. Aaron took off after him.

"Aaron!" Sam cried, chasing him. Ella wasn't far behind.

Aaron ran straight into the battling crowd of vamages and Hunters. He didn't pause, not even to catch his breath. He bolted right the way across and climbed over the tree, after the vamage. He tumbled down the hill. Quickly, Aaron picked himself up and peered through the darkness. He caught sight of the vamage scampering off in the distance. Aaron ran after him. The Hub was just a short distance away. He couldn't let the vamage get to it.

Aaron was running too fast. Even when he saw it, he couldn't do anything to avoid it. Out from the shadows stepped the vamage, right into Aaron's path. He raised his gun and pulled the trigger.

Aaron skidded to a halt, but he didn't have the clarity of mind, or even the time, to duck. The bullet came piercing through the air, aimed at Aaron's head. Before the bullet could bury a hole in Aaron's skull, it hit a block of ice that appeared out of nowhere. Aaron stared in shock and terror at the tiny metal bullet trapped in the thick, glass-like ice as it floated before him.

The vamage looked equally shocked, then glanced behind Aaron. An icicle zoomed past Aaron's ear and stabbed the vamage, straight through the chest. The vamage dropped his gun and staggered back, before falling to the ground. Aaron turned to see Sam and Ella running towards him. Ella had a hand still aimed at the vamage, her grey eyes narrowed with fury.

They came to stop next to Aaron, staring at the vamage lying on the ground. Ella cocked her gun, taking aim. The vamage glowered at her, still holding on to the icicle that had impaled him. Then, inexplicably, his expression cleared. He smiled, holding Ella's gaze. In a heartbeat, he disappeared, turning to mist before soaring up into the air; a white pulsing cloud against the night sky.

Aaron stared at it, brow furrowed in confusion. Before his eyes, the sky filled with more white clouds – countless in number. They merged as one and then took off, streaking into the distance. Aaron's breath was coming in fast, short rasps. He turned to look at Ella and Sam.

"They're gone?" Aaron asked. "We won?"

Somehow, he couldn't believe it. The vamages seemed to have given up all of a sudden, and all at once. Maybe they realised with Skyler and Ella back, there were enough Elementals to protect the Hub. That could be why they retreated.

Ella looked just as unsure as Aaron felt. Her narrowed eyes left Aaron and stared ahead. Her brow creased and she ran forward without saying a word. Aaron and Sam shared a look before chasing after her.

The moment they reached the grounds outside the Hub, they saw that they had, in fact, not won – not at all.

The ring that was used for Hunters' training was full of blue-robed Empaths, kneeling next to Scott's unmoving body. Scott's eyes were closed, blood on his clothes, on his skin, on the ground where he lay. Sitting next to him was Rose, crying uncontrollably, holding on to his arm. She looked up at Aaron and Sam.

"He's dead!" she cried. "Scott's dead! They...they did this to him," she sobbed. "They got inside the Hub and they attacked him. They killed him!"

Aaron's gaze moved to the circular building at the same time as Ella's. Both of them stood for a moment, frozen in sheer horror and disbelief. Then they were both running. They jumped up the bloodstained steps and into the building. They raced down the white corridor spattered with drops of Scott's blood. They saw the doors to their main meeting room hanging off the hinges. They burst into the room and stopped, the pair of them breathing hard, staring at the sight before them with growing denial.

In the middle of the room, where the gleaming round table was supposed to be, was nothing but a gaping hole in the floor. The Hub – the very *heart* of the mage realm, the device that gave mages control of the portals and allowed the formation of Q-Zones – was gone.

***

Aaron and Ella came back out of the Hub building, just as the rest of the mages and Hunters arrived. They didn't have to say anything. Everyone understood from the sight of Scott that the Hub had been attacked and taken. That's why the vamages had disappeared in a heartbeat. They'd got what they wanted and left, leaving a trail of bodies in their wake.

Aaron felt like his legs were about to give out from under him. Every step was heavy and took his full focus. He staggered his way towards the ring but he couldn't bear looking at Scott. He didn't have it in him to see another dead body. Empaths were still gathered around the Controller, their hands on Scott's body, their heads lowered and unseeing eyes closed.

"Rose?" Aaron called, collapsing next to Sam on the ground, close to the rocks that encircled the ring. "My mum...Have you seen my mum?" he asked, his voice trembling.

Rose was still at Scott's side, her bloodshot eyes on his pale face. She shook her head. "She went looking for you," she said quietly.

Aaron's heart plummeted to the pit of his stomach. He looked around at the crowd, desperately seeking her out. He couldn't find her.

Ella walked up to them and waved a hand, lifting the rocks that locked them inside the ring and kept them safe. Once the rocks were placed around the ring, nothing got in or out. It was a feature used to keep the spectators of the ring safe from the duelling Hunters inside the ring. But today it worked the other way around.

Being an Elemental, Ella was able to override whichever Empath had set down the rocks for their protection. "This was a good idea," she said, but her voice lacked any warmth.

"It was Rose's plan," one of the Empaths replied, still with her head dropped, eyes closed and her hand on Scott's arm. "She and Zhi-Jiya got us here, after our huts were attacked. The rocks forming the ring kept us safe. The vamages couldn't lift the rocks and anything they tried to throw at us was repelled."

Aaron looked at his friend, but no words of praise left him. How could they when she was sitting beside Scott's dead body?

The crowd of Empaths around Scott finally moved, sitting back on their knees and letting out deep breaths. Scott's brow creased, then his head tilted, just a fraction. Rose jumped in surprise.

"Scott?" she called, her voice shaking. "Scott? Oh my God, Scott!"

"He's alive," said one Empath, easily the eldest one out of the crowd, with an exhausted smile. "It was close, we almost lost him." She turned her head towards Rose. "Your effort paid off."

"Her effort?" Sam asked. "What did Rose do?"

"She left the protection of the ring to drag Scott's body to us so we could heal him," the Empath replied.

Sam looked back at his sister with surprise, and a little pride, too.

The mages helped to levitate Scott's body out of the ring. Aaron got to his feet and moved away to give them space. He wrapped his arms around Rose the second she walked out, with Sam quickly joining the hug.

Aaron pulled away, and that's when he caught sight of his mum, looking worse for wear, searching the crowd for him. Relief poured into Aaron. Kate saw him and she stopped in her tracks. Aaron quickly went to her, embracing her. She held him tight in her arms, whispering prayers of thanks under her breath.

Aaron saw Skyler, a frown on his face, eyes narrowed as he too looked for someone in the gathered crowd. He grabbed a hold of Zhi-Jiya's arm.

"Where's Armana?" he asked.

Zhi-Jiya turned to the crowd of Empaths, her dark eyes searching frantically. "They...they were the only ones I found in the huts," she said. "I didn't...I don't think I saw her," she said with mounting horror.

Skyler stared at her, his eyes wide. The colour drained from his face. He backed away.

"No," he breathed. He turned around, blue eyes searching the darkness. "Armana!" he called. "Armana!" He took off running.

"Skyler, wait!" Ella went after him.

Aaron pulled out of his mum's arms.

"Aaron, no!" Kate called after him but Aaron was already racing after Ella and Skyler.

They ran all the way back to the main street, passing the devastation. Aaron chased Skyler and Ella into the Empath huts, which were in complete disarray – the furniture broken and scattered on the floor, doors hanging off the hinges, lanterns smashed.

"Armana!" Skyler yelled.

He ran towards the room Armana usually used. The door was knocked down and the room trashed. Armana wasn't there.

"Armana!" Skyler screamed.

"Sky, please." Ella tried to calm him, rushing to his side. "We'll find her."

But Skyler wasn't having any of it. He went from one room to the other, shouting Armana's name.

Aaron and Ella did the same, searching room after room. Aaron turned from the room he had checked twice already to see Ella pause in the doorway of the room across from him. She didn't step in or back out. She was just standing there. Aaron hurried over to her.

"Ella, what–?" He stopped in his tracks.

There, lying on the floor, amongst the broken furniture, was Armana. Her long fair hair was drenched in blood, her robes torn. Two small holes in her neck were leaking blood, which pooled on the floor. She wasn't moving.

Skyler came in after Aaron and froze at the door.

"No," Skyler breathed. "NO!" He ran past Ella and Aaron. He fell to the ground next to Armana. "No, no, no, no, please, God, no. Armana! No! NO!"

Aaron felt like his body had turned to rock when he heard Skyler's cries turn to howls of anguish. He couldn't move. He couldn't look away. He watched helplessly as a distraught Skyler sat on his knees with the bloodied, lifeless body of Armana clutched to his chest.

30

PICKING UP THE PIECES

Dawn rose over a broken Salvador. The buildings and cottages were left smoking, charred black and thoroughly destroyed. The table was reduced to chunks of wood, scattered every which way. Reddish-brown marks tainted the cobbled street – the blood of mages or vamages, no one could tell which.

Aaron sat amongst the devastation, his eyes dry and tired, but he found he couldn't look away from the far end of the street, where the bodies of the fallen had been brought. So many had been killed in the attack: Jason Burns, an entire group of Orchard workers, many kitchen helpers and Hunters, including Danielle and Jean – the two Hunters who had once protected him from the Ichadaris on his first hunt. They were all there, laid on the ground, their bodies covered by white sheets.

Aaron found his gaze flitting past all of them to rest on Skyler, who was kneeling by Armana's body. He hadn't moved from her side. He had carried her out of the hut and laid her gently on the ground, and then just sat next to her.

The mages who had survived were left lost, not sure of what to do, where to even start. Their city had been ravaged, their people killed and their most prized possession – the Hub – stolen.

Aaron didn't want to imagine what that meant for them now. Hadrian had the Hub. He had a powerful hold on the entire realm now. What was he going to do? Nowhere was safe. Hadrian could now open portals, which meant he had access to any zone in the realm. Hadrian didn't even need to fight. He could map out a Q-Zone big enough to cover Neriah's zones and kill all the mages where they stood, in a single strike.

The air of Salvador changed, mages stopped in their tracks, staring at the gap where the Gate had once stood. Aaron turned his head too. His heart lurched in his chest. Neriah had returned.

The leader of the mages took small steps, walking in to see the city he had set up as a salvation to mages and humans alike completely broken. The Hunters who had left with him followed behind Neriah, mirroring his shock and anguish at the state of Salvador. Neriah's gaze swept through the street, no doubt picking up the burnt buildings, the bloodstained ground, but it was when he saw the bodies lined next to one another that Neriah came to a stop.

Mages ran to Neriah, crying and sobbing. They were all talking at once, telling Neriah what had happened, weeping the names of those they had lost. Neriah didn't say a word. His eyes were still on the sheet-covered bodies. Slowly, he made his way towards them, then crouched to the ground. Skyler looked at Neriah with red-rimmed, bloodshot eyes, but didn't speak.

Aaron felt someone come to stand over him. He turned to see his mum. Her eyes were on Neriah, though, searching quietly through his crowd. Her brow creased. It took Aaron a moment to realise why – his dad wasn't with them.

Aaron got to his feet and followed after his mum, heading towards Neriah. They had to push their way through the crowd of mages to get to the front. But once they reached him, neither Aaron nor Kate could find the voice to ask him anything. Neriah was devastated – completely and utterly devastated. He sat with his back curved, shoulders dropped, head lowered. Aaron watched as Neriah gathered himself and raised his head with visible difficulty.

"When?" he asked, and his voice sounded nothing like his usual strong baritone voice. It was quieter, brittle, on the verge of breaking.

"Just a little after sunset," Mary answered. "The Gate dropped and they flooded in." She struggled to keep herself together. "They took us by surprise."

Neriah turned to look at her with tears in his angry eyes. "Was *he* with them?"

Mary shook her head, her shoulders trembled as she fought to keep back her sobs. "No," she whispered. "He wasn't with them."

"He wasn't," Skyler said, drawing everyone's attention. "But his Scorcher was – he must have been. He's the only one out of them who could touch the Gate, but that cowardly son of a demon didn't dare come in with them. He just dropped the Gate and let his vamages do the work."

Aaron felt his mum stiffen next to him but he couldn't look around at her. His eyes were fixed on Skyler, staring at him with such shocked disbelief he could barely breathe.

"He did this," Skyler hissed. "He's responsible for every death here. He dropped the Gate. He let the vamages in. He told them exactly where the Hub was, which is why the vamages didn't waste time looking for it." Skyler's jaw clenched and the blue of his eyes gleamed with hatred. "Kyran sold out Salvador. He's the reason vamages got in and killed so many, killed Armana." His hand curled, taking a fistful of the sheet covering Armana's body. "I'm going to kill him."

"No." Aaron staggered forward a step. "Kyran didn't do anything."

Skyler didn't even look at him. "The vamages can't touch any of the Gates," he said. "And the Gate of Salvador was one of the most heavily protected. The only one who could drop the

Gate would be a mage working for Hadrian." He looked over at Aaron. "You know anyone else who fits that description?"

"It wasn't Kyran, Skyler," Aaron said. "I swear, it wasn't him."

"How do *you* know?" Skyler spat.

"Because..."Aaron faltered. "Because I was with him."

The effect of his words was like a thunderclap. The mages flinched with surprise, looking at Aaron in horror. Aaron tore his gaze away from Skyler's surprised expression to meet Neriah's narrowed eyes. "I called for him," he explained. "I wanted to see if...if he would hear me, if he would feel my call." He turned to glance at his mum. "I wanted to test my bond with him." His mum was staring at him, her expression full of shock and disbelief. "He came," Aaron said quietly. "He came when I called him." He looked back at Skyler. "Kyran wasn't involved in the attack. How that Gate fell, I don't know, but it wasn't Kyran."

Neriah stood up. "Where did you meet him?" he asked Aaron.

"Outside," Aaron replied. "In the woods next to the Gateway."

"What time?" Neriah pressed.

"Sunset," Aaron replied and then froze. The attack had happened just after sunset.

"He did drop the Gate," Mary gasped, voicing what everyone else was thinking. "Kyran dropped the Gate and then went to see you."

Aaron shook his head. "No, he wouldn't do that."

A hand grabbed him by the collar and he was pulled around to face a seething Skyler. "Open your eyes, Adams!" He shook Aaron roughly. "Kyran's the reason all of them are *dead*," he said, jostling Aaron towards the bodies lying on the ground.

"Let go of him!" Kate was trying her best to free Aaron, but Skyler's fingers were curled tight around Aaron's shirt.

"I'm going to kill him," Skyler raged. "Mark my words, Adams. I'll be the one to put a personalised bullet between his eyes!"

***

By that afternoon, the mages were slowly picking up the scattered pieces of Salvador. The bodies were taken away, to be prepared for burial at sunset. The Empaths worked endlessly to heal the wounded mages. Scott, Aaron learnt, was unconscious but was making a slow and steady recovery.

Neriah paused briefly next to Kate and Aaron. He told them that Chris couldn't wield the Blade of Adams. He had left Chris in the City of Hunda to recover from the drain.

So that settled it. The Blade of Adams was waiting for Kyran, for he was the legacy holder for Earth. No one could fight that truth now – Kyran Aedus was Benjamin Adams.

Kate left to help with the burial arrangements. Aaron, Rose and Sam helped the group of mages cleaning up the street, sweeping the debris to one side. They carried the remnants of the table and piled it before the Stove, or what was left of it.

They worked in silence, Sam and Rose avoiding Aaron's eye. After almost three-quarters of an hour working like this, Aaron's resolve broke.

"You both not going to say anything?" he asked.

Sam heaved a heavy piece of wood onto his shoulder and carried it away without replying.

"Come on, guys," Aaron said. "Talk to me, please."

"About what?" Rose asked, bending low to pick up a slab of the table. She began dragging it across the street. Aaron ran to catch up and lift it with her.

"I know you're mad at me," Aaron said. "You don't think I should've called Kyran."

Rose didn't say anything but her jaw clenched. She let go of the table three steps too soon and walked away.

Aaron dragged the slab to the pile of wood by himself and dropped it. "Kyran didn't do anything," he called after Rose.

Rose whirled around. "What is *wrong* with you?" she asked, her eyes full of anger. "You heard what Skyler said – the vamages could only get in if a mage dropped the Gate. What other mage do you know that works for Hadrian? What other mage would let vamages *destroy* an entire city in one night?"

"It wasn't Kyran," Aaron repeated adamantly. "He wouldn't let Salvador be attacked."

"He warned me about this," Rose said. "He told me to leave Salvador, said it wasn't safe." Her eyes bore into Aaron's. "Kyran knew an attack was coming."

Aaron stared at her, lost for words. Kyran may have known about the attack, but Aaron couldn't bring himself to believe he would drop the Gate and let the vamages in to Salvador. He shook his head.

"Rose–"

"He lived here," Sam interrupted, coming to stop in front of Aaron with an armful of broken wood. "He knew the layout. He knew where the Hub was and that's why the vamages went straight there." His brown eyes were serious as they held Aaron's gaze. "Argue all you want, Aaron, but Kyran is the one who dropped the Gate. You may have called him, but he didn't come for you. He was *already* here. He came with the intention of getting the Hub, annihilating everyone and everything in the process." He threw the wood onto the ground and began walking away.

"Sam, wait," Aaron said.

Sam turned. "But you know what gets me more than the fact that you called a known enemy to our doorstep?" he asked. "That you didn't tell me that's what you were thinking of doing." He stared at Aaron. "You used to tell me everything."

"Sam," Aaron started. "I didn't plan it. It was a spur of the moment thing."

"What about the time he came to see you in Hunda?" Sam asked. "Why didn't you tell me about that?"

Aaron didn't say anything. He dropped his gaze.

"Friends don't keep secrets, Aaron," Sam said. "I've never hidden anything from you."

"I know that," Aaron said.

"Then why didn't you tell me?" Sam asked. His eyes narrowed. "How many times have you met him in private?"

"Just twice," Aaron said. "That time in Hunda and last night."

Sam didn't say anything, but distrust gleamed in his eyes.

"Come on, Sammy," Aaron pleaded. "You know I'm not lying. It's just...I was confused about Kyran and why he wasn't attacking me, why he kept protecting me. That's why I didn't say anything. But now I know why. He protected me because I'm his brother."

"He may be your brother," Sam said, "but that doesn't stop him being an enemy."

"Sam," Aaron protested.

"You can deny it all you want, but Kyran's the reason Salvador was attacked last night," Sam said. "He didn't carry out the attack, but he dropped the Gate and let the vamages in. Every death in last night's attack is on his head."

He may not have used the same words, but Skyler had said the same thing to Aaron, and it hurt a thousand times more coming from Sam.

"Do you even realise that by dropping the Gate, Kyran made damn sure the human realm suffered along with everyone in Salvador?" Sam asked. "The Gate was gone, Aaron. There was nothing left to block the tear in the barrier. Every time a mage, or even vamage, used their powers last night, all that power went straight through the tear and into the human realm. God only knows how many people were killed or injured in our world."

Aaron was staring at him with horror. He'd forgotten that the ramifications of last night involved the human realm too.

"All of that is on Kyran's head," Sam said. "He had the power to stop the attack, but he didn't. Just like he didn't stop vamages from murdering my parents."

There was nothing Aaron could say. Sam's brown eyes had never looked so serious. Sam turned and walked away. Rose gave Aaron a long look before following after her twin, leaving Aaron all alone.

***

The sun set that day to the mages standing in a circle around the shrouded bodies. Wads of white cloth had covered each dead body, from head to foot, leaving only their faces bare. The mages stood in quiet mourning, listening to Neriah deliver one of Aric's sermons. Aaron tried to concentrate, but Neriah's speech was nothing more than mere words that made little to no sense to him. His mind felt clouded, his thoughts in disarray as he looked at the bodies on the ground. Twenty-four mages and one human – that's who they were burying today. How many would it be tomorrow? What was going to be the final count at the end of this war?

Aaron snapped out of his thoughts when he saw several mages step forward to each covered body and sit next to it.

"It is from Heaven that we came," Neriah said. "It is to Heaven that we shall return."

The mages seated beside the bodies lifted their hands and touched the soft grass. Before Aaron's eyes, the twenty-five bodies began to slowly sink into the ground.

"Bodies perish," Neriah read from memory, his deep voice laced with pain. "But the heart is immortal. It goes on living, forever alive in the whispers of the air it once breathed, in the current of the water it once swam, in the core of the fire it used to spread warmth, and in every grain of sand it walked on."

The bodies continued to sink down until they were gone. Slowly the ground reformed again. Small mounds of freshly dug ground marked each grave. Mages from the gathered circle stepped forward, each carrying a small headstone with the name of the deceased carved into it.

Aaron watched as a teary-eyed Ella carried a white tombstone to Skyler, who was kneeling next to the grave he had buried Armana in. Ella knelt at Skyler's side and silently handed him the stone. With shaky hands, Skyler took it and gently placed it at the head of the grave. Skyler's eyes hadn't dried. His tears fell on the grave as he fixed the stone. Even after it was placed, his fingers lingered on Armana's name, as if taking their last feel of her. Skyler's head dropped and his shoulders shook. Ella hugged Skyler from behind and buried her face into his neck as she cried. They stayed like that for a moment or two, lost in their pain, before Ella pulled back and urged Skyler to his feet. Skyler's pain was visible, raw and brutal on his tear-stained face. He stood but swayed a little. He clutched at Ella's arm, holding her close, but his eyes were still on Armana's grave.

Slowly, the crowd thinned. Everyone left, except for Skyler, Ella and Aaron. Wiping a sleeve over his eyes, Aaron approached Armana's grave and knelt next to it. He placed his hand on the ground. Pale blue forget-me-not flowers grew under his command, at the base of Armana's tombstone.

Getting to his feet, Aaron looked at Skyler and Ella.

"Skyler," Aaron started quietly, stepping towards him. "I'm so sorry about Armana—"

Skyler grabbed Aaron by the neck and pulled him close. His eyes were bloodshot, the blue as cold as ice.

"Listen close, Adams," he growled. "You tell that *brother* of yours the day I find him, that day will be his *last*." He shoved Aaron back and turned, walking away.

"Skyler?" Ella called. "Skyler! Wait!" She ran after him but Skyler didn't stop. He didn't even look back at her.

After a few minutes, the newly set up Gate flashed as Skyler left the City of Salvador.

***

Most of the cottages were left uninhabitable after the fire. There were only a few that had survived the attack. The mages crammed into the available space, taking the beds, sofas and even the floors to get some rest. If they had their Controller and the Hub, they could have easily set up a portal and gone to another city, but their journeys from now on were going to have to be made on foot or on their bikes.

Aaron slipped out of an overstuffed cottage and went for a walk. He needed to clear his head, to get peace from the tranquillity of the glassy pool. But it seemed someone else had the same idea. Aaron paused at the sight of Neriah at the bank of the lake. He turned to go back when Neriah called out to him, "It's okay, Aaron. You can come."

"It's cool," Aaron replied. "I'll go."

"Aaron," Neriah called. "Please. Come, sit."

Aaron hesitated, then slowly walked over. He sat under the floating lanterns, next to Neriah. For long minutes, both Aaron and Neriah simply watched the dark water before them in silence. Aaron glanced at him, but Neriah's expression was unreadable.

Aaron took in a breath. "Are you still mad at me?"

Neriah looked around at him. "For hiding your encounters with Kyran?" Neriah shook his head. "Not any more."

"Why's that?" Aaron asked.

"You're brothers," Neriah explained. "The instinct to protect blood is perhaps the strongest in us mages." He faced Aaron with a small, barely there smile. "You may not have known you were brothers, but your heart knew. Your core recognised his. You didn't raise the alarm when he came to you because you were trying to protect him – it's probably why you didn't mention it at all. I can't be angry with you for that."

Aaron kept his eyes on Neriah. "Because you did the same," he stated. "With Hadrian."

Neriah stiffened. His eyes continued to gaze ahead of him. After a long moment, he answered, "Yes. Because I did the same with Hadrian." He closed his eyes and pulled in a breath. "I protected him when I shouldn't have." He turned his head to look at Aaron. "I think about all the time I wasted, trying to find a cure, when deep down I already knew it was hopeless. I could have done the right thing. I *should* have done the right thing."

"Meaning you should've killed him?" Aaron asked.

Neriah didn't reply right away. He looked back over at the lake. "I saw what was happening to him," he said quietly. "I saw the light in him go dark. I could have done something then. I could have saved all of us from this fate. How many lives has Hadrian devastated? How many will he go on to destroy? All of them, all of this death and misery he's causing, it's on my head. I had a chance to stop him and I didn't."

"I don't agree," Aaron said. "Hadrian is responsible for what he does, not you. You tried helping him. You tried to find a cure. What's happening isn't your fault." Aaron paused, studying Neriah. "If you could do it over, would you kill him?"

Neriah didn't reply. He looked conflicted, his head dropped, eyes full of pain and guilt.

"I don't think you would," Aaron said. "You would always try to save your friend."

Neriah lifted his head, his eyes staring out into the darkness. "That's my error," he said. "I keep seeing my friend, when I should see a demon."

"Becoming a vamage doesn't erase the part of you that was a mage," Aaron said. "How can anyone expect you to forget the mage who was your friend?"

"He was more than that," Neriah said. "I cared for him like a brother. I loved him like he was my own blood."

"Do you hate him now?" Aaron asked.

Neriah didn't speak for almost a full minute. "Hate is a word that's greatly misused," he said. "It gets called on for everything, when really the word needed is dislike." His voice dipped low. "Hatred is a strong, crippling emotion. It destroys you from the inside, because the fact is you can't truly hate someone you never once loved." He turned to Aaron. "It's the abuse of the love we once had that gives us the ability to hate."

Aaron dropped his gaze to the ground. They sat in silence as the wind picked up, driving the chill into Aaron's body.

"What are we going to do?" Aaron asked quietly. "Hadrian has the Hub. He can now wipe out entire zones at a time." He raised his eyes to Neriah. "He could build a Q-Zone around us and kill us where we stand."

Neriah's jaw clenched. "Hadrian's done enough." The words came out with great strain, like he was struggling to speak past his rage. He looked at Aaron with dark violet eyes. "Now, it's my turn."

31

LAYING TRAPS

The plan was fairly straightforward. Neriah was going to take his Hunters and storm Hadrian's zone to take back the Hub. It sounded simple enough, but Aaron knew it was going to be anything but.

The Hunters all crowded in the street around Neriah, who had mapped out a copy of the realm on the ground with sticks.

"Zone K is Hadrian's securest zone," Neriah said. "No matter which corner we try to get in from, we're going to have to go through his other zones first." He sat back, crouching on the ground, brow creased. "That's where he's holding the Hub," he said. "At least, that's what he wants us to think."

"What do you mean?" Ella asked.

Neriah didn't answer right away. He was staring at his makeshift map with narrowed eyes. He reached out and touched one of their neighbouring zones.

"He's holding the Hub here," he said. "In Zone J."

Every eye turned to him.

"That's the closest one to us," Ella said. "It's literally the next zone."

"I know," Neriah said. "That's why Hadrian would put the Hub there."

"I'm sorry," Ryan said, shaking his head. "No disrespect to you, Neriah, but this doesn't make any sense. Why would Hadrian steal the Hub and then put it in the zone right next to us?"

"Because he's Hadrian," Neriah replied. "He would find it deeply amusing if we fought tooth and nail to get past his defences, only to find the Hub isn't there, but was under our noses the entire time." He looked at the map again and slowly nodded. "He would put the Hub in Zone J."

Aaron couldn't help it. He knew what he was going to say would upset many, but he had to voice his reservations.

"Are you sure Zone J is even one of Hadrian's zones?"

Neriah looked up at him with a frown. The Hunters, as expected, looked to Aaron as if he were mad.

"What do you mean?" Neriah asked.

"It might not be Hadrian's zone," Aaron said. "According to Kyran, Hadrian only actually has nine zones."

Neriah's narrowed eyes widened. The Hunters around him grew restless, shifting to look at Aaron.

"So who has the other ten?" Zhi-Jiya asked with a furrowed brow. "Evil, element-abusing fairies?"

"Demons," Aaron replied. "Kyran said demons have ten zones. They've found a way past Gates and are taking over the zones."

Murmurs of outrage rippled through the crowd. Aaron ignored them, his eyes on Neriah. The leader of the mages was staring back at Aaron, his eyes a dark purple.

"And you believe him?" Neriah asked.

"The Lycans that attacked us had found their way in without dropping the Gate," Aaron reminded. "Maybe what Kyran said isn't all that far-fetched."

Neriah was quiet for almost a minute. "What else did he tell you?"

"That you lied about him," Aaron replied. "That the attacks Scott reported as the work of the Scorcher was really Raoul and his Lycans. Kyran was here, in Salvador, at the time of the attacks. So how could he be responsible?"

The Hunters shifted in quiet fury, glaring at Aaron. Their hands were curled into fists, eyes narrowed and jaws clenched. Aaron held his ground. He knew calling the leader of the mages a liar in front of his loyal Hunters wasn't going to go down well. But he had to say it. He had to ask how Kyran could be blamed for crimes he clearly hadn't committed.

Neriah didn't move. He held Aaron's stare for a long minute, and then nodded.

"He has a point," he said quietly. "Maybe we were wrong about those attacks. Maybe some of them were in fact Raoul and the Lycans. I admit I don't know Kyran well enough to judge if he was the one responsible." His eyes grew fierce. "But I know Hadrian. And I know all nineteen zones belong to him. I know because he took them from me."

Aaron didn't fight back. Kyran had said the demons took the zones from Neriah, not Hadrian. Was Kyran lying? Or was Neriah blindly blaming Hadrian for something he didn't do? Like the mages did with Kyran?

Ryan took in a breath and stepped forward. "When do we leave for Zone J?" he asked.

Neriah took a moment before slowly straightening up. He looked around at his Hunters. "The day after tomorrow," he said. "I'm told by the Empaths that they hope Scott will have regained consciousness by then." He scanned the crowd. "Let's get our Controller his Hub back in time for him to wake up."

***

Two days later, the Hunters prepared to storm Zone J and take back their Hub. They gathered in the street, weapons of all kinds in hands and strapped on torsos, arms and legs. It was the largest crowd of Hunters Aaron had ever witnessed. He saw plenty of faces he recognised, including the red-haired Bella. She gave him a small nod in greeting but stayed next to her bike.

Despite the large numbers, the usual excitement for a hunt was missing. There was no boisterous laughter from the Hunters, no cheering from the watching mages, no positive energy in the air.

Aaron stood next to Ella in silence, waiting for everyone to assemble. Ella's bike stood to the side, ready for her to mount and take off with Aaron. Across the road, Ryan waited with his bike. Kate stood next to him but her eyes were glued to Aaron, watching him, silently pleading with him to change his mind. Aaron kept his eyes firmly away from hers. If it wasn't such an important mission, one that needed every Hunter, Aaron was certain his mum would've argued with Neriah until he agreed to leave Aaron behind.

Aaron spotted Neriah walking through the crowd, heading towards him. Peeking out from behind Neriah's shoulder was the hilt of a sword. Aaron didn't even have to see the rest of it to figure out it was the Blade of Afton.

Neriah walked up to Aaron but his eyes were on his niece. "Any sign of him?" he asked.

Ella's expression clouded with pain. She shook her head. "No," she replied quietly. "He hasn't come back since the funeral. I don't know where Skyler is."

Neriah didn't say anything, but Aaron could see sorrow in his expression. He nodded before scanning the crowd. "Another few minutes, then we must leave."

Neriah walked away. Aaron watched him go, his eyes on the magnificent sword slung on Neriah's back. Like the Blades of Adams and Avira, the Blade of Afton too had engravings along the gleaming silver. Neriah passed by Mary, who was standing to the side. Next to her were Sam and Rose. Aaron hadn't spoken much to either of them in the past few days, but he could see the worry in their eyes as they stared at him. Finally, Rose broke and ran towards him. Aaron moved too, making his way through the crowd to get closer.

Rose threw her arms around him, clinging to his neck.

"Please don't go," she whispered. "Don't go, Aaron. You'll get hurt."

Aaron pulled her away. "I need to do this," he said. "I have to help get the Hub back."

Rose's eyes were already welling with tears. She looked downright terrified. "You're going into *Hadrian's* zone," she stressed. "It's too dangerous."

Aaron smiled. "Are you channelling my mum?" he asked. "She said the same thing, word for word."

Rose held on to his hands. "Listen to her," she pleaded. "I've got a bad feeling, Aaron. I don't want you to go."

Aaron gave her hands a tight squeeze. "I'm going to say to you what I told her – I'm not sitting this one out. I'm fighting against Hadrian. I'm getting the Hub back."

Rose dropped her head and Aaron moved in to hug her again. He looked over her shoulder at Sam. It was clearly taking all he had to stay where he was and not come running like Rose. Aaron gave him a small smile and moved back. He left Rose and went back to Ella, who was getting ready to mount her bike. The Gate flashed and opened under Neriah's command.

***

The roar of the bikes filled the air as Neriah led the way, speeding through the forest on his liquid-blue Ducati Panigale motorbike. Aaron was seated behind Ella, holding on as she raced after her uncle, the rest of the Hunters behind them.

They went further than Aaron had ever been before. Usually, Scott had a portal ready and waiting in the middle of the forest to take them wherever they wanted to go. Now they had no choice but to travel the whole way across the zone to get to the next one.

They rode for what felt like hours. Eventually Aaron saw the trees thinning ahead. They came out of the forest onto a stretch of dry, sand-covered ground. The bright sunlight blinded all of them until their eyes adjusted from the dark woods they had left behind. Neriah slowed to a stop, halting the Hunters behind him.

For a moment, Neriah did nothing but scan his surroundings. There didn't appear to be anything there but sun and sand. Neriah revved his bike and turned, heading to his left. He took off and the Hunters followed in pursuit. Their bikes kicked up flurries of sand and dirt, which meant they couldn't follow directly behind each other. They spread out. Ella kicked her bike up a gear and raced to Neriah's right. They kept going until they saw a dark shape ahead of them. Aaron tried to make out what it was, but the sand was stinging his eyes.

It turned out it was nothing more than large rocks – a cluster of them, some boulders as tall as Aaron. Neriah came to a stop and dismounted his bike. Ella and the others followed his example. Aaron's legs had become stiff after sitting on the bike for so long. He stretched them as discretely as he could. Stepping past Ella, Aaron peered at what lay beyond the rocks: a steep hill leading the way down to more dry, sand-covered ground. Loose rocks sat on the surface. He pulled back to find his mum by his side.

"The path ahead is uneven. We should go on foot from here," Neriah instructed. "Stay ready. You don't know what we might find."

Guns clicked in response. Aaron saw the pistol in his mum's hand but refrained from taking out his own...yet. Neriah made his way past the rocks and down the hill. The other mages followed after him, carefully picking their way down the sharp slope. Aaron barely managed to get to the bottom without slipping and rolling the entire way.

The Hunters walked in tense silence, following Neriah, weapons clutched in hands. Aaron looked around, but he couldn't see any signs of a Gateway, or even a Gate. All that met his eye was more barren land. Then it occurred to him – they were going to one of Hadrian's zones. Everyone knew that Hadrian didn't use Gates. That's why elemental energy leaked out into the human realm through the tears and caused so much destruction, which the humans mistook as brutal acts of nature.

It was only Kyran who had argued that the nine zones they had were all Gated, that he himself had put them up.

Just as the thought came to Aaron, he spotted a glow in the far distance. As they moved closer, Aaron realised what it was. A Gate. A towering mass of glittering light. There was no Gateway to this Gate. It was just sitting there in the open, like the Gates that protected the Blades of Aric.

The Hunters shared looks, staring wide-eyed at the Gate, surprised at its presence. Ella turned to Neriah, looking as if she was about to start demanding explanations. Neriah didn't say a word, and continued walking towards the Gate. They finally reached it. Neriah stepped closer, examining the glowing white tower.

"Neriah?" Ryan called. "What's going on? How can one of our Gates be out here?"

"It's not one of ours," Neriah replied. "It's almost an exact replica, though." He stared at the Gate before a small smile came to him. "Looks like Hadrian taught Kyran well."

Aaron felt his mum tense beside him, but she didn't say anything.

"Kyran?" Ella asked. "He set this up?"

"He's the only one who could," Neriah replied.

"How are we getting in?" Zhi-Jiya asked.

Neriah turned to look at her. "It's a Gate," he said. "It won't be warded against mages." He faced the towering door again. "Not unless Hadrian wants to lock out his so-called son too."

He reached out and touched the shiny surface. He didn't have to say his name. With a flash, the Gate slid open. Aaron saw more of the dry, sand-covered land waiting for them beyond the Gate.

Neriah was about to lead the way in when Ella cried, "Neriah, wait!" She hurried to his side, her eyes wide and filled with unease. "This doesn't feel right," she said. "The Hub being kept here, right next door? Having a Gate that will let us through? It's too easy." She shook her head. "This feels like a trap."

"Smart girl," a voice said.

Everyone turned, their guns raised and aimed. Daniel Machado appeared before them from a swirl of mist. He smirked at Neriah, his glittery blue eyes alight with mirth. In the space of a heartbeat, large clouds fell to the ground, surrounding the Hunters. Countless vamages appeared out of the fog, guns clutched in hands and vicious, gleeful smiles on their faces.

"A trap is exactly what this is," Machado said.

The vamages moved in, tightening their circle. They motioned for the Hunters to walk through the open Gate. The Hunters didn't move. Neriah was watching Machado. The right-hand vamage of Hadrian waved a hand and stepped aside.

"Please," he said. "Do come in."

Aaron knew Neriah had seen how many vamages had appeared and surrounded them. They were outnumbered. Resisting would only get them killed that much faster. But as he watched, his heart going a thousand miles a minute, he was certain Neriah was going to fight back. To his surprise, Neriah walked in, head held high.

The Hunters, with their guns and swords still clutched in hand, followed after their leader. Machado stood like a mockery of a host, greeting each one as they passed by him. Neriah led the way across the barren land, until the last of the Hunters passed the threshold. Then the Gate closed with a resounding click.

A cloud, thick and pulsing, shot across the sky before hitting the ground before Neriah. It kicked up a mighty sandstorm. A man appeared within it, but it was only when the dust settled that Aaron and the others saw who it was.

Dark-haired and just as handsome as Aaron had witnessed in the memories and dreams, he didn't seem to have aged much in the last sixteen years. Hazel eyes, speckled with gold, ignored the rest of the Hunters, focusing only on Neriah.

Hadrian bared his teeth in a dazzling smile. "Neriah," he said in greeting.

Neriah bristled, like the sound of Hadrian's voice was physically painful. He didn't say anything.

Hadrian chuckled. "You're so damn predictable," he said. "Out of all my zones, I knew you would think this one would hold the Hub." He held Neriah's eyes and tilted his head. "If it makes you feel any better, this zone would've been the one to hold the Hub, if I didn't know you'd suspect it." He shook his head. "I guess that goes to show how well we know each other. Well, how well *I* know you."

Neriah held his silence. He stood with fists clenched at his side. Hadrian's gaze trailed leisurely through the crowd of Hunters. When it came to Aaron, Hadrian paused, but for no more than a heartbeat. He looked past him, giving Kate an almost smile.

"So many familiar faces," he said. "But what happened to you, Neriah? You haven't aged well." His eyes glinted. "What's the matter? Have the last sixteen years been tough on you?"

Neriah, for some reason, still remained quiet. Hadrian looked to Ella and paused. His expression changed. He looked genuinely surprised and awed.

"Don't tell me this is little Ella?" Hadrian laughed, turning to her. "You're all grown up."

Ella had her gun aimed at him from the moment he had appeared. "Yeah" she said. "Sixteen years do that to you."

"Not to everyone," Hadrian corrected.

Ella snorted. "Let me rephrase that – sixteen years do that to those without a tainted soul."

Hadrian smiled. "You're very much like your mother," he said, with something akin to fondness.

In the blink of an eye, his hand had lifted and Ella was yanked forward, landing straight in Hadrian's arms. Neriah was pulled out of his shocked stupor, but it was too late. Hadrian had Ella turned around, one hand wrapped around her neck, the other restraining the wrist that held her gun.

Aaron felt like his heart had stopped. He watched helplessly as Hadrian used a struggling Ella as a shield, but that didn't stop the Hunters from taking aim. The surrounding vamages clicked their guns in warning. No one fired. The Hunters watched in horror as Hadrian kept Ella in a chokehold, his eyes fast turning to a golden hazel, but never moving from Neriah.

"This must be like déjà vu for you, huh, Neriah?" Hadrian asked.

Neriah took a single step, holding out a hand. "Don't," he said, his voice not much more than a whisper. "Just let her go."

"She looks very much like Lily, doesn't she?" Hadrian asked, tightening his grip, making Ella grimace and pause in her fight to get free. "Talks like her, too. Don't you think she should die like her mother did?"

"Hadrian." Neriah's booming voice was panicking. "Don't."

Hadrian's eyes were a shade of liquid amber. He dipped his head to whisper into Ella's ear. "Like I said, déjà vu." His voice carried, so everyone could hear him. "Those were the same words he begged the day I killed your mother."

Ella's struggles ceased. Her eyes widened. "No," she managed to gasp. "Lycans...killed...her!"

Hadrian pulled back, looking thrown. His gaze darted to Neriah before the lines on his brow disappeared. He let out a breath of laughter.

"You never told her?" he asked.

Neriah didn't reply.

"What's the matter, Neriah?" Hadrian called. "Afraid the truth wouldn't show you in a *perfect* light?" His fingers dug into Ella's skin as he pulled her close to speak in her ear again. "Your uncle lied to you," he told her softly. "Your mother wasn't killed by Lycans. *I* killed her. I held Lily, just like I'm holding you today, before snapping her neck."

Ella looked to Neriah, holding his gaze. Tears welled in her eyes as she silently asked him if it was true.

Neriah didn't say anything, but his drooped shoulders, clenched fists and curved back told everyone he was breaking at the revelation. Ella's stare didn't move from her uncle, the only family she had – the man who'd brought her up, loved her like a daughter, and also lied to her about how her mother had died. Ella closed her eyes, spilling drops down her cheeks. She tried to get out of Hadrian's hold, but he wasn't letting go.

"Don't you want to know why I killed her?" Hadrian asked, his voice trembling with anger. His eyes darted to Neriah once more. "It's all due to your uncle," he said. "Lily's blood is on his hands."

"You're right," Neriah said and Ella stopped in her struggles, staring at him with an open mouth. The Hunters, including Aaron, were left shell-shocked at Neriah's confession. "Lily's blood is on my hands. I let her die." Neriah took a step closer. "I let all of them die, because I refused to kill *you*."

Hadrian gritted his teeth, but didn't speak.

"I should've killed you when I had the chance," Neriah continued. "If I had, I would have saved all the lives you've destroyed. So yes, every death at your hand, every family left devastated because of you, all that pain and loss is my fault, because I let you live!"

The fury on Hadrian's face was frightening. His eyes were glowing gold, his face taut with anger, jaw clenched. "You let me *live*?" he asked. "Is that what that was?" His grip on Ella must have tightened, because her face contorted with pain, her free hand scratched desperately at Hadrian's fingers. Hadrian barely seemed to notice. "What you did was worse than any death," he said to Neriah. "You should have just killed me – *that* would have been more merciful than locking my core."

Neriah straightened up to stand tall. "I guess it's the day to rectify mistakes."

The ground suddenly shook. A ripple tore through the ground, coming blindingly fast at Hadrian from the right. It hit him and Hadrian fell sideways, taking Ella with him. The surprise knocked his grip loose, only for a heartbeat, but it was all Ella needed. She rolled away from Hadrian, before crouching on all fours.

Out of the very ground, countless mages sprung up, spraying sand every which way. They grabbed the vamages from behind, holding the barrel of their guns to the vamages' temples before instructing them to drop their weapons. The vamages did so without protest. They wouldn't die if the mages shot them, but none of them wanted bullets in their heads. The excruciating pain would slow them down in the fight.

Aaron, along with the rest of the Hunters, stared in a moment of dumb confusion. The mages who had leapt out from the ground had sand and dirt stuck to their skin, sitting thickly in their hair, making it difficult to see who they were. But the one that had Machado in his grip was very familiar.

"Uncle Mike?" Aaron whispered in recognition.

Blue eyes twinkled at him and Aaron made out his uncle's grinning face behind all the sand.

Aaron looked through the sand-covered mages again, picking out Patrick Sweeney. Parts of his white robes were visible through the sand. Some of the other mages were dressed in robes too, a few blue, some green, but mostly white. Then it hit Aaron. Lurkers. They were Lurkers.

Attention quickly shifted from the Hunters and Lurkers who had come to the rescue, to Hadrian, who sat up like a wounded animal. The ripple that had thrown him to the ground led from him, all the way back to a furious Chris. Aaron stared at his dad with surprise, and a little awe. He looked undeniably fearsome – his bright green eyes fixed on Hadrian, his hands curled into fists as grains of sand crawled down the length of his body to pool on the ground.

Hadrian looked away from Chris, to find Neriah had stepped before Ella and was now looking down on him.

Neriah smiled. "I guess I know you pretty damn well."

Hadrian glowered. Neriah had played him. Neriah had known this was a trap, so he had Hunters and Lurkers already waiting in hiding, to flip the tables on him. The gold of Hadrian's eyes came alive and the ground lit up with fire.

Neriah leapt back, pulling Ella with him. Fire rolled like a wave, heading towards the Hunters. Neriah reached behind him and pulled out his sword – the Blade of Afton. The engravings on the sword shimmered an electric blue. With a mighty swing, Neriah brought forth a crashing wave of water that swallowed the flames.

The vamages, taking advantage of the distraction, attacked the Hunters and Lurkers holding them at gunpoint. Hadrian was back on his feet and sent a stream of fire that zig-zagged across the ground, spreading out in every direction. The mages and vamages broke into battle, with the flames licking at their feet. Aaron threw his own ripple at two approaching vamages, knocking them back. Kate pulled Aaron behind her, shielding him as she took care of the vamages, using her gun and her powers to keep them away.

Fire shot through the air at the slightest twitch of Hadrian's fingers. Neriah was fighting the flames, his Blade taking out most of whatever Hadrian conjured. Even so, at one point, it looked as if the sky was raining fire. Everything from fireballs to streaks of lightning fell on the Hunters.

Aaron fought with vigour, sending out ripples to throw back vamages, while dodging the retaliating attacks, as well as fireballs and lightning bolts that tried to catch him. His mum was by his side, shielding him, deflecting and throwing back what she could.

The vamages were focusing on Neriah and Chris, trying to take the Elementals out of the fight. Aaron caught sight of Ella, her face still stained with tears as she fought the vamages. Her grey eyes were on Hadrian, though, trying to get to him. She threw spears of ice at Hadrian, and one struck him in the shoulder, making him stumble back. Hadrian's eyes narrowed and he sent a fireball the size of a boulder at her. Ella dived out of the way, before sending another burst of power at him. Other Hunters joined in, directing their energy, their power at Hadrian.

Hadrian deflected the attacks and sent more of his own at the Hunters, sending them scampering out of the way. Hadrian was taking on five, six, seven Hunters at a time and fighting them like it was nothing.

Chris threw back the last of the vamages that had crowded him and turned to find Hadrian. He gathered his power and sent another ripple. Seconds before it could reach him, Ella's icy spear hit Hadrian, right in the chest. Hadrian staggered back a step and that's when Chris's ripple caught him, throwing him bodily into the air. Hadrian fell with a thump, the breath knocked out of him, the icicle impaled in his chest.

The fight between the mages and vamages was fast escalating, but Aaron couldn't take his eyes off his dad. He watched – all the while fighting back the vamages – as his dad held out his hands, taking aim at Hadrian again. A mighty ripple tore the ground open. It shot forward, straight towards the dazed Hadrian.

Someone stepped in front of Hadrian, and the ripple burst into fragments – thin cracks spreading out to both sides instead of making impact.

Aaron's heart stopped. Next to him, his mum's breath caught in her chest. Standing before Hadrian's fallen form – shielding him, protecting him – was a furious Kyran.

Chris froze. His eyes were on his son, who was glaring back with venom, his chest heaving after running full pelt to reach Hadrian. Kyran reached back to pull out the Blade of Aedus. With his eyes on Chris, Kyran slowly dragged a line in the sandy ground with his sword. It was as clear as day: Kyran was warning them – cross the line and come for Hadrian, and he would retaliate.

Chris, however, was too caught up in his own emotions to understand the warning. He took a step towards him, tears in his eyes. "Ben–"

"Kyran, no!" Aaron yelled, seeing what his brother was about to do.

Too late.

Kyran stabbed his sword into the ground. Flames erupted from the Blade with a mighty roar, ready to engulf everything in sight – the first being Christopher Adams.

32

DEADLY GIFTS

Fire spewed out from the ground, pulled from the earth's core by the Blade of Aedus. It filled the line Kyran had made, before spilling out as a fiery wave that swept across the dry ground – straight for Chris.

Aaron couldn't yell out. Terror strangled him as he watched flames catch his dad's legs, racing up his torso. That's when Neriah's counter-attack crashed around Chris, extinguishing the flames. Chris collapsed to the ground.

Neriah swiped his Blade and more water came gushing out, chasing after the flames, killing it before it reached the battling Hunters. The water turned the sandy ground into a thick mush that made running all the more difficult, but Aaron didn't care. He darted from under his mum's arm, racing towards his fallen dad. He ducked to avoid the crossfire, but kept going until he reached Chris.

"Dad!" he called as he skidded to his knees in the mud, falling to Chris's side.

Chris was in agony, his teeth clenched, eyes squeezed shut as he clutched at his thighs. Aaron's attention snapped to his legs to see how badly they'd been burnt. Fabric from his trousers had melted into his bloodied skin. Bits of his flesh had been singed off.

With tears in his furious eyes, Aaron looked up at Kyran. He was still standing in front of Hadrian, with his Blade in hand. He met Aaron's glare with eyes just as fierce, before turning away, not giving Chris a single glance. He helped Hadrian back to his feet, who had melted Ella's icicle from his chest.

"What are you doing?" Kyran yelled at Hadrian.

"Finishing this," Hadrian said breathlessly. He ignored the bloody wound on his chest and made to move past Kyran.

Kyran grabbed his arm. "We fall back," he said resolutely.

"Not until this is over." Hadrian pulled his arm out of Kyran's grip and headed towards the battle.

Kyran stared after him, his eyes dark and clouded. His jaw clenched. With a white-knuckled grip on the Blade, he followed after him.

"Chris!"

Aaron pulled his eyes away from Kyran to see who had shouted. He found his uncle Mike had come to kneel at his dad's other side. His eyes were wide, face pale. He met Aaron's gaze, looking just as terrified as Aaron felt. Not a moment later, Kate fell next to Aaron, staring in horror at her husband.

"Chris? Oh my God, Chris!" Kate put her hands on his face.

"I'm okay," Chris managed, his voice guttural with pain. "I'm okay."

Aaron looked across to his uncle, but he was watching Kyran. Michael's blue eyes stared without blinking, his mouth in a tight line.

"Uncle Mike?" Aaron called. "Uncle Mike!"

Michael turned to him and Aaron was thrown by the tears in his eyes. He pushed past the lump in his own throat. "Should we move Dad?"

Michael looked to Chris and shook his head. "No. Stay with him. Don't let anyone get close." He got up, drawing out his pistol and ran to join the fight.

Kate got up and moved to stand before her husband, gun in hand. Aaron was also by his dad's side, but both his and Kate's eyes were on Kyran, watching him fight the Hunters. Kate's tears rolled down her cheeks as she stared at the son she thought she had lost. Aaron could see her lips trembling, repeating the name *Ben* again and again.

Kyran had sheathed his Blade and was fighting using only his powers, a mix of all three elements under his control. It took Aaron a moment to see what it was he was doing: he was taking out anyone that targeted Hadrian.

The battle had turned chaotic. Vamages and mages were attacking one another with not only guns, blades and powers, but their fists too. A whole crowd of vamages tried to bring Neriah down. The leader of the mages fought them valiantly, flooring several in single strikes.

Neriah threw down the last vamage and turned, only to find Hadrian before him. For a fleeting moment, Hadrian did nothing but look at Neriah, before his hand shot forward, and the small blade in his hand disappeared into Neriah's stomach.

Aaron felt like he was the one stabbed, right in the chest. Somewhere in the crowd of fighting mages, Ella screamed.

Neriah's breath came out as a gasp, eyes widening. The Blade of Afton fell from his hand. Neriah leant forward, his hand clutching at Hadrian's arm. Hadrian pulled the knife out and grabbed Neriah by the back of his neck, bringing him closer. Tears lingered in his hazel eyes as he stared at Neriah.

"See you in hell," he said softly. "Brother."

He stabbed him again and again, the knife tearing into his stomach, his chest, his sides. Neriah keeled forward, his head lolled on Hadrian's shoulder. Hadrian pulled the knife out for the last time and threw the wounded Neriah to the ground.

The Hunters left the vamages, the battle forgotten, and ran towards their fallen leader. Their swords were raised against Hadrian, bullets rained towards him, but Kyran had his Blade in hand once more. The stream of fire he sent circled around him,

Hadrian and Neriah, cutting them off from the rest. The flames rose high, catching the bullets, deflecting them.

The Hunters fought the flames with desperate fury. Their shouts and cries filled the air. Ella was screaming, her element out of control as water crashed and battled with the fire. But Kyran's power was feeding the flames, refusing to let them extinguish. The vamages pulled some of the Hunters back, keeping them from finding a way past the flames.

Aaron found himself at the edge of the fire too, trying to get past – to get to Neriah and help him.

"KYRAN!" he screamed. "What are you *doing*?" he cried. "Stop this! Stop, please!"

Kyran looked at him, but then turned away.

"Kyran, no!" Aaron called. "Kyran, please don't do this!"

Neriah lay still, taking in shallow breaths. His front was covered in blood. It had seeped out to mix with the muddy sand underneath him. Slowly, Neriah turned, propping himself up painfully on his elbows. His bloodshot eyes went to Hadrian, who was standing before him, the knife still in his hand.

"Go on," Neriah rasped. "Do it."

Hadrian stared at him. The knife slipped out of his hand, hitting the damp ground. With glistening eyes, Hadrian stepped forward.

"You've brought this on yourself," he said. "You have only yourself to blame."

Neriah coughed and his lips stained crimson. "We both know where the blame lies."

Hadrian's hands curled into fists. "Damn you, Neriah," he breathed. "Admit it. This is your doing." He moved his head to look past the fiery wall, at the battling vamages and mages. He turned back to Neriah. "I never wanted a war. You're the one who instigated it when you locked my core."

"Because you became a demon!" Neriah spat, his expression one of agony and heartbreak. "You gave up your purity and chose darkness."

Hadrian's eyes glowed with fury. "And who was it that consigned me to this darkness?" he asked, stepping closer. "You turned on me when I did this, *all* of this, for you. I became what I am to fulfil *your* dream."

"I never wanted this," Neriah panted. "Not this." The tears that had lurked in his eyes from the moment he saw Hadrian finally fell. "Nothing is worth the price of your soul," he said. "No amount of power is worth losing yourself."

Hadrian smiled and tilted his head. "Is that right?" he asked. "So why did you do it?"

Neriah was breathing fast, agony laced in every line of his body, but he looked at Hadrian with a frown. Outside the ring of fire, many mages paused, halting in the process of extinguishing the flames. Aaron was staring at Neriah, seeing the confusion on his pale face.

Hadrian knelt to look the dying Neriah in the eyes. "You played me," he said. "You used me to take out James, then locked my powers. Chris left of his own accord, otherwise you would have got him out of the way somehow too. And all for what?" His eyes bore into Neriah's wide ones. "So you could take over. Rule the realm as the one and only Elemental; the one and only leader." He stared at Neriah, his eyes glistening. "All you had to do was ask me, Neriah. I would've happily handed you my power, even if it killed me."

"No." Neriah's voice broke. "I never wanted to rule on my own. I was *left* on my own, I didn't want it."

A bitter smile came to Hadrian. "You ruled as the only leader for sixteen years, Neriah. Now it's my turn."

Hadrian stood up and Aaron could see his eyes begin to darken. The golden hazel was steadily turning to red. When his lips pulled back in a smile, Aaron saw the fangs.

Dropping to the ground, Aaron took fistfuls of the damp sand and threw it onto the fire, desperate to get past the barrier. The flames flickered and dulled, if only a little. Aaron scrambled back to his feet, backed up and then ran forward. He jumped, just as the flames reared back up. Kyran must have seen him, because all Aaron felt was a brush of searing heat before the flames shrunk down for no more than a moment, lest it burnt him alive. Aaron hit the ground, and rolled to put out the flicker of fire caught on his jacket. He got up and ran, falling to Neriah's side.

In a flash Kyran was there, just behind Hadrian, staring at Aaron with alarm.

Following Aaron's example, the Hunters began throwing damp sand onto the fire, so they too could get into the circle and go to Neriah's aid. But Kyran's power fed the flames, making them stronger, so they didn't as much as flicker.

Aaron pulled out his pistol, but he didn't aim at the vamage before him. He placed it in Neriah's bloodied, shaky hands. Neriah held on to the gun, but he didn't raise it. He looked at Aaron and a small, barely there smile crossed his lips. Trembling in agony, he turned back to Hadrian.

"Go for it," Hadrian said, nodding at the gun. "You can't kill me."

Neriah's breath was laboured. His eyes fluttered but he forced them open. "I know." His voice was nothing more than a whisper. "I could never kill you."

Aaron's eyes darted to Kyran, who was staring back at him, clearly panicked. Kyran tilted his head to the side, gesturing silently for Aaron to move away. Aaron glowered at him and stayed put, remaining at Neriah's side.

The Hunters were almost done fighting the flames. Whether it was Kyran's distraction weakening the flames or the damp sand, Aaron didn't know, but soon the Hunters would be inside the circle. Hadrian was seemingly oblivious, his full focus on the dying Elemental before him.

"It's over, Neriah," he said softly, almost gently, as if he were consoling him. "I've won."

"No," Neriah panted. "You haven't. You did all of this for the legacies. But you don't have them." He nodded weakly at Kyran. "He does."

Hadrian smiled, showing his fangs. "Kyran may hold the legacies for now," he said. "But in due time, they will come back to me. And once I take your legacy, I'll have all four powers at my command." He looked down at Neriah. "No one will ever be able to stand against me again. I'll rule this realm as the most powerful leader."

Neriah's gaze rested on Kyran for a moment before his expression softened. He smiled and looked at Hadrian. "You're forgetting something," he croaked. "Nothing is more powerful," he whispered, "than blood."

Neriah dropped the pistol and slammed his hand against Aaron's chest.

Excruciating pain filled Aaron. It felt like a force had ripped him open and poured liquid lava into his bones. Aaron couldn't scream; his breath left him completely. But he heard Kyran's "NO!" thunder in the air around him, followed by Ella's agonised scream. The pain was over in seconds, and as Neriah's hand dropped, Aaron fell back, hitting the soft, muddy ground. He felt paralysed, yet his body was shaking, convulsing.

The sound of several shoes squelching against the wet ground reached Aaron but he couldn't see. His vision had turned white. Gradually, colours appeared as a mix of blurred images, slowly sharpening. He found a tearful Zhi-Jiya and several Hunters around him. Hands were on him, trying to hold him still, but his limbs still jerked painfully. His mum was screaming his name. Aaron's head lolled to the side, to try to find her, but all he saw was a distraught Ella sitting next to Neriah, whose eyes had closed, the life gone from his strong body.

Something in Aaron's aching core told him Kyran had left, taking Hadrian and the vamages with him. Aaron saw his mum running towards him and that's when his surroundings melted and Aaron's world slowly went black. But before he lost consciousness, Aaron understood what had happened: Neriah had given him the legacy.

***

Hadrian hurled the table across the room. It smacked into the wall and broke in half. It did nothing to appease his fury. He threw the chair, reducing it to nothing more than a pile of wood. He was cursing, throwing ugly words from his mouth, snarling like a wild, angered beast. Neriah had bested him. He had come so close – so *incredibly* close – to having all four legacies under his command, but Neriah had taken that away from him. Neriah had given his power, his legacy away. He had slipped it to another, right from Hadrian's very grasp.

Hadrian ran both hands through his hair before clasping his fingers behind his head. He stood like that for a moment with his eyes closed, in the middle of the destroyed room. When he opened them, his gaze fell on the only other person there. His son sat on the steps leading to the open balcony, his back to him.

Hadrian cursed Neriah under his breath again. He had given the last legacy to the youngest Adams. Why him? Why couldn't it have been anyone else? Hadrian rubbed at his eyes, breathing out a difficult sigh, before looking over at Kyran. He hadn't said a word since pulling out of the fight. Hadrian had known the battle was over, the minute he saw Neriah give the Adams boy his legacy. Distracted by them, Kyran's defence had fallen and the fire he had been feeding to keep the Hunters back went out like a candle in the wind. They'd had no choice but to retreat.

Hadrian pulled in a breath. "Kyran?" he called.

Kyran didn't move.

Hadrian walked towards him. "This is all Neriah's doing," he said. "He found a way to mess with me, even with his dying breath!"

Kyran dipped his head, but didn't turn around.

Hadrian came to stand behind him. "You know we have no other choice," he said. "We've come too far to give up now. I *need* that legacy. I must have the power of all four elements if I'm to rule the realm as the only leader." He put his hand on Kyran's shoulder. "I know you've vowed your obedience to my command," he said, "but I'm not going to say anything to you. I can only imagine how difficult this must be." His grip tightened. "But you do understand what has to happen, don't you?"

Very slowly, Kyran nodded. He lifted his head, fierce green eyes stared ahead.

"Aaron Adams," Kyran said, with a steeled voice, "has to die."

Look out for Book Three, *Thicker Than Water*,
in the Power of Four series by SF Mazhar.

Made in the USA
Charleston, SC
09 March 2015